SOMEONE'S WATCHING

Pescoli turned over in bed and she was instantly awake.

Something was wrong.

She could feel it in her bones.

She'd been back home less than two days and the feeling was back, that she was being watched by hidden eyes, that something bad was going down. Nothing in the last twenty-four hours had given her any fuel to feed this paranoid feeling, not even the ongoing investigation into her sister's death.

She hated all the self-examination and worry that had edged into her life. It had started with her pregnancy. Brindel's murder had only exacerbated it.

She threw back the covers and walked naked to the French doors, where, as she had hundreds of times before, she stared across the icy surface of the lake and then looked up to the black sky where no stars were visible, cloud cover erasing their shine and hiding the moon.

There is nothing out there, Pescoli. Get over yourself. Even the bears have the good sense to hibernate for the winter.

But it wasn't the bears or wolves or mountain lions that roamed the forests around her home that caused the little tingle of apprehension to crawl up her spine. No, it was something unknown, something insidious and evil that she felt observing her . . .

Books by Lisa Jackson

Stand-Alones
SEE HOW SHE DIES
FINAL SCREAM
RUNNING SCARED
WHISPERS
TWICE KISSED
UNSPOKEN
DEEP FREEZE
FATAL BURN
MOST LIKELY TO DIE
WICKED GAME
WICKED LIES
SOMETHING WICKED
WICKED WAYS
SINISTER
WITHOUT MERCY
YOU DON'T WANT TO KNOW
CLOSE TO HOME
AFTER SHE'S GONE
REVENGE
YOU WILL PAY
OMINOUS
RUTHLESS
ONE LAST BREATH
LIAR, LIAR
PARANOID

Anthony Paterno/Cahill Family Novels
IF SHE ONLY KNEW
ALMOST DEAD

Rick Bentz/Reuben Montoya Novels
HOT BLOODED
COLD BLOODED
SHIVER
ABSOLUTE FEAR
LOST SOULS
MALICE
DEVIOUS
NEVER DIE ALONE

Pierce Reed/Nikki Gillette Novels
THE NIGHT BEFORE
THE MORNING AFTER
TELL ME

Selena Alvarez/Regan Pescoli Novels
LEFT TO DIE
CHOSEN TO DIE
BORN TO DIE
AFRAID TO DIE
READY TO DIE
DESERVES TO DIE
EXPECTING TO DIE
WILLING TO DIE

Published by Kensington Publishing Corporation

LISA
JACKSON

WILLING
TO DIE

ZEBRA BOOKS
KENSINGTON PUBLISHING CORP.
www.kensingtonbooks.com

ZEBRA BOOKS are published by

Kensington Publishing Corp.
119 West 40th Street
New York, NY 10018

First Kensington Books Hardcover Printing: May 2019
First Zebra Books Mass-Market Paperback Printing: August 2019
ISBN-13: 978-1-4201-3609-8
ISBN-10: 1-4201-3609-7

ISBN-13: 978-1-4201-3610-4 (eBook)
ISBN-10: 1-4201-3610-0 (eBook)

10 9 8 7 6 5 4 3 2 1

Printed in the United States of America

Prologue

Near San Francisco, California
July Fourth

Dead.

Her son was dead!

Cold to the bone despite the summer's heat, she couldn't breathe, had to gasp for air.

Her throat clogged with grief, pain, and a deep, intense fury.

Standing alone in this cemetery where gravestones stood in sentry-like rows, she clenched her fists and wanted to rail to the heavens where, across the night sky, fireworks burst in thunderous booms and great sprays of light.

The demons that had tormented her mind hadn't lied.

As bitter as the harshest Montana winter, desperation cut through her heart. Blinking against tears, she dragged her gaze from the inscription on the small marble stone at her feet.

A low-lying fog was rolling in, swallowing the lights of the city situated on the far shore of the bay. The iconic Golden Gate was partially obscured, only the bridge's tall towers knifing through the fog to a black sky glittering with stars, a backdrop to the fireworks. She watched another shooting star rise high, streaks of fiery glitter bursting, then fizzling before her eyes. For a few awe-inspiring seconds, the pyrotechnics bedazzled, then faded, their short life spans over in quick, brilliant bursts. Over almost before they'd begun.

Like her son's brief life.

Her heart tugged so painfully she fell to her knees. She'd known this was possible, perhaps even probable, that he'd died, but throughout these past lonely years, she'd held out a glimmer of hope that he'd survived, that they would be reunited, that she would feel the warmth of his arms around her neck as she held him close. "Oh, baby," she whispered.

Once again she turned her attention to the small gravestone, a tiny marker in a sea of larger, more elaborate tombstones. In various shapes and sizes, some tall, some ornately carved, others more plain, the headstones stood unmoving, hulking along the slope that curved downward to the city and the dark, black waters of the bay.

Why?

Oh, God, why?

Closing her eyes, she drew in several deep breaths.

Don't question. It is what it is.

More importantly: What are you *going to do about it?*

Jaw clenched, she thought of those who had wronged her.

Those who had used her.

Those who had abused her.

Those who had taken out their animosity against her on the innocence of her child.

Still on her knees, she reached forward and traced the dates inscribed on the frigid stone with the tips of her fingers. Barely four years from date of birth to date of death.

Her heart cracked with the pain. "Oh, honey," she murmured, her throat catching as thoughts of that unlikely birth swirled in her brain. The agony of labor, the fear of the unknown, the rush in her blood at hearing the newborn's cry, and then the emptiness as her son was stolen from her, taken from that isolated delivery room. She'd heard the whispers in the hospital.

". . . deeply disturbed."

". . . mentally unstable."

". . . severe psychosis."

All spoken in hushed tones. As if she couldn't hear.

And now this.

She squeezed her eyes shut and brought to mind the manipulators who had made the decisions, those who had determined that she was "unable," or "unwilling," or "incapable." More words she wasn't supposed to hear. And then there was the harshest of all: "unfit." Her teeth gnashed as she remembered the callousness with which that word was tossed about. How would they know? Yes, she'd been unstable—she knew that—though the word "insanity," which she'd heard throughout her life, surely was extreme. She wasn't "insane," and never had been.

Especially not tonight.

No, as the rockets screamed into the sky, blooming in wild explosions of color and light, she'd never felt more sane. She'd spent so much time searching for her son only to find him buried here—that bit of hope she'd felt at the thought of reconnecting with him, of seeing him, of explaining to him and holding him . . . that tiny flame of expectation was now dead. Extinguished. And in its place rose a new emotion, raw and acrid.

Vengeance.

Swallowing the lump in her throat, she gazed at the small grave marker again and now, dry-eyed, thought of what lay ahead. "They'll pay," she promised her child, hoping that he would somehow know. Her fingers twisted in the drying grass of the hillside, the long blades and dandelions that were tucked close to the marker and had escaped the gardener's mower clutched in her fingers. "Every last one of them. I will hunt them down and, I promise you, they will pay." In her mind's eye she saw them all. As she pushed herself upright, a series of smaller fireworks exploded over the bay, flashes of kaleidoscopic colors disappearing in fading fingers until the darkness was unbroken again.

She knew who they were, those who had betrayed her.

She knew where they lived.

She also knew she had the element of surprise on her side.

And she would destroy them all.

Tossing the dried weeds from her fingers, she dusted her hands.

She had a mission.

As she headed down the hill, stepping carefully between the marble and granite sentinels of the dead, she plotted just how to wreak her vengeance against them.

A sense of cold satisfaction displaced her desperation.

She turned at the locked gate, then climbed atop the wrought-iron fence and looked back over her shoulder. Spying the tiny gravestone, she whispered, "I love you," and waited for an answer that didn't come.

Armed with her new purpose, she hopped lithely to the ground, shoved her hands into the pockets of her jacket, and felt the cold reassurance of the Beretta Pico, a small .380. Jaw set, she strode through the darkness, avoiding streetlights as the explosions burst overhead.

No one would stop her now.

No one would dare.

Chapter 1

San Francisco, California
Six Months Later

Brindel wanted a divorce.

Correction: She *needed* a divorce.

From Paul Latham . . . make that *Doctor* Paul Latham. He always did.

Self-important bastard.

Glancing out the bathroom window to the night beyond, the lights of the city pinpoints, the view even from this room stunning, she was ready to give it all up. But of course, Paul wouldn't go down without a fight. Not that it was about her or love. She actually laughed at that ridiculous thought, then took a sip from her second—or was it her third?—glass of wine. Didn't matter. She finished the last drop, considered pouring another, then decided against it, leaving the glass on the marble counter. Whatever love she and Paul had shared nearly fifteen years before had shriveled and died long ago, like a worm on a hot sidewalk. All that was left was a hard, heartless shell of their marriage. No, the reason he would fight her was that he wasn't a man who could lose. Not in his life, not in his marriage, not in his job, and especially not to her.

She shook her head. She'd been such a fool. She'd suspected early on, and discovered a few years into the marriage, that he'd expected her to raise his two sons, Macon and Seth. Which she had. Both disgustingly like their father.

Angrily she swiped off her makeup, scrubbing carefully, though she noticed a few irritating and stubborn lines on her face that needed a good shot of Botox. Afterward, she massaged cream into her skin, then brushed her hair until it gleamed. It now was blonder than her natural shade and streaked to hide any hint of gray, then cut in the most fashionable style money could buy, perfect layers framing her face to fall softly to her shoulders.

A glimpse of her closet showed off racks of shoes—heels, pumps, sandals, running shoes, a pair for every occasion displayed on lighted shelves that were slightly elevated. Neat rows. Each pair worth a small fortune.

How had she thought footwear costing thousands was worth the price of this hollow marriage? Along with the shoes, deeper into the wide walk-in were racks and racks of dresses, slacks, suits, sweaters, you name it, all designer, all expensive, all hung neatly, the gowns encased in plastic to protect them, purses, too. From the corner of her eye she caught a glimpse of the white gown she'd worn at her wedding—well, her second wedding if anyone was counting—and she saw the sparkle of beads, the cut of French lace, and cringed inwardly as she remembered wearing that gown and feeling as if her life, finally, had turned a favorable corner as she'd swept down the aisle to meet her handsome, successful groom. Despite his flashes of anger while engaged, his need to dominate, the warning knell from her sisters, she'd been determined to give herself and her toddler daughter a new, "perfect" life.

She'd had no idea how wrong she would be.

And now . . . now she needed to do something about it. Before it was too late. As it was, she was already over forty, for God's sake, her kid nearly grown. She stepped out of her robe and let it puddle on the floor. Turning sideways to the full-length mirror, she noted that her belly was flat and hard, her breasts high with the help of surgery and enhancements, her nipples pert and dark, her legs long and lean, even showing a bit of muscle, her posture erect. She was still very attractive, could compete with women ten, maybe even twelve years younger than she . . . well, maybe. If she had to. Not that she was looking for a new man. No way. At least not until she was single. She didn't want the hint of impropriety on her part. She'd already spoken to one of the best lawyers in town; she just hadn't pulled the trigger and filed for divorce yet.

"Tomorrow," Brindel said, mouthing the words as if her husband, who was in the next suite, could hear her.

More than slightly buzzy, she finally took out her contacts and finished getting ready for bed, which was basically undressing to slip between the soft sheets completely naked, a practice her husband had once found exciting, then disgusting, then had totally ignored. That had been before the remodel of the second floor into two master suites. His and hers. It had seemed perfect at the time, but now was claustrophobic. Silk wallpaper, coved ceilings, crystal chandelier, huge four-poster bed and private bathroom with its grand walk-in closet, all part and parcel of her jail cell.

And Brindel needed freedom.

More than anything else.

She'd only stayed as long as she had because of her daughter . . . and now . . . well . . .

She slid beneath the thick duvet, felt the polished cotton smooth against her skin, and turned off the bedside lamp. Her appointment was at nine, when she was certain her husband would be in the midst of his rounds at the hospital attached to the medical school, a short walk through the park from this house. She'd tell her attorney to file the papers and then let the chips fall where they may.

Smiling at the thought that she was finally doing *some*thing, well, actually the one thing he would abhor, she burrowed under the covers and drifted away, her dreams lulling her only to be interrupted by . . . what? The sound of footsteps? Oh, God, surely Paul wouldn't try to come into her room and slide into her bed. . . . Physically shuddering at the prospect, she opened an eye to darkness, the room lit only by the glow of the bedside clock.

Was that breathing she heard? Soft and low over the pounding of her racing heart?

She swallowed back her fear and stared, eyes narrowing, fingers curling at the edge of the duvet.

For a second she thought she saw movement—a shadow crossing in front of the armoire—but realized it was the mirror mounted over the antique, reflecting the sway of branches from the window on the opposite wall.

Don't be neurotic. You have one more night and then you start the fight for your freedom . . . and half of Paul's estate. He owes it to you for giving him almost fifteen of your best years. In her mind she calculated what she might receive, less attorney's fees. Three million? Maybe four? She'd earned every penny of it being married to the jerk-wad.

And it would be enough to last her the rest of her life.

Slightly calmer, she still listened for any sound that he might be stealthily walking down the hallway to her bedroom door, but she heard nothing . . . all her imagination. Her nerves were strung tight, that was it. Because of her meeting in the morning. She was alone. Safe. In her own damned bedroom. Closing her eyes again, she started to breathe easier.

And there it was.

The whisper-soft scrape of a footstep. Then another.

And a new smell. Musky and male and . . .

Brindel's eyes flew open and she gasped, saw the muzzle of a gun just before it was pressed to her forehead.

What??? NO!

She opened her mouth to scream.

Her attacker pulled the trigger.

An ear-splitting blast.

Then nothing.

"No, no, noooo!" Ivy threw a hand over her mouth to keep from screaming.

The carnage was horrible. Mind numbing.

Backing up quickly, the image of death seared forever in her brain, she wondered how everything could have gone so terribly wrong.

She knocked over a small table near the door, a vase with a single rose sliding to the floor, while on the bed . . . oh, sweet Jesus, on her mother's feminine bed . . .

Death.

A small dark hole in the smooth forehead, blood coagulated around the entrance wound, spatters of red on the creamy skin. And the eyes, God, her mother's eyes, sightless and open, seemingly accusing.

Blood on the ruched duvet and the lamp shades, flecks on the thick, white rug covering the ancient hardwood. "Oh, God, oh, God, oh . . ." Her stomach threatened to heave as she turned and fled, down the narrow hall with its long runner, pictures of the family placed perfectly on the hallway . . . and to the next room and the second body, lying facedown, the back of his head a mangle of blood, bone, and brains visible through a huge gaping wound that had destroyed the graying hair that had once been thick, his pride and joy. She backed up, ran into the wall, banging her shoulder as she raced through the familiar rooms, the acrid scent of blood chasing after her, the horrid images burned in her brain.

As she ran, Ivy retched, threw a hand over her mouth and tasted blood. Salty . . . or was that her tears?

Get out. Get out, now! Don't step in any of it, don't get it on your shoes. Run like you've never run before!

Images blurred in her vision, the old globe in the library, the books, never read but stacked in neat rows to the high ceiling, the mullioned windows overlooking the city, lights winking through the beveled glass. The banister—*don't touch it!*—smoothed by over a century of hands sliding along it.

She was gasping as she hurried down the runner of the steps, her feet flying, her hair streaming behind her as she reached the marbled foyer—*NO! Not out the front! What are you thinking? There could be people on the street. Old man Cranston walking his aging dachshund, or the Miller girl who was always running the streets at night, or a stranger . . . no, no, no! The back. You need to go out the back door, through the backyard, to the alley. Then, if no one's around, cut through the park. Fast. Run, damn it!*

She skidded around the bottom of the staircase and through a short hallway toward the rear of the old home.

A creak in the floorboards overhead made her stop short.

Was someone up there?

Someone still alive?

Or the killers?

Who? *Who?*

Holding her breath, she strained to listen over the frantic trip-hammering of her heart.

Was that a footstep?

A noise on the stairs?

Oh. Dear. God.

She didn't wait to find out, but flew through the darkened kitchen, her knee banging against a bar stool near the center island. "Ow!" Cutting off the scream, she saw the knife block resting on the marble top. Without a second thought, she yanked the butcher knife from its slot and raced to the back door.

Another creak on the stairs.

Shit!

Fear raced through her bloodstream as she found the doorknob and yanked on the door, the reflection of her own silhouette visible in the glass panels, the cold of winter rushing inside. She thought she saw movement behind her—the killer!

Oh, Jesus. No!

Ivy raced down the back porch, slipping on the last step.

She caught herself, but dropped the knife. It clattered against the brick path and she left it, flew through the back gate and didn't bother to stop as the gate slammed closed behind her. Running down the narrow, crumbling alley for all she was worth, she splashed through a puddle and scared a cat hiding near the garbage cans. It hissed and backed away, white needle-sharp teeth visible in the dim light of a security lamp on the neighbor's back porch.

Another screech.

The gate opening on its rusting hinges?

The damned cat scared again?

The killer chasing her down?

She didn't bother to look over her shoulder. Panicked, she sped headlong into the street.

A passing car honked and swerved, barely missing her, street water spraying beneath screeching tires.

She stumbled. Caught herself. Ran.

"Idiot!" a male with a deep voice proclaimed, rolling down the window of his white Volvo to make certain she heard.

She didn't care. Reeling back from the street, she kept going, scrambling away.

Adrenaline propelling her, she raced between two

parked cars and along the sidewalk. She didn't quit running at the gates of the park, but sped inside. Heart in her throat, she flew along the path. At a bend in the sidewalk, she veered into the undergrowth, away from the pools of light cast by the lampposts that lit the groomed path. Crouching, breathing hard, she scrabbled into rain-drenched thickets, where trees and shrubbery were her salvation. Her skin prickled. Rain slid down her bare head and under the collar of her jacket. She barely noticed, her fear was so intense, the images of the dead bright behind her eyes.

Don't panic.

But it was too late. Rational thought had disappeared, chased by pure terror. Was it her fault? When she'd agreed . . . ? How the hell had this happened?

She swallowed back a dose of guilt and took stock of her situation.

Ivy had played in this park as a child, knew all the hiding spots, and thought she might be safe, if just for a few minutes, long enough to catch her breath and gather her wits.

What now?

Where could she go?

Where could she hide?

Teeth chattering, body trembling, she tried and failed to dislodge the bloody images of the dead bodies from her mind. Her parents. Slaughtered in their beds. Unsuspecting. The brutality and unfairness of it all was too much and she started to cry, tears burning down her wet, cold cheeks. This wasn't supposed to happen, she thought wildly. No, not this. Not now. Not ever.

Calm down. Just calm the hell down!

She couldn't. Bile filled her throat. Her insides revolted. She threw up violently, the contents of her stomach emptying onto the bark dust by a thick-leaved rhododendron bush. Then again. This time bile came up and after wiping her nose and mouth with her sleeve, it was all she could do to prevent herself from dry-heaving. She scuttled backward, deeper into the bushes, distancing herself from the sour pool of vomit, creeping over rocks.

Hiding here was no good.

She'd be found soon.

Those who had killed might still be looking for her.

There was a good chance, she knew, that she was the ultimate target.

With that sizzling thought, she rimmed the park, keeping near the brick fence until she reached the far side. From her hiding spot, she had a clear view of the central fountain, lights directed at the rushing water tumbling over jagged rocks. No one stood gazing at the wet stone, no one appeared on the fringes of light.

And yet she felt the weight of someone's gaze, someone who was hiding just like she was, someone who would think nothing of taking her life.

Get a grip. No one's there.

Think.

Come up with a damned plan!

Her insides quivered and she nearly jumped out of her skin as the leaves rattled nearby. Biting back a scream, she scooted closer to the fence as a fat raccoon waddled from the cover of the bushes and padded around the base of a lamp near the path. She let out her breath and tried to pull her thoughts together. So far, it seemed, she hadn't been followed. The sounds of the city surrounded her, the even rumble of engines and whine of tires as traffic passed on the other side of the brick wall enclosing this block of greenery. Cigarette smoke drifted to her nostrils and she heard muted voices as people passed on the sidewalk on the other side of the brick barrier separating the park from the rest of San Francisco. A quiet cough. A far-off bark. In the distance a foghorn moaned. Yet no hurrying footsteps running toward the park.

Please, God . . .

Attempting to calm herself, to slow her racing heart, to force the fear back into the farthest reaches of her mind, Ivy frantically reviewed her options. She knew she had to escape. Now!

Going back to the house was out of the question.

Calling the police would be a major mistake.

Notifying anyone she knew would only put her in more jeopardy.

She could trust no one. Not a soul.

It wasn't supposed to happen this way! When she agreed to . . . oh, God. Her mother was dead. Killed.

Hands shaking, she slipped her fingers into the pocket of her jacket, felt her phone and the wad of cash that she'd hidden there. Four thousand dollars. Enough to escape and disappear.

Footsteps sounded. Someone moving fast.

Hurrying through these blocks of greenery.

Her heart lurched.

She bit her lip, trained her gaze toward the sound.

Her ears and eyes straining, her senses on alert, she heard the rapid footfalls, then spied a runner cutting through the park, slim and sleek, a man in reflective running gear striding easily, his breath fogging, earbuds visible as he flew past.

She couldn't stay here any longer.

It wasn't safe.

She was a sitting duck.

Ivy slipped through the dense, wet foliage, easing her way to the entrance on the far side of the park and out. Flipping the rain-soaked hood of her jacket over her wet hair, she walked rapidly through the city blocks where skyscrapers knifed upward into the dark sky, patches of warm lights visible in a few apartment windows, security lights in businesses.

By instinct, she headed downhill, toward the waterfront where, she hoped, she'd find a way to leave this city and her painful past forever. A bus out of the city. That's what she'd do. Find a bus and buy a one-way ticket.

She didn't care where.

Just as long as it was far, far away.

Chapter 2

An impatient little cry echoed through the house.

No. Please, just go back to sleep. From her side of the bed, Regan Pescoli glanced at the clock. 2:43 AM. Middle of the night.

What do you expect with an infant?

She eyed the somewhat blurry baby monitor, but as she focused she saw that Little Tucker was indeed awake, moving his arms and definitely making baby noises. *Great*. Then the screen went blank for a second, only to catch the image again. The monitor was wonky at best, useless at worst. She might have to break down and buy a new one.

Someday.

But not today.

With her husband snoring softly, she slid from the bed, found her robe tossed on a nearby chair, and stuffed her arms through its sleeves as she padded barefoot to the nursery where her baby was starting to raise a serious racket.

"I'm coming, I'm coming," she said in a whisper, then, in the dim illumination of the night-light, picked Tucker up and, after a quick diaper change, carried him to the nearby rocker, where she tried to nurse him. Of course that wasn't working. Hadn't for the past couple of months. He attempted to suckle and failed, sending up a wail loud enough to raise the dead in five counties.

"Okay, okay." Carefully she hauled him downstairs, heated a bottle quickly, and sat in Santana's recliner while Little Tucker ate hungrily. "There ya go," she said with a smile in her voice, though she was unhappy that she was no longer able to breast-feed him. With both her older children, she'd nursed until they were nearly a year old, but, of course, that had been a long while back, over twenty years for her oldest. "Sorry, little one," she whispered, placing a kiss on his downy head. "But that's what you get for having an old . . . er, let's make that *older* mother." Once he'd fallen asleep, she took him back to his crib, then walked into the master bedroom where Santana hadn't so much as moved.

Perfect.

Before sliding between the covers, she stepped into her slippers, then stepped onto the deck. Snow had piled across its bare planks, though now the night was clear and a million stars were flung across the wide Montana sky. Her gaze moved to the nearby lake, now iced over and serene, a calm vista where tall firs and pines, snow dusted and regal, guarded the far shore.

She loved this view of the lake and the mountains beyond. Loved her new home with her new husband

and her children. The air was still, no creatures stirring, and she should have felt at peace.

And yet . . .

As she squinted into the darkness, her eyes thinning on the distant shore of the lake, she felt a strange uneasiness. The hairs at the base of her scalp lifted in warning, as if something evil, unseen but malicious, was staring back at her.

You've spent too many years as a detective, seen too many horrific acts, witnessed too much carnage, and face it, though Tucker's six months old, your hormones are probably still out of whack, and on top of all of that you're sleep deprived—seriously *sleep deprived. There is nothing malevolent lurking in the shadows, no one or nothing evil hiding in the forest. Go to bed. Get some damned sleep.*

Turning, she reached for the handle of the door as a gust of wind swept across the frozen water, rushing past her and seeming to whisper:

I see you.

But that was crazy.

And then another gust.

I see everything.

"Who are you?" she whispered, her blood running cold, but as she heard her own words, she shook her head. For God's sake, no one had said anything. Just her own fears suggesting the words on the wintry air, just her exhaustion causing her to hallucinate. Hell, she was still half asleep . . . it was nothing. She didn't believe in ghosts or tarot cards or Ouija boards or Sasquatches—especially not Sasquatches—or anything the least bit supernatural. Pescoli would leave all that paranormal crap to Grace Perchant, the local "ghost lady" who lived alone except for a couple of wolf-dog hybrids. Grace claimed she could talk to the dead and see into the future.

Pescoli definitely didn't.

She walked into the house again, heard her husband's even breathing, and silently chided herself for being so susceptible. Everything was fine.

But as she locked the door she reminded herself that her service weapon was still locked in a safe in the closet. She then slid into the bed and nestled close to Santana. He murmured something in his sleep and flung an arm around her waist, the warmth of his body invading her own. She closed her eyes, willing herself to relax, but knew that it would be hours rather than minutes before she'd fall asleep again.

Pescoli was certain she'd barely shut her eyes when her cell phone chirped, then vibrated against her nightstand, buzzing loudly.

"No," she whispered, and pulled the covers over her head. She didn't care who it was—she couldn't answer the damned phone, not when she was more tired than she'd ever been in her life. Squeezing her eyes shut, she heard her cell fall onto the floor where it buzzed again.

Flinging off the duvet cover, she glared for a second at the bedroom ceiling before giving herself up to the fact that she never would get enough sleep. Not with two teenagers and one infant living under her roof. Glancing over, she noted that Santana wasn't in bed with her.

No surprise there; he was always up and at 'em early with the livestock, feeding the horses, cleaning stalls, getting ready to exercise and train the mares, geldings, and stallions in his care.

"Fine," she muttered, and leaned over the edge of the bed to scoop up the phone.

Alvarez's name showed on the small screen.

Great.

Why the hell was her ex-partner calling so early? Seven thirty in the damned morning. Then again, Alvarez had probably been up for hours, riding a stationary bike at the gym, or taking a yoga class, or sipping herbal tea, or already hard at work.

"Yeah?" Pescoli growled. She pushed herself up in the bed, propping her back with the pillows, shoving her mass of curls from her forehead. "Do you know what time it is?"

"I wanted to make sure you were awake," was the all-too-chipper reply.

"Hardy-har-har."

Alvarez, with her damned routines, by-the-book attitude, and even-tempered, logical brain, was a self-professed "morning person." Sometimes she bugged the hell out of Pescoli and right now was one of those times. "I thought you'd be up with the baby."

"Not yet."

"I assumed he was on a schedule."

"He didn't get the memo," Pescoli said, but grudgingly admitted, "but I gotta get up anyway. I don't hear anyone else stirring and Bianca's got school." Yawning, she flung open the covers just as she heard water running in the hall bath. Her daughter was stepping into the shower. Good.

"Blackwater's been on the warpath."

"What else is new?" The sheriff, a younger gung-ho type who had stepped into the job after the death of Dan Grayson, was always trying to improve the department, which, she supposed, was his right. But his take-charge and while you're at it take-no-prisoners attitude annoyed her. Then again, a lot of things annoyed her. Sleep deprivation had not improved her temperament.

"He's asked about you coming back."

"I know." He'd called several times.

"And?"

"I haven't decided. I've got another couple of months."

Actually she didn't. The department was allowing her to use years of accumulated sick leave after returning to the force briefly a few months earlier right after her maternity leave. Now she needed to make a final decision.

Alvarez lowered her voice. "Well, figure it out, okay? And let me know. He's got me paired with Ramsby and it's killing me."

Carson Ramsby, twenty-seven, a bachelor, and a know-it-all who never shut up, considered himself a walking/talking Wikipedia. "I thought you were going to get a new transfer from Helena. Amy Something-or-other."

"Amy Glass. Didn't work out. She took a job in Butte." A pause. "Blackwater has let it be known that he doesn't expect you back and he thinks I can be a good influence on Ramsby, if that's even possible." She hesitated, then added, "Look, I know that you and Dylan have been talking."

That much was true. Pescoli had spoken a couple of times to Dylan O'Keefe, Alvarez's fiancé. They'd discussed her becoming a PI as well as his partner.

Alvarez continued, "I can't tell you what to do—"

"But?" Finding the robe she'd tossed off earlier at the end of her bed, Pescoli slipped one arm through a sleeve, then the next.

"Give me a heads-up, okay?"

"I will. Really."

They hung up and Pescoli headed into the adjoining bath where she saw her image in the mirror and frowned. Not only were a few irritating gray hairs revealing themselves in her wild, red-blond hair, but also dark circles appeared under her eyes from lack of sleep, and those irritating ten pounds of baby weight. "You're too old for this," she told her reflection, then stripped and walked through the shower, feeling the warm jets douse her hair and body while chasing the remaining cobwebs from her brain.

Drying off, she threw on jeans and a sweatshirt, pulled her hair back into a quick ponytail, and didn't bother with any makeup. She peeked into the nursery and saw that Tucker was sleeping soundly, his little lips moving in a sucking motion, his eyes closed, his cap of dark hair mussed. Silently she backed out of the room and hurried downstairs to find that Santana had already made coffee, thank God, and Bianca was shoving books and her iPad into her backpack. Bianca's wet hair was pulled into a messy bun and she was wearing worn, holey jeans and a black sweater with a wide neck. For years Bianca had spent hours doing her makeup, hair, and nails before stepping one foot out the door. Not so much anymore.

A new worry.

To go along with a slew of others.

"You get breakfast?" Pescoli poured herself a cup of coffee and saw from the package left near the pot that it was decaf. Not her first choice, but necessary for as long as she breast-fed her baby.

"A yogurt."

"That all?"

"For now." Wide eyes looked up at her mother, silently daring her to argue.

Pescoli held up a hand.

"Tuck's not awake?"

"Not yet. And we want him to stay that way . . . for a while. So have you seen your brother this morning? Your *other* brother?"

"Nah." Bianca glanced out the window to the snow-crusted morning and the driveway where several vehicles were parked, including Jeremy's pickup. "But his truck's still here." He lived in a room, well, more like a studio apartment, over the garage. He was always talking about moving out, but so far hadn't done so and was still working part time while going to school. That was all good. The fact that he was still talking about becoming a cop wasn't.

Jeremy's father, Joe, had been on the force, killed in the line of duty, a fate she fervently prayed would not be her son's. The fact that she, too, was a detective was Jeremy's favorite fallback position whenever she tried to steer him away from law enforcement.

"I'll check."

"You don't have to check, Mom. He's an adult and . . . and, you know, he could have company," Bianca reminded her as her phone gave a quick ring tone and she glanced at the screen. "Oh, fu-frick!" Her lips twisted downward as she read the message.

"Trouble?"

"No. Just Dad. He keeps texting me." She slid the phone into her back pocket, then grabbed her jacket and backpack from a hook near the rear door.

"He probably won't stop until you reply."

"Can't you do anything about that?"

"We've been over this." But she didn't blame her daughter. Truth to tell, she would like to string Lucky up by his balls and read him the riot act over and over again or see him drop off the face of the earth. Yeah, that would be better. But she held her tongue. She'd said what she'd had to about her ex and what he'd done months ago, then had fought all her motherly instincts and let her nearly grown daughter deal with the dirtbag that was her father. It about killed her.

"I'm not talking to him. Ever." Again the challenge as Bianca glared at her mother, but Pescoli was staying out of that dog fight. Bianca's father, Luke aka Lucky Pescoli, had crossed a line with both Regan and Bianca just this past summer when he'd been instrumental in her kidnapping. Bianca had nearly lost her life and in the process had killed her captor, though no charges had been filed against her. Hence, Bianca was dealing with all kinds of thorny issues that included guilt, anger, fear, and, of course, there was no way she'd forgiven Lucky.

Regan got it.

Lucky Pescoli was handsome as hell, or had been, but was a prick of the highest—make that lowest—

order, but she didn't say it, just sipped her jolt-less coffee because like it or not, she'd picked him for husband number two and he was Bianca's father.

A big mistake, but there it was.

"And I'm changing my name—my last name."

"If you want to—"

"To Santana," she said, lifting her chin. "You should too!"

She swept out the back door.

On that count, her daughter was right. Pescoli was considering it.

Through the window she watched Bianca trudge through the snow to her ten-year-old Jeep. Once behind the wheel, she fired up the engine and took off, snow spraying from beneath the Wrangler's big tires.

Pescoli watched the SUV disappear into the trees just as the back door opened again. Along with a blast of cold air, Santana, three dogs trailing behind him, strode into the kitchen. Cisco, the oldest of the lot, a small, wiry terrier, took one look at Pescoli and did his little dance, rotating in tight circles and barking, while Sturgis, the black lab they'd inherited upon Dan Grayson's death, wagged his tail slowly. Nikita, Santana's husky, nosed around the baseboards hoping for a scrap of forgotten food.

"Hey, beautiful," her husband said, and she shook her head.

"Not feeling all that beautiful today," she admitted, setting her cup on the counter.

"Always are to me."

She eyed him warily. "What's with all the flattery?"

"Just the facts, ma'am," he drawled.

"Sure," she replied, fighting a smile as he settled

onto a stool at the kitchen island and skimmed his iPad. Where once there had been newsprint in their home, there were now only computer screens. "Alvarez called."

"Yeah?"

"She wants me to come back to work. Sooner rather than later."

He looked up and she saw the reservation in his dark eyes. "You tried before," he said, reminding her of her brief stint on duty once her maternity leave had ended.

"I know." She'd been excited to return to work but had missed her son to the point of being miserable. And then there was the fact that her emotions had been stretched to the breaking point.

"So?" he prompted.

"I don't know."

"For what it's worth—"

"I know where you stand." She cut him off. "But my decision, right?"

A muscle worked in his jaw. "Right."

"Glad to see you're so progressive," she said sharply, then regretted her tone. "Never mind. You want me here, I know. But you know I'm really not the type to sit at home and volunteer at the preschool or arrange playdates with moms who are probably, oh, I dunno, maybe half or at least only two-thirds my age?"

"You talked about becoming a PI," he reminded. "With O'Keefe."

She walked to the counter, found a loaf of bread, and popped two slices of whole grain into the toaster. "It wouldn't be the same."

"But it would be safer."

She threw him a glance. "Would it?" But she couldn't

argue the point. At one time or another everyone in her family had been in jeopardy, largely in part because of her job with the sheriff's department. And hadn't she crossed a line or two while on duty?

She hated to admit it but she missed working with uptight Alvarez, of being a part of the department, of the adrenaline rush of chasing down a killer, of being part of a team even if the new sheriff had no chance of ever filling Dan Grayson's size-thirteen boots. There were a few irritants in the department—Pete Watershed came quickly to mind—but still . . . The toast popped, she pulled out the hot slices gingerly, tossing them onto a plate just as she heard the distinct wail coming from the floor above. "Uh-oh. Sounds like the prince is awake."

"Come on," Santana protested. "Don't call him that. 'Sport' or 'cowboy' or 'buddy,' that's okay, but just not 'prince,' okay?"

She picked up her tepid coffee, took a big gulp from her cup, then tossed the remains into the sink where she left her cup. "Okay—maybe he'll be 'honey-bunny' or 'snookums' then."

"Right."

Hurrying up the steps, she heard Santana laugh.

In the nursery she found her son lying on his back in his crib, his dark eyes open wide. At the sight of her his little arms flailed wildly and he grinned.

That baby smile melted her heart. "You are a prince, aren't you?" she whispered, picking him up and smelling the clean baby scent of him. For the first time since the phone had woken her up, she grinned. "Huh, Tucker-Boy? Need a new dipe-dipe?" He cooed at her and she smiled back, then thought of what her colleagues at the department might say if they heard her making baby talk with her newborn. “Screw ’em, right?” she said before changing his diaper and onesie, then settling into the rocker to nurse. He latched on, suckled for a few minutes, then screwed up his face. “Sorry,” she whispered. “I guess it’s not in the cards for you and me anymore. Come on, let’s go see Daddy.”

Deftly she stood and, barefoot, carried Tucker down the stairs and into the kitchen.

“You’re up, Dad,” she said, finding Santana at the counter separating the cooking area from the family room. Tucker brightened at the sight of his father. She handed the baby into her husband’s waiting hands. “I’ll heat the bottle, you can feed him.”

“Hey, buddy,” Santana said, grinning at his son and letting the baby muss his hair. Tucker giggled, finding his father hysterical, his little legs moving jerkily in excitement. A fire was burning in the grate, blankets lopping over the edge of the couch, the dogs settled in their beds. Cozy. Warm. Home. Yeah, she loved it here, she thought as she finished making the bottle and handing it to her husband.

Her phone buzzed again.

“What is it this morning?” She read the screen but the number was unfamiliar. Punching the button to answer, she said brusquely, “Pescoli.”

“Regan!” a female voice cried. “Oh, God, I’m so glad this number still works.” Anxiety swept through the caller’s voice. “You have to come to San Francisco. Now.”

“Who is—?” she started to ask when she recognized

her sister Sarina's shrill voice. A sinking sensation settled over her. None of her sisters ever called unless something was wrong—seriously wrong.

"Oh, God. It's awful," Sarina cried. It sounded as if she was sobbing. "Just so awful."

"What is?"

"Brindel! She's dead."

"What?" Pescoli's heart nearly stopped. "Dead?" Brindel, second-born of the four Connors siblings, was tall and blond with a snarky sense of humor and a willingness to do whatever it took to get ahead.

"Yes! Dead! *Murdered!* Can you believe it? In her bed. I mean who would—?"

"Wait. Slow down." Regan leaned against the counter for support and noticed that Santana, who was holding the baby, was at attention, his gaze drilling into hers. Sarina was still crying. "Okay, okay, get ahold of yourself," she said to her sister. "Start over. At the beginning." Shaken, Regan was still trying to get her head around the news. But it was impossible. Maybe Sarina was mistaken—it certainly wouldn't be the first time.

"Not just Brindel, but Paul, too."

Paul was Brindel's husband. A doctor. Some kind of specialist. Heart, maybe. And a supercilious jerk, at least in Regan's estimation, but *dead*? She couldn't wrap her brain around it.

"It's just horrible. Horrible." Sarina was out-and-out bawling now, her words nearly indistinguishable. "You—you—oh, God, you have to do something!"

"Me?"

"You're a cop, aren't you? A detective?"

"In Montana. On leave."

"Perfect. Then you can fly out."

"I can't—"

"Sure you can! Regan, you have to. You just have to. You can stay with me. Or Collette."

"No." The thought of spending days with either of her siblings was out of the question.

"Our sister is dead. *Dead!* Someone came into her bedroom and shot her in the head. While she was sleeping. Do you hear me?" Sarina demanded, nearly screaming. "Brindel was murdered. *Murdered!* Oh, my God, Regan, I can't believe you won't help."

"Sarina!" Regan snapped. "I didn't say I wouldn't help. Now, calm down. Okay? Just calm down. I didn't say I wouldn't help, but I'm not staying with either of you. . . . If I come I'll get a hotel . . . or something."

"If? Just *get here*. This is so horrible! I can't believe it!" She began to wail again.

"Pull yourself together," Regan said, her own shock dissipating a little as she began to think like a cop. "Take a couple of deep breaths and then, slowly, tell me what happened."

"I don't know. That's just it, and the cops—the police—they're not saying much. I haven't even talked to the detective in charge yet. His name is Anthony Paterno, but I've only talked to a uniformed guy and he was pretty tight-lipped and pissed me off!"

Paterno? Why did that name ring a bell?

"So far Paterno won't talk to us. And I get the feeling, you know, that they, the police, don't trust us. Like we all might be suspects or something."

"We all?"

"Me and Collette. She's here too. Devastated."

Regan pictured Collette, the oldest of the Connors

sisters. Tall and pale blond with sharp features that matched her wicked tongue, Collette bulldozed her way through life, always got what she wanted, just like Brindel. An image of her sister came to mind and she had to deliberately set it aside to keep her emotions at bay. "The police will rule you out right away," Pescoli said, hoping it was true.

"Oh, God. I don't even know what happened. All I know is that Paul and Brindel were killed at home in their bedrooms."

"Bedrooms. Separate?"

"Yes, yes. It's . . . it's how they lived. You know, separate lives. Dona, their housekeeper, found them this morning. Brindel in her bedroom; Paul in his. Both in bed, at least I think so. I—I'm not really sure about that. Oh, dear God, I don't know. But poor Dona, to have walked into that—" She started to wail again.

"What about anyone else? Their kids? His boys? Brindel's daughter?"

"Oh . . . I don't know," Sarina blubbered. "The boys—Macon and Seth—they're away at school. Maybe? I'm not sure about anything. Brindel isn't . . . wasn't close to them."

"And Ivy?" Regan prodded.

"Ivy . . . Oh, Jesus. I think Ivy is missing!"

Chapter 3

Anthony Paterno, senior investigator for the San Francisco Police Department, surveyed the bedroom again while the ME's office was zipping up a body bag and loading the body of Brindel Latham onto a wheeled stretcher. Unfortunately, her sister had arrived and was having an emotional meltdown.

The crime scene guys were spread throughout the huge house, searching for trace evidence, photographing the rooms, vacuuming the carpets in hopes of finding hairs or tiny bits of evidence, dusting for prints, and going over all six-thousand square feet of the old house. The ME had finished with the bodies and now they were being hauled off to the morgue. No other victims had been found. No sign of the kids. In fact it seemed that the Lathams had been alone before being murdered.

The girl's room looked like it had been recently occupied, the bed unmade, but her purse and phone were missing along with her. Had she been kidnapped? Had she left of her own accord? He'd stared at her room as the techs had gone through the bedding and unhooked her computer. What the hell had happened to her? Hopefully nothing bad, but he'd thought about child/sex trafficking or the fact that she could be dead somewhere else. God, he hoped not.

Paterno had walked through the house carefully, disturbing nothing but eyeing it all. The home itself was grand, built in an era of pitched roofs, thick columns, mullioned windows, and the like. Over a hundred years old and upgraded with modern features that looked as if they'd been crafted in a previous century. Smooth tile, glossy marble, ancient hardwoods, grand chandeliers. . . . Still, the people inside, a man and a woman, were dead, killed in their beds—in their separate bedrooms though they were married. Dr. Paul Latham had been killed wearing only boxer shorts, the back of his skull destroyed, and his wife, Brindel, lying face up, a round bullet hole in the space on her forehead above her nose, the old "right between the eyes" shot, had been totally nude. Was that how she normally slept? Maybe. Had something sexual gone on first? Again, a possibility. There was evidence of a robbery, a safe in the library open and empty, a second one in the doctor's bedroom unlocked and cleaned out as well. On top of all that, Latham had a built-in armory, a gun closet with a sliding door, which seemed like it had housed a bevy of weaponry. It, too, was empty, the door left open, lights illuminating empty cases and racks.

So were these homicides the result of a burglary gone bad, he wondered, as he stepped outside and surveyed the gardens in the back of the house. Obviously that was what the police were supposed to think—the simple answer—but something was off. The victims were in their beds as if they'd been sleeping. Had they been killed before their valuables had been stolen, just to make sure nothing went wrong during the robbery, collateral damage as it were? Or was the robbery a mask for the murders?

He didn't know yet, he thought, glancing up at the gray sky, clouds with dark bellies moving steadily inland, the chill of a brisk winter wind piercing his rain jacket. The grounds were neatly tended, a fenced, sloped yard, boxwoods and other greenery, a gate that opened to an alley that ran between the backyards of half a dozen houses as grand and ornate as this one.

But he'd figure it out. He always did. This, he'd decided, would be his last case and then he'd retire. Put all the murder and mayhem, the brutal carnage and ugly side of life, behind him. Buy his brother-in-law's cabin cruiser, and leave the damp and cold of San Francisco for some warmer climate, sail south, past LA and San Diego, and find some little village on the coast of Mexico where he could drink tequila, fish for sierra or snapper, or sea bass, even a yellowtail, and spend his nights staring at the stars.

"Inspector?"

He was jolted out of his reverie by a sharp male voice and turned to find a uniformed policeman approaching. Short, fit, twenty-something, all business. Officer Nowak.

"I think maybe you should talk to Ms. Marsh. She's—"

"The sister of Mrs. Latham," he said, nodding. He'd known she would show up because of the woman who'd called in the crime, a nearly hyperventilating housekeeper with whom he'd been connected, Dona Andalusia. The housekeeper had told him, "The missus's sister in Oakland. Oh, my God. I didn't know what to do. I called her, *su hermana*, one of her sisters, the one who lives close . . . Sarina . . . Sarina. I'm sorry, I don't remember her last name. But I called her. I didn't know what to do."

"You did fine," he'd told her.

"I think she is coming to the house. To see—"

"That's okay. I'll talk to her, but she can't go inside. No one can."

"*Sí, sí.* I know. I know."

"She can't see her sister," he'd warned. "Not yet."

"*Dios.*" Something unintelligible in Spanish. He'd convinced her to stay at the crime scene so that she could speak with him. She had. A middle-aged, round-figured woman with apple cheeks and graying black hair tied back into a single long braid, she'd stood with a uniformed cop on the sidewalk in front of the house, inside the police barrier surrounding the Latham estate. She'd been wringing her hands, her brow furrowed, her big eyes dark with worry. He'd been introduced and Dona, nodding, gesturing wildly, had explained about finding the bodies.

Her story had never faltered: She'd come to the house as usual. When no one answered her knock, she'd let herself in with her own key and thought she was alone, even called out and received no answer. She'd started cleaning when she noticed the back door swinging open, and then, upon further inspection, the horrifying bedroom scenes. First she'd found "the missus" dead in her bed.

"It is horrible," Dona had said. "*Mal*. Evil. The work of *el diablo,* the devil. She was dead. I know. I feel for a pulse but . . . *nada* . . . nothing." Shaking her head, she'd swallowed hard before explaining that she'd peered into the second bedroom where she'd found "Mister Paul, oh . . . *Dios mío*, he was . . ." Dona had closed her eyes as if in so doing she could block out the mental image of Paul Latham's body. "And then I run," she said. "I run out of the house, to the neighbors and make the call to nine-one-one." Tears welled in her eyes. "Who would do such a thing? *Qué tipo de monstruo?* I mean, what kind of monster?"

"I don't know, but that's what we intend to find out," Paterno had assured her as she'd deftly sketched a sign of the cross over her chest. He'd given her his card, said he'd be calling, and had sent her off with a cop to take her to the station so she could give a complete statement.

So now he'd deal with the sister who lived nearby. He glanced at the cloud cover threatening rain, remembered that it was supposed to clear out by early afternoon, if the weatherman could be believed.

Following the deputy through the house to the front gate, Paterno saw a news van had double-parked on a side street, a reporter bustling out of the passenger side, a cameraman hefting a shoulder cam as he climbed from behind the wheel to eye the street.

Paterno ignored them for now as he followed Nowak to the front sidewalk, still cordoned off, where he found not one woman, but two, huddled together under a single umbrella though it wasn't raining, and the resemblance between them suggested they were sisters. Both in their early forties, he guessed, and taller than average. The shorter one had brown hair pulled into a drooping ponytail; the taller, thinner woman, with a plaid scarf draped over her shoulders and hoop earrings, wore her blond hair cut straight at the shoulders. In heeled boots and a long trench coat, her large eyes suspicious, her glossy lips tight, she seemed to be more in control of her emotions, whereas the shorter, rounder woman in a jacket and jeans was an obvious wreck. Mascara ran, her lips trembled, her eyes were rimmed in red, and her ponytail seemed forgotten, threatening to fall out of its band. "Inspector Paterno?" she asked in a quavering voice. "I'm . . . I'm Sarina Marsh, Brindel's sister, and this is—"

"Collette Foucher," the second woman cut in. "*Also* Brindel Latham's sister." Collette's words were clipped. "What happened here?"

"That's what we're trying to figure out."

"Was my sister murdered?" Foucher demanded.

He didn't like the way she glared at him and the fact that there were newspeople hovering nearby. "We're investigating."

"Murder-suicide, I bet. That prick!" she hissed, her face contorting in disgust.

"You don't know that!" Sarina said.

Collette shot her sister a dark look. "She was going to divorce him. Remember?"

"Yeah. But to kill . . ." Sarina shook her head, the wet ponytail slapping her shoulders. "I don't—I won't—believe it."

"Believe it," Collette advised. "Well, the murder part anyway. Paul is probably too much of a coward to kill himself. He was bad news. I told that to Brindel before she married him and now"—her voice cracked and her cool facade slipped a bit—"now . . ." She let out a tremulous sigh and her sister wrapped an arm around her taller sibling's waist.

Sarina's chin wobbled. "What about Ivy?"

Before he could answer, Collette said, "Ivy, if you don't know, is Brindel's daughter. Teenager and a handful, let me tell you. Sarina's been trying to locate her, calling and texting, but Ivy's not picking up or responding." She dabbed a finger beneath her eyes, drying them without messing with her mascara.

Sniffing, Sarina said, "It's not like her. Not to answer a text or return a call. I've texted about twenty times and called four." She shrugged and blinked. "Nothing." Frowning, she said, "I hope she's okay. . . . I wonder—oh, God, I hope not—but if she's been kidnapped?"

Collette's lips pursed. "Whoever kidnapped that one would have a fight on his hands." Then, realizing the conversation had strayed, she added, "We just need to know what's going on here. Find out what happened to Brindel."

"Maybe it's not her in there." Sarina's voice held little hope. "I mean, Paul . . . he . . . well, he wasn't entirely faithful."

Collette snorted. "What she means is that Paul Latham was a tom cat, what our mother used to refer to as a playboy, like it was—I don't know—kind of naughty but acceptable, back in the day, even something a man could be proud of. Thank you, Hugh Hefner! Anyway, Paul was one of those men who couldn't keep his hands to himself. Just ask some of the nurses he worked with. He even came on to me once at a Christmas party. All drunk and grabby. And he was in trouble with some of his patients, or had been." Her eyebrows arched. "If you know what I mean."

Paterno was starting to get a picture of the Lathams.

"He had weapons," Paterno said.

Collette rolled her eyes and clung to the umbrella as another gust threatened to pull it from her hands. "Not just a few. He was a major gun nut, and I mean major. He had everything from pistols to antique rifles to assault weapons."

"The boys too," Sarina agreed. "Paul's sons. Macon and Seth."

"It bothers—oh, hell—it bothered Brindel. She didn't like the guns, especially around the kids even though the boys had moved out. They're older." Collette shot a look toward the house. "And now this . . . It's just so hard, impossible to have sink in."

"I don't think it ever will." Sarina blinked.

"Let's go down to the station and you can fill me in. Give me names, phone numbers, and addresses of family and close friends, business associates. The couple had children, right? You mentioned they had 'sons.' "

Sarina was quick to say, "They're Paul's boys, not my sister's. They're around twenty now. . . ." She glanced at Collette, who lifted her shoulders in a beats-me gesture. "From his first marriage with . . . what's her name? Katrina. Yes, that's it. They lived with Paul and Brindel for the most part after the divorce. Paul wouldn't have it any other way. But as I said, they're grown, or should be. Sometimes I wonder . . ."

"And then there's Ivy," Collette said.

Sarina managed a fleeting smile. "Yes, my, er, our niece, Brindel's daughter. Ivy. The one we were talking about. She's . . . seventeen, I think. Her birthday's in

February, next month, so she'll be eighteen then." Again she glanced at her sister for confirmation, and again received a shrug as an answer. Obviously Sarina Marsh was closer to the dead woman than was Collette Foucher.

Collette's eyes narrowed a fraction. "Don't we need to identify the body, er bodies or something?"

Sarina let out a little squeak of protest.

"First, the station, then, if you want, the morgue," Paterno said. "We'll put out an Amber Alert for your niece and hunt down her stepbrothers as we've searched the house. No one other than the victims is inside."

"Maybe we should wait for Regan," Sarina suggested.

Collette rolled her expressive eyes, as gray as the San Francisco day.

"She's a cop. A homicide detective." Sarina was looking at Paterno now. "She lives in Montana. A town called Grizzly Falls."

From the corner of his eye, Paterno saw a uniformed cop at the barricade at the end of the street, the policeman talking to a man behind the wheel of a sporty BMW. The driver had his window rolled down and was gesturing angrily to the Victorian house next door to the Lathams. A neighbor. Someone to talk to. Later. Paterno made a mental note, then turned his attention back to the sisters huddled beneath the umbrella's plastic canopy. "Why would a cop from Montana be interested in this case?"

"She's our other sister," Sarina said, then hiking up her chin a fraction in defiance of her sister, added, "I've already called her."

Paterno didn't like the sound of that.

Collette groaned.

But Sarina barreled on, "Maybe you've heard of her? Regan Pescoli? With the Pinewood County Sheriff's Department? She's been in the news. Cracked quite a few bizarre cases."

Paterno was getting a bad feeling about this. "No."

"Really?" Sarina seemed surprised. "Just last summer there was a case involving Bigfoot and a television series—"

"Enough!" Collette cut in. "He can Google her if he wants."

The bad feeling just got worse. "I'm sure I'll meet her."

"She just had a baby," Collette argued. "I mean a few months ago." She didn't sound sure about the timing. "She can't come here."

"Of course she can!" Sarina added, "She'll bring Tucker with her."

"Oh, give it up, Sarina. Regan's not coming here," Collette snapped, her breath fogging a little in the brisk January morning. "And even if she did show up, what good can she do? Even Regan Pescoli can't bring Brindel back. No one can." Beneath the umbrella's ribs, Collette wrapped an arm around her sister's shoulders as the shorter woman soaked in the information and began to sob softly. "I know, I know. It's awful, just awful, unbelievable."

"Look," Paterno broke in as gently as he could, "I'm heading to the station. I could meet you there and then, if you still want to view the body, or . . . bodies, I'll make the arrangements."

"Fine," Collette said.

Sarina asked her sister, "You don't think we should wait for Regan?"

The taller woman rolled her eyes. "No, I don't. Sarina, you know as well as I do that Regan's always been a major screwup, cop or no cop."

Sarina's spine seemed to stiffen and, despite her grief, she said firmly, "Well, she's on her way. And she can help."

"We'll see," Paterno said carefully. He didn't like anyone butting into his case and that went double for anyone related to the victims. He only hoped Detective Regan Pescoli had enough sense to let the team of investigators in San Francisco handle the details. He'd listen to her opinion, if she wanted to give it, but if she turned out to be some crackpot in cowboy boots, a Stetson, and spurs who spit tobacco out the side of her mouth, they might have a problem. A problem he didn't need.

One more case, he reminded himself as he turned his collar to the January wind.

All he had to do was solve this one and then it was *adiós* SFPD and *hola* retirement in his thirty-foot Bayliner.

Right now, in the early hours of a bleak San Francisco morning, it sounded like heaven.

Chapter 4

Pescoli was frazzled. The quickest flight she could catch was out of Missoula, stopped in Seattle, then finally landed in San Francisco, all in all taking about ten hours when she added in the time to get from her home outside Grizzly Falls to the airport. The fight with her husband about her leaving and taking Tucker with her had been a doozie and it still chased after her.

"I just don't think this is a good idea," he'd said as he'd loaded the diaper bag and her carry-on into her car. His face had been hard and set as they'd walked into the garage and she'd strapped Tucker into his infant seat.

"Can you give me a better one?"

"Yeah, don't go."

"It's my sister," she'd said, tightening the straps and kissing Tuck's little nose before closing the back door and rounding the car, nearly tripping on an old skateboard of Jeremy's. Santana had been standing near the driver's side.

"You weren't close."

"Still my sister. Blood being thicker than water and all that. And she was murdered."

"Are you going in your capacity as a cop?"

She'd angled her chin upward, her gaze holding his, silently daring him to try and tell her what to do, to order her around. "And if I am?"

A muscle had worked in his jaw and his lips had thinned. "You're taking our son to a murder investigation."

"No, I'm not. Bianca will be with him when I'm not."

"In a hotel room."

"Right." She'd yanked her keys from her pocket. "I won't be away from him that long. I can't, you know, with the breast-feeding, such as it is, so even if I wanted . . . well, he'll be fine and again, Brindel is . . . was my sister."

"I know you, Regan," he said, using her first name to make a point and catch her attention. "It's the murder that's really got you going. Don't give me any BS about family ties. You don't have any, or at least none that are all that strong with any of your sisters. I'm not saying you're not sad or grieving, I'm just saying your curiosity is piqued and your cop mind is working overtime. Besides, I'm pretty sure the San Francisco Police can handle this without your help. You said the cop in charge is named Paterno, right? I met him. When I lived in California. Trust me, he's efficient. He'll get to the bottom of this. I don't think Paterno or the San Francisco PD want or need your help." He'd cocked a dark eyebrow, daring her to argue.

She'd wanted to go toe-to-toe with him. To lie. But

he knew her too well and she'd made a pact with him when they'd gotten serious: No bullshit. Complete honesty. Tell the truth and let the cards fall where they would. She'd suffered through two marriages, the second ending in divorce, worse than the first, which had ended in the tragedy of her cop husband, Joe, Jeremy's father, dying before she'd had a chance to straighten it out. So this time around she'd vowed to Santana and herself that their relationship would be bare naked truth. Always.

"I just have to do something, and to find out what happened, you know," she told him as she stood on her tiptoes to plant a chaste kiss on his cheek. She'd expected him to sweep her into his arms as he always did, thought she'd feel him pull her close, whisper something a little dirty into her ear, and then kiss her as if he'd never get enough of her. That's how it had always been with him, but standing in the cold garage she'd felt welling disappointment, and as she'd slid into the car, he'd taken the time to walk to the backseat, open the door and plant a kiss on his son's face. Then he'd shut the door, come back around the driver's side, and when she'd rolled down the window, he'd said, "Be safe," and that was it.

She'd backed out into the snow-covered landscape and, settling a pair of sunglasses onto her nose, seen him standing in the garage, barefooted, legs spread, arms folded over his broad chest. Her heart had given a silly little squeeze and the ridiculous thought that she might never see him again had swept through her mind, but then she'd given herself a quick mental shake.

Who was he to try to pressure her into doing what he wanted, what he thought was best?

Your husband, and more importantly, Tucker's father.

"Well, screw that," she'd said aloud as she'd put the car into drive and torn down the lane. The baby had given out a soft little coo, and she'd said, "That's right. You and me, buddy. Let's go get your sister and find out what happened to Aunt Brindel."

Her thoughts had darkened when she'd thought about growing up with her siblings and a single mother, their dad having left when she, the youngest, was eleven. There hadn't been another woman; the only reason for him leaving the declaration that he "couldn't live in a house full of females" a second longer. Later their mother had explained that he'd always wanted a boy and ended up with four daughters. Regan hadn't seen much of him after that, though he'd faithfully paid child support, but her parents had eventually divorced, he'd remarried, and lo and behold, fathered the son he'd always wanted.

"Bully for him," their mother had said through tight lips when she'd learned the news, and Regan had pushed any remaining feelings she'd had for her father down a deep, dark well, thoughts of him rarely bubbling to the surface. Until some family crisis occurred. Like this one. But she didn't have time to think about him now and pushed all thoughts of her parents out of her mind. Even her grief for Brindel was tucked away. There would be time enough for dealing with her emotions later. Right now she had to make the flight.

The only good news had been that she was able to

pull Bianca out of school. Baby Tucker would have care when Pescoli had to deal with her sisters or the police alone.

The flight had been uneventful once they'd made their connection in Seattle, and they were finally approaching the San Francisco Airport, located on the bay to the south of the city. Unlike Pescoli, her daughter was psyched for the quick trip, and with earbuds visible in her ears, Bianca pressed her nose against the window of the airplane and whispered "Awesome!" when she viewed the Golden Gate Bridge, the dark waters of the bay and the twinkling lights of the city visible as dusk settled over the peninsula.

They landed, grabbed their luggage, called for an Uber car that would take a baby carrier, and once the car arrived, were driven to the studio apartment she had reserved through Airbnb. Located in the daylight basement of a three-storied home in the Mount Sutro area of the city, the apartment was old, in the bottom level of a large manor that included a walk-out garden. The furniture was a blend of antiques, used junk, and modern pieces, kind of a cobbled-together "shabby-chic" style according to Bianca, who was thrilled at being in the city. It was nearly eight when they settled in, Regan and the baby claiming the double bed, Bianca relegated to a futon. Pescoli dropped her bags onto the foot of the bed. After a quick perusal of the apartment, Bianca said, "I'm taking a shower," before disappearing into the tiny bathroom.

Holding her son, Pescoli heard the ancient pipes groan and the hiss of spraying water as she scanned the display on her phone. Four messages from Sarina.

And one from a Detective Anthony Paterno with the San Francisco Police Department.

None from Santana.

Before calling anyone back, she climbed onto the bed, propped herself with pillows, and attempted to nurse Tucker again. No go. The baby fussed, and though she tried to relax, it just wasn't happening. After nearly ten minutes, she gave up. "I need a beer," she confided to the baby, then joked, "Maybe you do, too. You could help out with this, y'know."

"I heard that." Bianca, a towel wrapped over her wet curls, another draped around her body, stepped into the living area and started digging through her suitcase until she found a robe. "Why don't you just give up? The nursing, I mean. Obviously it's not working."

Cradling a crying Tucker, Pescoli migrated to the kitchen area that was little more than an undercounter ancient sink, small counter, and two-burner stove. She retrieved the can of formula. "Because it's best for the baby, for the mother, for the whole stinking planet and universe to breast-feed."

"Lots of people don't."

"I'm not lots of people."

"So you think it's better to be uptight and Tuck to be hungry and upset rather than just give him formula? Isn't this like approved by the FDA or whatever?" Bianca held up the can of powder, then studied the label.

"It's not human milk."

"Neither is coffee or Diet Coke." Two of Pescoli's weaknesses.

"I'm not an infant."

"I'm just sayin' it might be easier."

"Easier isn't the issue," Pescoli argued as her phone chimed. Balancing the baby, bottle, and cell, she returned to the bed.

"It never is with you, Mom. You should learn how to chill."

"Not going to happen." She saw that Sarina was calling again. "Hello?" she said as she clicked on the cell.

"Where are you?"

"Finally at our Airbnb. Just feeding Tucker. Then I'll Uber to the station."

"Well, hurry. For some reason Detective Paterno won't let us look at the body until you're here."

"You want to?"

"God, yes!" Sarina started to cry again.

"I'll be there as soon as I can," she promised, and hung up.

Bianca, wiggling the bottle, said, "I can feed him, Mom. With formula."

"Fine!" She handed Tucker to her daughter and had a second's out of body experience, looking down from above and observing herself handing down her infant son to her teenaged daughter, almost as a right, a passing down of generations. This was what she got for her unorthodox family planning or lack of it. She thought about getting older, even dying, a point Brindel's murder only reinforced. Whereas when she'd had the other two children, she'd been in her twenties, her entire adult life in front of her, an intrepid warrior ready to take on the world, now . . . well, by the time Tucker was out of college she'd be just shy of registering for Social Security.

Lots of people do it.

"Look, I'll be back as soon as I can," she said, pushing aside her grim thoughts and planting kisses on her children's cheeks before walking out of the apartment and punching up the app for Uber again. Outside, the darkness was put at bay by streetlamps and vehicles passing, headlights and taillights glowing. She spied the Uber car as it rounded the corner only to stop in front of the building.

"Regan Pescoli?" the driver asked as she slid into the back seat of the white Toyota Camry.

"Yes." She gave the driver the address for the police station, and waited as he cut through the steep streets of the city with ease. Crowded together, illuminated skyscrapers spired upward into the night sky. Alone for the first time since hearing the news of Brindel's death, the gravity of it all, the horror, sank in, delved deep. Pescoli felt it in her soul. Who had killed her sister? And why? Robbery gone bad? Someone with a serious grudge? Something else? She stared out the back window where the rain that had begun had collected on the glass, and she caught the image of her own face, faint and ghostly. Sarina was right. She had to figure out who had done this to Brindel, who would kill her sister in what appeared to be no accident.

No, someone—someone evil—had murdered Brindel and her husband.

"Here we are," the driver announced as he pulled up to an austere gray block building that looked to have been built in the middle of the last century. It occupied nearly, if not all, of a city block or two.

After finishing her transaction with the driver via an app on her smartphone, she climbed out of the car and, ducking against the rain, hurried inside. She stated her business, dealt with security, and was escorted to the Major Crime Unit of the Investigations Division of the SFPD where the Homicide Detail was housed. The place was quiet, the officers of the day shift having long departed, a few others scattered in the adjoining rooms.

Detective Anthony Paterno was waiting for her in an office straight out of the 1960s and showing its age. A stain on several ceiling tiles in the corner hinted at an old water leak, and all of the woodwork was faded and scratched. A bookcase covered one wall, the other displayed plaques, certificates, and awards. A file cabinet had been pushed into one corner. On its top was a picture of a much younger Paterno, fishing rod in one hand, baseball cap shading his eyes as he looked over his shoulder to the camera.

Now, he stood when Pescoli strode into the room. He sported a full head of graying hair, a jawline that was just beginning to sag, and sharp eyes that held little warmth but seemed quick. Intelligent. She'd put him somewhere around sixty, give a year or two. In a sport jacket, open-collared shirt, and slacks, he'd been seated behind a mound of paperwork, a computer monitor glowing on his desk.

"Detective Paterno?" Extending her hand, she introduced herself. "Regan Pescoli. I'm with the Pinewood County Sheriff's Department and I'm Brindel Latham's sister."

She'd already Googled him and, added to what she'd learned from her husband, had put together her own mental file on him. The inspector had been with the San Francisco Police Department for years, had moved inland for a while, and in that time had met

Santana. After a few years, Paterno returned to the city by the bay where he'd been quickly rehired.

"I was told you were coming by your sisters. I'm sorry for your loss."

"Yeah. Me, too. Thanks."

The woman officer who had led her to the department left, closing the door behind her.

"Sarina called and I came as fast as I could. I thought they'd be here," Pescoli said as he sat behind the desk again and she dropped into one of the two visitors chairs crammed into the tight quarters.

"They're waiting in the conference room. I thought we'd go through some preliminaries before we all got together."

Meaning: I want to hear what you know before you compare stories any further with the members of the family. She didn't blame him. First impressions and gut reactions were important; she relied on both when she was working a case.

"Fair enough."

"How about a cup of coffee? Or a soda? Water?"

She declined and he asked her about Brindel.

"She was a few years older, born between Collette and Sarina. I came along later and the truth is that she and I weren't all that close."

Paterno sipped what she assumed was coffee from a chipped San Francisco Giants mug.

"What happened?"

"Why we weren't tight? Nothing. It was just the way we were, not close even when we were growing up. We were just so diffcrent. Like night and day. She was into being popular and girlie things, had a whole closet of dress-up clothes and Barbie dolls. I was a jock. Grew up playing sports and outdoor stuff. The truth is I hadn't seen her in years."

He must've heard all this before from her sisters as he didn't press the issue. "When was the last time?"

"I don't know. Probably at a wedding or funeral. My—our—folks. They're both gone." She thought a minute. "Actually, it was at my mother's funeral. Brindel had remarried. Had been for a while. So that was about six years ago." She felt a little bad about that now, about the fact that she never really knew Brindel and now never would. "We didn't even exchange Christmas presents and I'm not big on cards." That was an understatement; Pescoli just didn't have time or the interest in once-a-year Hallmark greetings with some plumped-up, photocopied "Dear Friends" Christmas letter. She hadn't even sent out birth announcements for Tucker, at least not yet, and probably wouldn't. "I went to both of Brindel's weddings, but that's about it. And all I know about her husband is that Paul was married before and had a couple of boys who, I think, are in college? Maybe. But don't quote me. I'm not even really sure about that. They could be out by now. Graduated or dropped out. I don't know. As for Brindel's kid? Ivy is about my own daughter's age and so that would make her about eighteen." When asked if she knew where Ivy or her stepbrothers Macon and Seth were, Pescoli was at a loss.

"Ivy have a boyfriend?" Paterno asked.

Pescoli shook her head. "I'm not the one to ask."

"She have a good relationship with her father . . . ?" He checked his notes. "Victor Wilde?"

"Again, I don't know. But Brindel didn't. That I do

know. She could never say a kind word about her ex, at least she never did to me. Once, years ago, she asked me to check into his finances. Something about him not paying child support. She thought because I was a cop, I could pull some strings or something. I couldn't. Wouldn't even if I could." She met Paterno's eyes. "I declined. Didn't want to get into that catfight."

His bushy eyebrows quirked. "Don't blame you."

"Yeah, well. She didn't much like it."

"So, would you say you were estranged?" Paterno prodded.

"Estranged? No. That's so . . . defined. As I said, there was no big fight or rift or anything. Nothing we ever fought about. We just didn't hang out, never had much. We never had all that much in common. Other than the same parents."

Her throat was suddenly dry and she wished now she'd asked for water or something. "It isn't much different with my other sisters. The three of them—Collette, Sarina, and Brindel—they were closer. I was the youngest and kind of like the odd-man out."

He nodded. "What about Brindel's husband, Paul?"

"Didn't really know him, but what I saw, I didn't like. He was a doctor and not exactly the friendly local GP, if you know what I mean." She conjured up a mental image of Paul Latham. Slim, a runner and tennis player with a thick head of hair, rimless glasses, and a long nose that he couldn't help but look down on others with. "He was just . . . stuck on himself."

Paterno didn't push on that issue and Pescoli assumed she was only confirming what he already knew from her sisters' statements. He did bring up Paul's sons again, asked about any enemies and anything she might know that could help, which, at this point, she didn't.

When the interview was about wrapped up, she said, "I'd like to help with the investigation," and saw the shutters go down on his eyes.

His smile was far from warm. "You know, the department welcomes all the help it can get, so thanks. So far we've got it handled, but if we need you, I'll let you know."

Pescoli recognized the brush-off for what it was. Hadn't she said almost the same exact words time and time again when some eager relative wanted to "help"?

"I'd like to see the bodies."

He seemed about to argue, then nodded. "They're at the morgue. It's late, but there's a skeleton crew on staff. I can drive you over after we talk to your sisters."

At that moment the door was opened by a slim woman in her late twenties. Her black hair was layered around a face with high cheekbones, sharp chin, and thin lips, and her dark eyes hinted at an Asian ancestor somewhere in her gene pool. In boots, jeans, and a rust-colored sweater, she flashed a quick smile and introduced herself as Jasmine Tanaka, a junior detective. Paterno asked Pescoli if she would mind answering some questions for Tanaka's benefit, maybe covering some of the same material, and Pescoli agreed even though she sensed Tanaka's resistance to her before they even started. Though the junior detective's demeanor was friendly enough, Pescoli sensed beneath her civil exterior was an extremely competitive and hard-edged cop whose thin smile didn't quite hide her suspicion of Pescoli and probably just about everyone who crossed her path.

Tanaka started with the usual questions surrounding Brindel as well as Paul. How did the family get along? What was the status of the Lathams' marriage? Were there money problems? Work issues? Where were their children? What about ex-spouses with grudges? Was there another man or woman in the mix—a love triangle? Did Pescoli have any idea who would want to do them harm, who were their enemies?

That sort of thing. Paterno joined in and there was a discussion about weaponry as apparently Paul had been a gun enthusiast and his cache of rifles, shotguns, pistols, and the like was missing, most likely stolen, though the cops weren't saying that this was a case of a robbery gone wrong that ended in a double-homicide.

Which made sense if both Paul and Brindel were killed while sleeping in their beds, not in the act of confronting burglars.

Despite Tanaka's and Paterno's probing, Pescoli couldn't help with any suspects or motives. As she'd already said, she didn't know much about her sister or her relationships, less about Paul, and wasn't in contact with Macon or Seth Latham, Paul's sons, nor even Ivy Wilde, her niece.

Even though they'd covered the same territory several different ways, Tanaka didn't seem to want to give up, which irritated Pescoli. She'd handled many an interview by other members of the force, when she herself was being interrogated about a case, or when she'd used her service weapon. She recalled dealing with officers who didn't like her or would like to see her screw up. But Tanaka was something else; she could feel it. The woman didn't like or trust her, nor did she think Pescoli was a capable police officer.

"So you have no idea who would want to harm your sister?" Cool disbelief in Tanaka's tone.

"We've been over this. No." Pescoli couldn't keep a bit of irritation from her voice.

Still, Tanaka pushed. "Are you ever in contact with Victor Wilde?"

"No," Regan said shortly. Again, asked and answered.

Tanaka eyed her closely.

Pescoli lifted a palm. "The last I heard, he was remarried, had a couple of kids, but I'm not even sure about that. Maybe it was three . . . I didn't keep up."

Pescoli glanced at Paterno, hoping the older detective was satisfied, even if Tanaka wasn't. She decided to take the offensive. "What kind of leads do you have on Ivy? I assume you are getting her cell phone records and checking if she had a credit card." When they didn't respond, stonewalling her, she threw out a few more questions. "What about the wills? Have you found them? Discovered who had the most to gain if they died? What about Paul's business? Was it failing? What about life insurance policies? Or pawnshops where whoever robbed the Lathams might have tried to sell a gun?"

"We're on it. All of it," Tanaka cut in, obviously annoyed. "We know how to do our jobs, Detective Pescoli."

"Just trying to help. I know you have to talk to everyone in the family, eliminate them. This isn't my first rodeo, for God's sake. I can help with the investigation, but only if you let me." She looked from one impassive face to the other. "Okay," she said, "I get it. You have your procedure. But this interview is over. There's not a lot more I can tell you. It's been a long day—I found out Brindel was murdered just this morning. I haven't even seen my other sisters yet." She stood. "I think we're done here."

Tanaka's eyes flared.

Pescoli was definitely stepping on her toes.

Too bad. Brindel was dead. Murdered.

Paterno said, "Okay, let's go see your sisters. They've been waiting long enough."

Tanaka said shortly, "They can wait as long as it takes." Then before Pescoli could object to her hard attitude, she added to Pescoli with meaning, "This isn't your case."

"Let's move on, okay? Talk to your sisters, then move on." Paterno shot a warning look to his junior detective, as if expecting her to argue again, then added, "Once the forensic team is finished, I don't see any problem with walking you through the house." He rapped his knuckles on the desk, as if he'd just made a decision, and stood. Tanaka managed to keep her thoughts to herself, but resentment still shimmered in her eyes. "All right then. Let's go. This way."

Pescoli wanted to argue, to fight, to explain how she could help, to force herself on them if need be. But she didn't. It was all she could do to bite her tongue and follow Paterno.

He led the way walking down a short hallway to a room with an open door, large table, and chairs that had seen better days. Collette and Sarina were inside, waiting, their jackets folded over the back of an empty chair, an umbrella braced against the wall. Collette busy on her iPhone, her lips compressed, her makeup intact and apparently recently reapplied. Sarina hadn't bothered. She looked like hell as she rolled a can of Diet Pepsi between her palms. Though not crying, she was still blinking back tears as she glanced over her shoulder and her gaze met Regan's.

"Oh, thank God," she whispered, rolling back her chair, leaving the soda on the table. "You're here!" And then as Tanaka and Paterno hesitated in the hallway, Sarina flung herself into Regan's arms and the waterworks began all over again.

Chapter 5

"I don't like this." Tanaka placed a hand on Paterno's arm to keep him from stepping inside the conference room. They slid to the far side of the hallway as two uniformed cops, deep in conversation, passed by.

"I never would've guessed."

The Montana detective had joined her sisters, but Tanaka ignored the sarcasm and, keeping her voice low, said, "*She's* not calling the shots here. She's *not* with the department."

"So when does another set of law enforcement eyes hurt an investigation?"

"When those eyes are too close to the case—as in being the sister of one of the victims. Who knows what her motives are? She could be in the will. We haven't found that yet. Or the beneficiary of an insurance policy, or the appointed guardian of the kids or whatever."

Pretty much what Paterno had just put forth. "She's a good cop."

"Who admits she didn't know her sister, probably

didn't like her. And from the looks of it, the Lathams have money."

"She's legit. I Googled her."

"So did I. She's known to have bent the rules."

He gave her a look that said, *haven't we all? Haven't you?*

"But she's gone rogue. Killed a suspect in a kid pornography ring not long ago. No camera. There was talk that she killed him in cold blood."

"I spoke to her superior. Sheriff Blackwater. He vouches for her."

Her eyebrows slammed together. "What's he gonna say? That he's got a loose cannon in his department, that she's known to go off on her own? Of course he'd say that. To make his department look good."

"For the love of Christ, Tanaka, Pescoli's a dedicated police officer."

"And I'm telling you, I'm suspicious."

"You're suspicious of everyone."

"A good quality in a cop!" she said, defending herself.

"Maybe. You've got to layer that with reason."

"And gut feeling."

He grinned. "You could call it feminine intuition. That would work even better."

"That's sexual discrimination," she snapped, still fuming.

"Only if you call it that. Give it a rest, Tanaka."

"I will not."

He let out a long breath, showing that he was losing his patience. "Let's just talk to these ladies."

"Women. They're women. Not ladies. Not girls."

"To you maybe. Just try to be nice, would you?"

No way in hell. Nice? What did that get you? And if he laid on that old adage of "You get more flies with honey than vinegar . . ."

"Wait a second." Her phone had vibrated and she saw the message. "Looks like one of the Latham boys has been located. He's all right."

"Not a victim. Maybe still involved."

"We'll see." She read more of the message as he led the way into the room.

Jesus, Paterno could be such a stubborn ass. Caught up in his 1980s way of thinking. Make that 1970s. The guy was a dinosaur. *But a good detective. Dogged. Determined. Wouldn't let a case go until he solved it. All reasons you* requested *to work with him. Remember? To learn from the old guy, to give some depth to your tech skills, to find out how to dig deep without relying on computers. So here you are.*

Impatient, Tanaka waited while he gave the sisters some time to themselves.

Sarina, blubbering, disentangled herself from Pescoli's arms. "Sorry," she said, sniffing loudly. "It's just so . . . hard." Her eyes were red rimmed, her nose leaking so badly she had to find a tissue from her purse. "I never expected, I mean, who would do this . . . ? Oh, poor, poor Brindel." She was shaking her head, her ponytail sweeping the shoulders of her sweater. "What did you find out?"

"Nothing."

Collette scraped her chair back and she, too, gave Regan a hug, but it was cold and stiff, uncomfortable for both of them. "Nothing? Oh, come on."

"They'll come in and talk to us."

"And you'll be part of the investigation?" Sarina asked.

"If they let me."

Collette asked, "Why wouldn't they?"

"Well, I'm the sister of one of the victims, to begin with, and there're all kinds of jurisdiction issues. It's just not usually done."

"Desperate measures for desperate times," Sarina said, lifting her chin. "And if this isn't a desperate time, I don't know what is. Our sister and brother-in-law murdered, their kids missing—"

"—and who knows what the robbers took," Collette pointed out.

"They were robbed?" Pescoli hadn't heard this.

Collette's mouth tightened at the corners. "Dona, their housekeeper, said the safes were open. We don't know what was in them."

"The cops will figure it out," said Pescoli.

"With your help," Sarina sniffed.

"So far they haven't kicked me out."

"Would they?"

Regan thought of Tanaka's suspicious stare and her own need to find out the truth. Somehow she had to temper her tendency to bully her way into the investigation, or she could be shut out entirely. "We'll see. Let's not worry about that now." She took a second to text Bianca to check on the baby, then dealt with her sisters again.

By the time Sarina was somewhat in control of her emotions again, the SF detectives stepped into the room.

After quick introductions again, Paterno offered

water, coffee, or soda, and this time Pescoli opted for a bottle of water while her siblings shook their heads.

"I'll get it," Tanaka said, and disappeared for less than two minutes, returning with three bottles, handing one to Paterno, the second to Pescoli, and cracking the third as she took her chair, next to her partner and facing the Connors siblings.

Paterno explained a little about the case, bringing Pescoli and her siblings up to speed:

There were two victims, Paul and Brindel Latham, ID-ed by the housekeeper, who had found their bodies. Each victim had been alone, it appeared, in his or her separate bedroom at the time of the attack, which appeared to coincide with a robbery. There was no sign of forced entry—no broken locks or appearance of doors or windows being forced open—and so far the police had not been able to locate any of the children of the couple, but they were searching. Could they have been kidnapped, or victims themselves, or were they simply missing in action? Police were scouring the city and surrounding area, contacting friends and acquaintances.

Right now Pescoli didn't bother with notes. Time enough for that later, when she was dealing with Paterno and Tanaka on a professional cop-to-cop basis. Right now she'd try to rein in her impatience and just observe both her sisters and the detectives questioning them. She opened her water bottle and took a sip.

Sarina, as expected, was grief riddled and showed it. Always the most sensitive of the four Connors women, she dabbed at her eyes, blew her nose, and wept quietly throughout the meeting.

On the other hand Collette, firstborn of the Connors

sisters, was always hard edged and now obviously more pissed off than sad. No surprise there. Maybe anger was the way she expressed her grief.

Uncharacteristically, Pescoli held her emotions under tight wrap. If she were going to gain the trust of Paterno and especially Tanaka, she'd need to exude a calm exterior.

Paterno asked questions about Paul and Brindel, and as her sisters answered, she realized how little she knew about Brindel, much less than Sarina and Collette.

". . . we didn't see each other all that much, even living in the same city," Sarina said, "but then we were all busy with our own lives." Guilt flashed through her blue eyes. "We'd meet once in a while for lunch or drinks or coffee."

"How often?" Tanaka asked.

"I don't know." Sarina glanced at Collette as if her older sister might help out. "Maybe once every couple of months, maybe more often, depending on schedules."

"Sometimes it was half a year or more," Collette said, and Sarina sighed.

"I guess that's true . . . schedules, you know. But we always made time at Christmas or met for lunch to celebrate one of our birthdays, and parties, for the kids on occasion." She picked up her Pepsi can again, not drinking from it, and chewed on her lower lip, appearing for all the world as if she regretted every second she hadn't spent with her now-dead sibling.

For a second the room was quiet, only the rattling of air in the hidden vents and some conversation from the outer corridor breaking the silence.

"What about the kids? Your niece and nephews?" Paterno asked.

"Have you heard from them?" Sarina asked hopefully. "Seth, he . . . he's going to Berkeley, right? He's just across the bay. He should be here. . . ." And then she went quiet.

Tanaka looked at Paterno, who gave a short nod. "Seth Latham is on his way back here. He was out of town."

"Out of town?" Collette asked.

"Las Vegas," Tanaka explained. "With his girlfriend. The other son isn't answering his phone."

Sarina looked surprised. "So early in the term to be in Vegas. Or maybe not. Kids, these days, you know. But his brother? Macon? He's down at UCLA." When the two detectives didn't respond, she added, "Isn't he? Studying pre-law or something."

"Seth said his brother was taking a term off, that he was rarely at the house in San Francisco, just crashed there once in a while. Most of the time he stayed at an apartment in Oakland his friend rented," Paterno told her.

"Really?" Sarina said.

Collette rolled her eyes. "Come on, Sarina. You know he's got problems. School never really was his thing. He just went because Paul insisted." To Paterno, she said, "He's had issues, I guess you'd say."

"Collette!" Sarina gasped.

Her older sister shrugged. "They're going to find out anyway."

"What kinds of issues?" Tanaka asked.

Collette hesitated, fiddled with her earring, then sighed as she shook her head. "I guess you'd call it anger management. When he was younger he'd fight with his brother, put a fist through a door, kick a dent in a car, whatever, when he got mad."

"He's violent," Tanaka suggested.

"I don't think he'd hurt anyone, not seriously. . . . There's never been any, you know, animals who were abused, or bullying complaints or restraining orders or anything that I can remember, other than with his brother, but Paul always insisted it was just 'boys being boys.'" Collette lifted a brow.

"You didn't think so?" Tanaka said as Regan took another swallow. It seemed as if Collette was going to put all the cards on the table and air the family's dirty laundry, which was a surprise. She was usually so careful and uptight. Except of course Collette was one to always want to get the job done. Move on with life. Not get too wrapped up in sentimentality, or nostalgia. Collette was a doer. Had worked her way up in an accounting firm and now owned her own practice while on the side she planned events, or had in the past. Her oldest daughter, Elise, was grown and living somewhere south of Seattle. Sarina was an artist, who sold her work on some websites on the Internet, wore rose-colored glasses, and as a result was often disappointed or hurt, and now was going through her second divorce. And Brindel? Well, she'd been Brindel, always out for numero uno.

Collette said, "That 'boys being boys' thing is so old school, and if you ask me, an excuse for bad behavior. I raised three kids. Granted, they were girls and I grew up surrounded by sisters." She indicated Regan and Sarina. "We had our problems and snits and even got physical a time or two, as did my kids, but it's different with boys. They're so reactive, and don't worry about getting hurt, you know. The reason they become soldiers."

Sarina cut in, "Macon's a good kid."

Collette said, "It depends upon what you mean by 'good.' Yeah, he's never been arrested that I know of." She glared pointedly at Sarina. "However, the police need to know what's going on. All of it."

"I wasn't trying to hide anything!" Sarina bristled and blushed, her face infusing with color. "It's just personal. Private."

"It's a damned murder investigation, Sarina. You're the one who keeps reminding me of that."

Pescoli moved uneasily in her chair.

"I guess . . . yes, yes, Collette's right," Sarina finally acquiesced.

"Macon is . . ."

"A screwup." Collette met Regan's gaze. "Macon's had issues with Paul and never liked Brindel. He's a hothead. Certainly gets in his share of trouble. A bit of a violent streak, but"—she added, holding up a finger—"I wouldn't say he was their enemy and certainly not capable of murder."

Again Sarina shook her head, her hand over her chest. "No, no. Not at all."

Regan filed the info away, as did, she was certain, Tanaka and Paterno. The truth was Regan could barely remember them, having seen them only a couple of times, once being at Paul and Brindel's wedding. The boys had been young at the time, four and five maybe. Hardly old enough to realize what was going on. Ivy, Brindel's daughter, had been barely two, the same age as Bianca. The second time Pescoli had seen them had been much later. At her mother's funeral. The boys, then in their early teens, had each carried with them that attitude particular to boys of that age—sullen, defiant, angry. They'd sat glumly in the pews of the church throughout the funeral, then stared at their feet throughout the burial service and barely responded when spoken to at the gathering afterward. Ivy had been more outgoing, a gawky preteen with long limbs, braces on her teeth that she tried to hide. She'd seemed uncomfortable in her own body, but Regan could relate. Her own kids had been difficult. Angry. Rebellious.

And now they've both killed, haven't they? For the right reasons—Bianca in self-defense, Jeremy to protect Regan herself.

"So the older boy didn't get along with his dad. What about the younger one who went to Las Vegas?" Tanaka asked, breaking into Regan's thoughts.

"Seth," Collette clarified.

"Yes. Seth." Tanaka was taking notes. Regan felt her phone buzz in her pocket. Checking the screen, she saw that Bianca had texted back that everything was under control.

We're good. He's asleep. Stop worrying. I've got this. LOL. Three laughing/crying emojis were included in the text.

Regan didn't think there was anything worth laughing out loud about, but she did respond with a quick **OK,** then caught up with the interview as Tanaka asked, "How did Seth fit in with the family? Did he get along with his father?"

Collette said, "No one got along with Paul. That's because he's Paul. I know I shouldn't speak ill of the dead, but if you ask me, which you are, I'd say Paul Latham Junior is, er, was a supercilious prick. And he came by it naturally. His father, who lives in Arizona—retired doc, by the way—he's cut from the same cloth. A real jerk. Married four times. Oh—sorry, Regan." She cast her sister a quick somewhat abashed look as Regan was currently on her third marriage. "No offense."

"None taken," Regan said, lying. They both knew it was BS. Collette was needling her and she was bugged by it, but neither let on. Same old, same old.

Biting her lip, Sarina looked at the investigators. "I have to ask. Has anyone heard from Ivy? Have you located her?"

"Not yet." Paterno leaned over the table. "But we're working on it. Amber Alert's in place. We're contacting friends and neighbors, her father, of course, and checking local cameras and social media. We have both of the victims' cell phones—that's how we contacted Paul's sons, but so far Ivy Wilde hasn't responded. If you have any more information that might be helpful, have an idea where she might be or whom she might contact, please let us know."

Sarina's face fell. "I was afraid of that. What if she's been kidnapped?" Her voice sounded strangled as her thoughts ran wild. "She could be being held against her will and . . . oh, Lord, I hope not." She was starting to cry again.

"I assure you we're doing everything we can," Paterno said.

Collette put a hand over Sarina's arm. "We don't know anything. No reason to borrow trouble."

"Mom used to say that," Sarina said with a squeak as she tried and failed to staunch her tears. "I've tried to call or text Ivy, but nothing."

"Have your boys try," Collette suggested, mentioning Sarina's sons. "They've always been close to their cousins."

"Don't you think I have?" Sarina said, sniffing. "And . . . nothing."

They continued to talk to the detectives for another twenty minutes or so before Paterno wrapped things up by telling them that they'd be kept informed.

"And you're on the case, too," Sarina said to Regan.

"Not officially." Pescoli caught the tiniest bit of a reaction from Tanaka. The tightening of her jaw.

As Paterno stood, indicating the meeting was over, Sarina said, "Are you taking us to view the body? To ID Brindel?"

Regan shot to her feet. "Look, I'll do it, okay?"

Sarina wasn't about to be dissuaded, "But—"

"Seriously, you don't want to do this. You can . . . work with the funeral home when the bodies are released tomorrow. It's late now, but . . ." She turned her attention to Collette. "I'm used to this and do it all the time, and really, you don't want to go through the viewing. Not tonight."

For once her older sister actually listened to her. "I'm good with it. But Sarina . . ."

"I want to see her." Sarina glanced nervously from Regan to Collette.

"You will," Regan assured her. "But not now. Go home. Check on your kids. Get some sleep. I'll catch up with you tomorrow."

"I don't know—" Sarina was waffling.

"Sarina, seriously, I've got this," Regan assured her.

"Don't you think we've been through enough today?" Collette asked. She collected her scarf, wrapping it around her neck before reaching for her coat. "Let Regan handle this. She's the professional." She handed the shorter woman a damp jacket. To Regan, "You're staying over, I assume."

"With me," Sarina said.

Regan held up a hand. "I've got a small apartment, an Airbnb unit not far from Brindel's house. I'll stay there."

Sarina was dumbfounded. "The baby's with Nate?"

"Here. I brought Bianca with me. She's watching him now."

"I—I want to meet him," Sarina said. "I—just wish it was under better circumstances, you know." She swallowed back another spate of tears. "I really wish you would have taken me up on my offer and stayed at the house. Now that Denny's gone, I've got lots of room."

"Denny's gone?"

"You don't know?" Sarina's face crumpled. "He left me. Abandoned us. For . . ."

Oh, God.

". . . another woman," she squeaked out. "Left our sons. Can you imagine? Ryan and Zach are devastated. Devastated." Sniffing, she dabbed at her nose. "Who would do that to their own kids?"

Collette looked over the top of Sarina's crown to Regan and she gave the tiniest of shakes to indicate that the subject of Sarina's marriage shouldn't be pursued, at least not here. Not now.

They walked into the hallway and Collette said,

"Why don't you come over to my house in the morning?"

"No, no. Mine," Sarina insisted. "I'll have to get Ryan and Zach off to school."

Collette agreed. "Fine." To Regan, "Good with you?"

"How about in the afternoon?" Regan asked. "That will give me enough time to figure a few things out, I hope. And I'll need to spend some time with Tucker and give Bianca a break."

"That'll work," Collette said, before Sarina could protest.

"I'll escort you out," Tanaka said, and as Collette, carrying the umbrella, shepherded Sarina down the hall, the young detective led the way.

"Ready?" Paterno asked.

No. Not ever. "Yeah. Just let me call my kid. Make sure everything's okay with the baby."

Chapter 6

Standing in the morgue and staring down at her sister's body, Pescoli felt the blood drain from her face. For a second her knees threatened to buckle as she gazed down at the body of her sister. A kaleidoscope of sharp images cut through her brain: Brindel's birthday party when she was about ten and had broken her arm, all the kids who were invited signing her cast. Another memory of Brindel seated next to a boy in a convertible as they drove away. Still another when Pescoli was suffering from bronchitis and Brindel had come into the bedroom in the middle of the night to share a favorite book . . . No, they hadn't been all that close, but there had been moments where they had shared a sisterly bond.

"Yeah," she said, nodding, sucking in air through her teeth. "It's Brindel." Who had done this to her? And why?

The body was naked, a sheet rolled back, and Brindel's impossibly blue eyes were fixed, her skin bluish, tan lines visible. Most notably a small bullet hole was visible on her forehead, squarely between her eyes.

I'll find out who did this to you, and I'll get them. Trust me, Brindel, I'll hunt them down.

She glanced over to Paterno, who was standing a few feet away. "What about Paul?"

"You want to see him, too?"

Pescoli nodded.

Paterno spoke to the attendant, who wasted no time, found the right locker and rolled out another gurney. Lying upon it was the body of Paul Latham, dead as his wife, a gray tinge to his skin, appearing older than Pescoli remembered, his once brown hair threaded with gray, especially at the temples. She clarified, "It's Paul," then turned away, and the attendant began rolling the body back to what she'd always thought of as "cold storage."

They walked out of the building and Paterno, who had driven her the ten minutes to the ME's office and morgue, offered to drive her back to her apartment. As he maneuvered his SUV through the hilly streets, she said, "You know I need to be a part of this investigation, for myself."

Slowing for a traffic light, he said, "This isn't your jurisdiction and you're a member of the family. My advice: let us handle this."

"You can trust me."

"If the situation were reversed?" he asked, glancing at her as the light changed.

"Yeah, I know. But I could help you. I'm not going to mess things up."

"You have a reputation for . . . getting things done. If unconventionally."

So he'd checked on her. No surprise there.

"I know Tanaka doesn't like me, but I could work with her."

"She's a little territorial."

"I'd say 'a lot' territorial."

"Okay. Maybe." The rain had started up again and he flipped on his wipers as he rounded a corner and the house in which she'd rented the lower unit came into view. "This it?"

"Yes."

He double-parked in front of the home, dark, as it was close to midnight.

"I would like to be kept in the loop," she said as she opened the door. "My supervisor, Sheriff Blackwater, will vouch for me." She really wasn't sure about that.

"Already has."

Another surprise, she thought, as she leaned inside before closing the Durango's door. "Let me throw it back at you—what if the situation were reversed? What would you do if you'd just identified your sister in a morgue with a bullet hole in her forehead?" He just stared at her, so after a few moments of standing in the rain she slammed the vehicle's door and stalked back through the wrought-iron gate, ducking her head against the drizzle, taking the stairs to the lower unit.

She was pissed, but had to shake it off.

Time to take off her cop's hat and become mother to a seventeen-year-old and a baby.

For now.

Just for now.

* * *

Tanaka had logged in hours at the station, then returned home to her tiny bachelor apartment in Oakland.

But she wasn't finished working. Not by a long shot.

She was too wired, too determined to crack the Latham case, too irritated at the cop from Montana. Relative of the deceased or not, Regan Pescoli was a problem, even if her intentions were all on the up-and-up, which Tanaka didn't quite trust. Who cared that she was a detective? Even a decorated one. In Tanaka's mind, Pescoli was at best a grief-stricken relative of the victim, at worst a suspect.

She wasn't quite sure which yet.

There was just something about Pescoli that got under her skin.

And maybe rightfully so, Tanaka thought as she stretched her arms over her head. She was seated at her small corner desk on a supposedly ergonomic chair and had been for hours, a cup of now cold tea sitting near the opened laptop.

Pescoli had suffered through her share of scandals, both privately and professionally, though Tanaka hadn't had time to really delve deeply into Pescoli's life. Yet. There was too much going on with the murder investigation to waste any extra minutes on the pushy cop. Tall, and good-looking if not beautiful, Pescoli had a confidence that bordered on aggressive. She'd toned it down during the meeting, but Tanaka had sensed it, and whether she admitted it or not, Pescoli was sizing up Tanaka and Paterno and the whole damned department. As if they weren't up for the job. What a joke. How could the woman even compare the SFPD to some podunk sheriff's department in some backwoods Montana county?

Don't think like that. You know yourself some of the best cops have come from rural roots. Remember Watts?

Her heart twisted a little as she considered her first real love, a forensic pathologist whom she'd met while a grad student. He'd taught at the university and they'd had an affair that, each time she thought about it, could still turn her blood white hot. Roland Watts had been supremely brilliant, and supremely married. And she'd fallen for him anyway.

"Shit," she muttered under her breath.

She glanced at the clock. Three effin' AM.

She'd spent the last six or seven hours here, at her desk, getting information on every member of the Latham family, the exes involved, business partners, two women with whom Paul was rumored to have had affairs, and, of course, Detective Regan Pescoli. She hadn't eaten dinner, just snacked on salsa and chips and hummus and loaded up on tea to keep her going. Now, yawning, she brushed the crumbs from her desk, tore off her clothes, turned out the light to tumble into bed, her thoughts a jumble with details of the double-homicide. She couldn't help but wonder where the kids were. They'd found the one son, but what about the other, Macon? And Ivy, where was she? What had happened to her? She had been living in that huge house with her mother and stepfather and had just seemed to disappear. Nothing in her room had seemed out of the ordinary. Her bed had been unmade but she was a kid and the mess in her room appeared like many a teenaged girl's.

There had been no purse, ID, computer, laptop, phone, or tablet. Had she taken them all? She didn't have a car; Tanaka had checked. Both of the Latham cars, a BMW for him and Lexus for her, were in the garage, parked one behind the other, "buddy style."

So what had happened to her? She was already a person of interest; could she be something more? A scared kid, a victim herself, or maybe even involved in her parents' deaths?

Tomorrow they might know, if her cell phone company supplied the info. Or any debit or credit card information came through her bank account.

"In the morning," she told herself, thinking of the offspring of Paul and Brindel Latham. She'd caught a glimpse of Macon online, a college student who spent as much time protesting just about everything as being in class. He was handsome in that surly, bad-boy way. Even features, skin that always appeared tanned, deep-set, brooding eyes, while his brother was smaller and paler, with lighter hair and eyes. Ivy was just on the cusp of womanhood, but already beautiful by most American standards. Yeah, Tanaka would have to look into all three kids. She stood and stretched again only to hear some of her vertebrae pop. "Not a good sign," she reminded herself, surveying her small Oakland studio with its Murphy bed and kitchen that was little more than an induction burner, microwave, and mini-fridge. She lived here with her long-haired Siamese cat, her TV, and her books. Turning over, she pulled the covers to her chin and felt a soft plop onto the bed to indicate that Mr. Claus, the stray who'd shown up on her doorstep Christmas Eve, had decided to join her. She was just dozing off when she sensed him walking across the bed to stand on her shoulder. Soft fur from his fluffy tail skimmed her nose. "Move," she said into the darkness, but before he could comply she'd drifted off.

The first thing Pescoli noticed upon arriving at her sister's home the next morning was that Brindel's house was a damned mansion. Huge. As she looked up at the tall edifice she couldn't help but wonder how many places there were to hide in the restored Victorian. Probably lots of cupboards and closets and little hidey-holes.

Paterno met her on the front porch as rain lashed the city and a stiff breeze blew down the hilly streets. Dark clouds rolled overhead and, though it was ten in the morning, the day was already dark as dusk.

"You sure you want to do this?" he asked, probably remembering how she'd lost color at the sight of her dead sister.

"Absolutely."

"Okay then." He unlocked the door and they stepped inside a wide foyer that opened to the floor above. "This door was locked, the back door open. We can start in the kitchen."

"No," she said, looking up to the balcony on the second story. "I want to see it all. Can we start at the top?"

"Sure." Over the course of the night it seemed that his resistance to her interest in the investigation had somewhat ebbed. Though the place was a mess with fingerprint dust, the home was still lavish, every room decorated with expensive pieces, or at least they appeared to be worth a small fortune. He led her up the staircase to the second floor, then a narrower one to the third, and finally a back set of stairs leading to the attic. Not only did the steps go up to the rooms tucked beneath the eaves, but all the way down to the basement, he told her. "Servants quarters up here, and this was the staircase they used in the early nineteen hundreds when there was actually a live-in staff."

They trudged up to the attic where the windows were small, the series of tiny rooms dark and close, big enough for a bureau and twin bed, each with a small cupboard, a single bath, fixtures dry and showing signs of old rust, everything smelling of must. Boxes, old furniture, pictures in frames, and filing cabinets filled the space, and she saw a carton marked "X-Mas," another "Halloween Decorations," and yet another with "Macon's Schoolwork" and a date scrawled across it. The space felt empty and unused, a warehouse holding old memories.

There was nothing much to see and Paterno walked her down to the third floor, obviously used for guests and their children's bedrooms. "It looks like one of Paul's sons, Macon, I guess, used this room," he said at the first large room, where the bed was unmade, a towel was on the floor of the bathroom, and a baseball card collection along with a signed ball was still on built-in shelves over a desk. A second room, nearly identical, probably had been Seth's, and a fourth was decorated as if for guests. Ivy's room was at the end of the hall, done in shades of pink, accented with black, white, and silver. The bed was unmade, the bathroom, with its array of makeup, nail polishes, shampoos, and all sorts of body washes and perfumes, looked as if it had just been cleaned. "The maid said Ivy didn't come home that night, or she didn't think so—this room looked the way she left it. In fact, the whole floor did, except for what she described as Macon's room."

"The housekeeper came in every day?"

He nodded.

"Did she have any idea where Ivy was?"

"No. Tanaka's checking with her friends."

Pescoli had a bad feeling about that. "But she lived here."

"Yeah."

"And just happened to be gone when her parents were murdered."

"Lucky," he said, sending her a look.

"Or . . ."

"She was clued in, or part of it, or already gone missing."

The bad feeling got worse and didn't let up as Paterno led her down the stairs to the second floor where the murders had taken place.

The beds had been stripped, the bedding taken for lab tests, though there was no obvious sign that either of the victims had been sexually assaulted.

Paterno opened a set of double doors. "This was Paul Latham's suite," he said, and she followed him into a massive bedroom where a stripped bed faced a huge flat screen TV mounted on the wall. Oddly, in juxtaposition to all the rest of the furnishings, Paul's room was modern, a king-sized bed facing the TV, the headboard smooth, blond wood, the end tables wood and metal, the lamps chrome. Two sleek chairs sat next to a glass and chrome bar positioned near the French doors that opened onto a veranda.

"This connects to your sister's room," Paterno said, opening the blinds so that she could see the private outdoor space. "Only access is from one bedroom to the other. I wonder if they ever used it."

Looking outside, where rain was washing against the glass and running across the flagstones, she couldn't imagine her sister and husband—what?—sleeping separately but meeting outside on their private veranda for a drink? Still, it was a great place to hide between the potted plants. "Is there a ladder or some kind of fire escape?" she asked.

He nodded. "Doesn't look used much."

"But it could have provided access . . . ?"

"The doors were locked when we got here."

"So we're back to a key."

"Or someone inviting them inside." He motioned toward an open doorway. "The GSR on the bodies indicated that each victim had been shot at close range," Paterno said as they walked into the now empty gun closet. "Very close range."

GSR—gun shot residue—remained after a gun was fired, the closer the victim to the firearm, the more likely he or she would have traces of GSR on their bodies. The armory itself was the size of a small bedroom and filled with display cases, shelves, locking racks. Just no weapons.

"You think one of Paul's guns was used in the attack?" she asked.

"Don't know, but I'm leaning the other way, that they had their own weapons. It looks like two separate guns were used."

"You find casings?"

"Yeah."

"Different caliber of bullets?"

"Both .380s. We're checking to see if they came from the same gun, but I'm not betting on it. Two neighbors heard something. The guy across the street, Jerome Forrester, claimed to have heard only one shot that, of course, he thought was a car backfiring or something. The other neighbor, just next door to the west, Mrs. Margaret Rinaldo, thought the bang kind of stuttered, so maybe she heard two shots, but she couldn't say so. Neither heard the sound of two distinct shots."

"Huh. So . . . what? You're thinking two killers?" Pescoli asked.

"Possibly. Or probably." They started walking back through Paul's bedroom and down the short hallway separating his sleeping quarters from Brindel's. "No way could anyone shoot one of the victims close enough for the amount of GSR, then run out of the room, down this hall and cross the bedrooms to set up and shoot again. Not only would the first shot alert the second victim but the sounds of the shots would have been separated by silence. Two definite shots. There's just too much distance either by the hall or across the deck to have the sound of the shots not be distinct."

"They were executed?" she said, the thought chilling. "Two murderers with synchronized watches, or cell phones or just shouting, but firing simultaneously?" She had trouble believing it.

"I'm saying it's one possibility. A strong one," Paterno admitted, rubbing his chin as he stared at the bed trying to envision the crime.

She too, looked at the bare mattress, the spot where Brindel had drawn her last breath. Regan's throat closed as she considered those final moments. Had her sister known her attacker? Seen the gun before it went off? Recognized her killer? Or had she been blissfully unaware, sleeping soundly when her life had been ended so violently? Pescoli let out her breath slowly and realized Paterno was still talking about the plot.

"If that's what happened. The idea of the simultaneous shots is that neither victim has the time or presence of mind to wake up and try to get away, or confront the attackers or scream or even call the police. It's also less likely that anyone close enough to hear the shots would think it was necessarily a firearm going off." He made his way to the French door and tried the handle. It didn't budge. "And it worked. Forrester thought the sound was from a truck. Rinaldo wasn't sure what she'd heard but because it was over quickly, she ignored it and went back to sleep."

"No one could have saved them," she said.

"No. Don't think so. But if any of the neighbors had looked through the windows, maybe they could have seen something. As it is, so far, no one saw anything." He sounded frustrated and probably was, though, of course, it was very early in the investigation.

"Too bad," she whispered, reining in her emotions and eyeing her sister's private bedroom, trying to view it with a cop's eye rather than that of a sibling. Gauzy window coverings, a marble fireplace, vases of flowers and a spa-like bathroom with separate shower and tub, as well as a closet as large as the nursery in Pescoli's own home, surrounded the bed with its padded headboard, now spattered with Brindel's blood. French doors, identical to those in Paul's room, opened to the veranda connecting the two suites.

What the hell had happened here? She agreed with

Paterno. The victims weren't random. Someone knew how to get in and that there were safes with valuables and a closet full of guns, and they'd come armed. Probably with intent to kill. Her blood ran cold. Why in the world was Brindel so mercilessly murdered? And who would do it? Who would let the killers in or provide a key? Had it been carelessness, a key loaned to a friend or repairman or the housekeeper? Or were the murders intentional? Planned? The robbery only part of the cover-up, to throw the police off? How insidious was this crime?

Her gaze was caught by a large portrait of Brindel's daughter, hung on one wall, the picture taken when the girl was about seven, it seemed. Blond, with wide green eyes, and teeth slightly too large for her heart-shaped face, Brindel's daughter was poised on the edge of a gold chair. Wearing a dress that had a shimmery white skirt and black velvet bodice, she was half turned toward the camera. Her little legs were encased in white tights and dangled a bit, not reaching the floor. At first glance the picture was one of wide-eyed innocence, but if you looked a little deeper, past the pasted-on smile and curling blond hair, you could catch something more, just a subtle hint of something slightly darker than intended in the obviously posed shot.

Once more Pescoli thought of the hidden, malevolent forces she'd felt at her home in Montana, and her skin crawled.

What you thought you felt on your deck near the Bitterroots has nothing, nothing *to do with what's going on here,* she chided herself.

Jaw tight, she managed to push that disturbing idea aside. Tamped it down. What was wrong with her?

Yes, her sister was one of the victims here, but Pescoli was a cop, a detective, no less. If not always capable of separating her emotions from a case, Regan Pescoli had always been able to work through them, to keep doing her job. But this . . . this, of course, was different. This was her sister after all, no matter how far they'd drifted from each other. She cleared her throat and forced her attention to the details, the evidence that would help crack this case. "Did you find any footprints—something indicating the size or make of a shoe?"

He shook his head. "Nothing distinct, not in or out. No trampled flowers with a perfect impression of a boot print in the soil. No dirt tracked on the white tile in a perfect image of a shoe."

She almost smiled. "Nothing easy."

"Not like on TV. As I said, no forced entry."

"So we're back to the key and who had one, or who unlocked the house and let the killers in."

"Looks like. We're checking to see if any keys are missing. According to the housekeeper, only she and the family members had keys, but who knows? Also, there was an unlatched window in the powder room downstairs, but it's small, none of the vegetation outside disturbed. At least one of the killers would have to be small, slight."

"A woman?"

He didn't answer, but nodded slightly, still mulling the scenario over in his mind.

"But this was a robbery, right?"

"Yes."

"They might have just wanted to insure that there were no witnesses."

"Then they're not just robbers."

She agreed. Most thieves wouldn't cross the line and commit a homicide, some wouldn't even get into assault, at least until they were threatened, but to kill two people in cold blood, execute them in what had to be a premeditated plot, that was something far darker than burglary or theft. "This is . . ."

"Evil," he supplied, as if he, too, had experienced that skittering of dread that had danced upon her spine.

They wrapped up the tour, going through the main floor, eyeing the dining room, butler's pantry, living area, foyer, bath, and kitchen. Paterno showed her a hidden staircase straight out of Nancy Drew that led from behind the bookcase in the library to a private wine cellar in the basement. Also downstairs was the garage with its two cars, one parked behind the other, the laundry facilities, and a room with a TV, rowing machine, stationary bike, and treadmill.

She thanked Paterno for the tour and, as he locked up, used the app on her phone to secure another ride through Uber. Once she was in, the small Toyota took her to the nearest car rental office, and once there she rented a Ford EcoSport. Uber was all well and good, but she needed to be more mobile. With a baby in tow, an investigation to work on, a college campus or two to view, the rental seemed necessary. And now, after traveling the city streets and with the aid of GPS, Pescoli was confident she could navigate her way around San Francisco and the Bay Area.

Climbing behind the wheel of the white SUV, she drove first to a grocery store to pick up a few supplies, then back to the apartment where she found Bianca dealing with a fussy Tucker. "He's hungry," Bianca said. Her hair was a mess and she was still in pj's though it was going on noon. "I didn't feed him because you texted that you were on the way."

"Good. There's breakfast for you, too, or lunch," she added, recognizing the time. She left the two grocery bags on the small counter, then took the baby from her daughter's arms. "Hey, fussy britches, what's the problem?" she asked her son, and was rewarded with a toothless grin and bright eyes. "Yeah, you're a charmer, aren't you?" she said, then once more attempted to nurse. Again, it was a no-go.

And while Bianca fixed a bowl of yogurt, orange slices, and granola, Pescoli finally gave up the fight. "I guess you're going to be a formula baby from here on in."

"Finally," Bianca said. She dug in to her breakfast while checking her phone and texting as Pescoli made a bottle and fed her son. "Are the local police going to let you in on the case?" she asked. Pescoli had told her there might be problems.

"Maybe. The lead, Paterno, seems okay with it, but the junior detective, his partner, she doesn't trust me."

"Oh, gee. I wonder why. Could it be you came on a little too strong?"

"I'm always the soul of discretion."

Bianca made a disparaging sound just as her phone started buzzing. She glanced at it. "Oh, no."

"Let me guess. Your dad."

"He won't give up. Doesn't matter what I do, he won't give up."

"Have you told him outright you don't want to talk to him?"

"Duh. Like I've texted him a million times. He just won't listen or won't believe me!"

"I know." Boy howdy did she ever. Convincing Lucky Pescoli to change his mind or trying to get him to do something he didn't want to was nearly impossible. She remembered. Vividly. His take-no-prisoners attitude coupled with her stubborn streak had made living together impossible and had helped erode a marriage that had probably been doomed from the get-go.

"I'm going to get a restraining order against him!" Bianca declared.

Regan set the bottle aside, lifted Tucker, and burped him. "Do what you have to do." Gazing over her son's back, she said to her daughter, "This isn't how I envisioned it would be when I got together with your dad."

She snorted. "You thought we could be one big happy family? Like something out of a Norman Rockwell painting? If that's what you were looking for, you picked the wrong guy. Dad's a loser. No. He's worse than that. He's . . . terrible. For God's sake, Mom, he almost got me *killed*!" Her lower lip quivered.

"I know. I'll never forgive him for that," she said, and meant it. She'd like to strangle her ex with her bare hands for what he'd put Bianca through.

Bianca pulled herself together with an effort, clamping down on her emotions. She was nothing if not resilient. She found the TV remote, flopped onto the futon, and clicked on the flat screen. "Neither will I. Never. I hope Michelle divorces his ass."

"I think they're going to counseling."

Another snort as she channel surfed, images on the TV flashing by as Regan slid a sleeping Tucker onto the bed. The truth was that Pescoli had no love for Lucky's current wife. But, much as she hated to say it, Pescoli had to admit that Luke could have hooked up with someone far worse than his much younger, Barbie doll of a wife.

She caught a glimpse of Brindel's house on the television screen and said, "Wait. Stop there."

"What?"

"Back up to the news," Pescoli said, and with a quick look to make certain her son was sleeping soundly, joined Bianca on the couch. "There," she said as Bianca worked the remote and the screen settled on the front facade of Brindel's huge home, police barriers in place, no lights in the windows—a huge, dark behemoth gloomy in the falling rain.

A television reporter wearing a jacket with a hood and a serious expression stood in front of the home. Her face was composed, her dark eyes serious ". . . Police have revealed no new information on the double-homicide of Paul Latham and his wife, Brindel . . ." She continued solemnly with the story, offering up pictures of the deceased and their blended family. In each shot Brindel was smiling, appearing happy. But then, who knew what really went on in a marriage? What occurred when the doors and windows to the outside world were closed?

"That's Ivy?" Bianca asked, pointing at the screen.

"Uh-huh."

"Where is she?"

"Good question. One I intend to answer," she said, and as the screen returned to the in-studio anchor, her phone rang. She glanced at the cell and saw Sarina's name and number appear. Picking up the phone, she answered with, “I was just about to call you.”

“Why don’t you just come over,” Sarina said, and she sounded much calmer than she had the day before. “Seth’s coming over and I think you need to talk to him. And bring your kids, Regan. No excuses. You have a lot to do here and Bianca could use a break from Tucker, I’ll bet, so seriously, come over. I’ve made up the guest room. It’s yours and we can juggle cars. I can watch the baby. . . . I’d *love* to, if Bianca wants some space.”

“I don’t think—”

“Stop it, right there. Look, I’m sorry I fell apart yesterday, but I’m better today. Dealing with the shock, so think about what’s best for your family. Uh-oh, I’ve got another call coming in. See you in a few.” And she clicked off.

“Aunt Sarina?” Bianca asked.

“Yeah. She wants us to bunk in with her. You okay with that?”

“Haven’t you paid for this place?”

“Just for one more night. Tonight. But I can work it out.”

“Cool. Then let’s move already.” She slid her mother another look as she changed the channel. “Maybe being at Sarina’s will inspire you and you’ll figure it all out.”

“I wish,” Pescoli said. She had a couple of hours to do some research on the Internet before they packed up.

Chapter 7

"What's this?" Paterno asked, looking up from his work as Tanaka, in tight jeans and a tunic that reached midthigh, entered his office. She was carrying what looked to be a plastic-wrapped knife in one hand and a cup of coffee in the other.

"Maybe nothing, but I'm taking it to the lab." She set the knife on his desk and through the plastic he could see it was a butcher knife, one that looked as if it had come from a kitchen set.

"The Lathams'?"

"One was missing from the set on the counter. I checked. All accounted for except a butcher knife." She took a sip of the coffee.

"How'd you get it?"

"One of the Lathams' neighbors, Jerome Forrester? The old guy who lives across the street? Right next door to the park? He found it when he went out to get his paper this morning. Thought it might be important." She leaned a jean-clad hip against his desk.

"Or it might not have anything to do with the murders as the victims were shot," Paterno said, eyeing the blade. No visible blood. "But yeah, good to check it out."

"Maybe the killer dropped it while running away."

He rubbed his chin. "Any luck with cameras in the area?"

"Not yet. But we're still checking. There aren't many traffic cams up there, but a house two doors down has a security setup with a motion detector/camera, so that might help. And"—she pointed to the knife—"the entrance to the park near where the neighbor found that? There's a camera there. We're checking with the parks department."

He nodded. "The killers—"

"Or killer. Not sure about more than one yet."

He scowled. Tanaka could be so anal at times.

"Whoever it was had to have a getaway vehicle somewhere," he thought aloud. "They, or he, or she, or whoever, wouldn't want to be caught packing around all those weapons and whatever else they cleaned out of the safes. Too much to haul for any distance without looking suspicious. They'd want to put distance between themselves and the victims."

"Maybe we'll get lucky." She yawned, then disguised it with a quick sip from her cup.

"Maybe." Paterno didn't put much stock in luck.

Tanaka walked to the window and peered outside to the gray day beyond. "We've still got people canvassing the area."

"You got anything else?" he asked, and saw that she was stifling a yawn.

"Still waiting for results from the crime scene techs.

And I've pressed for a rush on the autopsies but that takes time and . . . well . . ." She shrugged and he noticed dark smudges under her eyes, circles that her makeup couldn't quite hide, discoloration brought on by a late night of work. "It isn't like we don't know cause of death." She took a final swallow from her cup. "I've done some checking on the MIAs, the Latham kids."

"Yeah?"

"Not exactly perfect citizens. Even for as young as they are, nineteen and twenty." Plopping down in a chair, she said, "Macon dropped out of college. Not to just take some time off, but because he was kicked out. Bad grades. Oh, he's smart enough. I checked. IQ off the charts actually, but he got involved with anarchists and was protesting everything he could. A privileged kid who got off on protesting against the privileged."

"He got a record?"

"Nothing serious. Picked up for MIP as a teenager, then was involved in protests that turned into riots, and there's footage of him caught on a reporter's camera, but he wasn't involved in any violence, at least not that we know of. I e-mailed you my notes before I came in here."

Turning to his computer, Paterno found the e-mail and clicked it open. A photograph of a man in his early twenties appeared. Unkempt dark hair, sullen deep-set eyes, and a scraggly beard that didn't quite cover a strong jaw. Macon Paul Latham. "And we still can't locate him."

"Not answering his phone, nor at his buddy's apartment in Oakland."

"Got a girlfriend?"

"Not currently that we know about. He's a bit of a mystery man."

"What about a job?"

"Doesn't seem so. Like I said, 'privileged.' As in the silver spoon clamped firmly between his orthodontically straightened teeth."

"While he protests the system."

"You got it." Her smile held zero warmth. "We've got a BOLO for his car—get this, a classic BMW."

Paterno leaned back in his chair until it squeaked in protest.

Tanaka went on, "As for the second Latham son, he's doing a little better. At least he's still in school and doesn't have a record. Not a stellar student by any means and has been known to party hearty, but he's never been picked up. Keeps his nose clean. Both of Paul's sons are into firearms, just like Daddy, but Macon is more into it than Seth."

Paterno straightened to look at the monitor again and scrolled to find Tanaka's notes on Seth Latham. He, too, sported a scrubby beard, but it was a little trimmer, his hair straight and combed, lighter in color though his eyes were the same brooding brown of his brother's, deep-set and slightly suspicious in the picture on the screen.

"He's got a roommate and a steady girlfriend. Been dating her for a couple of years. Supposedly, he's going to come into the office early this afternoon."

"You talked to him?"

"Briefly."

"He shaken up?"

She shook her head. "Hard to say. He seemed more mad than sad, but definitely upset. Accused the department of letting out the names of the deceased before the next of kin were notified. Apparently he doesn't count his stepaunts as that tight in the family. Claims he or his brother or his grandfather are next of kin."

"He has a point."

"We talked to Paul Senior. In Arizona. Scottsdale. Had a deputy go to his house and deliver the news. He called, so . . ."

"We've covered our asses."

She lifted a shoulder, finished her coffee. "Seth's also got an alibi. He was in Vegas and his girlfriend was with him. I encouraged him to locate his brother and bring him into the station with him."

"Does he know where the brother is?"

"If he does, he's not copping to it."

"What about Brindel's daughter. Ivy?"

"Still running down her friends to see if they know anything. Social media, so far, has given no clues, all of her pages on Facebook, Twitter, Snapchat went dead." Dead. That thought was chilling. He was worried about Brindel's daughter.

He scrolled down and saw the picture of a striking girl. Smiling into the camera, Ivy was blond and fresh faced, a dimple in one cheek, green eyes that seemed warm and friendly.

"Boyfriend?" he asked. Where the hell was she? Alive? Held against her will? Dead? His stomach churned at the thought.

"The maid, Dona Andalusia, said there was some boy who came around. Couldn't remember his name. Something that started with a T. I called the aunt, Sarina Marsh, and she said his name was Troy Boxer, so

I'm working on that now. Trying to track him down. All I know so far is that he is a little older, goes to school part time, and works for a shipping company, according to the aunt. So we'll see."

"Maybe she's with him." God, he hoped.

"But she should have come forward by now. This story is all over the news."

He nodded, had already thought as much, and as he stared at the girl on the computer screen, he couldn't help but worry. Had she met the same fate as her parents, or was she involved in something else, something dark? Once more, he considered all the horrors that could befall her, from kidnapping to human trafficking, to rape and forced prostitution.

He didn't like the turn of his thoughts. In fact, he didn't like much about this case. "Got to find her."

"We will." Tanaka started for the door, but paused at the threshold. "When I talked to Ms. Marsh, she said her sister, the cop, was on her way over and she seemed to think Detective Pescoli was, like, a part of the investigation."

"Not officially." Again he leaned back in his chair.

"Unofficially?"

"We'll see."

"Huh." She thought about that, obviously rolling it over in her mind, pulled a face, and then said, "Well, you're the lead."

"That I am."

"So it's your funeral if having her involved blows up in all our faces."

"Yep."

She flashed him a smile without a trace of warmth.

"Because it's not going to be mine." With that she slapped the doorjamb and took off down the hall, her boot heels clipping smartly.

With the aid of the GPS, Pescoli found her way to Sarina's condo and parked on the street in front of a fourplex that housed her unit. Bianca raced ahead with the diaper bag while Pescoli followed with the baby carrier.

"Oh. My. God. He's absolutely adorable!" Sarina gushed when she spied the baby. In jeans and a long-sleeved T-shirt, she'd answered the door, ushered them inside. She was more composed today, her brown hair curling around her face, her makeup intact. After hugging Bianca as if her life depended on it, she'd finally paid attention to her nephew. "It makes me want another."

"What?" Collette, who had been seated on the edge of a couch in the sunken living room, stood and walked toward the entryway. She stared down at Tucker's downy head. "Nope," she said, looking put together in black yoga pants and matching long-sleeved top over which she wore a looser silver tunic. "Two's enough."

"I know, I know, and . . . well, I couldn't even if I wanted to," Sarina said on a sigh as she looked from one of her sisters to the other. "With Denny out of his mind now . . . you know, having his midlife crisis with that . . . that slut, it's out of the question."

"Wow," Bianca said, staring at her aunt.

Sarina blushed. "I'm sorry, honey, but your uncle is . . . is . . . well, there's no getting around it. He's just being an ass. A stupid ass." Her lips twisted into a knot of disapproval and she blinked at a sudden spate of tears.

Regan kept her mouth shut, but shared a look with her daughter, who knew all about middle-aged men running off the rails. Neither of them brought up Lucky's name.

"Maybe we should talk about something else," Collette advised, and shepherded Sarina past a set of stairs leading to a loft overhead. "Regan can bring us up to speed about . . . the investigation."

"Oh, God," Sarina said, and looked about to burst into tears at the thought of her sister. "Of course. It's just . . . *He* just makes me nuts, and that woman—"

"Sarina," Collette said gently, propelling her forward. "Why don't you settle Regan's kids into the family room and we can stay out here and talk? The boys will be home soon, right?"

Sarina glanced at her watch. "Forty minutes give or take." To Regan she said, "You're staying with us tonight? That's still on?"

"Yes."

"Good. Good. I made up the guest bed and then there's the loft and I can watch the baby any time, *any* time you or Bianca need a break." She showed Bianca and Tucker to the guest room and then hurried back.

"We brought our stuff." Regan wasn't all that cool at the thought of bunking in with Sarina and her sons, especially not in Sarina's current emotional state. But she was right, Bianca and Regan could use another set of eyes and hands for Tucker.

"Please tell me there's some word on Ivy," Sarina pleaded.

"Nothing I've heard, though I'm not exactly in the loop."

"Well, get in it," Collette said, obviously worried.

"Trust me, I want to find her." She didn't add "desperately," but she was starting to really worry.

Sarina glanced at the clock on the stove. "Seth should be here any minute."

"Has he talked to the police?"

"Not yet," Collette said. "We asked him to come here first."

"You talked to him?" Regan said, her cop-brain taking over. This wasn't good. "Before the police could interview him?"

"Texted," Sarina said. "He finally got back to us this morning."

"But he should—"

"His father and stepmother were killed," Collette said sharply. "We—okay, *I* thought he might want to see us before being grilled by the cops."

"Not grilled—" Regan began to protest.

"Whatever."

"What about Macon?"

"Don't know where he is," Sarina said as she motioned them into a small kitchen attached to an equally sized family area where a huge flat screen dominated the room. An L-shaped couch had been squeezed into the tight area next to a sliding glass door that led to a patio currently being splattered with rain. "He runs with a pretty . . . out there crowd."

"Meaning what?" Pescoli asked.

"He's with the Anti-Christs," she said, opening the refrigerator door as Bianca plopped down on the couch nearest the TV.

"The *what*?" Regan asked.

"Anarchists," Collette said. "That's what she means." To Sarina, she added, long suffering, "Not 'Anti-Christs,' Sarina. He's not a devil worshipper, just against . . . I don't know, *everything*. Especially everything his father stood for."

"Except guns," Sarina reminded her.

"Yes, right. Except for any kind of weapon." Collette said to Regan, "He's . . . difficult."

"Too much testosterone and anger issues with his father," Sarina corrected.

"Unfortunately she's right." Collette's lips pinched. "About that, anyway. Macon is surly and . . . disturbed."

"I wouldn't say there was anything really wrong with him," Sarina denied. "He's just always acting out."

"You think he would harm his father and stepmother?" Regan asked.

"Oh, no!" Sarina pulled a couple of bottles of sparkling water from the fridge. "No, no, no. He's just, you know . . . testy."

Collette rolled her eyes and Sarina changed the subject. "This okay?" she asked, holding up the bottles. "Or, let me see"—she eyed the overstocked shelves of the open refrigerator—"I've got Coke and Diet Coke, but I thought it was too early for wine. . . ."

Collette said, "It'll be fine," and as Sarina busied herself with snacks and drinks, Collette motioned Regan to follow her back to the living area. In a barely audible voice, she said, "Try to keep any upsetting details from her." She glanced back to the kitchen, as if making certain Sarina couldn't overhear her. "She's trying to hold it together but she's a mess. The separation about did her in and now this . . ." Collette fluttered a hand to take in everything. "With Brindel's . . . passing . . . well, Sarina's not handling anything all that well."

"She seems better today."

"I think her Prozac has finally kicked in." Collette was less cold today, more worried. Lines appeared at the corners of her eyes. "I'd been up here for a couple of weeks to lend support when everything blew up with Denny. Sarina was driving Brindel crazy, so I came up a week ago last Sunday and was planning to head back to LA this next weekend, but . . . now . . ." She shook her head. "Thankfully Simon is busy with a major project at the bank." Collette's husband, Simon Foucher, was older, pushing sixty, and an investment banker who spoke four languages and worked with international clients.

"I don't know how this is going to go with Paul's kids, but I thought they should know that we're all in this together."

"As long as the police talk to them."

"For God's sake, Regan, give me some credit, would you?"

Sarina returned. She was balancing a tray holding three drinks, ice cubes dancing, and a basket of some kind of crackers. "I've got hummus and/or salsa," she said. "That's about it. And this."

"It's fine," Collette said, settling onto the couch again. "I mean it's great. Thanks." She waved her sister toward the couch. "Just sit down. Let's hear what Regan has to say."

Obediently Sarina set the tray on the glass coffee table, then found a seat in an old rocking chair positioned near the fireplace where a huge picture of their family was propped on the mantel. It had been taken about ten years earlier, when Ryan was about six, maybe seven, and blonder Zach around four. Denny and Sarina stood behind the boys, both smiling brightly, not knowing how their future would play out.

Sarina caught Regan looking at the picture. "I know," she said. "I just haven't had the heart to take it down."

"Do it." Collette picked up her glass. "The sooner the better."

"See how heartless she is?" Sarina appealed to Regan.

"I agree with her."

Sarina, rocking in the chair, sighed. "Of course you do."

"Tell us what you know," Collette said, effectively changing the subject.

Regan said, "I ID-ed the bodies, as you know. Brindel and Paul were both shot once, in the head."

Sarina clasped her hand to her mouth while Collette sent Regan a sharp, "be-careful-here" glare, and Regan reminded herself that her sisters weren't used to a "just the facts" discussion, so she dialed it back and was more careful as she explained about visiting the morgue, talking with Paterno, and walking through the Lathams' house.

Sarina ignored her drink and used a cocktail napkin to dab at her eyes. "Have they found Ivy? Have any idea where she is?" she asked.

"No, at least not that I'm aware of. But they're looking for her and I'll file an official missing persons report now."

"Hasn't that already been done?" Collette scowled.

Regan shook her head. "Enough time hadn't elapsed and there was the chance that she'd be found with a friend or something. As far as I know, that hasn't happened."

"Oh, that's not good," Sarina said, and her hand shook as she picked up her glass.

The doorbell chimed and Sarina glanced up sharply, nearly spilling her drink. "That must be Seth."

"I'll get it." Collette was out of her chair and across the room in a flash. She opened the door and not one, but two twenty-ish men strode into the hallway. Both wore baggy jeans and hooded sweatshirts whose shoulders were discolored by raindrops.

"Macon," Collette said, surprised, and Regan recognized him. At around six-two, Macon was the larger of Paul's two sons, taller than his brother by a couple of inches and heavier by what seemed around twenty pounds. With messy dark hair that curled over his ears and a scrubby beard, he took in the living room with the three sisters, then let his gaze land directly on Regan.

He didn't bother with a greeting. "You're the cop, aren't you?" Macon charged. "Brindel's sister from . . ."

"Montana," Seth supplied as he let his hood drop. His features were finer and sharper than his older brother's, his resemblance to his father more noticeable.

Macon nodded. "Yeah. That's right. Montana."

Regan stood. "I'm Regan. Yes."

"Good."

Sarina said, "We didn't know that you'd be here."

"Surprise," he said with more than a hint of sarcasm.

With Seth on his heels, Macon stepped into the living room, and Regan, not certain where this was going, felt herself tense. The scent of a recently smoked cigarette chased after him as he crossed the carpet to stand toe-to-toe with her, and, jaw set, eyes narrowed, said, "Since you're with the cops, maybe you can tell me what the fuck is going on."

Chapter 8

With Tanaka leading the way, Paterno stepped into the forensics lab. The working area, like so many parts of the department, was aging, the equipment a blend of old and new, half a dozen technicians and scientists working at tables and desks while carefully and clinically attempting to ferret out the truth of crime scenes with collected evidence. The bright lights, muted sounds, and the smells of evidence-processing chemicals mingled with the acrid odor of some kind of disinfectant.

Gus Varga, a senior lab technician was huddled over a large comparison microscope resting on a counter. A heavyset man with thinning white hair and a bulbous nose, Gus was somewhere north of sixty and a firearms specialist who had been promoted over the life of his career and now ran the department. Even so, he wasn't content to push papers in his office. Forever in his lab coat, he was a vital working part of the forensics department.

"Hey, Gus," Paterno said.

Varga looked up. "Thought you might be showing up."

"You thought right." Paterno nodded toward the microscope. "You working on the ballistics for the Latham case?"

"Got 'em right here." Gus rolled his stool backward and stood. Wincing, he straightened and rubbed his lower back. "Damned sciatica. Gives me fits." He motioned toward the microscope. "Striations on the bullets don't match. Take a look for yourself."

"You can just tell me."

Tanaka walked around the counter and checked out the bullet through the microscope.

"Pretty simple. Two weapons," Gus said. "And I checked with the GSR guys—point blank range."

Tanaka said, "Two shooters."

"Or one guy using two different .380s," said Gus.

"He'd have to be Superman to have pulled it off," Tanaka argued. "The neighbors only heard what they thought was one shot and the bodies were rooms apart."

Gus pulled at his lower lip and nodded, coming more slowly to the same conclusion. "Sounds about right, I guess. And both were shot at close range. GSR indicates point blank, each time."

Paterno nodded.

"Any trace?" Tanaka asked, still looking through the lens of the microscope.

"Still working on it. Quite a few hairs we're trying to match to others found in brushes in the home. We'll check for DNA of course, but that'll take a little while. And don't tell me you don't have a little while," he added, slapping the air as if to brush away a bothersome gnat. "I've heard it a million times. We can only work so fast."

"Has to be faster than it used to be," Tanaka said, no longer bent over the microscope. "Everyone does it. Finding out their ancestry, connecting to someone famous in history or whatever."

Gus just stared at her over the tops of his half-glasses.

Paterno asked, "Anything else?"

"The knife you brought in? Fingerprints match those found on a brush and the desk and bedpost in the daughter's room."

"Ivy had the knife?" Tanaka said.

"We don't have the daughter's fingerprints on file. Nothing to compare them to. But, since the same prints were all over the house, primarily in her quarters, her bathroom and bedroom, we're assuming they're hers. Thumbprint on the knife identical to one on her hairbrush."

"So she was there that night," Tanaka said, biting on the corner of her lip. "Dropped the knife when she left." She glanced at Paterno. "I checked with the housekeeper, who swears all of the kitchenware was accounted for the day before. She knows because Dr. Latham was one of those anal individuals who was big on 'everything in its place,' and since he was known to have a temper, everyone in the house complied. Dona Andalusia is about ninety percent certain that knife was in the block on the counter. Just as it was every night. The way I figure it, she was either a victim and ran, or part of the attack, then ran."

"Part of the attack?" Varga glanced from one detective to the other.

Tanaka said, "I know. It seems unlikely. A long shot. But it's a possibility."

Varga gave a crisp nod. "I've been in the business long enough not to rule anything out."

So had Paterno, but he just didn't see Brindel Latham's daughter being a part of putting the muzzle of a gun to her mother's head as she slept and pulling the trigger.

"Truth is stranger than fiction," Tanaka reminded him as they left the lab and walked outside to the wet January day where the wind was cutting, the drizzle having become rain. Tanaka threw up the hood of her jacket and Paterno dragged his beat-up Giants cap from the pocket of his raincoat and squared it on his head. They were going to interview the attorney for the Latham estate, find out who had the most to gain with the deaths of Brindel and Paul Latham, who, it seemed, had been headed for divorce, according to Brindel's sisters.

In the parking garage, they settled into a cruiser with Tanaka at the wheel. She always insisted on driving, called him an "old man" because of his caution, and so he usually white-knuckled it as she sped through the steep city streets, dodging other traffic and cable cars while avoiding bikes and pedestrians and somehow obeying the traffic signals—well, for the most part. Today was no exception, and by the time they'd parked in a space that wasn't quite legal and were taking the elevator to the offices of Casey and Casey, Attorneys at Law, Paterno's nerves were a little rattled.

Ten minutes later, after waiting at the front desk of the offices, they were ushered into the office of Armand Casey, a senior and founding partner of the firm.

Tall, lean, not quite fifty, with what Paterno assumed was a perpetual tan, Armand waved them into the two chairs next to his desk. The room, a corner office with two glass walls and a view of the Transamerica Pyramid, also had room for his massive desk, glossy credenza, and in the corner, two club chairs and a small table. "Terrible," he said, taking a seat behind his desk where two computer monitors glowed. "What happened to Paul and his wife. Senseless. Just mind numbing." He forced a smile, but seemed genuinely bothered. "Who would do such a thing?"

"That's what we're trying to find out," Paterno said.

"Good. Good." He seemed thoughtful, then looked up quickly. "Would either of you like coffee? Or water?"

"I'm good," Paterno said, but when Tanaka hesitated, Casey punched a button on his in-house phone and asked "Tom" to bring them each water. Almost before he'd hung up, three glasses of water, with ice-cubes and slices of lemon, along with a clear pitcher filled to the brim, were set on the desk by a sandy-haired kid in a suit who looked to be somewhere around twenty-five.

They got down to it and asked for a copy of the will as well as a list of the Lathams' assets and insurance policies along with any debts to the estate, all of which, it turned out, were held in a trust, and the attorney had no trouble handing over the documents.

"What about their divorce papers?" Tanaka asked as she picked up one of the glasses on the tray.

Thick eyebrows slammed together. "I don't have . . . there was no divorce. Not that I'm aware of."

Tanaka asked, "Mrs. Latham never mentioned wanting to file?"

A quick shake of his head. "It was obvious that theirs wasn't always a happy marriage, the second for both of them, but Paul never mentioned a word about them splitting up, and I never dealt with Brindel, except when we needed her signature. Paul handled all of the finances. No one filed for dissolution of the marriage, at least not that I'm aware of, and I think I would be."

"Do you know if Mrs. Latham had her own attorney?" Tanaka took a swallow from the glass.

"No . . ." He hesitated again. "No, no one that I know. But . . . it's possible, I suppose."

Paterno asked, "How about an Ivan Haas? He's a prominent divorce attorney, isn't he?" They'd found his name in her cell phone.

"Ivan? Well, yes, but . . ." Casey grew even more thoughtful. "I guess that's possible. Anything is and, as you said, he's one of the best divorce attorneys in the state."

"So, if they were splitting up, Mrs. Latham could hire, say, Haas, and you would represent Paul Latham?" Paterno suggested.

"I'd stay out of that mess entirely. Probably refer him to someone who specializes in divorce." He sighed and wrinkles appeared on his forehead. "Seriously, I had no idea that there was any talk of separation or divorce."

They talked a little while longer and Tanaka polished off her glass of water along with Paterno's untouched glass. "Thanks," Paterno said as Tanaka gathered the documents. "If we have questions, we'll call."

"Do." Casey walked them through the reception area. "And catch whoever it was who killed Paul and Brindel. They're . . . they were good people."

"That's the plan," Tanaka told him, and once they were through the glass doors leading to the hallway and elevators, she glanced at Paterno. "'Good people?'" she repeated. "First time I heard that about the Lathams." The elevator bell dinged and the doors opened. They stepped inside and punched the button for the lower level parking area. Tanaka reached into her pocket and withdrew a key. "Here. You drive," she said, handing him a key ring as the elevator car jolted to a stop. "I want to look over the will." As they exited the elevator and made their way through the gloomy parking garage, her cell phone rang and she answered. He only heard parts of the conversation and surmised it had to do with the case.

It did.

They settled into the Crown Vic as she ended the call. "That was the lab. It's all very preliminary, but it could be we have some hairs that aren't part of the family and don't match the housekeeper."

"Big house. Lots of people coming and going."

"It's a start," she argued as he turned the ignition and drove out of the underground lot to stop suddenly, waiting for a woman pushing a baby stroller to pass in front of the Crown Vic's grille. The woman was busy texting as she maneuvered the stroller through other pedestrians.

"Jesus," he said under his breath, a rush of adrenaline firing his blood. He was inches from hitting the woman.

"She never even saw you."

Paterno rolled down his window and said, "Hey!"

The young mother finally looked up. Saw the police car and frowned.

"Watch where you're going! I nearly hit you."

"And I'm on a sidewalk," she said angrily. "Your fault."

He steamed as the woman pushed the stroller away.

"She's right you know."

"But her kid—"

"I know. Just drive. Get over it." Tanaka reached for her own phone again and the sidewalk cleared.

Paterno eased the big car into traffic, his blood pressure lowering slightly.

"Let's see if Ivan Haas is in. If we can see him," she said, Googling the attorney's address. "Hey, not too far from here."

Paterno drove the half mile to the lawyer's office building and lucked out with a parking spot on the street as a UPS truck pulled away from the curb. The space was marked for loading only, but Paterno took his chances. He and Tanaka made their way into the glass-walled building housing the offices of Haas, Fielding, and Taft.

They dropped by the attorney's office on the seventh floor and were informed by a prim woman in her forties that Mr. Haas was in court until later in the afternoon. They would just have to reschedule. She smiled brightly, though Tanaka thought the pasted-on grin was fake. Smug.

Tanaka told her tightly, "We'll be back later today."

"Oh, no, no. Today just won't work. Nor tomorrow, either. Mr. Haas won't be in. He'll be out of town. But week after next, uh, on Thursday possibly? I might be able to squeeze you in." This time the grin was more sincere, as if she'd just done the impossible.

"Don't bother," Tanaka said. "Have him call." And she left her card with the receptionist.

Once the glass doors to the offices swung shut behind them, Paterno said, "You rolled over pretty quick on that one."

Tanaka punched the call button for the elevator and shot him a look. "Apparently she didn't get that we're the cops. And I'm not waiting for Haas's damned call. We're coming back." The elevator doors whispered open. "Today."

"That's the Tanaka I know."

"And love," she added testily once inside the car. "Remember? 'And love'? You forgot to add that."

At least they were fast enough to keep from earning a ticket in the tow-away zone.

"I just want to know what the fuck happened," Macon repeated once Sarina had herded everyone into the kitchen where she offered them soft drinks and a snack of crackers and cheese hastily tossed onto a platter.

"Me too." Seth was nodding, but already reaching for a slice of cheese as they all crowded around the peninsula.

Bianca was flopped on the couch next to Tucker

sleeping in his infant seat. The television was turned on to some reality show Pescoli recognized as one where a bunch of twenty-somethings try and fail to live together, this one focused on what seemed to be C- or possibly D-list celebrities. She thought she recognized a face or two in the crowd of a dozen, but she couldn't be certain and really didn't care.

Using the remote, Bianca turned off the show, pushed herself to her feet, then joined them at the counter.

She got a nod as a way of greeting from Seth.

Macon didn't bother. "I saw on the news that Dad was murdered," Macon said, his voice tinged in disbelief, though he showed little, if any, grief.

"Brindel too," Collette reminded him.

"Yeah." He plowed on, "So after I see what happened on the news, even before I can phone Seth, I get a call from some chick cop who wants me to come in."

"You talked to her?" Pescoli asked.

"Not then," Macon said. "She left a message."

Pescoli: "So you did call her back?"

"Not right away. I wanted to talk to Seth and then, because I still didn't believe it, thought there had to be some mistake: I phoned Dad like a million times and texted him, too. I left all kinds of messages. Voice. Text. I even tried to get through to Brindel, which was stupid, I know. Seth had told me she was dead. When I couldn't get through to anyone then . . . I called the cop just to confirm." He ran a hand through his wild hair, pushing it from his eyes. "Man, this is all just so bat-shit crazy!"

Amen, Pescoli thought.

Macon grabbed one of the bottles of Coke and twisted off the cap. "I just can't fuckin' believe it, you know? Why would anyone want to kill Dad? He was a doctor. He *saved* lives. That's what he did for a living. It's just so wrong for him to be *murdered,* you know? Shit." He took a long gulp from the bottle, then added, "I hope they get the fucker who did it and string him up by his balls."

"If it's a guy," Seth said.

"You think a woman would shoot him?" Macon asked.

Seth grabbed a bottle of Dr. Pepper and cracked off the cap. "Maybe."

"Nah."

"C'mon, man. He's had, like you know, other . . ." Seth lowered his gaze as if realizing where he was, the company he was keeping. His brother took a long pull from his bottle.

"Other women. Lots of them," Macon finished. "Fine. But none of them would want to kill him. I mean, they weren't psychos."

"How do you know?" Seth skewered his brother with a hard look.

"Christ, Seth, you're such a dumb shit!"

"Hey!" Pescoli said. This was getting them nowhere. "Why don't we go see what the police have to say? You said you'd be in, right?" she asked Macon, who didn't reply. "They just want a statement from you . . . from both of you." She wagged a finger between the two brothers.

Macon said tautly, "You're a cop. You know what happens and so do I. They're going to grill me in some little interrogation room with no window, a camera recording me, and two-way mirrors and shit."

"You think the police suspect you?"

"Yeah! Dad and me didn't get along. At all. Everybody knew it. We got into it all the time when I lived at home. Ask Seth."

No one had to. Seth shrugged and nodded as Macon continued to rant. "The cops were called a couple of times when I lived with Dad and Brindel. And that chick cop? I forget her name, something Asian." He scowled as he thought. His phone vibrated loudly, but he ignored it. "Japanese, maybe. Lots of syllables."

Pescoli supplied, "Tanaka."

"That's the one." He nodded, near-black curls shaking. "Tanaka! She kept asking me where I was, y'know, when the shit went down. Like I was suspect numero uno."

"They're just weeding out anyone close to the family, checking alibis."

"I *know* that. I'm tellin' ya. But I've seen enough cop shows to know what's going down. And if they're looking at family members, what about Ivy?" he said.

Sarina gasped and Collette backed up a step.

"Like she's so lily-white? Oh, come on. She's been seeing a shrink for years." A sideways glance at Regan. "Bet they didn't tell ya that, did they? No bad words for little niecey, but I'm lettin' ya know, she had nothin' good to say about Dad. Nothin'."

"He's right," Seth said, finally chiming in. "Called him a 'perv.'"

Macon was incensed. "A goddamned perv, that's what she said. About our father. Nice. Just real . . . nice. Psycho-bitch."

"Stop it!" Collette ordered. "Ivy isn't 'psycho' or a 'bitch,' for that matter. And she would never hurt her mother. They didn't get along all the time, but . . . Sarina help me out here."

"The idea's ridiculous!" Sarina was flushed, as angry as Regan had ever seen her.

"No more ridiculous than me or Seth being looked at. And neither one of us was ever in the nut-house." He chugged down the rest of his Coke and tossed the empty bottle into the sink as his phone buzzed again.

"Ivy was under psychiatric care? Hospitalized?" Pescoli asked.

Sarina sighed. "Severe depression after trouble with a boyfriend."

"What did I tell ya?" Macon said. "Psycho."

"But she was fine, after. Did some out-patient care but Brindel said she'd much improved," Collette added.

"And the boyfriend?" Pescoli asked.

"That useless piece of shit?" Macon threw his aunt a get-real look.

Pescoli said, "Who is he?"

"Troy Boxer," Seth answered, his hair flopping over his eyes with the movement. "Macon's right. Big-time trouble."

Regan made a mental note.

Macon looked at his phone, scowled, and pocketed it again.

"They broke up," Seth said. "Ivy and Troy."

Macon turned to his brother. "You sure?"

"Yeah. Ivy told me."

Macon wasn't convinced. "When?"

"Couple of months ago, I think. Maybe around Thanksgiving." Seth paused. Thought. "Yeah, I remember now. She told me about it over Christmas break."

Macon shrugged. "Whatever. Good thing. Boxer's a loser. Anyway, I'm outta here. C'mon, Seth."

"Wait." Regan wasn't going to let him just walk away. "You really need to talk to Detective Tanaka. I'll go with you."

"No." The look he sent her was a mixture of disgust and deep-seated suspicion. "I'm not goin' to talk to any cop and that includes you." He added, "Not without a lawyer."

"Seriously?" Collette asked.

"Yeah, seriously," he mocked, grabbing a cracker and cheese. "Damned fuckin' straight."

He seemed unable to be moved, so Pescoli backed off for the moment. She felt her phone vibrate and pulled it from her pocket to see on the screen that Santana was calling. Her heart lightened a little bit and she slid outside, onto the covered deck off the family room, before answering. Rain was pouring down, pounding on the roof and gurgling through the gutters.

"Hey."

"'Hey,' back," Santana said, and she had to plug her free ear to hear him over the storm. "Wondered how you were doing."

"Could be better. Could be worse. I guess we're going to bunk here with Sarina for a couple of nights. She's pretty upset. Collette's handling Brindel's death a little better."

"And Tuck? How does he like his first road trip?"

"He's okay. Sleeping through a lot of it. Bianca's been on duty most of the time."

"She okay with that?"

"Mmm. Think so." Still straining to hear over the gurgle of rain in the downspouts, she gazed through the slider door to the group gathered inside, clustered around the peninsula in the glow of the hanging light fixture, deep in discussion. "But that's one of the reasons I came to Sarina's—to give Bianca a break. Sarina's all about the baby." She decided not to let on about her sister's impending divorce. For now. "How're things there?"

"A little quiet for my taste."

"Is that a backhanded way of saying you miss us?"

He let out a laugh. "I guess. You didn't leave on the best of terms."

"And that would be because . . . ?"

"It couldn't be that you're mule-headed."

"No, sir. Don't think so."

"But maybe I was a little out of line." That was a big admission from Santana.

Pescoli's eyebrows arched. "A little?"

Another snort and, over a gust of wind, she heard the dogs, suddenly on alert, start barking. Nikita's deep woof, Sturgis's raspy howl, and Cisco's sharp yips. A chorus. Her heart twisted. Santana said, "I just want what's best for all of us. The kids, me, and you're included in that."

"Nice to know."

"It's your life, Pescoli. Do what you want. As I've said before. You will anyway."

"You got that right."

"I know."

She walked to the edge of the deck, felt the sting of icy raindrops against her cheeks, and took a step back, under the overhang of the roof. "So, if it's any consolation, I miss you, too."

"I'll expect you to demonstrate just how much when you get home."

"In your dreams, Santana."

"Morning and night."

She felt a corner of her lip twitch upward. "Look, I'll be home in a couple of days; I'm not waiting around for the body to be released and a funeral. I'll come back later. Collette was like an event planner at one point in her life. She and Sarina and Paul's sons can handle it, once we find Ivy."

"She's still missing?"

"So far, and if the San Francisco cops have any idea where she is, they're not saying, at least not to me. My guess is she's a person of interest."

"They're not letting you in on the investigation?"

"Just peripherally. I've got a bit of a personality clash with one of the investigators."

"No!"

"Oh, shut up, Santana. It's not my fault. Kind of a territorial thing. She's like Alvarez on steroids and has the attitude to go with it. Doesn't want me messing up her investigation, or whatever."

She could almost see him smiling. "Don't let her intimidate you."

"She doesn't."

"Go get 'em, tiger." He started to sign off, then said, "Oh, wait . . ." and then there was some muted conversation before he returned. "That was Jeremy. He says hi."

"He could call."

"Yeah . . . well . . ." She heard a door slam on the other end of the connection as the rain peppered down in San Francisco.

"Well what?"

"I think he's got a new girlfriend."

"Really?" As far as Pescoli knew, her son wasn't dating anyone exclusively. "Is it serious?"

"Who can tell? He's just twenty-one."

"Too young," she said, then remembered that by her son's age she was already married and had a baby—him.

"He seems all about it."

That was the problem. When Jeremy fell, he fell hard. "You met her?"

"Not yet."

"Why not?"

"Don't know."

Warning bells began to clang inside Pescoli's head. Jeremy's last steady girlfriend, Heidi Brewster, had been a piece of work. "Tell him I want to meet her . . . never mind, I'll let him know myself. Look, I gotta go," she said as she noticed Collette heading her way. "I'll call ya later."

"I'll hold you to it."

"All right." She clicked off just as Collette opened the slider and stepped onto the deck.

"God, it's cold out here!" She closed the door and peered back inside, as if making certain she wasn't followed. "But quieter. I thought it was a good time to escape. Sarina's boys just got home." She rolled her eyes.

Pescoli looked through the glass to verify that yes, Sarina's sons, two blond boys who each took after their father, had joined the group. Their backpacks and jackets had been slung unceremoniously onto the couch near the baby carrier. Fortunately Tucker was still sleeping.

That wouldn't last for long.

"Too much testosterone for me," Collette said with

a mock shudder. "Besides, I wanted to talk to you. Alone."

"What about?"

"Paul's boys. Macon and Seth. I didn't want to say too much in front of Sarina. You know how she is—kind of a Pollyanna. She always wants to see the best in everyone."

"Not so much with Denny's girlfriend."

"Well. That. She's pretty wounded right now. And they're still married. Just you wait, though, give it time," she said, as from a nearby condo a dog began to bark. "Even that will change."

"I wouldn't bet on it."

"Hey! Bruno!" a male voice yelled. "No barking! You get in here! Aw, Geez, not on the deck! Oh, no . . . come on! Inside. Now! Sarah? You'd better take *your dog* for a walk. Now. Come on, let's go." Then the distinctive sound of a slider door slamming shut.

Collette, distracted slightly for a second, continued, "Anyway, the point is Macon and Seth really are trouble. Where Sarina's boys still have some, oh, I don't know, not exactly innocence to them, maybe more like naivete, Paul's kids are different. Trust me, I'm not just saying that because they're not related by blood. That's not it. It's just that Macon's as explosive and deep-down angry as Paul was. A chip off the old block. And dear Lord, how he loves all of Paul's weaponry. The man had a damned arsenal, you know."

"Yeah."

"Still," Collette went on, "Macon and Paul were like oil and water. Macon couldn't stand to be in the same room with his father for more than about five minutes. And, I think, the feeling was mutual. Macon was opposed to everything Paul stood for, especially his money, if you can believe that."

"He didn't like the wealth?"

"I think he didn't like the ostentatious show of it because he sure as hell always had his hand out. Anyway, I think we already discussed this." She adjusted one of her earrings and stared at the curtain of rain pouring from the heavens. "Macon is like a time bomb about to go off."

"You think he's capable of a double murder?" Pescoli asked, glancing into the room where Macon, the oldest of the cousins, was holding court, Sarina's boys and Seth taking in his every word. Even Bianca was listening intently as Macon spouted off about something.

"I'm saying I don't know and I hate to admit it." She let out a long, drawn out sigh and walked to the railing, ran her finger along its wet edge, and retreated to the covered area near the door. "But at least he's not leaving, yet. He's cooling down a bit, so maybe you can talk him into speaking with the police."

"If he doesn't, they won't clear him."

"I know. He has to figure it out."

"Yesterday you told Paterno and Tanaka that he wasn't all that violent."

"I toned it down, but truthfully? I just don't know how far he would go," Collette said, obviously disturbed. "You saw how he was when he came in, all militant and ready to punch walls. He's always been like that as far as I know."

"What about Seth?"

"Oh, pfft." Collette fiddled with one of her earrings, tightening the back. "He's not in the same category as

Macon, not nearly as mercurial. But there's something off with him, too. He does okay in school and he at least accepted his parents' divorce and Brindel as a stepmother, but he's soft around the edges, kind of a mama's boy, if you know what I mean."

"He's close to his mother."

"Oh, yeah. He and Katrina, Paul's ex?" she asked, then held up her hand, her middle finger crossing over her index finger. "Just like that. Tight as you can imagine, and at his age, you know, it's a little weird."

"Did Katrina have a problem with Paul or Brindel?"

Collette shrugged. "They seemed civil enough. They weren't palsy-walsy, but after the initial shock of Paul's affair with Brindel, Katrina seemed to get over it. Moved on. Didn't remarry, but dated, and Brindel said they all 'got along.' That's how she described it. Whatever that means. But back to your question. I don't think Seth is capable of murder," she said, staring through the glass at her nephews. Her gaze traveled to the larger of Paul's sons. "But Macon? Him, I'm not so sure."

Chapter 9

Ivy Wilde stared out the grimy window of the bus as it rolled across the high desert of New Mexico. Some kind of sage was sprinkled in the dust, along with cacti that she recognized as yucca and prickly pear; the rest of the terrain was foreign, desolate, as the ground met mountains rising in the distance. The bus's loud engine continued to rumble, the tires whining, and far off, the sprawling city of Albuquerque was visible. At least she hoped it was Albuquerque, her temporary destination. She'd picked this part of New Mexico because it seemed remote, worlds away from San Francisco.

But it wasn't far enough.

Though it seemed impossible, Ivy was certain she was being followed. All the way from the Bay Area.

Ivy glanced over her shoulder. She'd picked a spot in the middle of the bus, the row of her seats placed in front of the back tire wells. No one occupied the seat beside her. Thank God. Then again, the big Greyhound wasn't all that full. Twenty-eight people, if she'd counted correctly, most of them older, senior citizens reading books, playing on their phones, or just dozing, mouths open for the most part. A family of four, the kids under five, the couple continuing to bicker, sat not far behind the bus driver, and in the very back a couple in their twenties were all over each other, apparently believing the coats they'd tossed across their entwined bodies could disguise what they were doing.

None of those people worried her.

It was the singles who caused her stomach to churn: the men.

Scattered around the lumbering vehicle, some of the people traveling alone appeared to be sleeping. Some had earbuds in their ears, others with their heads down, staring at the small screen of their phone or iPad or other device, playing games or texting or surfing the Internet.

Most didn't pay any attention to her.

Two did.

She'd caught each of them casting her surreptitious glances when they thought she wasn't looking. At first she'd thought it was because she was pretty and traveling alone, but then she wondered if there was something more to their furtive glances.

She checked them again.

One of the men was near the back of the bus, just two rows in front of the couple making out. He sat on the opposite side of the big vehicle from Ivy, but had a clear view of her seat. Wearing a baseball cap low over his eyes, he pretended to sleep, but if the fading sunlight hit him just right there was a slight reflection beneath his lashes. His eyes were open. He was faking it. Watching her.

The muscles in the back of her neck tightened, knowing his gaze was centered on her.

The other guy was just as bad. And closer. Again, across the aisle, but only one row back from her. He was leaning against the window, angled slightly toward her, earbuds in place, arms folded over his chest, sunglasses hiding his eyes, gelled hair slicked back, a cell phone in his hands. She supposed he was trying to appear as if he was engrossed in the hand-held device, but Ivy wasn't buying it.

No.

He was staring at her behind his dark shades.

Why? What did they know? Were they working together, trying to throw her off by sitting separately? Or were they independents?

That's crazy. No one could have followed you. No one! Don't let your paranoia get to you. Remember what Dr. Yates said . . . how to fight this . . . She drew in a long breath, let it out, and counted slowly in her head: *Ten, nine, eight . . .*

But the psychiatrist's trick didn't work. Not on this bus. Not now. Instead her anxiety ramped up as the bus driver passed a slow-moving van. Her throat closed and her hands gripped her own phone as if it were a lifeline.

By now the police would be looking for her, putting out APBs or whatever they were called now. BOLOs, she thought. Be On The Look-Out for. She bit her lip. With everyone hooked into the Internet and her picture floating around, how would she ever escape?

Her heart clenched and a little shred of fear whispered up the back of her arms, raising the hairs though the interior of the bus was warm.

The kids in the front started acting up again. The father, his LA Dodgers cap on backward, snapped at his exhausted-looking wife, and she yelled right back, then dug into a backpack to retrieve a bag of chips. The sack crinkled as she struggled to open it, and the husband snatched it away, ripping it so fast that some of the chips sprayed and the kids laughed.

"Oh, for the love of Chr—Christmas!" he said as the smell of barbecue flavoring mingled with the faint odor of diesel.

Almost everyone on the bus saw the exchange.

Well, except for the couple who were too into themselves, the few who were sleeping, and the guy in the sunglasses, the man who, like the guy in the baseball cap farther back, would not be distracted by the potato chip incident.

Whether he was malicious or not, she had to shake Sunglasses. At the next stop. She'd been careful, leaving San Francisco via BART, the Bay Area Rapid Transit system, heading across the bay to Oakland, but maybe they'd found her.

How? Had she given herself away somehow? She'd been totally freaked out when she'd climbed onto BART and had hoped since it was the middle of the night, she might just appear to be strung out if any of the other riders had noticed her. She'd been shaking and pale, her hair and makeup a mess from running in the rain, but no one had seemed to notice another young person dealing with what appeared to be the after effects of a bender.

At the nondescript cinder-block building of the bus station on the east side of San Francisco Bay she'd had to wait for several hours before she could board the next bus to LA, and she'd been so upset trying to buy the ticket, she'd dropped the cash onto the counter and had scooped it up, only to fumble with the bills, a couple of fifties drifting to the floor. She'd scrambled for the money, chasing one bill under a bench. As she'd hurried back to the counter, she'd felt more than one set of eyes watching her.

That southbound bus had been crowded, more of a mix of riders, a pregnant woman seated next to her. Ivy had tried and failed to sleep, her stomach rumbling from lack of food, her nerves shot. She hadn't had a plan when she'd fled San Francisco, just to get as far away as possible.

In LA, she'd been delayed until early morning, something to do with a bus breaking down, so she'd adjusted her plans and instead of heading to Phoenix, she'd taken the bus to Albuquerque, New Mexico. She was tired and hungry and needed a shower after nearly two days of being on the road, not to mention the vision of her mother, a bullet hole in her forehead.

Now, catching the guy in the baseball cap peering at her again, she swallowed back her fear. Told herself she was imagining things, that she was the only woman under forty on the bus and so it was natural.

Still . . .

Her heart hammered and her palms were sweating.

What if they got off when she did?

What if they followed her?

So far she hadn't let anyone know where she was.

Not even Troy.

Nor her aunts, the closest people to her.

How could she?

She glanced out the window and in the reflection

caught the guy a row back looking her way again. Studying her.

Sweet Jesus.

Panic threatened to take hold of her as the big bus lumbered into the station, a sprawling stucco building with a red tile roof and an arched doorway, a mission-like facade to blend in with the Spanish architecture of the city. As soon as the doors to the bus opened, she bolted outside, hurrying into the chill of the New Mexico afternoon. Dusk was fast approaching, the shadows of the surrounding buildings crawling across the street. Inside, she bought her next ticket and in her peripheral vision caught sight of some of the other passengers, some hauling bags into the cavernous building. She was first in line at the counter. "One way to Missoula, Montana," she said, remembering the name of the town nearest to Grizzly Falls.

"First train out is early in the morning," the woman behind the counter, an African American with high cheekbones, rimless glasses, and a gold cross around her neck, advised her. "And I do mean early. Two thirty-seven." She handed Ivy a slim schedule.

"What about Helena?" she asked as an announcement of a bus departure echoed through the building.

"Same difference." The woman's graying eyebrows drew together. "You okay, honey?" she asked, and Ivy had trouble finding her voice.

No. I'm not okay. I'll never be okay again! My mother and stepfather were killed in cold blood in their bedrooms. I am definitely not *okay.* "I'm fine," she squeaked out. "I'll take the ticket to Missoula."

The woman looked as if she didn't believe her as again Ivy fumbled with her cash and waited, feeling a nervous tic in her eye as the terminal employee made change. Ivy stuffed the ticket into her jacket pocket and hurried out of the terminal. Using her phone, she found a diner a couple of blocks over and, inside the small mom and pop establishment, she ordered a burger and fries, Diet Coke, and while waiting to be served, headed to the restroom. She used the toilet, splashed water on her face, then repaired her makeup and hair, but the reflection in the mirror stared back at her with wary, worried eyes. She looked like hell. Like she'd just witnessed a murder scene and no amount of mascara, blush, and lip gloss would change that.

Worst of all, she was recognizable.

Despite the fact that she looked like a ghost in comparison to the smiling head shot on her driver's license, the photo she'd seen of herself on the Internet—already they were looking for her—she was still Ivy Wilde. That would have to change. She couldn't chance being identified, or turned in, not until she did it on her own terms, not until she was certain she would be safe. If that were even possible.

She had hours before she could leave, so she'd have to find a place to crash. A dive of a no-tell motel, and while there she would change her appearance. Cut her hair. Dye it. Find a pair of sunglasses for herself and some kind of hat that didn't stand out, but would cover her forehead and shade her eyes. And buy an oversized sweatshirt to wear over her jacket, to make her look heavier.

Back at her table, she found her order waiting, the hamburger still warm, the French fries crispy. She was hungry and dug into the burger with gusto, washing the first couple of bites down with swallows of her Diet Coke. Then her stomach seized. Threatened to hurl. She waited. Sipped the soda, glanced out the huge plate glass window to the parking lot where a few dusty cars and pickups were scattered.

She tried again.

The next bite stuck in her throat.

Another swallow of the diet drink. Maybe the fizz would . . .

Something caught her eye. A shadow outside. Quick movement. She squinted to a hedgerow separating the burger joint's parking lot from that of a neighboring brick building.

Then nothing.

Everything seemed normal.

Four teenagers, loud and laughing, walked into the restaurant and found a booth where the two girls giggled at whatever it was the boys were saying. They fell onto the benches and sprawled, high on life or whatever.

Ivy couldn't handle another bite. What she had eaten felt like a brick, heavy in her stomach. She took another swallow of the soda, then peered through the window again, her gaze scouring every inch of the parking lot, but as she did, she let her mind wander . . . and it returned once again to the image of her mother lying naked and dead in her bed.

Forcing her eyes back to her plate was no better. The small pool of catsup near her fries looked so much like blood she felt her stomach start to quiver.

No. She couldn't do this. Couldn't eat. Not yet. She wiped her mouth with a napkin and pushed her plate aside, up against the napkin stand. Then she peeled off a twenty from the wad of bills in her pocket and got the hell out of there.

Outside, the wind was cold enough to steal her breath. Traffic rushed by and night was on its way. Headlights glowed white, taillights red, the hum of tires on dry pavement ever present. She had to keep moving, keep thinking. Clicking on her phone, she noticed it was about out of power. Time to recharge. She Googled convenience stores and found one a few blocks away.

Did she hear footsteps behind her?

Pulse jumping, she glanced over her shoulder as she walked, nearly running into a woman bundled in a bulky ski jacket who was forced to step out of Ivy's path. The woman sidestepped her and muttered, "Watch where you're going!"

"Sorry," Ivy mumbled.

She saw no one else on the stretch of sidewalk behind her. The streetlights were just starting to glow.

Darkness was falling. Quickly.

Spying the convenience store, she waited until a pickup with a camper drove past, then jaywalked across the street. Still no one was behind her. Opening the door, she felt a wall of warmth and smelled the odors of nacho cheese and onions and hotdogs that looked roasted to death coming from a small deli case. Near the back of the store, a single clerk stood behind the counter, a skinny, pimply faced boy of about eighteen who paid more attention to his phone than the near-empty store.

For once she lucked out; the store sold cheap makeup, hooded sweatshirts, hair dye, scissors, and baseball caps. All of which she needed and grabbed. She swept through the few aisles and threw in a cell phone charger, oversized hoodie, and a travel-sized bottle of hair spray. Then, thinking of the long night and day ahead, tossed a couple of bottles of water and three candy bars and a large bag of Cheetos into her basket. Her mother would kill her if she saw the junk food . . . oh, God. Mom.

Ivy's knees nearly buckled at the thought of her mother. With an effort she forced herself not to break down as she approached the counter.

Nervously, on one foot and the other, she waited for the cashier, whose name tag read COLLIN, to ring up her items. He was incredibly slow and as he scanned the oversized sweatshirt, she heard the front door whisper open, then caught sight of a man perusing the magazine rack.

Her heart nearly missed a beat.

One of the men from the bus.

She recognized his shades and the beard-shadow covering his jaw, the gelled hair.

She didn't doubt for a second that he'd followed her.

Oh. God.

She had to get out of here. Fast.

"Do you know the closest motel?" she asked the cashier under her breath. "A cheap one that, you know, won't ask many questions."

Collin focused on her for a second, then scanned her items, including the hair dye.

"Seriously," she said. "I need a place to crash."

"Uh." He lifted the cap from his head, squinted, and scratched his head. "Maybe the Lakesider?" He didn't sound sure of himself.

She didn't care. "Okay. Sounds good."

"Yeah, uh, it's about six blocks that way." He pointed in the direction of the parking lot, over the top of a shelf holding over-the-counter sleep aids and other medications.

Seeing the guy in the sunglasses approaching, she repeated the name of the motel under her breath, as if memorizing it. "The Lakesider."

"Yeah, but there ain't no lake anywhere nearby," Collin said on a wheezing laugh. "Why they call it the Lakesider beats me."

"No problem," Ivy lied, irritated.

The cashier was an idiot and he'd just given away the location and name of the motel to the other patron in the store.

She scooped up her bagged items and change as the man in the hat stepped closer to the counter.

"Pack of Marlboro Reds," Sunglasses said.

Heart thudding in her chest, she hurried from the register as Collin reached for the pack of cigarettes.

It could all be innocent, she told herself. This little store wasn't that far from the bus station, anyone could have wandered over here without following her. The guy in the sunglasses just needed a smoke.

"Yeah, right," she whispered once outside, where the temperature seemed to have dropped another five degrees. She didn't believe that rationale for an instant. Had he hidden in the shadows and watched her through the plate glass window of the diner, then tailed her to the market?

Or was she overreacting?

Either way, she couldn't take a chance.

Chapter 10

Paterno stopped by Tanaka's desk where she was chewing on the rim of her paper coffee cup as she worked at the computer. The cup was nearly shredded with her teeth marks. "Just got a call from Regan Pescoli," he said. "She's bringing Paul Latham's sons in."

"Both?"

"Turns out they're both in the city. They'll be here in half an hour."

Her eyes narrowed. "It'll be interesting to hear what they say and if they've heard from their sister." Her lips pulled down at the corners. "I got information from the cell company on all their phones."

"That was quick."

"I know a guy," she said cryptically, then didn't elaborate. "We're checking the numbers from the sons' phones, but it's been radio silence since that night for Ivy Wilde's phone. I'm checking with the people she talked to in the days before the murder, but so far have struck out. Just friends who said everything was normal. Or as normal as it could be. Turns out Ivy was dealing with psychological problems."

"Serious?"

"Not good, but if you're asking if she's violent, I haven't seen any evidence of that, and I spoke with Dr. Yates, who is Ivy's psychiatrist. She couldn't confirm anything, nor tell me much because of doctor/patient privilege and HIPPA, but I gleaned she hasn't heard from her. She seemed concerned. She wouldn't give me a diagnosis but said she seemed to think Ivy wasn't capable of the violence one would need to commit murder, but even that was couched in all kind of cover-her-ass vernacular and there was a very big 'don't quote me' attached to the sketchy information she provided." They talked about Ivy's friends, a couple of girls and one boy, none of whom had heard from her since before the murders. "One of the boys seemed concerned, but said that she'd been moody over the past few weeks, kept to herself."

"He know why?"

"The boy I talked with—not a boyfriend, totally platonic—says so, and the girlfriends confirm. He said she was worried her mother was going to divorce her stepfather and though she didn't like Paul, she wasn't up for the upheaval of a divorce. She'd already been through that with her own parents. The girlfriends, though, think she's been more upset with the breakup with her last boyfriend, Troy Boxer."

"You talk to him yet?"

"No, but soon. He works for a shipping company."

"That's right. That's what you said." Paterno paused, thought about it. "A kid by the name of Boxer works delivering packages?"

She rolled her eyes. “I know. Life’s full of fun little ironies, isn’t it?”

“Let’s just solve this case.”

“Yes. Find and arrest the murderers and locate a missing, runaway, or kidnapped teen.” She actually smiled, then finished her coffee and tossed the cup into her trash bin. “Maybe we can wrap this up early.”

“Then you can go on a hot date.”

“Wouldn’t that be nice.”

“You need a life, Tanaka,” Paterno said, fully aware she spent her supposed downtime working cases or hanging around with her cat.

She rolled back her chair and gazed up at him. “Forgive me if I don’t get all hot and bothered at the image of being on a boat trolling off the coast of Mexico.”

“That’s because you’re forgetting the part of the fantasy that includes clear aquamarine water, the sun high overhead, a fishing pole in one hand, and a chilled margarita in the other.”

“Maybe you have a point,” she said. “But put that aside and let’s figure out who killed the Lathams.”

Pescoli expected a cool reception from Detective Tanaka.

She wasn’t disappointed.

The San Francisco detective was definitely not thrilled that Pescoli had driven her two stepnephews into the station. Though Tanaka tried to hide her feelings under a mask of indifference, Pescoli felt the other woman’s hostility. Thc plain fact of the matter was that Tanaka didn’t trust her. For that, Pescoli didn’t blame her. Didn't she herself feel the same sense of ownership when she was deep into a case?

As Macon had suspected, he and Seth were split and interviewed separately, Pescoli kept out of the loop. She'd finally convinced Macon to talk to the authorities and just tell the truth, but she'd also advised him that if at any time during the interview he thought he needed counsel, he could stop answering questions and demand a lawyer.

"Fine," he'd finally acquiesced, "but you need to be with me. If not in the room, then watching . . . otherwise, it's a no-go."

Now, standing in a darkened chamber with Paterno and a couple of other cops, Pescoli was allowed to observe both interviews in progress. Macon had been correct. The interviews were filmed by a technician at a desk in the room with the cops.

On his side of the glass, Macon slumped in one of the two molded chairs, arms crossed over his chest, answered succinctly, without much expression, and didn't elaborate a lot. Somehow he kept his anger in check.

His alibi was simple and straightforward. He'd stayed at a friend's apartment, which he did often.

When pressed, he said further, "I didn't get along all that great with my father and he wasn't happy that I was taking a term off from UCLA. It wasn't always comfortable at home. Dad thought since it was 'his' house, I needed to play by 'his' rules. I didn't see things that way so I spent a lot of time at Corey's . . . Corey Mendicino. I've known him since junior high. He knew the situation. Gave me a key to his apartment."

"Gave it to you?" Tanaka repeated.

"Yeah, it's here. On my key chain."

"Was Corey with you that night?"

"Not all night. Not until around two when he got home. He bartends down at Culpepper's Ale House. When he got home I was on his couch."

"There were beer cans in your room at the house."

He shrugged. "Probably from earlier."

"The housekeeper comes in every day."

"Then I can't explain them." He looked irritated at Tanaka's insistence.

She changed tack and asked about the firearms.

"That's the one thing Dad and I had in common, I guess. Otherwise he was always on my ass, telling me to get my act together—that's how he put it—and think about my future."

"You liked his guns."

"Yeah. His collection's bitchin'. Man, really great, y'know."

"Was it insured?" she asked.

"Well, yeah. Had to be. Some of the pistols were from like World War II, and I think he said the Colt, yeah, that was from like 1848, I think. Five shot. Six-inch barrel. Baby Dragoon. Really sweet." He then went on about some long gun, a musket from the period of the Revolutionary War.

"He's not holding back," Paterno whispered to Pescoli. "We have an inventory of Latham's collection from the insurance company, and both those guns were listed."

"But missing. Stolen."

"Along with jewelry also listed and probably papers. Don't know for certain on that count. Only certain about what was insured."

"Were Paul and Brindel killed with one of his guns?"

"Don't know yet. He did own a .380, so it's possible that one of them was killed with it. But the victims were killed with separate guns by what appears to be two different killers, working in tandem."

"Premeditated," she said, thinking aloud as she envisioned the scene in her mind. "And orchestrated."

He nodded, his gaze never leaving the viewing area.

Tanaka showed Macon the knife and didn't get much of a reaction, just knit brows. "Is this from the kitchen block?" he asked. "What does it have to do with anything. I thought . . . didn't you say Dad and Brindel were shot?"

"This was found outside the house."

"How did it get there?" he asked.

"I thought you might tell me."

"I have no fuc—effin' idea." His eyebrows collided and he shook his head. "Is this from the kitchen? Dad had a set, kept them razor sharp, like a surgeon's scalpel. That's what he'd say anyway. He was always sharpening them and . . . Jesus, I don't know."

He seemed genuinely confused as was she, unless the police were hoping to trip him up and shock him, maybe thinking he was in cahoots with Ivy. It didn't make a lot of sense, but they had to cover all their bases.

After about an hour of answering questions, Macon pushed back his chair. "I've told you everything I know. Really. I didn't kill my father or his wife. I don't know who did." Before Tanaka could argue, he was on his feet and reaching into his pocket for a pack of cigarettes.

Seth's interview was more emotional. He was near tears throughout, but stuck to his alibi that he was with his girlfriend in Las Vegas. Tanaka had already spoken to the girlfriend, Laura-Dean Ellerby, who backed him up. The trouble was, Laura-Dean was underage and couldn't have accompanied Seth into the casinos. Which wasn't a cause for serious suspicion, just something to think about.

As they were leaving the darkened room and the two interviews, Pescoli asked Paterno, "You got anything on Ivy?"

"Not yet." He shook his head. "We're checking her phone records and still looking through camera footage around the scene." Tanaka came out and joined them, and Paterno added, "Tanaka has talked to some of her friends. They don't know anything, or at least that's what they say."

"They're teenagers," Pescoli said. "They lie."

Tanaka raised an eyebrow at that remark.

"What about that boyfriend, Boxer? I'd like to hear what he has to say," said Pescoli.

Shaking her head, Tanaka said, "I don't think—"

"We're hoping to catch him when he goes off duty today," Paterno cut in. "He gets off at five, brings the delivery truck back to the warehouse where they ship from."

Pescoli asked, "What do you know about the guy?"

"Not much. He has his own place, basically just a room in a house south of the airport."

"The landlord is George Aimes," Tanaka broke in. "A widower with a big house. Rents out empty bedrooms and the renters all agree to help out with repairs around the place to get the affordable rent, which is hard to come by in this city."

"Or anywhere in the whole Bay Area."

Pescoli checked her watch. "Why don't I meet you there? I'd like to hear what Boxer has to say but I have to get back to my sister's house and my kids, so I might have to leave early."

She saw Tanaka's lips tighten at the corners. She obviously disapproved. Tough.

"That'll work," Paterno said. "Afterward we hope to meet with Brindel's divorce attorney. We tried earlier and missed him."

Tanaka checked her watch. "But we might have missed our window."

Paterno was obviously torn. "I'll report back on that one," he said, and his partner shot him a look.

It wasn't really good enough for Pescoli and she didn't trust that she would hear what she needed from him, but she backed off, would get back to the family for now. There were other ways to get the information. Ways she'd never admit to if pressed. Nothing totally dishonest, she told herself. Just expedient. This was the murder of her sister and brother-in-law after all. And her niece was missing. So, the rules could be bent a little.

Or maybe even a lot.

Pissed beyond pissed, Tanaka drove steadily south through the driving rain and the tangle of traffic that clogged the street. She and Paterno were headed south through the city to the warehouse of A-Bay-C Delivery where Troy Boxer worked. The wipers were working overtime, slapping the heavy rain away at a vicious pace.

"You shouldn't have invited Pescoli," she said as she was forced to slow for a red light. Through the windshield she noted the sky was blackening. Sunset came early this time of year and the storm and gloom only seemed to speed up the return of darkness.

"She invited herself."

"You should have said no from the get-go," Tanaka pointed out as they idled behind a silver Prius with a "Coexist" bumper sticker. The interviews during the day hadn't gone all that well and she'd even tried to trip Macon up by bringing up the beer cans found in his room even though they already knew there weren't any prints on them. He hadn't been rattled.

Nothing was coming together.

Yet.

But Tanaka was damned sure including Pescoli wouldn't help. The plain fact of the matter was that she didn't like Pescoli nosing into the case. It was out of line. She knew it, Paterno knew it, and most important of all, Pescoli knew it. She was just used to bullying her way onto a case. Tanaka could smell it on her.

As soon as one of her sisters had brought up that one of Brindel Latham's siblings was a cop, Tanaka had immediately suspected the detective from Montana would be trouble. The oldest sister, Collette Foucher, was tough and cold, and Sarina Marsh, the younger one, was shorter and rounder and an emotional mess, and could barely stop crying to breathe.

And the cop. Pescoli was more together but Tanaka wasn't about to trust the detective with her messy bun of reddish blond hair, suspicious green eyes, and no-

nonsense set of her jaw. Cool on the outside, there was something more to her, a fire and impatience that Tanaka recognized in herself.

Nope. Tanaka couldn't trust her. Not as far as she could throw her. And she was the sister of the victim, so that should disqualify her straight out.

What the hell was wrong with Paterno? He should never have allowed Pescoli within a hundred yards of the case. All his talk of "another set of eyes" and Pescoli being a "well-respected" cop was just a load of BS. Allowing a victim's relative into the investigation was a huge breach of protocol, at least as far as Tanaka was concerned.

The light turned green, but the Prius didn't move.

"What the—?" She laid on the horn and the driver, who had been looking down, visibly started.

"Texting," Paterno guessed as the Prius leapt forward.

"Or surfing the damned Net." Tanaka was right on the Prius's tail. "We should ticket the idiot." But she wouldn't. They were already pushing it. She wanted to find Troy Boxer and get some kind of a statement.

They pulled into the lot for the company and, as they were walking inside, from the corner of her eye, Tanaka caught a glimpse of Pescoli parking her rental nearby, then pulling the hood of her jacket over her hair. At least Paterno had nixed her joining them at the divorce lawyer's office.

The Montana cop caught up with them at the counter where a slim man in horn-rimmed glasses, clipped hair, and a bored expression offered to help them while glancing pointedly at the clock that read four fifty-three. They displayed badges and Tanaka noticed his spine visibly stiffen and his Adam's apple move up and down. Nervous. When they asked about Troy Boxer, he loosened up a little.

"He just got in," he said, looking up at a monitor mounted over the counter. "Truck seventeen. Do you want me to call him in . . . ?"

"No, just show us how to get to him."

"Through this door." The clerk jabbed a finger toward a red door, then hustled around the end of the counter and, using a keypad, punched a code into a locked door. "This way," he said over his shoulder as he half ran down a wide hallway and through another door to open bays of the warehouse. The entire parking area in front of the building was surrounded by a high fence topped with razor wire. Cameras were mounted on the corners of the warehouse. "Loading dock three," the clerk said. "I have to get back to my station. I could be fired for leaving the office."

Tanaka spied Troy Boxer. "We've got it."

The manager didn't wait for a response, but peeled off and jogged back to the hallway and disappeared inside.

Tanaka, Paterno, and Pescoli walked to the third bay where a burly-looking man in his early twenties was unloading the driver's area of a yellow delivery van painted with the logo of A-Bay-C Delivery. His brown hair was clipped so short that his skin showed through and the hint of a tattoo was visible over the collar of his shirt, another one peeking out from beneath the sleeve of his yellow A-Bay-C Delivery jacket.

"Troy Boxer?" Paterno asked as they approached the van.

Boxer looked up sharply, his bushy eyebrows drawing together. "Who wants to know?"

Paterno said, "San Francisco Police Department."

Again they displayed their badges and introduced themselves, including that they were with the homicide department.

Before they could explain further, he cut in.

"Homicide? I don't . . . oh, fuck!" His pale blue eyes widened as the light dawned. "This is about Ivy's parents! Son of a—is that why you're here? Because of the Lath—wait a sec! Did something happen to Ivy?"

Paterno said, "She's missing."

"I know . . . I mean, I heard." He was nodding, rubbing the scruff of a three-day beard shadow. "I saw it on the news. But you said 'homicide.' Don't tell me Ivy's dead." He was shaking his head and Tanaka tensed as he reached into the pocket of his baggy jeans.

"Hold it!"

But he pulled out an e-cigarette. "What?" he asked, startled. A long moment later, he said, "Oh, you thought I had a gun? Oh, hell, no. I just need a vape." He fired up the device and drew a great lungful of vapor, then let it spew out in a cloud around his face.

"We're investigating the deaths of Paul and Brindel Latham, and also trying to locate Ivy Wilde," Tanaka said, waving her hand in front of her nose.

"She hasn't turned up yet?" Another huge cloud of sweet-smelling vapor swept out.

"You don't know where she could be?" Tanaka pushed.

"No, I don't know. Anywhere, I guess." He sucked on the e-cig hard. Outside, through the open doors, the rain finally began to slacken. "But she's alive."

"You know that? She contacted you?" Paterno pounced.

"No, no, but I just . . . I mean . . . she can't be dead." He sounded as if he were trying to convince himself. Then, while a forklift loaded a pallet of merchandise onto a flatbed, the light seemed to dawn, as if he finally understood why the cops had shown up where he worked. "Oh. You think I might know something about what happened?"

Tanaka asked, "Where were you two nights ago, between nine at night and two in the morning?"

"Where was I?" he asked. "Jesus Christ. I don't know." He raked one hand over his head, smoothing the stubble. "Shit, what night was that?"

"Wednesday."

"Wednesday night? At that time? God, I was home, I think. Yeah. That's right. I was in bed. I had to work the next day—yesterday."

"Can anyone confirm that?"

"Of course," he said, then didn't look so sure. "I live in a house, kind of a rooming house. Four guys rent from George. George Aimes. I saw him when I was using the microwave . . . at . . . umm . . . maybe seven, seven thirty. Oh, and Ronny Stillwell was there. He's one of the other guys who rent from George, works at some plumbing company. Anyway, Ronny and I BS'ed about basketball, y'know. He's a Lakers fan cuz he's from somewhere around LA, and I'm Warriors all the way. So then I ate, took a shower, and went into my room. Had a couple brewskies and watched the game. The Warriors were playing." He looked from Tanaka to Paterno.

"Did George or anyone else see you after seven thirty?"

"No. I told you I was in my room. God . . . wait . . . look, I don't know anything about what went down at Ivy's house."

"When was the last time you saw her?"

"I don't know. Maybe . . . in November, or December? . . . Wait. No. It was around Thanksgiving, so a couple of months ago. She and I are history."

"You didn't talk to her? Text her?"

"No . . . I . . ." He started to lie, then said, "Maybe she texted me around Christmas, but I didn't reply. Didn't want to start something up again."

"Did she?" Paterno asked. "Want to start something up again?"

"I didn't want to find out. She's a little . . . strange. Kind of off."

"How so?" Tanaka asked.

"I don't know. Just weird." Then, as if he regretted confiding in them, added, "Forget it. I shouldn't have said anything."

When pressed, he wouldn't say anything more.

A bell sounded, then steady beeping as an automatic gate began to slowly slide open. Headlights glowed as another yellow A-Bay-C Delivery van waited, only to roar through as the gap widened. The driver, a woman, parked her vehicle next to Boxer's.

"Look," he said, his voice lowered as the woman driver, dressed as he was, cast a glance in their direction, raised a hand, then walked into the warehouse. "I had nothing to do with what went down. Ivy and I dated for what? Less than a year—she kept track of that shit, I didn't—but it was over and last I heard she was dating someone else, so go look for him."

"Got a name?" Tanaka said.

"Nah. I already told you all I know, which is nothin'."

Pescoli said, "Do you know of anyone who had something against the Lathams?"

He snorted. "Christ, yeah. The old man? Ivy's stepfather? He was a real douche. One of those guys who thought he knew everything, so yeah, according to Ivy no one liked him. Not even his own kids. If I were you, I'd start with them."

Chapter 11

Heart drumming, Ivy glanced over her shoulder and kept moving.

Someone was definitely following her. She could feel it.

Someone who was probably a killer.

She left the convenience store and took off walking fast, moving quickly in the direction of the Lakesider. With a quick glance over her shoulder to make certain Sunglasses wasn't behind her, she jagged sharply, veering around a corner, and broke into a jog for two blocks before backtracking.

"Come on, come on," she whispered, hoping the battery on her phone wouldn't give out as she Googled nearby motels. Her pulse was thundering in her ears, her nerves stretched to the breaking point. Never missing a step, she found the name of another motel, not too far away, and following the guide from the GPS, veered abruptly and cut through a narrow, darkened alley where trash cans were overflowing and a shadow moved.

Someone crouching.

Shifting toward her.

She bit back a scream.

Her heart nearly stopped before seeing that the movement was from the edge of a black garbage bag flapping crazily in the breeze.

Keep moving. Just keep moving. You can do this!

The alley opened to a street. She forced herself to slow her steps, didn't want to attract unnecessary attention. Cars and trucks rolled by, headlights and taillights glowing in the coming dark, a desert wind cutting through her jacket and flinging her hair in front of her eyes. Her teeth were chattering by the time she cut through a parking lot and back to a side street leading to the Sunset Valley Inn, an L-shaped cinder-block building in desperate need of a paint job.

Steeling herself for a confrontation, she headed into the reception area, brightly lit with fluorescent lights that hummed softly. The interior was small and smelled of day-old coffee, a fake wood-grain stand of brochures about "What to Do in Awesome Albuquerque" was positioned next to a rolling cart where two pressure pots of coffee stood at attention and half-empty packets of powdered creamer and sugar had been left. The girl running the desk looked like she was younger than Ivy despite an overload of makeup.

Ivy approached and the receptionist, her bored expression never changing, checked her in. She wore no name tag but the tattoo on her wrist was of two names held together by a heart. "Tammy heart Drake." Ivy assumed the girl was Tammy, but she didn't ask, didn't want to make any unnecessary conversation, and was grateful that "Tammy" didn't worry too much about Ivy's lack of ID.

"I lost it and my credit cards on the plane. In my carry-on." The girl's plucked and darkened brows drew together. "I know, crazy, huh? It's just that I'm so upset." Ivy swallowed hard. Called up the lie. "I'm going to my mother's funeral. And my brain just isn't in gear." Tears sprang to her eyes. "The airline is supposed to call if they find my bag; until then I'm effed-up, if you know what I mean."

Tammy gave her the what-kind-of-idiot-leaves-her-bag-on-the-plane look, but said, "I'll need enough to cover any damage. A security deposit, y'know?"

"Sure. Sure. How much?"

"I dunno. Fifty? Maybe—"

"I've got it. Okay. Fifty. And then for the night. I'll pay in advance. One night."

Ivy filled out a registration card with the first name that came into her head—Macie Smith—and fortunately the girl at the desk didn't so much as blink, just handed over an old-fashioned key and said, "Check out's at eleven."

Ivy's room faced the parking lot and she carried her meager belongings with her as she left the warmth of the lobby and headed outside where night had definitely fallen, taking the temperature with it. She raced up the exterior staircase to room 214.

Inside the bare bones room, she locked the door, threw the dead-bolt, dropped her bag of purchases onto a battered TV stand with a bubble-faced television, and cranked the heat up to nearly eighty. The bed, dressed in a floral print bedspread, appeared to sag in the middle. At least it was a place to sleep, she thought, then stripped off her clothes on her way to the tiny bathroom with its telephone-booth-sized shower. After fifteen minutes under a measly spray that was just hot enough to warm her skin, she dried off with a threadbare towel and threw on her oversized T.

Before she could second-guess herself, she swiped the condensation from the face of the mirror over the sink, twisted her hair into a taut ponytail, and with her new scissors, started cutting, clipping off the long strands of her pale hair. It took a little bit of work and a lot of clean-up snips to get the uneven cut manageable. She even chopped the bangs that fell just below her eyebrows. "Ugh," she said to her reflection, but was determined to see her transformation through and meticulously followed the steps to changing herself from a golden blonde with pale highlights to a blend-into-the-woodwork mousy brown.

After all the processing was done, she showered again, careful with her hair, then rinsed out her clothes.

God, how had she come to this?

She felt the sting of tears again as she thought of her mother, and her heart ached. Blinking, she hung her clothes over the towel rack, then started charging her phone. She flopped onto the bed. The room was warm if dingy, the door locked if not completely secure. The best she could do.

But now, as the events of the past nearly two days washed over her, she felt weak again. Alone. The wind whistled outside, the heater rumbled throughout the small room, and she heard the television from the next unit. The urge to call someone, *any*one, overtook her, and she went to her favorites on her contact list and nearly pressed the number, but her thumb hovered over the screen and before she made a stupid mistake, she switched the phone off. She'd heard about the police or parents tracking their kids down by looking through phone records and she couldn't risk it. Of course, she was probably already screwed. If they were really intent on tracking her they could by her cell phone, she was pretty sure.

But if she could just get on that bus tomorrow.

Briefly, she considered reading about the murders online or switching on the news and finding out if the horror of San Francisco had made national headlines and was broadcast here, but she couldn't face thinking about her mother or the fact that she'd never see her again.

She turned out the lights and eased to the window, opening the blinds a fraction with the wand and staring out to the parking lot where only one security lamp lit the uneven asphalt. A few cars were parked near the building but no one seemed to be loitering around the lot. Light traffic. Nothing out of the ordinary . . .

Or was there?

She squinted and gazed across the street, past the cars and trucks driving by to a gas station on the corner and strip mall directly across the street. Was there someone hanging out by the back of the gas station? Maybe not. She was probably just conjuring up the image, nothing to worry about. . . .

A small flash of light appeared.

Her throat tightened.

"No!" The shadowy figure became more distinct. Definitely a man. He bent his head forward to the flame, lighting a cigarette. She thought about Sunglasses buying a pack of Marlboros.

Her heart froze.

The flare of the lighter reflected in his dark lenses.

"Oh, Jesus."

Her fingers tightened over the rod controlling the blinds.

He couldn't have followed her. No way. She'd been so careful, even trying to distract him to the Lakesider Inn.

All the spit dried in her mouth and she snapped the blinds shut. Now what? She checked the door and windows. Everything locked tight. If only she hadn't dropped the knife. If only she had some kind of weapon. She thought of all of her stepfather's guns and the ammo he kept in his private walk-in safe. If only she'd grabbed a firearm . . .

Well, you didn't. So somehow you've got to get out of this mess you made for yourself. Just figure it out. It's what Mom would say. You know it.

Pacing, she wanted to stare through the blinds, but didn't. Five minutes crept by, then ten, and fifteen. She resisted. But after forty-five minutes had passed in the dark, she couldn't stand it a second longer and risked a tiny peek.

Nerves stretched tight, she adjusted the blinds and peered out.

The street was empty. And across the street, no one stood in the umbra, at least not that she could see. An attendant was behind the counter of the cash register of the office of the gas station, another one in a red coat filling up the tank of an older sedan parked beneath the brightly lit awning covering the pumps, but no other strangers loitered nearby. She hazarded opening the blinds a bit more and her gaze swept the street as a semi, bed empty, rumbled to the stoplight and cruised through beneath the light as it changed from amber to red.

He could still be out there, of course, but she tried to calm herself, by snapping the blinds shut, double-checking the lock on the door, and dropping onto the bed again. She turned on her phone, set the alarm, switched on the ancient TV with its oversized remote and, as some ball game blared, opened the pack of Cheetos and unwrapped a candy bar.

Her mother would freak if she saw what Ivy was calling dinner. . . .

Mom.

Ivy closed her eyes and felt tears well behind her lids. "I'm sorry," she whispered. How had the plan she'd worked out so carefully backfired into something so awful? "I'm so, so sorry."

Pescoli decided to make the call.

Even though the Latham case wasn't hers.

Knowing full well that Sheriff Blackwater would read her the riot act.

Despite the fact that she could easily lose her job.

And disregarding any sense of protocol.

She glanced at the bedside clock in the loft that Sarina had converted into a temporary guest room. Not even two AM yet. But that was normal. Tucker had awoken just after one. She'd fed the baby, cuddled him until he'd dozed off, then laid him on the Aerobed where he was currently sleeping peacefully. Afterward, she'd taken his empty bottle downstairs and checked on Bianca, who was sleeping on the couch in front of the flickering TV while some old movie from the eighties was playing.

Pescoli had clicked off the television and tucked a blanket around her daughter. For a second she'd paused, wondering how the years had flown by with Bianca thinking about college while Tucker was just working on rolling over.

Too fast, she'd decided, but hadn't given herself too much time to ponder it.

She had too much to do and too little time.

She'd headed back upstairs, saw that Tucker hadn't moved, and as she'd stared at his sleeping innocence, she'd felt it again—that particular anxiety, a little sizzle through her nervous system that he was so vulnerable. She'd told herself she was going nuts, that everything was fine, that there were no hidden eyes lurking in the spreading branches of the oak tree that shaded the upper deck.

"Idiot," she'd whispered as she double-checked the lock on the slider. She was being foolish. The malevolence she'd felt . . . *no* . . . imagined at her home in Montana hadn't even existed, much less traveled to San Francisco.

Still, the hairs on the back of her arms had been at attention, and only with the passing of ten minutes of silence, with the baby sleeping peacefully and safely nearby, had Pescoli calmed and let down her guard.

Now, she noticed that the rain had stopped, the night

still, only the sound of Sarina's soft snoring from down the hallway and the quiet rumble of the furnace breaking the silence.

She slipped her cell phone off its charger, then walked to the slider. She stared out at the night where streetlights were visible through the spreading branches of the oak tree.

"Now or never," she whispered.

Ignoring all of her interior arguments to the contrary, she called Tydeus Chilcoate and in so doing, crossed that thin, invisible line between legal and not so legal.

She'd done it before.

Always on the sly.

Because no one knew about her secret source. Could never. Not Alvarez. Not even Santana. And Pescoli planned to keep it that way.

A night owl, Chilcoate was an electronic and technical genius who happened to be a loner and hacker and lived isolated, in a cabin outside Grizzly Falls. She'd met him during a case years ago, where a serial murderer dubbed the Star-Crossed Killer had terrorized the area surrounding Grizzly Falls. Chilcoate was one of those antigovernment types who had no qualms about hacking or surveillance or wiretapping or anything technical for the right price. Pescoli had rarely used his talents, but sometimes his ambivalence about the law and his technical genius was an asset. As in this case. Pescoli needed answers and she needed them quickly.

Working with the San Francisco PD was burdensome. Tanaka was putting up roadblocks right and left, and going through the usual channels at the sheriff's department in Montana would only send up red flags to Blackwater and create too much jurisdictional red tape that she didn't have time to cut through. The fact that she was one of the victims' sisters would only make working the case and getting information more difficult.

Not so with Chilcoate.

They had a deal: she tended to look the other way if his name came up in any investigation as long as it didn't pertain to a crime of violence, and in turn he gave her a private number and access to his hidden computer system with its GPS, tracking systems, and the like along with his unique ability to hack undetected into corporate, government, and private computer systems.

Sometimes it would take several days, but usually he could get the information she needed much faster than through the usual and "legit" channels.

She listened in the dark as the phone rang once. Twice. And then he answered, his voice gravelly from years of cigarettes. "Yeah?"

"This is Pescoli."

"I know."

Of course he did.

"And I figure you want something that you'd rather not have anyone else know about," he said, a smile in his voice.

Chapter 12

Ivy woke up with a start.

Her phone was bleating.

Where was she?

What was she doing . . . ?

Then she remembered: Mom and Paul were dead and . . . and someone was *following her*. She sat up straight in bed, the covers shifting, the half-eaten bag of Cheetos sliding to the floor.

She pushed her hair out of her eyes, but it felt weird, her long tresses missing. The horror of the past few days came back as her eyes adjusted to the half-light of the shoddy motel room with the TV turned on to a rerun of *Seinfeld*, giving off a surreal glow. She was in Albuquerque, heading to Montana and . . .

The phone was still making that god-awful noise, so she shut off the alarm and saw that it was 1:45.

Time to get moving.

She was cutting it close as it was, didn't want to linger too long, didn't want to attract any unwanted attention and cameras. . . . Didn't they have cameras in bus stations? No, she planned to get to the station with only five minutes to spare.

So there could be no slipups.

She changed into her still-damp clothes, then slipped into her jacket before adding the zippered, extra-large hoodie. Most of her money was tucked into her bra, with spending money in her jeans pocket with her bus ticket. She thought about wearing sunglasses but decided they would create more interest in her as it was the middle of the night and they reminded her of the man who'd been following her.

Instead, she went with thick, dark eyeliner, dark gray eye shadow, and heavy mascara coupled with pale face makeup and no lip color. With her newly dyed and cut hair, she looked far different from the girl who had registered a few hours earlier. Tugging the baseball cap low over her forehead, she snagged the few items she owned, made certain she still had her cash and bus ticket, and worried for a second about discarding the garbage, the leftover packaging from her hair dye and other trash, in a dumpster somewhere, to cover her tracks. But that would take time.

Which she didn't have.

No.

Whoever had been following her knew she was in Albuquerque already, and the police . . . Oh, hell, she'd deal with all that later. Now, she had to get going. But first she slid the scissors into the side of her boot and made certain her hair spray was in her pocket.

She checked the street again, through the blinds. Spying no one, and noting the same five cars and one pickup that had been in the parking lot earlier hadn't moved, she headed out, moving quickly past the other second-floor rooms on the long exterior porch and down a set of stairs at the far end of the building, away from the office where the lights glowed brightly, the interior counter and waiting area awash in fluorescent light.

No one seemed to be following her through the near empty streets.

Traffic was almost nonexistent.

She headed straight for the bus station, past a tavern where a couple of men in jeans, western shirts, and cowboy hats leaned against the building while smoking. A couple of trucks growled to life in the parking lot, the bar shutting down for the night.

She walked past the smokers, feeling their eyes on her, but their low conversation never faltered and they didn't bother her.

Just keep moving. The bus will be leaving soon.

No doubling back. No sneaking through alleys. Just a steady line for the next eight or so blocks. She didn't run, but walked quickly, seeing no one, hearing no footsteps behind her, the map on her phone guiding her with its small illuminated map.

Still her heart thudded and her nerves were strung tight as bowstrings. She heard a train chugging on far-off tracks and felt the chill of winter in the wind. A block from the bus station a police cruiser rolled through the intersection and Ivy slowed near the darkened doorway of a pawnshop, now closed, lights dimmed. Her gaze followed the police car. God, wouldn't that be the worst if right now she were picked up?

She swallowed hard.

Had the cop seen her?

Would a lone woman on the deserted streets give an officer pause on this quiet night?

Would he circle around and—

A huge hand grabbed her face!

What!

She tried to scream. Reacted. Flailed as another arm wrapped around her waist and drew her into the alcove.

God, no!

Who was this?

He's going to kill you.

Like Mom. Like Paul.

No! NO! NO!

She fought. Twisting and turning, her arms reaching backward, as she clawed, catching the edge of his sunglasses, sending them clattering to the sidewalk. Panic screamed through her blood. Where was the cop car? The one that had just passed? Oh, God, please let the officer have seen her and be at this moment rounding the block!

Her screams were muffled by his thick glove.

She bared her teeth. Tried to bite his hand.

The glove was too thick.

"Stop it!" he ordered.

She didn't.

"If you don't, I'll fuck you up," he growled into her ear, the smell of his last cigarette heavy on his hot breath. "Real bad. I swear. Cut your face to ribbons."

So where was the knife? For the first time she thought about a weapon. The fact that he hadn't put a gun to her head, or a knife to her throat.

His hands were busy holding her down.

Panicked, she fought harder. Wriggled and kicked

with the heel of her boot. *Bam!* She connected with his shin and he let out a howl.

"You *bitch*!"

Hadn't anyone heard?

Where was the cop?

Or one of the cowboys from the bar?

Or *any*one.

With the hand on her face, he pinched her nose between his thumb and index finger and held her jaw closed. "Stop it!" he growled as he cut off air to her lungs.

Ivy struggled harder, trying to hit or scratch or kick. To maim him in any way. She was only three damned blocks from the bus station, for God's sake. Couldn't anyone hear or see his brutal attack?

Please, please, please!

Her lungs began to burn.

She tried to draw in a breath.

Failed.

If only she could reach the scissors in her boot. If only . . . Her hand fisted and she struck. Hard. Her knuckles connecting with his head, the greasy hair. He barely flinched.

It was too late.

She needed air.

Bad.

She couldn't think.

Her thoughts swam and blackness threatened to pull her under.

The bus! She had to get to the bus!

She swung again, this time her arm flopping ineffectively.

Pain radiated from her chest and her eyes bulged. She felt them, felt every nerve ending in her body.

"Give me the money!"

The money? He'd followed her to rob her?

Too woozy now. Lungs going to burst. Legs buckling. Thoughts disconnected. Dying. She was dying. Here on the empty Albuquerque street, she'd . . .

He released her suddenly, dropping her as if she'd burned him.

She collapsed. *Thud!* Her head smacked into the cement of the alcove. She opened her mouth to scream but only sputtering noises erupted.

"I warned you." He yanked a knife from his pocket. The blade glinted in the weak light from a streetlamp on the corner.

She sucked in another breath, her thoughts clearing, her gaze on the blade.

Freaked, Ivy scooted away. Her head throbbed and she felt something sticky—oh, God, blood—on her cheek. He was blocking the doorway, but for an instant she considered trying to get past him, throwing herself onto the sidewalk and screaming, attempting to run and catch the bus. . . .

Oh. God.

"The money." He reminded her. He was standing over her, breathing hard. Gripping the knife. "Give it up," he ordered, and she tried to think. "I saw your stash. At the bus station."

What the hell was he talking about?

She could just hand over her cash.

Or she could try to get away.

As if reading her thoughts, he crouched down and

she was staring into pale gray eyes that seemed to glow in the night. The knife blade touched her cheek, just below her eye. "Don't scream," he ordered. "I see you're thinking about it. Just hand over the cash and you'll live and that pretty face won't be messed up forever." His face was inches from hers, tanned and taut, with cruel lips and a jaw covered in beard shadow. "You owe me a new pair of glasses," he said, his gaze never leaving hers, his one hand balled into a fist, his other reaching out to pick up the sunglasses where one lens was cracked, one of the bows missing. "Now, girlie, let's do this, before I have to hurt you."

"O-okay," she said, and decided at least to appear to acquiesce, maybe get him to let his guard down. "It's . . . it's in my jacket . . . under my sweatshirt, but please . . . please don't hurt me."

His eyes narrowed as if he were sizing her up, suspicious of her intent, and she let down the tears she'd been fighting earlier, feeling one trickle down her cheek, allowing her lips to tremble in real fear. Her hands were unsteady as she unzipped her sweatshirt.

"Don't try anything," he warned, but somehow he must have realized she didn't have a gun. He must've observed her long enough to know that she wasn't armed, and she couldn't reach for the scissors in her boot.

The tears and shaking, all real, seemed to convince him. With his free hand he reached into his pocket for his pack of Marlboros, shook one out and jammed it between his teeth. Then, lips drawn back in a cold smile, he found his lighter. All the while his gaze was locked into hers, wary, almost daring her to try and defy him. Ivy slid her hand into the pocket of her jacket and felt the small canister of hair spray.

Did she dare?

She withdrew the money and watched his eyes gleam at the roll.

"Well, my, my," he said, his grin widening. "What the hell did you do to get so much cash? Rob a bank?"

If you only knew.

She felt a coldness settle into her soul, that familiar and unwanted sensation that rarely appeared.

He snatched the wad with the hand holding his lighter and, satisfied, stuffed it into his pocket. He glanced back to the deserted street and Ivy saw a little bit of indecision cross his eyes. "You know, I was gonna leave you alone. But you've seen me now. Too bad about the glasses. You shouldn't have ruined 'em. Now, you could pick me out of a lineup. And that . . . that wouldn't be good. Besides, I think maybe you and me . . . we've got some unfinished business." His unlit cigarette bobbed as he talked, the lips surrounding it stretched wide. "It won't take long," he promised. "And you'll get one last thrill."

Her insides turned to water.

He was going to rape her. Then kill her.

The iciness within grew.

Just try it.

She heard the rumble of a huge engine only a few blocks away.

The bus.

Her bus.

Her escape route out of here.

Panic swept over her.

He was still contemplating what he might do as he flicked his lighter to the tip of his cigarette.

She reacted.

In that split second, when his gaze focused on the small flame, she reached for the can of hair spray, flipped off the lid, and sprayed, straight at his lighter.

"What the—? Oh, Christ!"

In a puff, blue fire enveloped the cigarette and crawled up his face, sizzling and catching fire in the gel in his hair.

"Shit! Fuck!"

He fell backward, his face contorted in agony.

His knife clattered to the sidewalk.

Ivy kept spraying.

The top of his head was on fire, crackling and burning, sizzling light spreading over his scalp, blue flames threatening her hands.

She dropped the canister just as it exploded, with a bang, shards of metal flying out like burning shrapnel.

"Aaaaah!" Screaming, he rolled on the ground, his hands to his eyes, his body coiled. His knife clattering on the sidewalk. "Owwww . . . Jesus! Ow! Ow! What the fuck . . . oh, owww, you fucking bitch!!" The acrid odor of charred flesh and burning oil filled the alcove, the smell burning her nostrils. Fire reached down to the collar of his jacket.

Oh. God.

"Help me! Help me! Owwwww! For the love of God!"

Get out now! Run!

Ivy didn't think twice.

Scooping up the knife, she launched past the rolling,

wriggling man, his head aglow, his pained screeches loud, the edge of his collar burning as he shrieked.

Get away. Just run. Don't think!

Racing as fast as her legs would carry her, she flew along the street, her boots pounding the cement, the horror behind her propelling her forward.

Was it too late?

Had the bus already left?

Oh, God, was he going to die?

Who cares? He was going to rape you. Probably kill you. Just fucking move!

Breathing hard, she raced forward, the lights of the Greyhound station a beacon, now only two blocks away.

Faster, faster, faster!

Could she make it?

If only she was in time . . .

She saw the bus, a big silver beast, parked in the loading area.

Idling.

Exhaust spilling into the night.

No one around.

Not one person on the platform.

Because they've already boarded. They're on the bus. It's leaving!

Forcing herself even faster, she sprinted.

The doors closed with a *whoosh*. The bus started to move, big tires rolling, the beast lumbering forward.

No. No. No!

"Hey!" she cried, her lungs burning, her throat a rasp. "Wait!" Oh, please, God!

Taillights glowed an eerie red.

No, no, no! This couldn't happen! Not after all she'd been through! Heart crumbling, adrenaline propelling her, she threw herself forward.

Miracle of miracles, the Greyhound slowed for a traffic light.

Redoubling her efforts, she ran and saw the light change from red to green.

With a growl and belch of diesel fumes the huge bus moved forward again.

Shit!

Frantic, her heart beating a thousand times a minute, Ivy tried desperately to flag the driver down. Couldn't he see her in his huge mirrors?

"Stop!" she yelled, wildly thrashing her arms. "Stop!" *Oh, please, please!*

With a squeal of brakes and flash of bright taillights, the bus jerked to a halt.

"Yes!" She picked up the pace again, her breathing fast and hard. Obviously the driver had spotted her. Finally. A bit of hope appeared just as she saw a flash, a quicksilver movement caught in the beams of the Greyhound's headlights.

A scrawny coyote zipped through the swath of illumination to scurry into an alley near the station.

Good enough.

Again the bus started to inch forward, but Ivy was alongside the silver beast now and began pounding on its paneled sides. "Stop!" she cried, banging her fists on the metal until she reached the door, still running alongside the moving bus. "Let me on! Stop."

The driver's gaze jerked to the door and in an instant the bus ground to a stop.

A burly man with thick jowls and a bulbous nose, he squinted through the smudged glass to stare and take stock of her.

"Let me in!" she yelled, gasping for breath.

For a second he looked as if he might reach for some kind of weapon or drive off. "I have a ticket!" she cried, freaked that he might leave. As she pleaded with him, she saw the ghostly outline of her reflection in the doors—a pale woman with strange hair, smeared make-up, and a desperate, wild look contorting her face where blood was running from a cut above her eye and a bruise was beginning to show over her cheek. "Please!" she cried, and reached into her jacket pocket. "Please, sir. Let me in."

His eyes widened as if he expected her to pull out a semiautomatic, but she retrieved her ticket and waved it at him.

From the corner of her eye she saw movement a few blocks behind the bus, an eerie shimmer that didn't belong to a vehicle.

Oh. No.

A man staggered into the street behind them, his head still glowing from the fire burning through his hair.

She held her breath, and silently prayed the driver didn't see him as he collapsed onto the street.

No! No! No!

"I'm supposed to be on this bus!" she yelled.

Oh, God, the figure was on his feet again, heading this way, the aura around his head still visible.

The driver seemed to make a decision and opened the doors. Scowling, more at himself than Ivy, he said, "Fine. Come on, then."

"Montana?" she asked, stepping inside, climbing the steps. "Missoula?"

"That's where we're heading." He eyed the ticket, then turned his attention to her, still regarding her warily. "You look like you should go to a hospital."

"I will," she lied. "Once I get to Montana."

He stared at her with eyes that suggested he'd seen it all in his lifetime. "You'd best do that. You don't look too good."

"I'm fine."

Thick eyebrows quirked over his eyeglasses.

"Look, I'm sorry I didn't get here on time. . . . It was my boyfriend," she babbled, hoping beyond hope that he didn't notice the injured man, wouldn't throw her off the bus. "He, um, he . . ."

"Hit you." His lips tightened. "Honey, he's no 'boyfriend.' More like a psycho. You should call the police."

"I will, but I have to get away," she said, pleading, her voice shaking. From her vantage point, in the mirror she saw a flare, the glow of shifting light as the dark figure of a human scrambled forward, his hair afire as he crumpled to the ground.

Stay down. Just stay down.

"Well, okay then. Take a seat," the driver said, squaring a baseball cap with the company's logo of a racing greyhound above the brim and apparently not noticing the figure in the street a few blocks behind. "I'm getting too old for this crap."

To keep her balance as the bus started forward again, Ivy held on to the sides of the seats lining the aisles. The bus was mostly empty, only a few seats occupied by people trying to sleep, only a few interested eyes following her. As the bus lurched ahead, gaining steam, she sat in the last row and heard the first wail of a siren.

Oh, no. Just keep going!

Surely the driver wouldn't stop the bus again.

Heart in her throat, she stared out the back window and down the empty street. The man, head still glowing, had fallen into a crumpled heap in the middle of the street. Headlights appeared, a pickup rounding the corner, screeching to a stop.

The pickup driver flew out of the cab, and a cop car, siren blasting and lights flashing, appeared and slid to a stop.

Keep driving. Oh, please.

If only the bus driver wouldn't notice, wouldn't feel compelled to stop. The distance was getting farther by the second, but if he did stop, would he put two and two together? He'd seen her wounds, knew she was running from something . . .

But the bus kept moving, engine loud in her ears. Huddled in the corner, she stared through the glass. She caught a glimpse of the coyote again. Nosing out of a side street, the shaggy beast eyed the scene, then turned quickly, avoiding the vaporous lamplight to vanish into the shadows.

Chapter 13

Morning came early.

As it always did for Pescoli.

With the dawn came the need for a warm bottle of formula, a fresh diaper, and now a gallon or two of coffee, as she was no longer nursing, all coupled with lots of baby smiles and baby coos.

Thank God for those toothless grins, Pescoli thought as she made her way to Sarina's kitchen where a fresh pot of coffee was lacing the air with its morning fragrance. A good thing, too. Pescoli was exhausted from the interrupted sleep and long hours worrying over the case.

Not your case. It belongs to the SFPD.

Balancing Tucker on one hip, she poured herself a cup and joined her sister at the table. Sarina was already showered and dressed, her hair dry, fresh lipstick and mascara visible.

Pescoli stifled a yawn as Sarina, frowning, chewed on the end of a pencil as she sat at the glass-topped table. A newspaper was spread in front of her, the Sudoku puzzle barely started.

"I can't concentrate," she said, tossing the pencil down. "With Brindel gone and Ivy missing and Denny . . . probably screwing his brains out somewhere." Her lips twisted down at the corners. "But then the Saturday puzzle is always rough." She looked up and zeroed in on Tucker. "Here, let me take him," she said, wrinkling her nose at the baby as she made "goo-goo" noises that delighted him. He kicked his little pajama-encased feet as Pescoli passed him off and Sarina touched the tip of his nose with her finger. "Oh, I miss these days." Her gaze moved to her sister's. "You're lucky."

Pescoli didn't look at life in terms of bad luck or good; more in mistakes made or opportunities taken.

Sarina nuzzled Tucker's cheek and he giggled in delight. "You go on upstairs and get ready and I'll take care of this little man."

"You don't think I'll wake the boys?"

"This time of day? Morning? Or anytime before two in the afternoon? It's like trying to wake the dead. Case in point." She hitched her chin toward the family room couch where Bianca was curled up, the blanket over her head, oblivious to the world.

"Okay, I'll take you up on that." Pescoli dragged herself and the cup of coffee upstairs. The caffeine flooded her bloodstream about the time the needle-sharp shower spray hit her skin. By the time she'd changed and returned to the living area, she felt like a new woman.

And Sarina seemed a little more relaxed. As if holding the baby had given her a new lease on life. "So what's on the docket?" she asked.

"Bianca and I are heading home."

"What? No." She'd been washing the baby's face and hands despite his protests. "We had a little burp accident," she admitted. "Some of his bottle came back up." She tossed the disposable wipe into a nearby trash can. "What do you mean you're leaving?"

"Just that. I've done what I can. The SFPD will handle it from here."

"You're kidding!"

"There's not a lot I can do. Paterno promised to keep me in the loop, and I've got a life back in Montana." She'd almost said "husband" but had changed her mind at the last minute, didn't want to set Sarina off about Denny again. "I have a family and a job waiting." That last part was a bit of a lie, but it worked.

"I thought you would stay until they found out what happened to Brindel and what happened to Ivy—where she is—and . . . oh." It must've hit Sarina for the first time that the investigation could take weeks, or months or longer. "Oh . . . dear." Her eyes grew sad and she flipped the newspaper over to page one where the headlines blared:

NO CLEAR SUSPECT IN LATHAM DOUBLE-HOMICIDE.

"I hate this," Sarina said as she skimmed the article.

"I think you'll have to get used to it."

"Don't I know it. I've had reporters calling at all hours, and this morning at eight a reporter for one of the local TV stations was already knocking at the door. I got rid of her right away, told her I had 'no comment' other than she might wake a sleeping baby."

"Did she leave?"

"Yeah, about an hour later."

"Let the homicide department handle them. Or the

public information officer. Refer anyone who calls to the police department. It's all part of the job."

She worried her lip. "I'd talk to them, you know. The reporters? If I thought it would help to find out who did it, bring them to justice and get Ivy home . . . or at least here."

Pescoli said carefully, "Macon seemed to think Ivy might have had a hand in it."

"Of murdering her parents? Of course not. He's just . . . upset." She saw the next question in Pescoli's eyes. "Yes, Ivy was in a hospital for a while . . . up in Portland."

"Why there?"

"I don't know, really. Brindel said Paul wanted it all kept quiet, that his stepdaughter was you know, 'troubled.' That's what he called it. If you ask me, Paul just didn't want anyone to find out that his family wasn't what it seemed on the outside. He was very concerned with appearance. Very. All the while having affairs on the side." She sighed and pursed her lips, no doubt her thoughts wandering to her own straying husband. "Anyway, it's no wonder Brindel wanted a divorce. She was going to file, you know. And Paul had no idea. I'm sure it never occurred to him that a woman might want to leave *him,* might need some independence, that all the money in the world wasn't worth it if you were kept on a twenty-four-carat leash. He's . . . he *was* a piece of work."

"It was that bad?" Pescoli asked, and felt a jab of guilt that she'd known so little about her sister.

She shrugged, gently bouncing the baby on her knee and cradling his little head. "Now, it looks like we'll never know."

"Could one of them have hired someone to take out the other and then was double-crossed?"

"As in *kill*?" Sarina's eyes rounded. The idea had obviously never occurred to her. "I don't think so. Oh. Dear. No." She was shaking her head, ponytail swishing along the tops of her shoulders as the notion took root. "Why would you say that?"

"Anything's possible."

"Is that what the police think?" Sarina was horrified.

"It's not even what I think, but we can't rule anything out, not yet. And I'll keep working on it, in my own way, from Montana unless I think I need to come back, but I just can't stay here indefinitely."

She sighed. "I suppose not."

"So, I'll check in with Paterno later this morning. He said I could call him regardless that it's Saturday. Then Bianca and I will look at a couple of colleges in the area and we'll roll out of here tonight."

Sarina swallowed hard as Tucker began to cry. Pescoli picked up her son from Sarina's arms.

"Hey now," she whispered, kissing his downy head.

Sarina said, "I know Collette plans to leave on Monday and we'll have a service . . . well, we don't know. Once the police release the bodies . . . It would be nice if Ivy were here for . . ." Her voice thickened and she cleared her throat, blinking back tears. "Well . . ." she said. "We'll just have to see, won't we?"

"I'll still be working the case," Regan said again. "As much as I can. Remotely." She thought of the information she'd requested from Chilcoate, data he'd promised by late afternoon. "And if anything comes up, I'll change my plans."

Before Sarina could argue, Pescoli, carrying Little Tucker, walked over to the couch and touched her daughter's shoulder, gave it a shake.

"What're you doing?" Bianca grumbled, reaching for the covers.

"If you want to look at some of the schools around here, today's the day."

"Now?"

"Yeah, now. Rise and shine."

"You're so mean!" Bianca said.

"I know. It's a problem I have to live with."

"Oooh, Mom." She pulled the blanket over her head but Pescoli was having none of her teenaged petulance.

"You've got an hour. If you're not ready by then, we'll skip UCSF, and Berkeley, Stanford or—"

Bianca threw off the covers and scowled at her mother. "I'm not going to Stanford."

"Or any of the others unless you get a major scholarship."

Bianca let out a huff of disgust as she climbed to her feet. "So I've heard."

"You're not even a resident."

"She could live with me," Sarina chimed in, and Bianca sent her mother a don't-you-even-think-about-it glare.

"I'm thinking Montana State or the junior college that her brother went to. But it doesn't hurt to see what's out there."

The glare got decidedly more intense. "I'm taking a shower." Bianca marched up the stairs, obviously thinking that whatever choices she was given, all were a fate worse than death and all meted out by a mother who didn't understand her.

So be it.

That was life.

Bianca would have to get used to it. Despite her jerk-wad of a father, or her mean mom, or the fact that she didn't have the grades or money to live the California dream. At least not yet.

She'd survive.

That thought stopped her short as she realized how closely Bianca had come to death barely six months earlier. Maybe Pescoli should cut her some slack. Some more slack. Then again, maybe not. Bianca had to learn to be tough, no matter how hard the lessons.

"Hell's bells," she said under her breath as Tucker let out a sharp little cry for attention. Sometimes being a parent was a real pain in the butt.

Tanaka was getting nowhere fast.

Though it was still early in the investigation of the Latham double-homicide, she sensed things starting to stall.

In her studio apartment, with Mr. Claus doing figure eights between her bare feet, Tanaka stretched her arms high over her head, bending her knees slightly, grasping high in the chair pose. Closing her eyes for a second, she felt her muscles lengthen. "Let go," she told herself, her mantra. "Let go." She was standing in front of the television, playing a recording of a yoga instructor and following the routine.

She'd spent the last forty-eight hours running down leads, going over notes, statements, and trace evidence, rereading the autopsies, checking phone records, bank statements, insurance inventories, and the damned will. As far as they could reconstruct the last hours of the victims' lives, it seemed that the housekeeper, or possibly Ivy Wilde, was the last to have seen Brindel Latham alive. Paul was at his clinic until the afternoon, then played squash at his athletic club, and the man who'd been his opponent said he'd left around six thirty. Camera footage had confirmed.

"So who killed you?" Tanaka said aloud, thinking about both victims.

Brindel Latham's will left everything to her husband, and then in the case that he died before her, to her daughter and Paul's sons equally. In trust. Paul's will was different, leaving only a portion of his estate to his wife and her child from a previous marriage, the bulk going, again in trust, to his sons, the snarly Macon and more reticent Seth.

Taking in a deep breath, Tanaka tried to clear her mind. She forced herself to mimic the flexible instructor on the tube. Stretching and bending her body, she attempted to lose herself in the stretches and breathing.

But she was too focused on the case to get into it. Who, who, who? she wondered, then turned her thoughts back to why. If she knew why, the who would follow. She'd thought the ex-spouses might have been holding a deep and murderous grudge, but so far that theory hadn't panned out. Both Brindel's ex, Victor Wilde, and the previous Mrs. Latham had solid alibis that Tanaka hadn't been able to break. So far.

Of the two sons, Seth had been cleared . . . well, mostly. Tanaka wasn't completely convinced. And Macon was too much of a smart-ass for his own good.

"Doesn't make him a killer," she told the cat as his long tail tickled her calf. "But it doesn't mean he's not, either."

She rotated her neck slowly, breathing out as she did, trying to count the seconds away.

Ronny Stillwell had seen Troy Boxer the night of the murder, though the hours of the actual killing were up for debate. If Boxer had stayed in, he would no longer be a suspect, but if not . . . the jury was still out on that one.

George Aimes, the owner of the rooming house where Boxer and Stillwell resided, had insisted Boxer's car had never left the parking area that night, but there wasn't a security camera on the property to back him up. Tanaka was checking other traffic cams and security footage from businesses in the area. And also with the other tenants of the rooming house other than Ronny Stillwell.

The alibi bothered her somehow. Didn't seem as solid as it should have been. Probably because Stillwell had done time for burglary three years earlier. He'd been eighteen at the time and clean ever since, but Tanaka wasn't convinced that Stillwell's larcenous instincts had been totally rehabilitated or quelled by his light, slap on the wrist sentence of three months in jail and a year of probation.

Maybe that was prejudice talking.

Or perhaps it was gut instinct.

Or even just plain reasonable.

"I'll find out," she informed the cat. Neither Ronny Stillwell nor Troy Boxer had come off as a Rhodes scholar.

Downward-facing dog was the next position.

Tanaka bent from the hips, lowering her head toward the yoga mat. "Your favorite," she told Mr. Claus, who lifted his nose so that it met the tip of Tanaka's. "Silly, silly boy."

He meowed and she actually smiled, felt the tension in her body release and told herself, she could do this. She could solve this case. She probably didn't even need Paterno, but he had one foot out of the department already, and as for that Montana detective, she wouldn't be around long.

Nope, the Latham double-homicide was her baby.

She intended to solve it.

"By hook or by crook," she told the cat, and wondered, for a second, just how far her ambition would take her. How far would she go?

"Doesn't matter. All that matters is that the case is solved and yours truly gets the credit she deserves."

Mr. Claus just stared at her. But he understood. She was certain of it as she finished the routine, grabbed her towel, and headed for the shower. Next up? A few more hours at the computer, or on the phone, or actually going out and knocking on doors.

Tanaka was never happier than when she was on the trail of a killer.

Tomorrow she planned on meeting a few of the people she hadn't been able to track down during the week.

A road trip.

She didn't care that it was the weekend.

There was work to be done.

* * *

Pescoli never thought she'd be so glad to see snow.

As she drove around the final curve to her home and saw the house, lights glowing inside to reflect in shimmering patches on the snowbanks outside, her heart rose. Snow was falling, drifting against the house, and the lake looked frozen and still. Peaceful. Heaven after the last six hours of her son being fussy, first during the college tours, then at the airport and on the flight as well. She'd hoped he would settle down in the car, as usual. But no such luck. Tucker had fussed and cried all the way from Missoula.

"Wake up," she said to Bianca. "We're home."

From the passenger seat, her daughter opened a bleary eye. She stretched and yawned and, by the time the garage door rolled open, Bianca was awake. Before Pescoli cut the engine, the door to the interior of the house opened and Santana, in a T-shirt, jeans, and bare feet, stood in the threshold.

"Hey!" he said, walking into the garage as Pescoli climbed out of her Jeep.

"Back atcha."

"Bianca?" He nodded at his stepdaughter as she got out of the passenger side, then he pecked Pescoli on the cheek and opened the back door to retrieve Tucker. "Hey, little man," he said, and the baby let out a sharp cry. "I see you missed me."

"He's hungry," Pescoli said, "and you're up, Dad."

"And I missed you, too," he teased, grabbing one of the bags and toting it and Tucker inside as she gathered the rest of her things and followed after him.

"I did miss you," she said as the dogs greeted her, tails thumping wildly, each barking out a greeting. "You know that."

He glanced over his shoulder. "You can show me how much later."

"Still here," Bianca reminded them as she headed toward the stairs. "I can hear every word and it's gross."

Santana whispered, "When did she get to be such an old lady?"

"Maybe she was born that way."

"Like her mother."

"Still hearing this!" Bianca said.

"Okay, we're done," Pescoli laughed, petting the three dogs, each of which acted as if she'd been gone a year rather than a few days. "Where's Jeremy?"

"Out. I think." He shot her a look as he mixed a bottle. "I don't keep tabs on him. He's an adult."

"Living under our roof."

"Well, kinda." As the bottle warmed, he toggled his palm to indicate maybe yes/maybe no.

She wanted to argue and point out that Jeremy wasn't paying rent, but that was because she'd allowed it. As long as he was going to school nearby. So she said, "Look, I'm going to take a shower. You've got daddy *and* mommy duty for a while."

"You got it." He slanted her another smile, this time a little more wicked, his eyes gleaming, a hint of a dimple visible beneath his beard stubble.

"You're . . ."

"Perfect?"

"I was going to say 'impossible.'"

"Close enough."

"All right, because you *are* so perfect, why don't you haul my suitcase up to the bedroom?"

"You got it. Once I deal with Mr. Crank here." He

touched the baby on his button of a nose, then glanced up at his wife. "You know, your every wish is my command."

"Uh-huh. That's just how our relationship works." Swallowing a smile, she made her way to the upper story and peeled off her clothes, listening with half an ear for any noise coming from the kitchen.

But Tucker had quieted; Santana apparently had everything under control.

Good.

She took a quick, hot shower and was just stepping out when her phone began to ring. Throwing a towel around her body, hair dripping, she picked up the phone and recognized Chilcoate's number.

"Pescoli," she answered.

"I know. I called you."

Pointing out the obvious. Chilcoate could be such an arrogant ass. "You got anything?"

"Some. Still working. But I thought you'd want to know about Ivy Wilde."

"I do."

"She's in Albuquerque."

"New Mexico?"

"Yeah. Well, at least she was. Last night. According to her phone. Well, I guess what I mean to say is that her phone was last on in Albuquerque. Someone else might have it."

Pescoli didn't want to think about that. "You hacked into phone records? Or cell towers?"

He was silent, and she said, "Sorry." Unwritten rule: she never asked how or where he got his information.

"Can you tell me who she called or texted in the days before the murders?"

"I can e-mail the info to you. The e-mail will come from a private source. You won't be able to reply. If you need more information, call."

"Okay." This was a start. Maybe she could at least locate her niece. If the phone was with Ivy. "Anything else?"

"Bank records. Several different banks. So far, money wise, the Lathams were in good shape. No major outstanding debt. But the husband had a girlfriend. Roberta, aka Robbie Grogan, RN, also married, but separated. Worked for him in the clinic. Previous girlfriends, two I've located, also worked for him, both moved away. One in Tulsa, recently married, cell phone suggests she was in Oklahoma this past week, and the other in Nome, Alaska, and she hasn't been out of the state that I can see."

"What about Brindel?" Pescoli asked.

"If she was having a fling, she was extremely discreet. I've found no evidence of an affair. Not by text or e-mail or phone call. Like her husband, she had no major debts, but her e-mail indicates she was in contact with a law firm, Ivan Haas being the attorney, and she was ready to file for divorce. She did open a separate bank account about fourteen months ago where she siphoned money to the tune of about five grand a month."

"Her escape stash," Pescoli thought aloud. "She'd need money if she were going to file for divorce."

"I'm still working on a few other angles," he said.

"Send me everything you can. Bank statements, insurance claims, phone information, whatever you've got."

"Will do." And then he was gone. Pescoli clicked

off the phone, towel-dried her hair, and was about to get dressed when Santana entered the bathroom.

"Where's Tucker?"

"Sleeping. In his crib. I just put him down."

"Good. He was fussy all the way from the airport."

"Maybe he'll sleep through the night," Santana said.

"From your lips to God's ears."

"That's the way it usually works."

She chuckled.

"Okay." And he grabbed the edge of the towel, stripped it away from her, and swept her off her feet.

"No, no! Put me down," she ordered, but was laughing as he carried her into the bedroom and kicked the door shut. "Oh, for the love of God, Santana, we're not a couple of horny teenagers."

"Since when?"

"We don't have time for this."

"No?"

"No . . . no . . ." But her protests were slowing down. They looked at each other and then he rolled with her onto the bed and kissed her hard, in a way that turned her insides to molten lava. She wanted to feel his naked body against hers, wanted him deep inside her.

"Okay . . . yes . . ." she said breathlessly.

Chapter 14

Chilcoate was as good as his word. While the baby napped, Pescoli sat at the kitchen table where she pored over phone records and bank statements, insurance information, and e-mails. She'd printed out most of the data Chilcoate had sent, and was double-checking some of the information on her laptop, trying to put some of the pieces of Brindel's last few days together. She needed to figure out what was going on in Brindel's life as well as Paul's and Ivy's in the days and weeks prior to the murders.

Santana was out of the house, taking the two big dogs with him as he checked the stock at the Long Ranch where he was still manager of operations. Bianca was studying, or supposed to be, in her room, and the baby was napping, so Pescoli had a few minutes alone with a cup of real coffee, the fire crackling in the grate, snow falling lazily beyond the windows.

She considered drawing Alvarez into the case, but decided against it. She had enough roadblocks with

Tanaka and didn't need a lecture about jurisdiction, or getting personally involved as a relative of a victim, or just getting in the way of the San Francisco investigators assigned to the case.

She had no intention of compromising the investigation, of course.

But she had to do her own detective work from a distance and on the sly.

Chilcoate was right. Brindel had been siphoning off money and how Paul hadn't noticed it surprised her.

Paul's cell phone records indicated that he was very much in contact with a nurse in his office during the day, and during the night. Robbie Grogan. Their texts and e-mails were carefully worded, but as Pescoli read between the lines, it wasn't too hard to imagine that if the two parties hadn't been involved in a full-blown affair so far, they'd been on their way.

And then there was Macon, Paul's oldest son, the kid who said he hadn't been in contact with his parents all that much. The cell phone records indicated that he'd texted both Brindel and Paul often, including the day of their deaths.

A good sign or bad?

It could all be innocent, of course, but then why lie about it? Macon's alibi was far from rock solid.

As to the missing Ivy, the clues were few and far between, but she, too, had some texts to Macon as well as quite a few to a number with no name or ID attached, a burner phone.

That didn't look good at all.

With whom was she communicating?

Troy Boxer's number had ceased to appear around

the time of the holidays, but not long thereafter the unknown number had started to show up. Was it Troy's? Or a new boyfriend's? Or a legitimate friend? Pescoli was tempted to call the number and had even punched in the first five digits before she realized that she would be stepping over the line and stopped herself. This was information she would be forced to hand over to Paterno and Tanaka.

"Pisser," she said under her breath.

She couldn't help but be drawn into the case. At that moment she realized that she could never give up being a cop. She loved it too much.

So what about Tucker? Will you be able to stand being away from him as much as you will have to be?

Who knew? She'd worked when both of her other kids were young and they'd survived, though there had been some very hard years. She wasn't out of the woods yet as far as Jeremy and Bianca were concerned, but there was definitely light at the end of the tunnel. Also, Tucker had some advantages her older kids hadn't. First of all, his siblings were old enough to tend to him and yet be delighted by him, and his father was very hands on and in the picture, much more so than the other kids' biological fathers.

He'd survive.

Because he was so loved.

And wasn't that what mattered most? At least according to every greeting card she'd ever picked up.

Or was she kidding herself? Rationalizing because selfishly she wanted to go back to work?

"Damn it, Pescoli," she chided, "when did you get to be such a pansy?" Is that what came with age?

Being on the damned fence all the time? Not just following your gut? If so, she didn't like it. Not one little bit.

She took a sip of the tepid coffee, climbed to her feet, and stretched. From his bed near the fire, Cisco lifted his head, then, spying her, stood and shook himself so that his collar jangled when he did his own stretching. He trotted over to her and she petted his graying head. "So is this going to be it? Me a working mom again?"

The dog barked and at that moment the baby let out a cry from his bed in the nursery. Her heart did a quick little jump. "The prince is awake," she told the dog, and hastily tucked all the papers into her computer case. It was time to make a change, and if Santana didn't like the fact that she was returning to the force, he was just going to have to get over it.

"I tell ya, I haven't heard from her," Victor Wilde insisted as he stood in the doorway of his Modesto town house Sunday afternoon. A compact man in his early forties, he was prematurely gray, his hair receding, his eyes sharp and suspicious. A mechanical engineer, his résumé claimed, he wore slacks and a golf shirt, was going a little soft around the middle, and was very wary of the two detectives standing under the overhang of his porch.

"Mind if we come in and ask a few questions?" Tanaka asked.

He hesitated, but only briefly. "Sure, sure," he said, eyeing first Tanaka and then Paterno, whom she'd dragged away from his oversized flat screen against his better wishes.

"This way we catch him at home," Tanaka had explained when she'd called to convince Paterno to ride with her. "Wilde's a workaholic, always at the job, probably to avoid the three kids he fathered since he and Brindel split."

Paterno had reluctantly agreed, deciding he could record the 49ers game and try to avoid the news so he could watch the football play action later without having the ending spoiled. He'd been propelled by a bit of a lead. The phone records for Ivy Wilde's cell had finally arrived and it looked like she, or at least her phone, had traveled to New Mexico.

They'd driven an hour and half east into the Central Valley and as they passed under the iconic Modesto arch, the fog had thickened. Paterno had read the words of the motto aloud as Tanaka cruised beneath the arch.

"'Water, Wealth, Contentment, Health,'" he said, then added, "Everything you could ask for. Maybe I'll give up the Mexico dream and retire in the valley."

"Lots of wine here."

"I know. Sounds good." He'd been smiling, looking more rumpled than usual. Usually clean shaven, he'd forgone the razor for the weekend.

"But, what about that boat?"

"Ah, that's the problem, isn't it?" He'd glanced out the passenger window to a strip mall and rubbed his chin thoughtfully. "I bet there's a lake or two around here, somewhere."

They'd found Victor Wilde's town house in an area of Modesto that appeared to have been developed sometime in the eighties, the connected homes mostly ivory stucco and trimmed in a darker tan color.

And now, he'd invited them inside where music, something from the nineties, she thought, was blasting through the house. Wilde said, "Alexa, turn off the music," and the rooms quieted.

Tanaka saw that the place was beginning to age. Between the living area and kitchen nook, the old paneling had been ripped down, new wall board evident around the eating area where a round table was covered with tools and wall spackling, two cans of paint and several brushes. The carpet had been pulled from the wall near the stairs where baskets of toys overflowed onto the exposed subfloor.

He waved them onto a worn blue sofa with lumpy cushions. "Excuse the mess. We're planning on selling this spring and according to our real estate agent we need to 'update' the place for top dollar. I thought we could sell 'as is,' but Elana, my wife, she disagrees, so . . ."

"Is your wife here?" Paterno asked.

"No, no. She took the kids to an indoor park for the day and I'm supposed to finish a project or two."

His way of saying: "I'm busy. Keep this brief."

Wilde added, "Do you . . . do you have any information on Ivy?"

Tanaka shook her head. "We were hoping you did."

"No." He let out a sigh, rubbed the knuckles of one hand with the fingers of the other, then he settled into one of a well-worn set of recliners that faced a small flat screen mounted over an electric fireplace. "Oh, Lordy. I hope she's okay." He worried his hands as they hung between his knees. "You know, Ivy and I haven't been close in a long while," he admitted, getting right to the point. "I think I already told you that on the phone. In fact I told you everything. I thought . . . I mean I was afraid when you showed up that you were going to bring me bad news. Worse news." He rubbed a hand over his mouth. "It's no secret that Brindel and I didn't get along. Never did. Married out of college, were gonna split up, and ooops, she's pregnant, so we gave it a go for another couple of years, but that woman was way too high maintenance for me. She found Paul Latham and I thought, great! To be honest I was glad she agreed to a divorce. In fact she was the one who wanted out. No muss. No fuss."

"What about Ivy?" Tanaka asked.

"Well, that was a little tougher," he admitted, and he seemed to sweat a little.

"During the divorce Brindel insisted she get full custody and I . . . well, Ivy would spend every other weekend with me, but that didn't last long." He looked away from Tanaka's gaze, staring instead at the stained carpet. "I should have tried harder, I suppose, but I got involved with Elana; we got married and she and Ivy didn't exactly click, y'know. So, it was just easier if Brindel and Paul raised her." Then, as if hearing his own words, he added, "She was always welcome, of course."

"But she never came."

He nodded. "That's about right. Elana and I started our own family and now we have three girls. We're outgrowing this place and . . ."

There was no room for Ivy.

He didn't say it.

He didn't have to.

"When was the last time you saw her?"

"Christmas," he answered, which is what he'd said on the phone. "Well, actually it was the week before. We always celebrate with Elana's family and Ivy had never felt comfortable with them, or with our kids. They were half sisters and all, but . . . well, as I said, Elana and Ivy didn't mix and she didn't want our girls around her as Ivy was always . . . rebellious."

The door opened at that moment and a thin woman with short black hair and a weary expression swept into the room. In jeans and a black puffy coat, she was juggling two grocery bags. Three girls, stair-steps with dark hair and curious eyes, spilled in through the front door behind her. "Who is—? Oh, dear God," Elana said. "You're the police? Emery, close the door for God's sake, it's freezing outside!" She turned to her husband. "I have two more bags in the car." She race-walked to the kitchen, set the sacks on a cluttered peninsula, and returned to the living area. "It's about Ivy, isn't it? Oh. My. God." She froze, as if understanding for the first time. "Is she—?"

She let the sentence dangle as if aware that her daughters had suddenly gone quiet and had clustered near the front door, all three staring at the group in the living area.

Paterno said, "We're still trying to locate her. Her cell phone records were held up, but we're going over them now and we think she may be in New Mexico. Not sure yet."

Elana let out her breath and sketched the sign of the cross feverishly across her chest. "Thank God."

"Do you have family or friends in the Albuquerque

area? Anyone she might want to meet, or who might put her up, even hide her out?" Paterno asked.

Both Victor and his wife shook their heads.

Useless, Tanaka thought.

Then, as if the subject were closed, Elana turned to her husband. "I said there were other groceries in the car. Could you get them?" Her mouth turned down at the corners. "Please?" An afterthought.

"Okay," he said to her, then to the officers, "I don't think I can help you."

"Did she have a room here? Any personal property?" Tanaka was reaching and knew the answer before she asked the question, but she didn't want to leave any stone unturned.

Elana rolled her eyes. "I guess you didn't tell them, did you?"

"Elana," he said quietly, warning.

His wife plowed on, "Ivy wasn't welcome here any longer. Yes, she was here at Christmas for what—two hours, max? That was long enough, let me tell you. That girl was a klepto, a thief. Lived in a damned mansion, given anything she wanted by Mommy and Stepdaddy, and yet when she came here, she stole."

"You don't know that," Victor argued, but the glare she sent him caused him to shut up.

"I do. She took a ring out of my jewelry drawer and some of Larissa's things. Tell them, honey," she said to the oldest girl, who was around twelve, all arms and legs, dressed in leggings and a short dress, just as her sisters were.

Larissa averted her eyes. "My phone," she said.

"Your new iPhone!" Elana corrected. "She hadn't had it two months."

Tanaka said, "And you're sure Ivy took it."

"It went missing that same day that she was here! I tell you, that girl is trouble. She's on a path to nowhere good." She cast a glance at her husband as if daring him to disagree. "I banned her from the house. Gathered up every bit of her things and shipped them back to her."

Victor winced, but either Elana was oblivious or just didn't care about his feelings as she added, probably not for the first time, "I won't have Ivy peddling her bad attitude around my girls. Who knows what she's into? Boys. *Older* boys. Men, really. And they're not from the country club where Paul plays golf, let me tell you." She was on a roll now. "She was even sent to a mental hospital, up in Washington somewhere."

"Oregon. Portland, Oregon," Wilde said.

She rounded on him. "The point is, Victor, she's psycho!"

"No." He stood then and shook his head, but he was still sweating. "She just needs some guidance."

"Not from you. Or me." Elana was poking an index finger at her husband now. "I don't want to wish anything bad to happen to her, I'm not saying that, but she's not welcome here ever again. Not around me. Not around the girls. And not in this house!" She was breathing hard as she unzipped her coat. "I'm sorry," she said to the detectives without a trace of regret, "but that's how I feel."

"She's not psycho," Victor said tensely, getting to his feet.

"'Troubled' then. Yes, let's say 'troubled.'" She turned to the detectives and her husband's face reddened as she went on. "That's the word we use for it now. 'Troubled.' But there's something wrong with her. No friends to speak of, at least none that we know about, and there's something deep and disturbing and . . . well . . . evil about her." She angled her chin up defiantly, daring her husband to deny it. "There, I've finally said it. Out loud. What you and I have thought for years."

"For the love of God, Elana."

"It's the truth." Then, as if realizing for the first time that her children were hearing her every word, she added, "She went to a mental hospital for a while and, if you ask me, her stay there did more harm than good."

"That's not true," Victor said, challenging his wife. "Ivy . . . did have problems. Was suicidal. Brindel and Paul put her into a place in Portland, Oregon, and she came back better."

"Did she?" Elana asked, then to Tanaka, "And now her mother and stepfather are dead."

Victor shook his head. "Not connected! Don't even put the two thoughts together. Jesus, Elana, what's wrong with you?"

"With *me* . . . ?" His wife gave him a hard look. "I think we're done here. We, I mean, Victor and I, have no idea where Ivy is, and as for Brindel and Paul . . . 'As ye sow, so shall ye reap.' Still, it's a shame, I know. God rest their souls."

She said it without a lot of conviction.

"Larissa." Paterno caught the attention of Elana's oldest daughter. "Why do you think Ivy took your phone?"

A beat. A glance at her mother. A slight nod of Elana's head. Finally, the girl replied, her voice barely audible. "Cuz I showed it to her."

Elana said, "What did I tell you?"

Larissa's gaze was glued to the floor. She looked like she would rather be anywhere other than this living room.

"Did you show it to a lot of people?" Tanaka asked. "A new phone and all. To your friends?"

Larissa swallowed visibly, then snuck a glance to the stairs as if she wanted to bolt.

"Of course she did," Elana answered for her daughter. "Who wouldn't? But what does that have to do with anything? It was Ivy. She snatched the phone."

"You saw her take it?" Paterno asked.

Elana opened her mouth to say something and then, as if tasting the lie, she decided against it. "No, not actually take it, but Larissa had shown it to her and Ivy had played with it."

"She was showing her how to download some apps," Victor cut in.

"As if Larissa didn't know how," Elana sneered. "In this day and age? She's twelve. She was practically born with apps." With a huff, she crossed her arms over her chest. "Now . . . can we wrap this up?" Her attention swung to the detectives. "I've got groceries in the car."

"Yeah. I know."

Her gaze swept to the kitchen table and the untouched do-it-yourself tools. "And we've got work to do." She was frowning now, clearly unhappy that Wilde wasn't involved in his home project.

After a quick trip outside to unload the car, Victor answered a few more questions, but the detectives didn't learn anything else. In fact they seemed to leave the town house with more questions than answers.

"Step-Mommy Dearest," Paterno said as Tanaka, at the wheel, pulled away from the curb.

"Sad," Tanaka said. "I know I come across as a hard-ass and I am." She slid a glance at Paterno. "Don't argue with me."

"I wasn't going to."

"Well, okay, but you know, when it comes to kids? I get really pissed when adults don't put their children's needs above their own. Even if Ivy was running with the wrong crowd, or taking up with the wrong guy, or giving her old man a hard time, it's his job to do what's best for her. Doesn't matter if she ends up living with a super-rich stepfather, or spends time in a mental hospital or whatever. Victor and his wife need to step up with Ivy, know what I mean?" With Paterno on his phone, she drove out of town, making only a slight detour to drive under the iconic arch one more time, just for kicks.

Pescoli turned over in bed and she was instantly awake.

Something was wrong.

She could feel it in her bones.

She'd been back home less than two days and the feeling was back, that she was being watched by hidden eyes, that something bad was going down. Nothing in the last twenty-four hours had given her any fuel to feed this paranoid feeling, not even the ongoing investigation into her sister's death.

Santana's arm was draped around her waist, aftermath of their lovemaking. For the last two nights, they'd been insatiable. Pescoli couldn't get enough of him. Her own sister's violent death made her feel more vulnerable, more concerned with death, and she was hanging on to Santana for dear life.

"Oh, hogwash," she whispered, hating all the self-examination and worry that had edged into her life. It had started with her pregnancy. Brindel's murder had only exacerbated it.

Or maybe you're just cracking up.

She threw back the covers and walked naked to the French doors, where, as she had hundreds of times before, she stared across the icy surface of the lake and then looked up to the black sky where no stars were visible, cloud cover erasing their shine and hiding the moon.

There is nothing out there, Pescoli. Get over yourself. Even the bears have the good sense to hibernate for the winter.

But it wasn't the bears or wolves or mountain lions that roamed the forests around her home that caused the little tingle of apprehension to crawl up her spine. No, it was something unknown, something insidious and evil that she felt observing her.

Paranoia is not a good look for you.

Still she stared into the quiet night, as if in looking through the glass she could discern whatever it was that was disturbing her subconscious and causing the hairs on her nape to stand on end.

Who are you? Or no, what *are you?*

And what the hell do you want with me?

With no answers, she returned to the bed and snuggled close to Santana once again. His warm breath ruffled her hair. "You okay?" he asked groggily.

"Fine."

His arm tightened around her and he mumbled, "Go back to sleep."

And she did. So close to him that she could hear his heart beat, she finally fell into slumber only to dream of her sisters, all four Connors girls, as they were in school, young and full of life, but something was wrong with Brindel . . . something she couldn't figure out.

Beautiful and ethereal, Brindel suddenly was holding a baby in her arms and walking quickly away, crossing a bridge over a span of dark water. Somewhere a dog barked and she began to run. "It's all your fault, Regan," she whispered as she looked over her shoulder, and the flesh on her gorgeous face started to peel away, showing bits of her skull. "All your fault . . ."

Regan gave chase, realizing that the baby in her sister's arms was her own.

"Brindel, stop!" she yelled, though her voice was muted, and then she heard the gunshots.

In rapid fire succession.

Bam! Bam! Bam!

Brindel's body jerked. She was a skeleton. The baby vanished.

Pescoli's eyes flew open. She was breathing hard, her heart racing, but she was in her own bed, her husband right next to her.

Bam! Bam! Bam! Bam!

"What the hell?" Santana said, rolling out of bed and yanking on the pair of jeans he'd kicked off the night before. "It's five in the morning."

Pescoli was instantly awake.

It was all a dream. A horrible nightmare.

The dogs were barking loudly from the laundry room

downstairs, Cisco's gruff yips audible over the deeper growls and barks of the larger dogs. Pescoli snatched her robe from a hook on the door and threw it around her body, only pausing to check and see that both Bianca and Baby Tuck were still fast asleep in their rooms despite the cacophony rising upward from the first floor.

Thank God!

Down the stairs she flew to catch up with her husband in the lower hallway. "If Jeremy lost his keys again—"

"He wouldn't be pounding on the door. He would've texted or gone through the garage."

"And pulled down the stairs onto my Jeep? I don't think so."

Santana had already crossed the living area and was peering through the peephole.

"Wait!" she said. "Be careful." Why had she left her service weapon up in the bedroom in the gun safe? No one ever showed up on their doorstep in the middle of the night.

"What the hell?" Santana threw back the dead bolt and yanked open the door to expose an ashen-faced girl with choppy hair and smeared makeup shivering on the porch. Snow had collected on the gray hood of her sweatshirt. She looked beyond Santana's frame to Pescoli, her eyes round, blood evident on her forehead. "Aunt Regan?" she whispered, teeth chattering, snow swirling behind her.

"Let her in," Pescoli said, stepping forward and realizing that Ivy Wilde, her missing niece, was alive, but nearly freezing to death on her doorstep.

Chapter 15

Ivy's tale was a little hard to swallow.

But Pescoli was listening, trying to believe.

She and Santana had brought her niece into the family room, and while he quieted the dogs, allowing them inside to sniff and greet the newcomer, Pescoli had pointed Ivy to the couch and given the girl a comforter to wrap herself in. She looked awful: pale and distraught, her hair chopped off and mousy brown, her overdone makeup fading.

But then she'd been traumatized. On the run, to hear her tell it.

Santana stacked wood and kindling, then lit a fire in the hearth where flames caught and crackled. Satisfied, he made his way into the kitchen and scraped a bar stool backward. He glanced at Pescoli as he took a seat at the island, reclaiming his morning spot and coffee, glancing at his iPad where he'd been perusing online news.

Pescoli had offered breakfast to Ivy, who'd insisted

she wasn't hungry. Coffee had been declined as well, but finally she'd settled on a cup of instant hot chocolate.

With a little prodding, they'd learned that Ivy had taken a circuitous route from San Francisco via Albuquerque and Missoula, then had hitchhiked to Grizzly Falls with a nice man who'd helped her connect with people in town whereupon she'd learned Pescoli's address. All of that information had been hair raising enough—the people of Grizzly Falls were too damn trusting by far, Pescoli thought, seeing how easy it apparently was for someone to find her address—before Ivy had launched into her tale of finding the bodies of Brindel and Paul when she came home from seeing "a friend." She told Pescoli how she'd run through the kitchen, grabbed a kitchen knife, only to lose it while stumbling on the street near the entrance to the park. Freaked out, she'd then decided to run away. She'd taken the first bus she could find out of the Bay Area, all the while planning her trip to Grizzly Falls and connecting with her aunt "the cop."

Now that some color had returned to her face, Pescoli asked, "Can you go over it again? I have a few questions."

Ivy seemed to want to argue, opened her mouth, then shut it again. She bent her head to the steaming mug she was cradling and looked like she wanted to disappear completely.

"I'm just trying to put it together," Pescoli explained. "Your friend's name?"

"Anna. Anna Jordan."

"What about your boyfriend?"

"I don't have one." Ivy's gaze narrowed on her aunt. "I broke up with Troy."

"I thought there was someone new."

"No. After Troy . . ." Her voice drifted off as if she'd lost her train of thought.

"What?"

"It just wasn't good with Troy," she said, "so I lied about another boyfriend. To get him to leave me alone. Troy was . . . aggressive, I guess. When he drank, it got worse. He was really nasty." She met the questions in Pescoli's eyes.

"He hit you." She'd seen it a hundred times.

"Well, he mainly punched holes in walls or kicked something. His truck once, I saw that. Put a dent in the side panel."

"But he hit you." Pescoli could hardly control her rage at the thought.

Ivy's voice was soft when she said, "Just once."

"One is one too many times."

"Yeah, I know."

"I'd love to run him in or worse," she admitted.

"No. Don't. It's over."

"Were you drinking with him?" she asked. Ivy was far from legal.

"No. But I got angry with him and he hit me, slapped me hard across the face, then his fist balled, but he backed away. I broke up with him the next day. I remember it was the day after Thanksgiving."

"Did you report it?"

"I just told you, I ended it."

"But if he's violent, he could hurt someone else."

"Like my mother and Paul? Is that what you're

thinking? Jesus. You cops. He slapped me. He's *not* a killer, for God's sake!"

Pescoli wasn't convinced, but seeing her niece's reaction, decided to let it go. For now. "So, back to that night when you got home from Anna's?"

"I already told you. I found them . . . dead." She swallowed. "The house was quiet at that point."

"Did anything seem disturbed?"

"Not that I saw. There was no furniture turned over, if that's what you mean. I went up the stairs and . . . and I found Mom." Her gaze dropped back to the cradled cup. "I went to Mom's room first. I saw her on the bed and I don't know . . . it was horrible, and I went to Paul's room." Her face contorted at the memory. "He was all bloody and . . ." She broke off, shook her head. Her hands quivered as she forced the cup to her lips again. "And then . . . and then, I thought I heard something . . . someone else in the house, and I ran. I just took off . . . out the back."

"Did you take anything?"

"What do you mean? Oh. The knife. And just what I had with me. My phone and wallet."

"That's all?"

There was a beat of hesitation. "I took some money from Paul's safe," she admitted in a small voice. "That's why that guy attacked me."

"What guy?" Santana's gaze was boring into her, the iPad forgotten.

"Yeah, what guy?" Pescoli repeated.

"He must've seen the cash I dropped at a bus station," Ivy said, then gave them a horrific story of how she'd been accosted by a man who'd stolen her money and how she'd gotten away from him by spraying him with hair spray, turning his cigarette into flames, which caught in his hair gel and set his head on fire.

Both Pescoli and Santana went silent for a moment, taking that in. The way Ivy described what had happened made Pescoli think the bizarre event would most likely hit the news. She could follow up on that later.

"Do you think this man followed you from San Francisco, that he could've been in the house that night?" Pescoli asked.

Ivy bit her lip and muttered, "I don't know."

"Let's take this a step back. Did you see anyone in or around your mom's house?"

"No, just heard them." Chewing on her lip, she thought. "I mean, I thought I heard them."

"More than one person?"

"I don't know," Ivy said again, and her eyebrows slid together as she concentrated.

There was something about her that made Pescoli question the veracity of her tale. Not that she was lying . . . more that it felt there was a lot left unsaid. Was she involved somehow? Lying? Covering her tracks? Were there two perpetrators? Her thoughts went to Paul's sons, the two people who would gain the most from their father's and stepmother's death. Collette hadn't trusted Paul's sons, nor had Sarina, not really. Was it possible? For Seth and Macon to have simultaneously pulled triggers on their father and stepmother? Her stomach soured at the image that played through her mind—Paul's disbelief, though he may not have seen who had put a bullet through the back of his head; but Brindel's eyes had been wide open, rounding with fear as she recognized her assailant.

Was it possible?

Of course.

Anything was.

She eyed her niece.

Ivy had closed her eyes, as if she were replaying the scene of her escape from the house in her head. "I was downstairs," she said. "And I heard footsteps . . . on the floor above, and it sounded . . . I mean, I think it was more than one set. It sounded as if there were at least two people, maybe more. But . . . I'm not sure. All I know is that I ran through the park to the waterfront."

"You didn't call anyone?"

"No."

"Why not? Your father—"

"Victor's not an option. I don't get along with him or his wife. Not even what happened to Mom changes that."

"But—"

"He's not there for me!"

Pescoli nodded. She'd never liked Victor Wilde, not when he was married to Brindel, not after the divorce. He'd been pissed that his ex had taken up with a rich doctor whereas he'd always struggled. But she didn't think he was a killer, not by any stretch of the imagination. Not for revenge for Latham being married to his wife and not even for being in control of the inheritance Ivy might have received.

Still, one never knew.

"You could have called your Aunt Sarina. She lives in the city—"

"I was freaked! Beyond freaked, for God's sake! Someone killed my mom and stepdad! Murdered them in their beds . . . oh, Jesus." She looked away, blinked.

"I thought whoever did it might be following me, planning to kill me, too. I still do."

"You could have called nine-one-one."

"Yeah! I could have, but I didn't!" She stood quickly and a few drops of cocoa sloshed onto the area rug. "Oh, shit! Shit, shit, shit!"

"It's okay."

"No, it's not. Nothing is okay and nothing ever will be again!" She set her cup on the table, wrapped her arms around her middle, stalked to the fire.

"Do you have any idea who could have done this?"

"No!" She said it so sharply, so quickly, Nikita lifted his head and gave a soft husky bark. "Of course not."

"No enemies?"

"Probably tons! Paul's a dick!" Then she rolled her suddenly wet eyes toward the ceiling. "I guess I shouldn't say that about him now. But he was. A real dick. Cheated on Mom all the time, bossed her around. She was getting a divorce, you know, and I was glad. He was just awful."

"So who were his enemies?"

She'd been warming the back of her legs, but now she crossed the room toward the couch again. "I've asked myself like a million times, but I just don't know. I was scared, so I ran, but Mom . . . oh, God." Her voice caught and trembled and she sank into the cushions at the opposite end from where Pescoli had perched. She admitted, "I don't like cops."

Pescoli had run into that attitude before. Even with her own kids. The distrust of the police. Or the school administration. Anyone in authority. But especially the cops.

"Mom told me if I ever got into trouble and for some reason I couldn't reach her, I was to call you."

"You didn't call."

"I was afraid! And it's not like I keep your number on my phone's contact list." More belligerence. "I. Just. Ran."

Maybe a natural reaction. Maybe not. Pescoli wanted to believe her but experience had taught her to tread carefully, especially with family members. It was too easy for people close to her to try and pull the wool over her eyes.

Her jaw set, Ivy stared at the fire, watching the flames. Then as if seeing something disturbing in the embers, she turned away and focused her gaze on the three dogs, all curled on their beds and sleeping near a stack of firewood on the hearth. She looked haggard and rung out, pale, bruised, and haunted.

As if she'd been through hell.

She probably had.

Pescoli said, "It took you quite a while to get here."

"Yeah, well, it's a long way."

"A long way, and then you hitchhiked in a snowstorm," Santana reminded. He was still as tuned in to Ivy's recap as Pescoli was. "Lucky you found someone so willing to help you."

Ivy lifted her chin, giving him a long look. "Yeah, it was."

"If you'd called, I would have come and gotten you," Pescoli said quickly. Santana practically radiated skepticism. Clearly he was having some trouble with Ivy's story as well.

"Call where? I didn't have your number and I wasn't

"Five. Ugh. I just got up to use the bathroom."

"Use ours."

"Is she okay?" Bianca asked as they walked through Pescoli's bedroom where the bed was as they'd left it, covers flung back, over an hour earlier.

"Would you be?"

"'Course not." Another yawn. "Can we talk about this later? Oh God, the boss is awake."

Pescoli, too, could hear her baby making noise over the sound of the shower running. "I'll fill you in after school."

"I'm just gonna sleep a little more."

"Don't think you have time, but you figure it out."

"Geez, Mom, it's still dark." She closed the door to the master bath as Pescoli made her way to the baby's room.

Tucker was wide awake, his eyes bright, cooing to himself in his crib. At the sight of her, his little arms and feet started moving frantically. "Hey, there, Buddy," she said, picking him up and kissing the top of his head. She carried Tucker to the window and pressed the tip of a finger to the glass. "Look out there."

Outside, all three dogs at his heels, Santana was trudging through knee-deep snow, blazing a trail to the stable. Cisco, the smallest, was nearly buried in the drifts; Sturgis, the black lab, plunged steadfastly at Santana's side, while Nikita ran hither and yon, the furry husky bounding through the untouched snow and sending it spraying as he landed, only to leap up again. "There's Daddy," Pescoli told her son. "He's gonna feed the horses."

As Santana and dogs disappeared into the stable,

Pescoli saw the ghostly reflection of herself holding the baby, backlit by the night-light, an almost eerie image of mother and child. As she turned, the baby in the reflection vanished from her arms, a trick of light.

But a chill skittered up Pescoli's spine and she glanced across the lake. Placid and snow covered, the trees on the far bank, fir boughs, bending with the weight of their icy white mantle. Cold. Clear. The rising sun just beginning to turn the black of night into a deep, shadowy gray.

Goose bumps rose on her arms and she tightened her grip on her child. "It's gonna be all right," she whispered, though she didn't know why. She heard Bianca return to her room and close her door just as the shower turned off in the hall bath.

Thinking about the day ahead, she decided to let her niece sleep for a while and call her sisters to let them know Ivy was safe. Pescoli would also phone Paterno in San Francisco, and once Ivy was awake, have her text or call her father.

Then she'd get down to the nitty-gritty.

Because the girl was lying. Not about all of her story—some of it rang true—but in Pescoli's opinion, Ivy knew more than she was telling. About what, Pescoli could only guess. But it was time to come clean. She was obviously scared, no doubt about it. And affected deeply by her mother's murder, but still, Ivy was leaving something out.

Something important.

And probably something incriminating, but for what, Pescoli couldn't imagine. It didn't seem likely that Ivy had pulled the trigger, and that part could be figured out probably by a GSR test on her clothes. Unless she'd changed. Even now she could be washing away evidence in Pescoli's very own shower, but still, it seemed really unlikely that Ivy had killed her own parents.

That's the aunt in you talking. The reason you're not on the case. It's not just about jurisdiction but objectivity. Alvarez's voice rang in her ears. *And you just can't trust your gut, Pescoli. You know that. You need facts.*

Attempting to shove that nagging voice out of her head, she decided it was time to put a call in to Chilcoate again. Pescoli wanted her facts straight before she and Tanaka talked and she wanted to ferret out how much of her niece's story was straight-up facts and how much was a load of bull crap.

You might not like what you find.

"Too bad," she said aloud, startling the baby. He began to cry.

"Sorry. Come on, let's get you ready for the day." With her mind half on the mystery surrounding her sister's murder, Pescoli bathed and changed Tucker, then watched him play, lying on his back and trying to touch the toys and mirror that dangled from an arch that was secured to a padded mat on the floor. His private "baby gym" was one of the gifts she'd received from a surprise baby shower that was thrown in her honor by Joelle Fisher, the receptionist and self-appointed maven of all things celebratory in the department. Over Pescoli's objections, and after the baby had arrived, Joelle had mounted her coup and lured Pescoli to the station. She'd gone reluctantly to find the conference room decorated in baby blue ribbons, onesies, and booties, the table piled high with gifts. Pescoli had been surprised, and a little angry, and eventually gracious, though it kind of killed her to admit that Joelle had been right. It was nice to have a party for the baby. This little gym was part of the bounty she'd received.

Now, lying on his back, Tucker swiped at the colorful objects. He grinned and kicked and was delighted when Pescoli swatted at the little paisley elephant that swung over his head.

With Tucker occupied, she gave one last glance out the window as she put in another call to Chilcoate, pushing aside the eerie feeling that had been with her earlier. Her attention switched back to her son, which was the reason she didn't notice the reflection on the lenses of the field glasses trained on the house.

"I see you," the woman dressed in white whispered, her breath fogging in the freezing air. Lowering her binoculars, she stared at the snow-crusted cottage built recently on the opposite shore. Warm patches of light glowed in the windows, reflecting on the ground, and behind the panes, people moved about. A family. Close and feeling safe, a fire sending curling smoke out of the chimney, lights visible even over the garage in what, she assumed, was an apartment.

For the older son.

Who came and went as he pleased.

The daughter lived in the house along with the man, wife, and newborn.

So cozy.

So safe.

A haven nestled in these imposing woods.

But not for long, she vowed, thinking of her own

son ripped from her arms and now, she knew, not among the living.

The cold pain filled her chest at the few memories she had of the boy—the sterile birthing room, an unknown doctor wearing a face mask, the wriggling, squalling infant with his shock of wet dark hair and wide mouth. Red-faced, little fists clenched, he'd been placed on her belly for the briefest of instants as the cord was cut. She'd reached for him, wanted to comfort him, but before she had a chance to pull him to her, feel his tiny heartbeat against her own, a nurse—a big woman with blond hair escaping her cap—had swept him away from her. With gloved hands and a heart of ice, she'd quickly walked out of the room, the baby's cries lingering long after the swinging doors had slowed and closed.

And as she'd felt tears wash down her cheeks, the doctors and nurses had swiftly and efficiently cleaned her and the bed where she'd birthed her son to eventually leave her alone in a private room, a sterile spot where an empty bassinet beside the bed reminded her of her loss.

Never had she felt so bereft.

Never had she been so alone.

Even now, she felt a shimmer of emotion.

Tears started to burn in her eyes as she'd finally found her son.

She'd finally found her son, but it had been much too late.

She focused on the house across the lake again.

A shadow passed in front of a downstairs window. The woman—Regan Pescoli—holding her infant, cradling his head, a moving silhouette.

"You will know," she whispered, at the thought of her vengeance. "And you will feel my pain."

She thought about her rifle, high powered and far reaching, its laser sight able to pinpoint a target so that the shot would be accurate from over five hundred yards.

Just far enough.

Chapter 16

"Detective Tanaka?" a male voice asked when Tanaka answered her phone in the department on Monday morning. "This is George Aimes. Remember me?" She did, but he clarified, "I own the rooming house. Troy Boxer rents from me."

"Of course I remember you, Mr. Aimes," Tanaka said, catching Paterno's eye as he passed by her desk. She waved him over.

"Well, remember you told me to call you if anything odd happened? Anything out of the ordinary?"

"Yes." She'd been sifting through e-mails and reports, but now he had her full attention. "What is it?"

"We have a pretty steady routine around here, you see, and when neither Ronny or Troy did their assigned duties, I tried to roust them, y'know? Both their cars were here, all weekend, still here in fact, but neither of them answered their doors. I checked—their rooms are empty, beds don't look like they've been slept in, though with Troy, it would be hard to tell."

Tanaka's pulse jumped. "You think they're missing."

"Like I said, hard to tell with boys that age, but I got a call from A-Bay-C Delivery asking about Troy. He didn't show up for work and was scheduled to. His route starts at eight. Then Ronny, his boss calls. Works for Stillwell Plumbing, company owned by his uncle. S'posed to be on the job at eight and he's a no-show, too."

"When was the last time you saw either of them?" she asked.

"I thought about that. Both of 'em were here Friday night and up and about on Saturday, but I didn't see either of 'em on Sunday, or Saturday night for that matter, but that's not surprising. They're both young and single and tend to kick up their heels on the weekend. But I don't know either one to have missed work like this."

She asked a few more questions and, getting no further information, hung up and caught Paterno's attention.

"What's up?" he asked.

"Troy Boxer and one of his roommates, his alibi, Ronny Stillwell?"

"Yeah?"

"Both men appear to be MIA."

She was already standing and reaching for her jacket. "I've got more information, too."

"You must've gotten in here at four."

"Four thirty, but close enough. Come on." She hurried into the hallway and nearly ran over Dani Settler, another detective with the department, someone Paterno had known for a long while. Settler had been carrying a cup of coffee and juggled it quickly. "Sorry," Tanaka said.

Paterno said, "She's onto a big lead. You know how that is."

"No prob," Settler said, and turned into her office. "Go get 'em."

Tanaka didn't bother responding. She was too hyped. Had no time for any kind of chitchat unless it had to do with the case.

"Ultra-focused," her mother had said of her once, to which her engineer father, who had been sitting at the small kitchen table in their apartment, had snapped his newspaper and from behind the screen of the financial page said, "It'll serve her well."

And it had, Tanaka thought.

She was one of three, firstborn and determined to be a standout, not that her father would ever notice. Her siblings were sons and to Takami "Tom" Tanaka, that was what mattered: gender. It wasn't that he didn't love her; no. He did. Tom just didn't have the same aspirations for his daughter that he did for his two boys. Fortunately her mother had always pushed her, and when her father had mentioned her being "too stubborn for her own good," or "bullheaded," Mom had thrown his own words back at him: "It will serve her well."

She smiled at that thought now.

No one was more proud of her for making detective than her old man. *Thank you, Dad.* He'd come around.

But she couldn't get caught up in nostalgia. Things were finally breaking in the Latham double-homicide.

She walked swiftly through the old hallways of the department. "The cell phone records for Ivy Wilde came in," she told Paterno as they made their way out the back exit. "She's been in Albuquerque, but that was as of a day or two ago."

"Or her phone's been there."

"Right. It could have been stolen. I'll drive," Tanaka said.

"No. You talk. I'll drive."

For once she didn't feel like arguing; let the old man get behind the wheel. As they drove out of the parking garage, she saw the city coming alive, pedestrians in long coats or thick jackets, some with hats, others with umbrellas, all hurrying along the wet pavement. A thin fog was drifting through the city streets, giving an ethereal glow to the scene.

Paterno turned at the light and Tanaka filled him in. "I talked to the Albuquerque Police after I got the phone records. Then I e-mailed the missing persons report to the officer I talked with."

"So Albuquerque's looking for her."

"Yeah, but the thought is she's already taken off. They're checking motels and the bus station, airport, trains . . . the usual. But he did say a strange thing happened the other night and he wouldn't have mentioned it, but it happened during the time we think Ivy was there. Only a few blocks from the bus station a man was attacked by a woman. Around two in the morning."

"The guy was attacked by Ivy? She's all of what? Five-two and maybe a hundred pounds soaking wet?"

"That's what he claimed. Said that she tried to rob him, maybe was strung out at the time, but she set his hair on fire. Turned him into a damned human torch."

"What? She torched him?" Paterno glanced at her as he flipped on the wipers. "Jesus."

"It's an off-the-wall story. The guy's suffering from second- and third-degree burns. Can barely speak. Barely hanging on. Lucky to be alive."

"Maybe."

"That's why the detective I spoke with brought it up." She was thinking about the information she'd received early this morning, still working things out in her own mind. "It might have nothing to do with anything. Maybe it was a junkie looking for a big score and she jumped him. The guy did have about four thousand bucks on him. In cash."

"Huh." Paterno's eyes narrowed as he, along with the traffic ahead of him, slowed for a traffic light. "Lotta money."

"Uh-huh."

"But Paul Latham could have had money stashed in one of his safes."

"My thoughts exactly."

"You think Ivy robbed her folks and took off."

"Something scared her. Say she grabbed the cash and a knife in the kitchen, ran out the back door and lost the knife as she crossed the street before cutting through the park. That's the way I see it. And there's something more. The burn victim? The New Mexico cops ID-ed him."

"Let me guess: He's got a record."

"In three states. Wynn P. Ellis, and that would be Junior, no less. There's a senior in Reno where Junior hails from. The charges run the regular gamut: possession, resisting, burglary, and assault. Turns out there's an existing warrant out for him, so his ass is grass. After the hospital, he's going back to jail."

"So you think his version of the attack scenario could be erroneous."

"If I were a betting woman, I'd say yes." She glanced out the side window, past the condensation on the glass, to stare up at a huge crane working at a construction site where another skyscraper would soon rise.

Paterno changed lanes, passing a slow-moving RV. "You think Ivy was involved in the murders?"

"Dunno. Maybe." She thought about it. "Would she really be party to putting a gun to her mother's head? Paul, her stepdaddy, maybe . . . That's a different story. But Brindel? Doesn't seem likely."

"And yet Troy Boxer and his roommate are missing," Paterno reminded her. "They could be meeting up with her."

"Yeah, well. Then there's that." She rolled the idea around in her brain. Was Ivy a part of the double-homicides? A willing accomplice? Unwitting victim? Was she any part of it at all? "We're looking into the bus schedule that night."

"Ellis ID-ed her?"

"Yes and no. The woman who attacked him had shorter, darker hair and was heavier than Ivy, but she could have been disguised. They've already got a picture of Ivy, so they're going to check with Ellis, but might not get anything concrete."

They arrived at the rooming house, and with Aimes's key, went into the living quarters assigned to Boxer and Stillwell. Both rooms were a mess with unmade beds and half-filled garbage cans, beer bottles in each, a pizza box in Stillwell's. But in neither space did they find car keys, cell phone, computer, or any hand-held device. No indication of what had happened to them. They peered into the interiors of the two vehicles owned by the men, but saw nothing. "Cars are locked. We'll need a warrant unless you have keys," Paterno said to Aimes.

Aimes shook his head. "If they have spares, I don't know where."

"Okay," Paterno said.

"I think we've got all we can here," said Tanaka.

Paterno instructed Aimes to lock the rooms and not allow anyone inside and to call when either man reappeared.

"They obviously planned on returning," Paterno said as he opened the driver's door. "They left their cars, most of their clothes, and their TVs and gaming sets. No twenty-something would leave those things."

"Unless they left in a hurry. Something spooked them," Tanaka said, thinking as she checked her phone and ran through a couple of reports that had come into her e-mail account. "Uh-oh."

"What?" Paterno was checking his side mirror, waiting for a minivan to pass before pulling onto the street.

"I don't know what took the lab so long, but there's a match on the beer can left in Macon's bedroom at the Latham house."

"And?"

"Wonder of wonder, it turns out to belong to Troy Boxer. The last known boyfriend. I haven't found any trace of the new guy Boxer mentioned. I've got calls into her friends, but most say they didn't know of a new guy and that she'd been in a bad mood since the breakup with Boxer." It was more than that. Ivy Wilde had few friends and the ones Tanaka had interviewed all said the same thing: they avoided her.

"She's okay, I guess," Anna Jordan had said in a phone interview. "I was with her the day her mom and stepdad were, you know, found dead and all. We hung out until about ten, I guess, just watching movies."

Paterno grinned without a trace of humor. "With Boxer's fingerprints it shouldn't be a problem getting those warrants now."

"I'm on it." Tanaka felt a little sizzle of anticipation as she made the call, that rush of adrenaline that came with the first real break in the case.

Soon Boxer's car at the very least, and probably Stillwell's as well, would be impounded and examined with a fine-tooth comb by the forensic techs. They'd also check out the rooming house and any locker space at A-Bay-C Delivery along with the truck assigned to Boxer.

Ivy Wilde's ex had just been elevated to suspect number one.

Alvarez liked to get into the department early.

Today was no exception.

Dunking a tea bag into a cup of hot water, she made her way to her office. She loved this quiet time of morning when she could spend time alone at her desk, mentally getting ready for the day, reading through e-mail and reports, catching up on leads or whatever else she needed to do before the Pinewood County Sheriff's Department came to life.

At her desk as she sipped the hot Earl Grey, she checked her e-mail and got lost in an autopsy report of the victim of a bar fight. She'd just flipped the page when her peaceful hour of solitude was destroyed.

By Carson Ramsby.

Junior detective and her partner. For now. Hopefully it would be a temporary, make that a *very* temporary, partnership.

From the corner of her eye, she saw him approaching the half-open doorway to her small office. Tall and fit, he had the easy, confident gait of an athlete. She eyed him critically. He was handsome, she supposed. His jaw was tight, his cheekbones sharp, his skin swarthy, his hair a warm brown that curled a bit. In khakis, a polo shirt, and open jacket, he was already through the doorway. He hadn't bothered to shave, his weekend stubble visible, his hazel eyes bright.

"Hey!" he greeted as he slapped a newspaper onto her desktop, her neatly arranged reports fluttering before she secured them with one hand.

"What?"

He swung one of his long legs over the corner of her desk and leaned forward. "This guy—" He pointed a finger at a small column to one side of the front page. The headline read: MAN CLAIMS TO BE MISSING SON. "Says he's Brady Long's illegitimate son."

"No person is illegitimate," she said, thinking of her own life, the child she'd given up for adoption when she was a teen.

"Oh, right, right. Let's be politically correct about it." He leaned. "Anyway, this alleged biological son of Long, what's his name?" Ramsby pulled the paper back and scanned it quickly. *Garrett Mays*. He claims that Brady Long might not have known about him. That he was the end result of an affair with a woman thirty years ago, an affair that went sour. And the woman, Mays's mother, kept his father's identity a secret from him and probably from Brady Long as well."

"Unlikely. Brady Long was one of the richest men in Pinewood County. He owned thousands of acres of land, a huge ranch that Nate Santana now manages, and mining and logging companies."

"He lived on the ranch?"

"Some of the time, I guess. The Long family also owned a place on the top of the hill. You've seen it, right?"

He nodded. "The big Victorian mansion with a view of the river. Massive."

"That's it. It's a museum now, donated to the city by Brady's father before he died. It's closed for the winter, but pretty damn impressive. My point: Brady Long was a major player in these parts. Married and divorced a couple of times, no kids, and single when he died. He had a girlfriend, Maya something or other, I think, and she claimed that they were engaged at the time of his death, but that was unproven. Again, no children. It's pretty damned unlikely that anyone who had an affair with him, especially one that produced a kid and heir, would keep quiet about it."

"Could be Mays's mother was paid off—you know, one of those 'Do Not Disclose' agreements to keep quiet."

"Could be she and her son aren't legit." Alvarez kept to her side of the argument, wondering where the hell this was going. Hearing the distinctive click of Joelle Fisher's ever-present high heels in the hallway,

Alvarez glanced toward the open door. The shift had changed and the station was beginning to fill with office staff, deputies, and detectives.

"Santana? As in Detective Pescoli's husband?"

"That's right. He knew Brady Long and his sister when they were growing up, at least I think so. Pescoli mentioned it, but you'd have to ask her. Or Santana." She rolled her chair back and eyed Ramsby as her computer dinged, indicating she'd just received a new e-mail. "Why all the interest?"

"It's a mystery. Is he the unknown son? Is he a con artist? A grifter? What's the real story?" He slashed her an off-center smile that probably had broken its share of hearts. "Come on, Detective, aren't you curious?"

"Mildly."

"Of course you are; we all are. Otherwise it wouldn't be on the front page of the *Reporter.*"

"Maybe it's just a slow news day, er, week for the paper. This is Grizzly Falls, not Chicago or New York."

He laughed. "I suppose you've got a point."

"And this guy, Mays? He's not the first, you know," she said. "There have been others who've laid claim to the estate. It's been in limbo for several years. Ever since Brady died. Tied up in the courts. That's what happens when a lot of money's at stake."

He shrugged, obviously not completely convinced. "The reason this is different is that Mays has already taken a DNA test and hired a hotshot attorney out of Helena. He swears the DNA will prove that he's Long's son." He smiled wistfully. "Wouldn't that be somethin'? To wake up one day and figure out you're the son of a multimillionaire."

"A dead multimillionaire."

"Well, that's the point, isn't it? Talk about winning the dead-father lottery." Ramsby's smile gained wattage, thinking of the possibilities. "Oh, yeah. That would be great. Really great!" His cell phone gave off a sharp, insistent beep and he glanced at the screen. "Gotta take this," he said, swinging his leg off the desk and walking briskly out her door, leaving the newspaper still sitting on the desk.

More intrigued than she admitted, Alvarez skimmed the article quickly and wondered if, indeed, a new Long heir had been found.

It would certainly change things if Garrett Mays turned out to be legit.

But it would be a long shot.

Make that a Brady Long shot.

Chapter 17

Tanaka didn't waste any time.

"Come on," she said, just as Paterno was sliding his arms from his coat and hanging it on a hook in his office, positioned near the door. "Let's go."

"Go where?"

"Road trip. To Albuquerque to interview Wynn P. Ellis, who had the misfortune of tangling with Ivy Wilde." Paterno frowned, started to say something, but Tanaka ran right over him with, "I finally got to pore over her phone records and the cell tower pings. Tracked down the motel in the area where I think Wilde stayed. One of the receptionists at the Sunset Valley Inn ID-ed her. Local deputies had canvassed the area with pictures of Wilde that I'd e-mailed to the PD there once we thought she was in the area. I'm still betting she tried to turn her victim into ashes."

Paterno was still standing near his coat, but he didn't pick it up again, which made Tanaka feel impatient. He said, "I just got off the phone with Pescoli."

"Okay . . . ?"

"Ivy Wilde is camped out at her house."

"What? In *Montana*?" Tanaka was stunned. Hadn't seen this coming.

"She showed up in Grizzly Falls early this morning after a long bus ride or two and hitchhiking."

"You're kidding." Tanaka leaned against the wall, tried to put the pieces together. Why the hell would Ivy Wilde be in Montana? With Pescoli?

"And you're right," Paterno said. "Ivy Wilde did tangle with the human shish kebab, claims he attacked and robbed her and tried to rape or kill her. She set him on fire and took off, hailing down the bus she'd nearly missed."

"That's quite a way to fend off an attack."

"She worked with what she had."

"How did she do it?"

"With aerosol hair spray and a victim with a lit lighter and copious amounts of gel in his hair."

"Man." The fiery image that came to Tanaka's mind made her shudder. "How's Wilde doing?"

"Well, she survived the attack pretty much unscathed, at least physically."

"That kind of thing'll mess you up bad, and from what we know, that girl isn't exactly even-keeled to begin with. First her parents are killed and then she's attacked by this guy, probably. She might've got the better of him, but it was ugly. Even if she's somehow involved in her mom's death, it's hard to push it away unless you're a complete psycho."

He nodded.

"But at least we know where she is."

"According to Pescoli, Ivy changed her appearance

and, like you said, spent some time in a motel not far from the Greyhound station. Got attacked on her way to hop a bus north."

"Huh. Okay." A pause. "What are we waiting for?" she said, her mind whirling. "Looks like the road trip just got extended to include—what was it? Bear River?"

"Close enough," Paterno said, and plucked his jacket from the hook again.

Tanaka was already making her way to the door.

"By the way, I told Pescoli about Boxer and Stillwell going missing," said Paterno.

"You know that she's—"

"—not on the case. Yes. But if she's got Ivy Wilde, I figured we'd better bring her up to speed. Forewarned is forearmed."

"Thank God!" Sarina's voice trembled over the wireless connection.

Pescoli had called with the news that Ivy had arrived at her home in Montana. Now, in her family room, the television turned on but muted, she could picture Sarina, ever the drama queen, now nearly overcome, crumpling against the wall and sliding down it.

Sarina whispered, "I was so afraid, I mean, I didn't know what happened to her. How did she end up at your house? Not that it matters, of course. I just thank the good Lord that she's there and safe. She's okay, isn't she?"

"Fine," Pescoli lied. The girl was a wreck. But then who wouldn't be after what she'd been through?

And then there was the niggling suspicion that Ivy wasn't on the up-and-up.

With the phone to her ear, Pescoli walked onto the deck and watched as Santana let out the horses. One by one, bucking and prancing through the snow, they ran from one end of the long pasture that bordered the lake, to the other. The gelding was an ebony streak, the buckskin mare, black mane and tail flying, followed close behind, with the bay pausing to give Pescoli the eye before tearing after the others. Only the older gelding, a rangy chestnut, eyed the others as if they were crazy and strolled slowly along the fence line while Nikita bounded over to Santana, who watched the display, then bent down to pat the husky on his furry head. Tall and lean, an irreverent cowboy, he stood with his back to her, not realizing she was watching him.

God, she loved that man.

Even though, often as not, she wanted to personally throttle him.

". . . live with me. We'll make room in the loft," Sarina was saying.

"What?"

"I just said she could come and live with us. We've got room now that . . . well, *you know who* isn't coming back, at least right away."

Sarina had taken to not saying Denny's name as if in so doing she was denying her cheating husband's existence. Pescoli understood. She'd been through the same scenario herself.

"I don't know what Ivy's going to do. First off, she needs to talk to the authorities. Paterno and his partner are coming here to take her statement."

"She's not coming back to San Francisco?"

"Of course she is. Eventually. We just haven't gotten that far. She's pretty shaken up."

"I thought you said she was 'fine.' "

"I meant physically. There's bound to be emotional trauma."

"Oh, right. So much trauma. And for one so young." Sarina's voice broke. "What that poor girl saw . . ."

Pescoli thought about the man who was lying in the hospital now in Albuquerque, the assailant that Ivy had so handily dispensed.

Poor girl? Well, yes, but . . .

"She has a psychiatrist here. Dr. Yates," Sarina said.

Pescoli already knew as much. From Chilcoate. "Good. Look, I won't know what she has planned until she talks to the detectives from San Francisco."

"Can I talk to her?" Sarina asked anxiously.

"Ivy's sleeping now. I'll have her phone when she gets up."

"Okay. You know, she knows me better than anyone. . . ." She drew a breath. "I assume you've let Victor know she's all right."

"Yes."

"And Collette?"

"I thought I'd leave that to you."

"Okay," Sarina said, always the one who wanted to pass along news of any kind, bad or good. "I'm sure Collette will want to talk to Ivy as well."

"Yes," Pescoli said again.

"What about Macon and Seth?" Sarina asked. "Have you talked to either of them?"

Macon and Seth. Heirs to their father's estate. Pescoli hadn't cut them from the suspect list despite their alibis, which were, in her estimation, wobbly at best. "You can call them if you want."

"Oh, good. I do," she said enthusiastically, then sighed. "You know, my boys want them to come and live with us, too."

"Seriously?"

"I know, crazy, huh? Just what I need. Two more. Holy moley."

"They're men, Sarina. Basically on their own. Or they should be."

"These days boys grow up slower," her sister advised, as if she were an authority on all things male. "Look at Den—you know who, forty-two and going on fourteen."

"I guess."

"Isn't Jeremy still living at home?"

"That's different. He has his own apartment over the garage."

A pause as Sarina let Pescoli hear her own excuses.

"When he gets out of school, he'll move on," Pescoli said, irked.

"Of course," Sarina said with forced sincerity. All of a sudden Pescoli remembered why she didn't get along with either of her sisters, not the two remaining and not Brindel, though, with the current situation, the thought made her feel guilty.

"I doubt Macon or Seth, either one, will want to come and live with you, but hey, what do I know? You're right—they're a lot more familiar with you than me. So, go for it." The last thing Sarina, in her current emotional state, needed was the Latham boys/men hanging out, but maybe she needed to learn by experience. "Just be careful, okay? Right now . . .

with everything up in the air as to the homicides, everyone's a suspect."

"Including my nephews."

"Technically they're not, you know. They're Paul's kids. They have a mother."

"Katrina?" Sarina let out a snort. "She's never been a mother of any kind and after the divorce, she let Paul raise them. With Brindel. She was more of a mother to them than Katrina ever was."

"Still—"

"And now you think Macon and Seth killed Brindel and Paul?"

"I didn't say that."

"But you insinuated it. That's the trouble with you, Regan. You're so suspicious. You see the bad in everyone!"

"Oh, come on, Sarina."

"It makes me crazy. The boys, Paul's boys. They're not perfect, but none of us are. Deep down they're good kids."

"If you say so."

"I do!"

Pescoli thought of the Menendez brothers. Convicted of murdering their rich parents. Probably some people might have described them as being deep-down good. Until the truth won out.

"All right. I just wanted to let you know that Ivy's here."

"Well, thank you. And thank God for that. I'm . . . I'm sorry I got a little . . . upset. It's a hard time."

"I know. I'll have Ivy give you a call when she wakes up." She ended the call and kept any other thoughts she had to herself. That was the trouble with advice. Everybody wanted it, solicited it, but for the most part, ignored it when given. Better to keep one's mouth closed.

How much more could she tell?

What should she hold back?

Ivy lay in the spare bedroom in her aunt's home and feigned sleep, though slumber hadn't come.

She was dead tired. Exhausted. But at the same time wired, her brain running in circles.

She wondered if she'd ever sleep again. Or would she forever see her mother's gray face, a bullet hole front and center in her forehead every time she closed her eyes. Surely the image would fade.

How had she ever gotten herself into a mess like this?

Why had she listened?

What desperation had made her agree?

She started to cry and fought it. God, she hadn't cried in years. Maybe since she was around nine, and now she couldn't seem to stop the waterworks.

She could hear her mother: *You've made your bed, Ivy, so now you get to lie in it.*

But the pain wouldn't go away.

And the fear wouldn't stop chasing at her, nipping at her heels. She thought of the man she'd set on fire. Had he died? So now she was a killer? A murderess? Even though he'd robbed her and surely meant to do her harm?

How had things gone so wrong? she wondered miserably.

From its hiding spot under her pillow, she pulled out

her phone and started to call. If she could just talk to *him,* hear his voice . . . find out if he'd . . .

NO! She couldn't think that way. She slid the phone back under the pillow, didn't want to chance losing it.

Even though she had a backup. One that would have to be activated, if she so chose, but at least it was something. Stealing Larissa's phone had just felt right. It was deactivated, of course. No way would her father keep paying for service for a missing phone, but still it was there if she needed it. She could sell it or somehow find some computer nerd to get it up and running. And wasn't that fair? Larissa had Daddy. Now Ivy had the latest iPhone.

Ivy glanced at the bedside clock. Ten AM. She could still carve out a few hours if she could just relax enough, forget for just a little while the images of her mother, Paul, and that horrid man who had attacked her.

She could hear all the activity in the house—the doors opening and closing, dogs barking, coffee being ground, the baby crying. Had she made a huge mistake coming here? Aunt Regan was a damned cop. Sooner or later she might learn the truth.

Not if you keep your mouth shut.

Not if you play it cool.

Not if you don't blow it.

Remember: this is the place you were told to come to.

By more than one person, though her mother's voice was the one she heard again, telling her to go to Aunt Regan if she was ever in trouble. She'd given Ivy that same advice many times over the years, and as a child Ivy had wondered what it meant. "Won't you always be around?" she'd asked her mother once, when Brindel had picked her up from the private elementary school she'd attended.

"Of course I will be," her mother had responded, though she hadn't smiled, just kept her eyes on the road ahead.

"Then why would I have to call Aunt Regan?"

"Oh, honey, I mean if . . . you know, I get waylaid or Daddy and I are on a trip and out of town or—"

"You mean Paul, don't you?" Ivy had declared. "He's *not* my daddy."

"Yes, yes, honey, I know that. Yes, I'm talking about Paul. Of course, but I meant—Oh, for the love of St. Jude, did you see that?" she'd said suddenly. "Holy Jesus, they issue licenses to total morons these days!"

Ivy had looked to see what her mother was talking about, but the only car on the road wasn't anywhere near theirs. Mom had wanted to drop the subject when Ivy started asking too many questions. That was the nature of their relationship, she realized.

Now, lying on the bed, her head pounding, Ivy knew she was in trouble. Big trouble. What could she tell the San Francisco cops? They wouldn't be as understanding as her aunt, and Ivy wasn't certain she could really trust Pescoli. Though her face had remained calm, even passive, Ivy had sensed that her aunt had reservations about her story, and that might develop into a problem.

But if it did, she knew how to solve it.

Her gaze moved to the closed door of her room, which, as it so happened, was right across the hall from the nursery.

Which was perfect.

Chapter 18

Oh. Joy.

Bianca could see her father was waiting for her in the school parking lot, behind the wheel of his idling Mustang convertible, his latest shiny toy. She was already halfway through the door near the gym when she caught sight of him. Why the hell wouldn't he just leave her alone? Setting her jaw, she decided to once again ignore him. Swept up in the tide of other students, she beelined for her Jeep, which was parked several rows away from his vehicle.

She hated him. *Hated* her own father for the way he'd played her, used her, nearly costing her her life itself, all for fame, glory, and of course, money, some of which had gone into the purchase of the new car with its vanity plates that said simply: "Lucky."

Sick jerk.

Of course he would show up here.

Over the noise of car engines revving, laughter, and wheels spinning, kicking up loose gravel, she heard

Annie, one of her friends, call out to her. "Hey, Bianca! Wanna hang out?"

She couldn't deal with Annie now. Or anyone else for that matter. She just lifted a hand and kept trudging through the crisp winter air and across the parking lot where snow, ice, and gravel made walking a bit of a trick. As she neared the Jeep, she pulled her remote key from her pocket and hit the button to unlock the driver's side door, sliding quickly inside.

Before her dad could chase her down.

But as she started the engine and clicked in her seat belt, he appeared outside her window.

And he looked like shit.

He'd always been handsome, had an easy, happy-go-lucky demeanor that attracted women like bees to honey, or moths to a flame, or, more realistically, like flies to raw meat.

But now, not so much. Lines that had once made his sharp features rugged in that Hollywood cowboy way had deepened to age him. Worry and regret had started turning his hair gray, and that easy smile that had turned so many heads? It now seemed forced, his eyes having lost their spark. He was shivering in the cold, his bomber-style jacket losing a battle with the January chill.

He now looked desperate.

Sad.

Afraid.

Well, too bad!

Her heartstrings tugged a little. They had once been close. He had once, she believed, adored her. And pain came from grieving for the daddy she'd lost and how deeply that man she'd trusted had betrayed her. She wouldn't be stupid enough to trust him ever again. She would not, would *not* let him close to her. Not ever again.

He tapped on the window as she twisted on the ignition.

"Go away!" she yelled, her breath fogging in the Jeep's cold interior as the engine turned over.

"Princess, don't do this." He was yelling. Other kids' heads turned.

"Watch me!"

She pressed the window's down button and as the glass lowered, she ground out, "I'm not your princess."

"I just want to talk to you."

"No!"

He leaned closer, his head coming through the window opening. "Don't do this, Bianca. Don't shut me out."

She couldn't believe him. "Are you serious? You expect me to talk to you after what you did? You almost got me killed! You planned to have me kidnapped! And now you're upset that I'm shutting you out? Well, fuck that! I never want to see you again!"

"You don't mean that."

"Yes, I do. I really do. And you may as well know. The minute I turn eighteen? I'm changing my name to Bianca Santana!" With that, she slammed the gearshift into reverse and hit the gas. Lucky just managed to pull himself back before her tires squealed and she shot backward.

"Hey!" A sharp falsetto voice rang out as she nearly clipped Marv Pointer's Toyota RAV4 and the kid himself. A skinny red-haired kid in a hooded ski jacket, he hopped out of her path. “Jesus, Pescoli! Just cuz you’re a cop’s kid doesn’t give you the right to mow me the fuck down!”

“Just get out of my way,” she ordered, ramming her Jeep into drive.

“Bitch!” Marv yelled.

“Hold on!” Lucky again. Well, she wasn’t holding on. No way. Especially not for him. She caught a glimpse of Marv hoisting his middle finger into the air. Fine, let him flip her off all he wanted. She didn’t care.

Fuming, she drove out of town, through the suburbs, along the ridge and into the countryside where snow covered wide fields before the road angled upward into the stands of fir and pine, needled branches bowed with the weight of the snow. Why the hell had her life turned upside down? First her mom got pregnant, which was just gross, then she married Santana, who Bianca had decided was a good guy, though at first she’d resisted her mother dating him. Then Little Tuck had been born. Bianca had been mortified by her mother’s pregnancy, then accepted it, but wasn’t convinced she needed a baby brother when she was told the news her mother was going to have a boy. Not that a baby sister would have been all that much better. But then once Tuck was born, she’d warmed to him . . . a lot. He was just such a happy, sweet little soul. So, yeah, he brought some joy into the house and Santana and her mother were over the moon. And Tuck’s arrival had taken a lot of the attention off her, given Bianca some freedom. So, Tucker Grayson Santana had been a benefit after all. Kind of a surprise, but an okay one.

Her father, however, was another story.

By the time she turned into the long drive, Bianca was calmer. She let her death-grip on the steering wheel relax a little. Her cell phone buzzed, but she ignored it as she was almost home. When she pulled into her parking spot at the side of the garage, she checked the screen and saw that her father had texted her again.

She growled low in her throat, then erased the text and ran up the front walk and into the house, where she heard Tucker's gurgles and another voice, a girl's she didn't recognize, drifting down the stairwell.

Ivy.

"I know," Ivy was saying, a wheedling quality to her voice. "I'll come back. Promise. Just not now. It's not . . . it's not safe, okay . . . ? No. I'm not living with you and Elana. Ever . . . What? . . . C'mon, Dad, you know why. For God's sake, she thinks I stole Larissa's phone. I mean really? When I have my own. Geez, I was just showing the kid some apps, but would Elana believe me? Hell no! She thinks I'm a damned thief! . . . What? . . . Okay, but face it, Dad, she hates me and really, the feeling's mutual. . . . No, I'm not kidding. Of course I mean it! . . . Oh, for crap's sake, just forget it. I'm not coming to live with you. It's *never* happening! Just leave me the hell alone. You're good at that!"

Feet suddenly hit the floor overhead as Ivy, obviously off the phone, stalked out of her room and into the upper hallway. "Yeah, right, old man," she muttered, probably thinking no one could hear her. "In your fucking dreams."

So Ivy had daddy issues, too.

Now, Bianca and her cousin had something in common. Maybe they could have a contest: whose dad was the worst.

Bianca would win. Even if Ivy's dad had abandoned her, Bianca was willing to bet he hadn't set her up in a bizarre kidnapping scheme and almost gotten her killed.

At the reminder of Lucky Pescoli, Bianca scowled. Her bad mood resurfaced. Even the welcoming scents of garlic and sausage emanating from the kitchen didn't help as she walked past the stairway.

Her mother was working at the table, phone to her ear, papers strewn around her. Tucker was on the floor of the family room in his little gym with its dangling mirrors and baby animals. Pescoli looked up. "Hey! How was school?"

"Boring," she said. She decided she wouldn't mention that Luke had been waiting for her. It would only set Mom off. Though she tried to pretend she was cool with her ex, she never had been. She hadn't liked it when he'd married Michelle, who was only a few years older than Bianca, and she didn't like it now that Luke and Michelle were separated. "What smells so good?"

"Santana discovered the crock-pot. He's making . . . something . . . I'm not really sure what."

She dropped her backpack onto a bar stool and walked into the family room to play with the baby, something she *never* thought she'd want to do.

The back door swung open and she glanced up to spy Jeremy stride in. "Hey," he greeted them both. He shook the snow from the dark strands of his hair and it was obvious he hadn't shaved for a few days, his jaw sprinkled with stubble. He was tall, whip-thin, with broad shoulders, deep-set eyes and, Bianca's friends told her, "hot." She didn't see it. He was just such a . . . dweeb for lack of a better word.

"I wondered when you'd show up." Mom looked up from her laptop, closed the screen, then scooted all of her papers into a pile and slid them along with the small computer into her case.

"Been busy." He made a beeline to the crock-pot on the counter. "What've you got?"

"Something Santana's making."

Without a thought Jeremy opened a drawer, found a serving spoon, then after lifting the lid of the pot, dipped out a healthy portion of some red sauce.

"It's not ready."

"Sure it is." He blew on the spoon, then slid it into his mouth.

"Didn't your mother teach you any manners?" Mom demanded, obviously irritated despite her joke. "Don't. Okay. This is Santana's thing."

"He won't mind." Jeremy shoveled another spoonful into his mouth.

"Enough!" Now Mom was mad.

"Geez, you don't have to go all bat-shit crazy on me." Jeremy replaced the lid.

"I'm not going crazy, just pointing out that you could be more polite."

"So what's got into you? Suddenly you're Miss Manners?"

Mom hesitated, her lips tight. Something was going on, but before she could respond, footsteps from the hallway could be heard and a few seconds later Ivy walked into the room. She didn't look the way Bianca remembered her. She was a lot older and her hair was darker than it had been, now lying in short, uneven layers. Her makeup was light, but maybe she hadn't taken the time to apply it, because Bianca was pretty sure she'd worn a lot, the last time she'd seen her.

But the big thing she noticed was that Ivy was wearing a pair of leggings and a long-sleeved T-shirt that belonged to Bianca.

She was about to say something, to protest, when she got a swift knowing look from her mother. The silent message: go with it.

Jeremy's head nearly swiveled off his neck. His eyes narrowed and he visibly straightened. A slow, interested smile crawled from one side of his jaw to the other.

He found her attractive?

Of course.

Jeremy was such a horndog.

"Hi," Ivy said, lifting her fingers, her gaze centered on Jeremy's.

"Jer, this is Ivy, you remember, and, Ivy, you know Jeremy and Bianca."

"Yeah." Still appraising her, Jeremy was nodding enthusiastically.

"Hi," Bianca said. "Sorry . . . sorry about your mom and dad, er, stepdad."

"Thanks."

"You hungry?" Pescoli asked. "Dinner's still a few hours off, but help yourself to anything in the fridge."

Ivy hesitated, but Jeremy, still near the stove, was quick to the rescue. He opened the door of the refrigerator. "Coke? Water? What else do we have?" He held the door open, leaning inside like a big goof. But he came up with a tub of hummus and Mom found some crackers.

Ivy smiled, almost shyly. "Thanks," she said softly as he handed her a bottle of water and practically melted under her gaze.

This was no good, Bianca thought with an inner groan. In fact it was big trouble. Jeremy had always wanted to play the part of the hero. Hell, he'd even gotten an award for saving Mom's life once, and he was always rescuing someone or something. Girls were his favorite, of course. And Ivy, the girl who'd lost her parents so brutally, would be the perfect new mission.

Even though he had a new girlfriend, one no one in the family had met yet. All anyone knew about her was her name. Becca Johnson, someone who had recently moved to Grizzly Falls. He'd seemed all about her as recently as yesterday. But maybe things had changed since Ivy was flirting with him and Jeremy, that jerk-wad, was eating it up, flirting back, laughing a little too loud, his eyes riveted to Ivy's pretty, but sly face.

In fact, from the way Jeremy was hanging on Ivy's every word, it looked like Rebecca Johnson might be history.

And Bianca thought that could be real bad news.

Chapter 19

"This was not supposed to go down this way!" Ronny Stillwell pounded on the steering wheel with one hand and glanced at Boxer in the passenger seat of the stolen truck. "We are so fucked. You know? So fucked!"

Troy noticed the speedometer needle inching over eighty-five. "Just keep it under the speed limit. We'll be fine."

"Fine?" Ronny croaked. "Fine? Are you fucking kidding me? We'll never be fine again!" Instead of slowing he punched it, the truck flying along the highway. They were in Montana now with the dust of California, Nevada, and Idaho in their rearview. They'd entered Montana west of Yellowstone with a change of clothes, tools, weapons, and the contents of the Lathams' safes and were heading north toward Missoula. Theirs wasn't the quickest route to their destination, but Boxer figured it might be the safest, with less traffic and fewer cops. They hoped no law officer would notice their stolen pickup, an eight-year-old Chevy Silverado they'd found in a parking garage in Oakland with a spare key hidden in a wheel well. They'd placed Paul Latham's gun collection, all cased up, into the bed of the truck, then slid into the cab, with Troy at the wheel. In Reno they'd switched drivers and license plates, stealing from a like-modeled truck in a public parking lot near a casino. Once they'd slipped into Montana, they'd done the same thing, so that the pickup they were driving was equipped with Montana plates. The only trouble was that this time, though they'd traded plates of the same make and model truck, this one was navy blue rather than black, so on close inspection, it might not pass muster.

It had taken time to find plates in the different states, extending the length of their road trip, but Boxer figured it was worth it to elude detection. That part had made sense. Dragging Stillwell along and into this whole mess had been a mistake. From the get-go Stillwell had been nervous. Antsy. Worse yet, on this trip, he'd gotten more hyped up rather than calming down the closer they got to their destination. As the desert of Nevada and most of Idaho had given way to grassland and finally the forested hills surrounding the Bitterroot Valley, Boxer had thought Stillwell would chill out. He'd expected Stillwell to breathe a little easier as the miles between them and San Francisco and the murder investigation had lengthened. But no way.

"We were cool," he said now as he eyed the passing countryside. Hills and mountains, stark white in the coming night, cut upward and framed this valley with its meandering, icy river.

"You think we're cool?" Stillwell gripped the steering wheel so hard his knuckles blanched and, in the illumination from the dashboard, his face was a mask of dread, skin pulled tight over his bony features, his eyes ever-shaded from the bill of a baseball cap with a New York Yankees logo.

"I think we should be," Boxer said as the beams of headlights from an oncoming semi washed through the cabin. "As long as we cover each other's ass, the cops can't get us."

"You don't know that."

"Yeah, I do."

"Then we should have stayed, man. Instead of stealing vehicles and running. We should have just stayed."

"Too late now." And it wouldn't have worked. Ronny had already been ready to turn on him back in San Francisco. Troy had seen it in his eyes.

The trouble was that Stillwell was weak. The weakest link in all of this.

"We're fucked."

"You've said it enough."

"I don't know how I got into this in the first place."

"Come on, Ronny, we both know why. A hundred K each? That's why."

Teeth clenched, Stillwell was shaking his head, his lips barely moving. "It's not enough." He was freaking out, sweating, his eyes narrowed on the highway ahead of the truck, his mind spinning.

"Murder," Ronny said, as if talking to himself. He fumbled around the console, found his cigarettes and lighter and, one-handing it, lit up, sucking in a deep drag.

Hopefully the nicotine would calm him down.

"I just don't understand it, man," he said around the cigarette. Darkness had completely fallen and he turned on his high beams.

Boxer didn't ask what. He knew.

"Why is it you're following your dick, no, why're *we* following your dick to bumble-fuck Montana? She's crazy. You know it, right? Didn't you tell me she was in some psych ward in Oregon?"

"That's over."

"She's fuckin' nuts, buddy."

He wanted to argue, but Stillwell did have a point. Not that Boxer would admit it—the truth was that Stillwell wasn't far from the truth. She had him. By the balls.

Stillwell passed a sedan puttering down the highway, a silver-haired woman huddled over the wheel.

"What is it about her that you can't say no? Huh? Even to fuckin' *murder*? I should never have gone along with that." He inhaled deeply, the tip of his Winston glowing red in the interior.

"It'll be okay."

"It won't! Not ever," he said desperately, in a rush of exhaled smoke. He cracked the window a bit. Cold air rushed in. "You didn't have to look at her, man. See her starin' at you when you pulled the fucking trigger." He was shaking now. The cigarette between his lips vibrating, smoke curling out the slit of the open window.

"Think about the money."

"I can't."

Stillwell was cracking up. Losing it. Something would have to be done about that.

Ronny's gaze cut back and forth across the windshield as snow began to fall, heavy flakes reflecting in the truck's headlights. "No woman and no amount of money is worth this."

"Oh, shut up!" Boxer was done with all this moaning and complaining. "It's over. You knew what you were getting into before you pulled the damned trigger. We just have to keep moving. We've got a plan."

"*She's* got a plan and it's probably for shit."

"Have some faith, asshole."

Stillwell snorted, sucked on the cig, then rolled his window farther down and flicked the butt outside, tiny red embers visible into the night. "Faith."

"We just have to keep moving."

"And 'following orders' from that nut job."

Boxer sent him a hard look. "We don't have much of a choice now. If you wanted out, you should have said something before you iced Brindel Latham."

"Don't say her name! I don't want to think about it!" He was yelling now, the speedometer stretching toward ninety.

"Slow the fuck down! The last thing we need is to be pulled over by the cops!"

Instantly Stillwell let up on the gas and closed the window. "Speed limit's higher here than in California."

"Keep it under eighty for Christ's sake! It's dark as shit. You can't see any cop hiding and waiting."

"Where?" At this point the road was arrow straight, cutting through snow-covered fields and farmland.

"That's just it, you don't know where."

Frowning, Ronny let out a sharp breath. The pickup slowed to seventy-five, keeping pace with a van a hundred yards ahead.

That was better. But Stillwell was still obviously shaken, close to cracking up. Boxer hated to think it, but Ronny was a liability.

A major liability.

Sooner or later, he'd have to be dealt with.

The man in the hospital bed looked as near death as just about anyone Tanaka had seen. Wynn Ellis's face was seared, red, and oily looking, so puffy that his eyes were the barest of slits, the top of his head, where bandages didn't hide it, was charred skin. He lay in the burn unit of the medical center in Albuquerque hooked to an IV with monitors surrounding him. He didn't move his head, but his eyes followed Tanaka and Paterno as they stood near enough to him to be heard.

"Is this the woman who attacked you?" Tanaka asked, showing him a picture of Ivy Wilde.

His cracked lips moved slightly. "Maybe," was his raspy whisper.

Oh, so he was going to be cute and play coy with her. She didn't have time for games and sure as hell wasn't going to play any. "But you're not sure?"

"Looked different. But her maybe."

"What about this one?" She held up photo number two, an unaltered picture, one she'd had Photoshopped showing Ivy with choppy darker hair and more make-up, as this man had originally described to the officer on the scene when they'd found him on the street, his hair ablaze.

"Yeah, it's her."

Ellis's eyes moved as he turned his attention from the altered photo to the original picture of Ivy. "That one. The girl with the long blond hair. I saw her at the motel."

"The Sunset Valley Inn?"

"Yeah," he said slowly. "But I never seen her come out. The other girl did. The fat one with the weird haircut. She jumped me."

"This girl," Tanaka said, holding up the doctored photo of Ivy.

"Yeah."

"She's the woman who attacked you in the doorway of a pawnshop?"

He hesitated, as if he sensed a trap but couldn't quite see it coming. "Maybe."

"The pawnshop only a couple of blocks away from the bus station."

Ellis didn't reply. In her peripheral vision she saw Paterno shift, fold his arms over his chest, the corner of his mouth lifting slightly. She pressed, "How would you know who went in and out of the motel, the Sunset Valley Inn, if you were attacked by the bus station?"

"It was earlier. That's when I seen her go inside."

That much was probably true and they'd already confirmed with the clerk on duty at the time that a woman matching Ivy Wilde's description had, indeed, rented a room for one night and been gone early the next morning.

"So you were following her?" Paterno asked, and Tanaka saw a look of panic flare in the bandaged man's eyes.

"No."

Tanaka said, "I guess it's a good thing that the gas station across the street from the Sunset Valley Inn and Good and Plenty Pawnshop and the bus station all have exterior cameras. You know, to confirm your story."

Beneath the bandages and seared skin, Ellis actually lost color. "I ain't sayin' anything else. I know my rights. I want a lawyer."

"You've got a record," Paterno reminded him, stepping closer.

"I said I want a lawyer. I ain't sayin' one more word."

That was their cue to leave. "You got it, Wynn," Tanaka said, and they headed out, past the guard stationed at the door. "And, I'm guessing you'll probably need an attorney, so make sure you get a good one. You're going to need it."

They left the room, a guard posted at the door, and made their way out of the hospital. Tonight they had a few more loose ends to tie up, double-checking camera footage, interviewing a store clerk and the motel clerk, then they'd wrap it up for the night and hop a plane in the morning. Destination: Missoula, Montana. They would rent a car and drive to Grizzly Falls to meet Ivy Wilde face to face.

Tanaka could hardly wait.

Brindel's daughter was the key to this entire case; Tanaka could feel it in her bones. She'd gone through the obvious suspects, interviewing Paul Latham's ex-girlfriends, his old business partners, his ex-wife, anyone who might have wanted him dead. She'd checked into Brindel Latham's past as well and come up dry. Though she hadn't cut Macon and Seth Latham off her list of suspects, and of course the missing Troy Boxer and Ronny Stillwell, the one person who might be able to point them in the right direction was Ivy Wilde,

Brindel Latham's daughter, who had been at the scene and taken off.

But there was a stumbling block squarely in her path.

She'd have to confront Regan Pescoli again. The person to whom Ivy Wilde had run, albeit in a circuitous path, and almost killing Wynn Ellis in the process.

Yeah, she was looking forward to interviewing Ivy. But dealing with Detective/Auntie Regan Pescoli was something Tanaka could definitely do without.

Chapter 20

Brooding in her room, Bianca tried to force herself out of her bad mood. Nothing was working. She'd tried listening to music, texting with her friends, playing video games, but she was still bugged. She walked to the window seat and stared through the panes to the lake. She usually liked the view, but today, with the gray clouds lying low against the treetops on the far shore, she found no peace, no tranquility.

The Ivy thing bugged Bianca.

But she had to put up with her cousin. Like it or not.

After all, Ivy had just lost her family, so Bianca needed to cut her some slack, but come *on!* Ivy just seemed so fake and she was really doing a number on Jeremy. And then she'd even given attention to Little Tucker and that seemed weird, too. And made Bianca uncomfortable. Not to mention that Ivy seemed to be helping herself to all of Bianca's things, her clothes, her brush, her hair products, everything. It burned Bianca. Even if the girl had just lost her family.

At that thought Bianca frowned and told herself she was being childish and petty and totally without empathy.

Besides, there was a chance Bianca was being too hard on her because her own life seemed to be going to crap. Her father—ugh—she didn't even like thinking of Luke Pescoli as her father, so let's rethink that. Lucky had wounded her and she'd never forgive him, so there was that. His wife, Michelle, whom Bianca had heretofore adored as she was so funny, smart, and cute, now seemed like a fraud. Bianca was pretty sure Lucky and Michelle were going to divorce.

Already, it seemed Michelle had moved on. Her interest in her stepkids had waned along with her interest in being married to their father. It seemed Mom had been right about the woman Pescoli had referred to as a "Barbie Doll" all along.

She ran a finger along the glass and sighed, then crossed the room and flopped onto her bed. Even the pink paint on her walls bothered her. Maybe she should repaint. Black sounded good, or a dark charcoal gray.

No one understood her.

They tried.

And they failed.

School was another nightmare. Her senior year was a bust. She didn't have a boyfriend, which was okay, but could admit she liked being part of a couple, if only to herself. Then there were her friends. They'd seemed to drift away after Bianca had been involved in the kidnapping and subsequent death of one of her abductors at her hand. Yeah, she'd had a little fame, or infamy, after the horror of last summer, but over the school year, her friends had found excuses to avoid her.

Which wasn't exactly their fault.

Bianca had changed.

From the inside out.

You didn't take a life, even in self-defense, and return to the way you had been before ramming a weapon into another person's body. Suddenly, boy crushes, and fashion, the next party, and the latest reality series on TV didn't seem all that important.

All the shrink sessions in the world couldn't change the past or how profoundly it had affected you.

So, yeah, it wasn't a surprise that for the first time in her life, Bianca felt completely and utterly alone.

She had her family, so that was something.

A lot more than Ivy has, her ever-guilty conscience reminded her.

And Mom was trying her best to "connect." That was the word she used. So sometimes connect meant be a mom, other times be a friend, other times it meant Mom thought she had the right to look at her text messages or check whatever she was doing on the computer, always on the sly, but Bianca knew. But the bright spot was Tucker. He was a charmer with his dimpled, toothless smile.

"What a dork," she said, but grinned at the thought of him.

But the rest of her life was garbage.

She rolled off the bed and found her jacket. Though it was getting dark, she'd go riding. That always helped her get out of her lousy mood.

Pulling on warmer socks and boots, she slid into her jacket and headed downstairs, only to find Jeremy and Ivy, laughing and talking, playing with the baby as Mom was on the deck, in the cold, bundled up, cell phone to her ear. Cisco was dancing on the snowy boards beside her and as Pescoli looked up, Bianca waved. Her mother shook her head and slid open the slider. "Where are you going?"

"Riding."

"It's freezing."

"You're outside on the phone." And why was that? Because she didn't want anyone to hear the conversation.

"It's dark."

"It's a full moon and snow everywhere. Almost like day. I'll be back soon." She saw the protest forming on her mother's lips and held up a hand. "Seriously, Mom. I promise. And I'll take Sturgis."

"Half an hour."

"Sure," she lied. Didn't care. She just needed to get out. Away from . . . everything, but especially Jeremy and Ivy. The sight of them together soured her stomach a little and she wondered if she were jealous. It had been a long time since she'd seen a boy look at her the way Jeremy was staring at Ivy.

But they were first cousins, right, so . . . She gave an inward shudder, found her gloves in the pocket of her jacket, and with a sharp whistle to Sturgis, who was curled in a ball on his bed by the fire, said, "Come on, boy. Let's go."

The black lab pushed himself to his feet and stretched, yawning, then with his tail wagging, followed her outside. Mom hadn't lied; twilight was long past descending and it was cold enough that her breath fogged. The dog didn't seem to mind and trotted after her to the stable. She'd adopted Sturgis, who had come to live here when his owner, Dan Grayson, the sheriff who had been her mother's boss, had been killed a while back. The big dog had settled in and seemed happy, but, Bianca guessed, he missed the tall, even-tempered man who had raised him.

"Things change, life goes on," Bianca said to him as she followed a path through the snow that Santana had broken earlier, and wondered at her own philosophical look at the world. That was new. For her. Her younger self had never pondered anything more weighty than the most popular shade of lip gloss.

What a self-involved twit she'd been.

"Come on." She unlatched the door and as she stepped into the stable, the scents of oiled leather, straw, horses, and a whiff of urine hit her nostrils. Obviously Jeremy, taken with Ivy, hadn't tended to mucking out the stalls. That wouldn't fly. Part of Jeremy's deal was, that for free rent, he helped out around the small ranch, and Santana held him to cleaning the stables, helping mend fences, feeding the stock, oiling the machinery, and whatever else needed to be done to keep things running. Jeremy, to his credit, had stepped up and handled whatever task had been shoved his way.

But then, Ivy Wilde hadn't been around to distract him.

"Get over it," she told herself, and saw her favorite horse, a black gelding with a crooked blaze running down his nose. Sinbad was small and feisty, a foal who'd nearly not made it as he'd been born early and struggled for the first few months. Now a three-year-old, his ebony coat was glossy, his eyes bright with intelligence, his head lifting over the edge of the stall as Bianca approached.

"How about a quick one?" Bianca asked, and petted

Sinbad's silky nose. He snorted and tossed his head. "Sounds good, eh? Let's do it." Within minutes she'd saddled and bridled Sinbad and was leading him outside, the dog, as ever, a few steps behind.

Once in the fields, she swung into the saddle and then took off, across the unbroken snow and riding the perimeter of the lake. The sky was beginning to clear with the night, clouds high overhead, the moon rising over the frozen landscape. The trees were thin along the shoreline, making the cattle trail easy to follow. Bianca let the quietude of the coming night settle over her, the tranquility of the wintery forest sink into her bones. Why was she so upset about Ivy? She was just here a little while, only until she could get her life back together and find a permanent place to stay, either with her father and his family or one of her other relatives, like Sarina or maybe Collette. No way would she want to camp out long in Montana as she barely knew "Aunt Regan" anyway. And Mom's life was full. She was talking about going back to work full time at the sheriff's department, if she could find someone she trusted to care for Tucker.

Ivy, like Bianca, should be planning for the coming year, going off to college. Maybe university wasn't in the cards for Ivy, especially now. Her life had really turned upside down and inside out.

As they passed beneath a pine tree, Bianca ducked her head to avoid a low-hanging branch. The needles brushed her hat and clumps of snow fell from the limb, startling Sinbad. He tried to bolt, but Bianca reined him in. "It's okay," she said, though as the words crossed her lips, she wondered. Would anything ever be okay again? Her eyes were focused on the snowy trail between Sinbad's ears. A snowshoe hare suddenly appeared and bounded into the brush and Sturgis gave chase. "Sturgis, no! Come," she yelled from the saddle, but the dog took off in a flurry of white powder. "Great." She let the horse continue on the path, her thoughts drifting as deep as the snow, and when she finally focused again, she saw the old ranch house where Brady Long had once lived. Nestled in the trees, the huge cedar and glass home stood empty, had been for years, and yet . . . was there a light in one of the windows? She clucked to the gelding, urging Sinbad into a trot so she could have a different view of the house, and sure enough, between the branches and trunks of the surrounding trees she spied a glow from within the structure, a soft light emanating from under the eaves, barely visible behind drawn shades.

No one should be there, right? Isn't that what Santana had said? The place was completely empty, or at least devoid of life other than rodents, insects, and birds that may have nested in the abandoned property. No one had lived here for years. It was Santana's responsibility to keep the place up.

A little niggle of apprehension skittered along the back of her neck, like a spider running across her skin. Her flesh prickled in warning, but she rode closer still, skirting the house and surveying the windows. There it was again. Another bit of lamplight through a window over the back porch. The rest of the building was dark as death.

She pulled back on the reins.

Paused and listened.

Heard the horse's breathing and in the distance a dog's deep bark.

Sturgis.

God, she hoped he hadn't caught the hare.

She strained to listen. Did she hear the almost indistinct sound of music? Or was that all in her mind?

She shouldn't go closer.

She should go home.

Tell Santana.

But . . .

Again she clucked softly to Sinbad, and the horse moved forward, then stopped suddenly and snorted, backing up.

"Come on." She leaned forward.

Was that music? Really? Or was she imagining it?

Still twenty yards away, in the cover of the surrounding trees, she dismounted and tied the reins of the bridle to a tree, then hesitated, listening hard. The snow lay in soft folds all the way to the house. No trail. No tire tracks near the closed door of the garage or on the long lane, at least none created recently.

All her senses told her to go home.

But her curiosity kept her going, so she broke her own path and as quietly as possible walked to the house, to first a darkened window and then to the one where she thought she'd seen light. The blinds or curtains were drawn, but around the edges she could see a slit of lamplight. She leaned forward, peering in, all her muscles tense. Wasn't this the scene in the movies where the bloody killer tore open the blinds and swung his ax through the window, cleaving the unsuspecting, stupid teen in two?

Heart pounding, ears straining, she leaned close enough that her breath was visible on the glass. Was there someone . . . a dark figure . . . inching toward her? Holy shit! Someone was inside! She started backing up, nearly tripping in the process.

The blinds snapped up and the dark figure of a man was backlit by a single lamp.

She turned as he tapped hard against the glass.

She flashed back. To the abduction. To the feeling of powerlessness. To knowing her life was about to end.

Running toward her horse, she expected to hear the sound of shattering glass, or the sharp report of a rifle. Any second she could be shot. Why had she been so stupid?

A door creaked open near the garage on the other side of a wide car port.

This was it! She braced herself for the shot. The pain. God, would she die now? After she'd killed the last man who'd attacked her? Frantic, she reached for Sinbad, stripping the reins from the branch, fir needles, cones, and snow falling.

"Bianca!"

Her name rumbled across the icy grounds and she froze.

"What the hell are you doing here?"

Santana?

She whirled to see her stepfather marching toward her. His expression was grim, dark eyes beneath the rim of his hat dead serious.

"I was just out riding."

"Over here?"

"Yeah."

"Why?"

"No reason," she said. "I just needed to get out of the house. I was just riding and thinking and . . ."

His expression softened a bit.

"What're you doing here?" she asked him.

"Same as you. I was riding. Exercising Benson. I saw the light and checked with the housekeeper who lives in the guest house." He pointed a gloved finger toward the back of the main house and she saw a spur off the lane where there was a widening in a copse of pines. "She said she must've left on a lamp when she cleaned yesterday. I double-checked."

She swept her gaze over the snowy terrain. "But there are no tracks."

"I'm careful, didn't want to disturb anything or give myself away, just in case the housekeeper was wrong and someone was holed up in there. I wanted to catch him in the act."

"And Benson is where?"

"A quarter of a mile up the ridge." He hitched his chin toward the surrounding hills to the west.

She was calming down. "So what did you find?"

"Nothing. Everything clean as a whistle. Ellen must've just left the lamp in the den lit."

It all made sense, she supposed. Santana didn't seem worried at all. And it was his job to take care of the place, so she'd let her imagination run wild.

"Come on, let's go home. My guess is your mom is going to be worried about you."

"What else is new? It's because of her job, you know. Because she's a cop."

"And because you've been in danger before."

Their gazes locked and she remembered last summer when she'd been kidnapped. Santana was remembering as well.

"She freaks out." But she climbed into the saddle and looked down at him.

"So do I."

"Not so much."

"Enough," he admitted. "I worry enough." He was thoughtful for a second, then looked up at her and pushed the rim of his Stetson back from his forehead to see her better in the darkness. "Race you back to the house?"

"You'll lose," she said. "My horse is right here. And I'm already on it. You said yours was up on the ridge." She pointed to the spot he'd mentioned and felt the bite of January against the back of her neck as the wind kicked up.

"Five bucks says I'll win anyway."

Really? He seemed sincere. "No way."

"Way." His grin was a slash of white. "Unless you just admit defeat now."

He knew she couldn't resist a dare. "Okay," she said, picking up the reins and whistling for Sturgis. "You're on!" With that, she took off, leaning forward and sending Sinbad into a quick trot and then a lope. From the corner of her eye she spied Sturgis, no rabbit, thank God, but Nikita was matching him stride for stride as they all ran along the path toward the lake.

She knew she'd beat Santana back to the house, but it wasn't until she was halfway home that she wondered if he'd made the bet to get rid of her, that something was going on at the Long house that he didn't want her to know about. Was that even possible?

Sinbad broke from the trees, galloping along the shore of the lake again. The wind ripped at her stocking cap, so she grabbed it with one hand and let her hair stream behind her as she felt the horse's strides lengthen, saw his neck stretch with each stride. The air was cold on her face and drawn into her lungs, but she felt better, freer than she had in weeks, and when their own house came into view, she was a little disappointed that the ride was over. She brought the gelding down to a trot, then walked him, letting him cool down internally. As cold as it was outside, he'd still heated with the run. Santana was nowhere in sight and, even after she'd seen to Sinbad, taking off the saddle and bridle and making certain he had water and feed, her stepfather had failed to return.

"I think we were snookered," she told the horse, but didn't care. The exhilarating ride and scare at the Long house had brought her back to center, at least for now. And really, she could always use an extra five bucks. Her father had always quoted a line from an old movie. *The Color of Money*. One of Lucky's favorites. The quote was: "Money won is twice as sweet as money earned." One of the characters, Fast Eddie, had said the line, and Luke Pescoli had attempted to live his life by that premise. It hadn't worked out all that well for him, she thought, then pushed Lucky Pescoli out of her mind.

Hopefully forever.

Chapter 21

At the dinner table, Pescoli pointed at her husband with her fork. "If this horse-training thing for you doesn't work out, Santana, maybe you could become a chef." His meal of *pasta e fagioli,* compliments of the slow-cooker, bread from the local bakery, and a tossed salad, had been spectacular.

No one seated with her seemed to find her joke funny. Jeremy and Ivy, sitting next to each other, were caught in their own conversation.

Bianca, though she'd taken one of the horses out for a ride and that usually improved her mood, seemed lost in her own thoughts, and they didn't appear happy ones. Even Santana kept one eye on the muted television where the news was playing throughout the meal.

So much for family togetherness.

Pescoli glanced at the baby, who, usually active at dinnertime, had passed out in his swing and was still rocking rhythmically to and fro, eyes closed, hair falling over his forehead.

"Well, that was delish. Thanks, Santana." She motioned around the table for her kids to chime in, but it didn't happen. Only the dogs appeared to appreciate what had been served as they'd each staked out a spot near the table in hopes that someone might drop a morsel.

She pushed her chair back and said, "Jeremy, you clear tonight and take out the garbage. Bianca, you're on dish duty."

No one argued, at least until Bianca opened the dishwasher and said something under her breath.

"What?" Pescoli asked, but could guess.

"It's full." She skewered her brother with a glare meant to cut through granite. "You were supposed to unload it."

"Hey, I'm busy," he argued, "and I don't really live here."

"You do too. The garage is like attached. And the stables need to be cleaned."

"Who put you in charge?"

"She's right," Pescoli said, "but he's right, too. The stable and barn and outside stuff is between Santana and Jer."

Ivy said, "I can do it. Just tell me where to put things. It was my job, too, at home. . . ." Her voice had trailed off and she swallowed hard.

"Nah. It's okay." Jeremy placed an arm around her and she nestled her head into the hollow of his shoulder.

"Oh, brother." Bianca turned on the water in the sink and reached for the sponge.

"You've got Tucker?" Pescoli asked her husband, and Santana lifted a hand in response, but he'd already gravitated to the family room and the TV, which, for some reason tonight, he found more fascinating than usual. "Don't forget."

"I won't." He didn't bother glancing at Tuck, but Pescoli did and saw he was still sleeping in the swing. Rocking back and forth. *Tick, tick, tick.*

Good enough. Pescoli left, letting them sort it out while she ran to the store for essentials: diapers, formula, and a six-pack of Diet Coke, her newfound vice, or refound, as she'd spent years drinking the soda. She'd given it up because of the caffeine, but now, she could indulge. And as for all those studies saying it was bad for you? Tough. "Everything in moderation," she told herself, eyeing the cigarette display at the check stand with a little tug. She'd given up smoking years before, but every now and then, especially when a case became difficult, she'd break down and smoke a filter tip from the emergency pack she kept in her glove box. She'd thrown out the few crumpled cigarettes left in her last pack when she'd found out she was pregnant, and though the urge caught up with her once in a while, she wasn't about to go down that slippery slope again.

At least she hoped not.

As she drove home her cell phone chimed and she saw Paterno's number on the screen. She clicked into the Bluetooth and listened as he brought her up to speed with the case. He wrapped up about the time she pulled into the drive. She grabbed the two bags of groceries and carried them into the house where she was met by the exhilaration and cacophony of the dogs. The rooms were dim, the only illumination in the family room provided by the fire and television. Jeremy and Ivy were on the couch, almost snuggling, a blanket over them, watching some old romantic comedy, a movie from the nineties with Hugh Grant flickering on the television.

Really?

She'd never known Jeremy to watch what he'd referred to as a "chick flick" since he was around twelve. Her radar clicked on. Hmm . . .

"Hey," she said, setting the groceries on the counter.

Jeremy looked over his shoulder. "Get any Red Bull?"

"That's on you," Pescoli said.

Ivy just smiled, cuddled up as she was to Jeremy. Didn't she have a boyfriend? A new guy in the picture? Hadn't Troy Boxer said as much? So what was she doing with Jeremy?

Pescoli was getting a bad feeling about the dynamics between the two. Though Pescoli's niece had been here a very short while, Jeremy, with his raging hormones and need to be a savior, seemed already smitten with his cousin. It was wrong on so many levels. Yes, undoubtedly Ivy needed emotional support and a shoulder to lean on, but Pescoli was damned sure Jeremy didn't need to provide either. Or at least not to the extent to which he seemed committed.

Maybe the infatuation would pass.

She sure as hell hoped so.

Looking around, she noticed the baby, no longer in his swing, was already in his pajamas and seated in his little baby carrier.

Ivy followed Pescoli's gaze. "I changed him," she said brightly, then at a sudden thought, became more serious. "But I didn't bathe him. Is that okay?"

"Sure. Thank you." Pescoli hadn't expected her niece to do anything.

"I was a babysitter for the kids down the street last summer. None of them were as little as Tucker, but one was still in diapers, so it doesn't gross me out or anything." She offered up a smile just as her phone chirped. She pulled it from beneath the blanket and glanced at the screen. Her expression darkened and she rolled her eyes. "My brother," she said to Jeremy, then, "At least he thinks he's my brother, but we're not even related."

"Who?" Jeremy had asked.

"Macon. You remember him? Paul's son?"

Jeremy looked blank and shook his head.

"He's soooo bossy. Thinks he can tell me what to do. Always in my face." Another dramatic roll of her eyes. She ignored the text.

So where was the grief? Where was the worry? What was with all this flirting?

Pescoli left the groceries on the counter and walked over to pick up Little Tucker. "Hey, little man," she said, and blew across his face, which made him giggle and kick. "Yeah, I missed you, too."

"He's a good baby," Ivy said just as Bianca, in pj bottoms and a T-shirt, came downstairs to shoot her a look.

"Hey, did you take my flat iron?"

"Oh," Ivy said, her eyes rounding. "Yeah, I borrowed it. Sorry. It's in my room."

Bianca's eyebrows quirked a little, but she didn't totally freak out. "Okay, but just, if you use something? Put it back."

Ivy slid a glance at Jeremy as if she expected him to

come to her defense, and like a puppet on a string, he did.

"Chill out," he advised his sister.

"I'm not wrong. If she uses something, or wears something, she should ask. And put it back. Clean."

Ivy sighed. "I'm sorry. I guess I'm kinda, you know, overwhelmed. But yeah, I'll ask next time. For sure. It's just that I have nothing." And then the tears began to flow again. Jeremy comforted her.

Bianca sent her mother an I-can't-believe-this-is-happening look, then filled the empty water bottle she was carrying and headed back upstairs.

"Where's Santana?" Pescoli asked.

"Don't know," Jeremy said. "He left a little after you did and said he'd be back. That was . . . fifteen minutes ago?" He glanced at Ivy as if she could confirm.

"Yeah. About that."

"So what does Macon want?" Pescoli asked, collecting Tucker and carrying him to the counter and the fresh tin of formula she'd picked up.

"I don't know. Probably to tell me what to do. He thinks I should go back to San Francisco and talk to the police and move in with Aunt Sarina." At that thought, her lips twisted downward. "With Ryan and Zach?" She shook her head. "Shoot me now." And then she realized what she'd said. "Oh . . . oh . . . God." This time when she fell apart it seemed genuine. "I didn't mean to . . . I mean . . ."

"Shh." Jeremy comforted her and pressed a kiss to her temple.

That seemed a little too intimate, even for the situation.

"It'll get better," he promised, which he had no business doing.

The girl seemed to calm, so Pescoli said, "I'm going to put the baby down, but then, Ivy, I think we'd better talk."

"You want to talk about what happened again?" she asked, and her face twisted into a mask of disbelief.

"I just want to prepare you a bit for tomorrow. Detective Paterno called. He and his partner with San Francisco PD will be here in the morning, probably sometime after ten."

"They're coming *here*?" She appeared to shrivel at the thought. "Do . . . Do I need an attorney or something?"

That stopped Pescoli cold. "I don't know. Do you?"

"If you mean did I do something wrong, then no! But . . . on TV. You know those cop shows, they always get attorneys before they talk."

"The suspects."

"Am I a suspect?" Horror rounded her eyes.

"Mom!" Jeremy shot his mother a harsh glare, reminding her of the tragedy Ivy was living, the gruesome scene she'd gone home to. "Come on. Lay off. Give her a damned break."

"I'm just letting her know."

Then, because she knew it would be on the news and maybe that's what Santana was so keen on, she added, "I think I should tell you that Troy Boxer is missing."

"Troy?" Ivy whispered, disbelief evident.

"He and a roommate of his. Ronny Stillwell."

She blinked. "Why?"

"Unknown."

"What happened?" Her voice was a squeak and Jeremy's grip on her shoulder tightened.

"That's what the police are trying to find out. I talked to the detectives on the case and Detective Paterno told me that both men are missing."

"But I—I don't understand. Why are the police coming here?" She made a circular motion with her hand, to include everything in the house and probably the entire county. "Are they looking for Troy and Ronny?"

"No, they're coming to talk to you." *They're following your trail. . . .*

Pescoli thought about what else Paterno had told her. That the man in Albuquerque who had been set on fire had identified Ivy as the person who'd tried to make him into a human torch.

She decided she'd let the SFPD handle that one. They needed to see Ivy's reaction first hand.

Despite the fact that Pescoli was the girl's aunt and she felt a tremendous amount of empathy for Ivy and the horror she'd so recently lived through, Pescoli sensed Ivy was holding back. She knew something she wasn't telling. And two people were dead. No matter how much or how little Ivy Wilde was involved in her parents' deaths, the truth had to be uncovered.

Pescoli was, after all, first and foremost a cop.

Chapter 22

It had to be done, Troy thought as the pickup bounced down an abandoned logging road.

Troy knew it and she did, too.

In fact, she'd given the order.

He glanced at his "friend" who was still at the wheel, squinting through the windshield, fingers curled over the steering wheel in a death grip.

Ronny Stillwell had to go.

He wasn't even hiding his second thoughts any longer. No, Ronny-Boy was already planning ahead, ready to turn himself in and work a deal with the cops. He'd been jabbering about it for the last hour.

"What kind of deal do you think you can get?" Boxer asked him again. "We both pulled the triggers, and it was premeditated. No question about it. So, I don't know about you, but I'd rather spend the rest of my life in Mexico or Canada or Costa Rica, or any other place you can name, with a hundred grand in my pocket than sitting in a six-by-eight jail cell with a four-hundred pound roommate."

"Jesus, you make it sound like we don't have any choice," he whined.

"We don't. Once we pulled those triggers, our options became limited. Okay? Very limited. You know that." He couldn't believe Stillwell was so stupid, so weak. Frowning, Troy added, "Just drive . . . It's only a little farther and then we get our money and take off." Why was the guy being such a moron? He added, "You know the plan, take Ninety-Three due north through Kalispell and Whitefish, cross into Canada with our fake IDs and we're in like Flynn. We'll be in Calgary in eight, maybe nine hours. Now, what's wrong with that?"

"A million things could go wrong. We could have trouble at the border. The cops could figure out our car switching. Someone might have ID-ed us on some camera we went by—like at the convenience store where we bought gas or when we went through the drive-thru back in Idaho. Hell, *she* could double-cross us. I wouldn't put it past that psycho-bitch."

"Nah! Don't worry about that," Troy snapped. Though Ronny was making some legit points.

"She's mental, man."

Boxer forced a smile. "Hey, aren't we all a little crazy? To pull off what we did?"

"A little nuts is different from fuckin' crazy, the kind that puts you in the psycho ward." A tic had developed near his eye. Boxer watched it pulse in the weird illumination cast by the dash lights.

"We knew it was risky going in."

"Risky? It was damned near suicidal, and y'know, the jury's still out on that one."

Boxer didn't like talk about juries or psych wards or getting caught. They were so close. So damned close. He glanced out the side window where branches were scraping the sides of the pickup. At least he wouldn't have to hear Stillwell's bitching and moaning and worrying aloud much longer. He drew a little line in the condensation on the glass and then let his hand drop down to his side, to the spot between the door and the passenger seat where his pistol was waiting. "Come on, bro, relax," he suggested in the most calming voice he could find. "We're almost home. Hey. Over there." He pointed with his left hand. "There's the turnout. Just like she said. See."

The beams of the headlights showed a gap in what had once been a fence, and a rusted gate had been left open, yawning wide. A single set of tire tracks had crossed into the denser brush beyond.

Ronny, bless him, turned the wheel, the pickup shimmying a bit as the tires slid, and they drove through the open space, following the tracks. Like a lamb to the slaughter.

"I just don't get why we had to meet up here," Ronny said, squinting as he guided the truck through the trees, thick stands of fir and pine, branches laden with ice and snow. "I mean we passed by a dozen cheap motels on our way here. What was wrong with the Shilo or Motel 6? Or Double Tree?"

"Cameras, man. That's what's wrong. And people at the front desk, or guests or maids. Someone might recognize us. With the gear we've got in the back of the truck, we might look a little suspicious. Those aren't golf clubs in those bags and it ain't the weather to hit the links."

"Lots of guys bring guns. Hunting rifles. No big deal." But he was chewing on his lip, thinking it over as he studied the ruts leading deeper into the woods.

"But why risk it? Trust me. This chick knows what she's doing. She's careful. Y'know? Takin' no chances that we'll be spotted. The police in San Francisco have to be looking for us."

"That's far away."

"My point exactly. No reason to fuck up now. Especially if there's a BOLO out for us. Right now, we're ahead of the game, on a roll."

Or at least I am. You, Ronny, well, sadly, that's another story.

The pickup bounced along the ruts of packed snow and Boxer relaxed against the passenger door, seeming aloof when inside he was strung tight as a bowstring, every muscle tense, electricity pulsing through his nerves. He had to ice Ronny quickly. Get it over with. He felt his jaw knot with tension and forced it to relax, to appear as calm as a clear water lake while inside he was churning. But he couldn't tip his hand. Stillwell was already antsy, ready to run. It was Boxer's job to keep him loose and sane.

At least for a few more minutes.

"What the fuck?" Ronny said as they pulled into a small clearing behind an aging Jeep Wrangler that was idling, exhaust blowing from its tailpipe. As the Silverado's beams washed over the back of the dirty rig, the shadowy outline of the driver was visible behind the wheel.

"I told you she'd be here."

"But what is this place?" Stillwell looked nervously around the isolated terrain.

"Hunting spot, I think." Boxer was pulling on his gloves. "She said there's a cabin not far and a duck blind."

"Well, it's in the middle of fuckin' nowhere."

"That's the idea."

"It still gives me the willies."

It was a little eerie, the white landscape with its shadows where moon glow couldn't reach, tall trees rising like sentinels, the undergrowth covered in frigid powder. "Let's finish up and get the hell out. Cut the lights, will ya? No reason to attract any attention," Troy advised.

"Right." Ronny was already opening the truck's door, wasn't bothering to turn off the engine, only paused to switch off the headlights and grab his pack of smokes from the console as he stepped outside. But he wasn't as quick as Boxer, who had slipped his pistol from the floor before opening his door and now held it in his right hand, away from Stillwell's vision as he approached. Together they broke a path through ankle deep snow, their boots crunching into an icy layer as they made their way to the driver's side of the Jeep.

She powered down the window. "About time." Her face was as pale as the surrounding landscape. Ashen. White.

"We had to make sure we weren't being followed," Boxer said.

Stillwell was glancing all around, as if he expected to see a SWAT team, weapons drawn, leap from behind the trunks of the surrounding trees. As if he expected a setup.

Not as dumb as he looked.

"You got our money?" Stillwell asked, his gaze returning to the woman.

"All right here." She held up a black bag that had been resting on the passenger seat. "Load the gear in back." Up the window went.

Boxer slipped his gun into the pocket, then helped Ronny haul the heavy cases of weaponry, Paul Latham's collection of pistols, knives, and larger guns that had been disassembled and neatly packed in the cases they'd found in that mother of a gun closet the doc had kept. Like a damned museum for his arsenal. The weapons displayed in cases with lights as if they were pieces of fucking art.

Paul Latham . . . *Doctor* Paul Latham had been one weird dude.

"Give a hand, will ya?" Ronny grunted, and Boxer realized he'd been daydreaming. Getting ahead of himself. Here in the damned forest. When there were still serious last details to wrap up. He hauled the last of the gun cases from the truck and crammed them into the cargo space of the Wrangler.

So they could get paid.

Finally.

And his share had just grown over the past few hours.

The deal they had struck was that she would take care of the stolen items, pawn them, private sale the guns, whatever. And they would get their hundred thousand each for the murders and the robbery. Boxer would even get a little bonus. Twenty-five grand. For taking care of Ronny. And, of course, Stillwell's share. All in all, he was going to leave this forest a rich man tonight and Canada was only a few hours north.

He grinned despite the fact that it was cold as a mother out here. His breath steamed and his flesh was tight where it was exposed to a brisk wind that rattled the limbs of the surrounding trees and froze Boxer's nose and cheeks. Once they'd loaded the stolen guns, they walked to the driver's side of the Jeep.

Again the window slid down.

"Okay. You got it all. Now we need to get paid. Let's get this over with." Ronny paused to light a cigarette, bending his head over his lighter, inhaling deeply.

"Yes, let's," she said, turning away toward the bag on the passenger seat. "Now."

Boxer raised his pistol.

Before Stillwell straightened or knew what was happening, Boxer placed the barrel against the taller man's temple and squeezed.

Blam!

The blast was loud. Echoed off the surrounding hills.

Stillwell's body jerked wildly.

Blood spurted.

His lighter flew from his hand.

His lit cigarette fell to the ground, sizzled out.

He weaved a split second before his legs gave out and he fell to one side, landing with a quick *whumph* on the ground.

Boxer watched him fall and felt just a bit of remorse for the man.

Ronny Stillwell had never really been much of a friend, but, still, they'd drunk pints together, talked sports, and shot the shit. He wasn't a bad guy, just a . . . problem.

If only he'd been able to stay focused and keep his damned mouth shut.

"I get his share," Boxer reminded her, turning and seeing the barrel of her own gun raised, pointed straight at his chest.

"Not this time."

What?

Blam!

A flash of blinding light.

He instinctively ducked.

Too late! Before he could react he was hit. His body jolted backward. His pistol flew from his hand, spinning wildly before dropping into a drift.

What the fuck?

He landed hard. Snow sprayed. White and red.

Oh, shit. Blood? *His* blood?

Instinctively, he put a hand over his chest. It came back sticky and wet. Blood smeared, dripping on his glove. Dazed, uncomprehending, he staggered to his feet. "What're you doing?" he said, his words garbled, the earth and night sky spinning in his vision. Blood and spittle running from his mouth. Pain radiating from his middle. He was hit. Bad. He needed to get to a hospital.

"Collateral damage."

With difficulty he focused on the Jeep, on the woman in the window. Her pistol was tracking him as he staggered, as if she intended to shoot him again. Dully he wondered what had gone so wrong. *Collateral damage?* Blinking, he saw her taking aim. *What?* "No—"

He held up his bloody hand, fingers splayed, begging her to stop. This wasn't supposed to happen! He was on his way to Calgary, a rich man—

"Sorry." But the word held no meaning. She wasn't sorry at all. Her face, a beautiful face, was set in stone. Evil. Jesus God, she intended to kill him! Like he'd killed Ronny.

With effort, he twisted, turning away, intending to run, to try and dig his gun from the snow.

Blam!

From the corner of his eye he saw the deadly flash.

His body jerked wildly as the bullet ripped through him, singeing flesh, doing all kinds of internal damage.

Jesus!

He stumbled. Pain ripped up his spine. This was all wrong. All wrong.

His legs wobbled. He tripped over something—oh, shit, it was Ronny's body.

The gun. Get the gun. Kill her before she kills you!

Boxer reeled. His legs tangled.

The ground rushed up at him.

Thud!

He tried to get up, pushed himself to a sitting position.

Blam!

The forest seemed to shudder with the blast.

He fell back again, his head cracking against a rock buried in the snow, blood blooming from his rib cage.

Fuck.

The world started to go dark.

God, it was cold. So damned cold. He tried to blink, but his gaze was fixed, his eyes refusing to respond.

Somewhere far in the distance, from deep in the blackness, he heard a soft voice.

Her voice. "No, you don't get his share this time," she said, sounding as if she were speaking from far, far away, her voice a whisper on the wind. "And, I'm afraid, Troy-honey, not ever."

Chapter 23

"We talked it over," Tanaka said from the other end of the wireless connection as Pescoli leaned a hip against the kitchen counter and waited for the coffeepot to finish brewing the first pot of the day. Santana had already left, running into town for some supplies, the baby was cooing in his play area on a blanket by the couch, Bianca had taken off for school, and Ivy hadn't yet arisen. "And we decided it would be best if we interviewed Ivy Wilde at the station."

"I thought you were coming here. To the house."

"Change of plan."

"Paterno's in on this, too? He agrees?" she asked, refusing to keep the edge out of her voice. It was a little after eight in the morning after a loooong night of sleeplessness and she was two steps beyond bitchy. She glared at the slowly filling glass carafe.

"You're a cop. You know the drill."

Of course she did.

Earlier they'd agreed that Ivy could be interviewed

at the house where she would feel more comfortable and relaxed, but of course, there was no two-way mirror here at the house, no cameras to record Ivy's reactions, no other cops to watch the interview.

Tanaka was right: Pescoli did understand, knew the drill.

"She'd be more comfortable here," she tried.

"Yeah. I know. But, along with her mother and father being shot and the attack on Wynn Ellis in Albuquerque—"

"She says he attacked her," Pescoli reminded.

"That's possible. Probable. We're going over footage now, but we need to hear her side of the story and record it." There was a beat, a hesitation, then she said, "We just want to clear this up ASAP."

That, too, Pescoli understood. "Okay, we'll meet you there, but it will have to be this afternoon."

A pause. "Why is that?"

"My sister's coming to provide emotional support. She's going to decide if Ivy needs an attorney or not."

Another pause. "Your sister?"

"Sarina Marsh. Remember. She's Ivy's aunt. Brindel's sister. Ivy's father can't make it."

"Can't you handle this? You're her aunt as well."

Pescoli held on to her patience with an effort. Didn't want to admit she was a bit overwhelmed herself and glad that Sarina wanted to be involved. "Ivy's seventeen, a minor. She just lost her mother and stepfather. Found them murdered. She needs all the support she can get. Do I really need to go into this again? And then there's the fact that I'm a cop, involved in the investigation."

The coffeepot was still filling. Drip by incredibly slow drip.

"You're not involved—hold on a second." The conversation grew garbled as Tanaka turned to speak to someone who was with her, probably Paterno. Pescoli couldn't make out the words. With her phone to her ear, she took the opportunity to pull out the coffeepot and fill her waiting cup, seeing a bit of black liquid drip onto the hot plate and sizzle before she stuffed the carafe back into its spot on the warmer. Tanaka's voice became clear again as she came back to the phone. "Fine," she said, though from her clipped tone, it clearly wasn't. "What time does Sarina Marsh get in?"

"She should be landing in Missoula a little after eleven, if there are no delays."

Again there was muted conversation, as if Tanaka was holding the phone against her body to keep it private.

Pescoli took a tentative drink from her cup, nearly burned her tongue, but gulped anyway. After the night she'd had? She needed this coffee with its jolt of caffeine in a big way.

Tanaka was on again. "All right. This afternoon. Just after lunch. One o'clock? Hopefully Paterno and I can take a later flight back to the city."

"We'll be there. If there's any problem, I'll let you know."

"Do that." Tanaka cut the connection and Pescoli wondered if she'd made a mistake in asking Sarina to come. She still didn't trust Ivy. She took another swallow.

Innocent until proved guilty, remember?

She made a face, wondering about her at least somewhat untrustworthy niece.

Nate Santana wouldn't admit it to anyone, but he was worried. Though he'd told Bianca the night before that nothing was out of the ordinary, it had been a lie. And now, on his way to the feed store in Grizzly Falls, he drove to the Long property and went through the ranch house, room by room once more. Last night he'd done a quick scan, discovered Bianca, and left. This morning he'd headed over to the house to give it more than a quick once-over. And, so far, as was the case last night, nothing inside appeared out of the ordinary, nothing was disturbed. Unlike what he'd told Bianca, the housekeeper had sworn she hadn't left any lights on the night before, and yet a table lamp in the den had been lit and there was just the feel that the air had been disturbed, almost as if the house smelled different.

Or was that just his imagination running away with him?

He walked through the living area, kitchen, and den, then down the hallway to the bedrooms, the master that Brady had claimed once his old man had passed away and the other three rooms, one for his sister Padgett, who had moved away years before, and still bore a few reminders of its occupant, an old corsage pinned to a bulletin board, a few dresses that looked over ten years old, a couple pairs of shoes, and the same pink striped bedspread over the canopied double bed, faded now, the canopy threadbare and showing a few rips, vacuum cleaner tracks visible on the aging carpet.

The same was true for Brady's original bedroom,

the one where he and Santana had played early versions of video games, talked girls and sports, flipped through *Playboy* magazines, and smoked cigarettes on the sly. It still had sports paraphernalia resting on shelves and tacked to the paneled walls, just as Santana had remembered, though one tack had given way and a once maroon and silver banner for the University of Montana Grizzlies was threatening to fall.

The other bedroom, always a guest room, was clean and neat, looked as if it was ready and waiting for anyone who wanted to visit the Long family.

The furnace, which he kept on low to hold the house above freezing, rumbled softly, and through the few windows that weren't shuttered, he saw the snow was falling again.

Everything was fine.

And yet . . .

Feeling as if he were wasting his time, he drove into town, to the cliff overlooking the river, where some of the original settlers had homesteaded over a century and a half before. Those acres had been cut up into city blocks as the town had grown, but the Long property occupied several of those blocks. The Victorian house, a massive five-thousand-square-foot stone and brick structure complete with turret, had been restored. The original carriage house, guest house, and laundry house occupied over three acres of tended lawn shaded by ancient larch, aspen, and pine. All of the property had been donated to the town by the Long family, whose riches from mining and logging in the area were legendary. This house was now owned by the historical society.

Santana had driven here because he remembered spending time here, where Brady's mother spent most of her winters, when he was younger. Of course that was years ago.

Maybe he was jumping at shadows.

First his wife's sister and husband were murdered.

Then Brindel's daughter showed up at their door.

About the same time some yahoo blew into town claiming to be Brady Long's long-lost son.

Then someone left a light on at the ranch. . . .

Did it all add up to something?

He parked along the street and stared at the old house. The museum was closed today and no one was about.

Just like no one had been in the ranch house.

He looked in his rearview mirror to pull out onto the street when he saw a familiar car round the corner.

His jaw tightened and he felt the same dark fury he always experienced whenever he was face to face with his wife's lowlife of an ex, Bianca's biological father, Luke "Lucky" Pescoli.

For some reason Lucky's Mustang was now heading this way and the bastard himself was at the wheel, driving slowly, his gaze fixed on the Long Museum, his head turned away from Santana, who was parked on the opposite side of the street. If he'd caught a glimpse of his ex-wife's current husband, Lucky gave no indication, and the way his gaze was locked onto the museum it seemed doubtful that he noticed anything other than the three stories of brick and natural stone of the house; the other buildings that were part of the vast estate didn't interest him.

No, Lucky Pescoli just kept his eyes on the manor.

What the hell was that all about?

The Mustang cruised past, drove to the end of the

street, turned around in another stately drive, then, once more, rolled past the grounds so slowly that Lucky nearly stopped in front of the now-closed wrought-iron gates before driving on.

Using his side-view mirror, Santana watched the Mustang reach the corner again and then drive down the hillside toward the heart of the old city sprawled on the shores of the Grizzly River.

So what was Lucky doing here?

Probably nothing. Don't make a big deal of it. Free country and all that. He can cruise down any damned street he wants to.

But . . .

Santana started the engine, his thoughts still spinning out.

Manny Douglas, a reporter for the local paper, had already written a column about Garrett Mays and his claim to the Long estate, a person everyone assumed was a con artist trying to get his hands on some of the Long fortune. Then there was Lucky Pescoli, always ready for a quick scam and now perusing the old Long property. Were the two events linked?

Unlikely.

But worth noting.

Maybe it was time to have a chat with the kid who claimed to be Brady Long's unknown son. As the manager of the Long estate, Santana figured he had the right to talk to the would-be heir, to question him. And even if it wasn't any of his business, he was going to make it so.

As Santana pulled away from the curb, he told himself he was borrowing trouble.

Yet he couldn't shake the feeling that something bad was about to go down.

After feeding, bathing, and changing the baby, Pescoli decided she'd waited long enough for Ivy to appear. Though they still had a couple of hours until it was time to pick up Sarina, she knew how long it sometimes took for a teenaged girl to get ready and Pescoli wanted her niece with her when she picked up Sarina at the Missoula airport. From there, they'd grab a quick lunch if there was time, and if not, head directly to the sheriff's office. It was too bad they'd have to take the baby with them, as Santana wasn't yet back.

Pescoli set her empty coffee cup in the sink before hauling Tucker up the stairs where she knocked softly on the door to the guest room. Funny, she'd started thinking of the bedroom as "Ivy's."

"Hey, time to get up," she announced as she opened the door to the darkened interior. "Ivy?" Her eyes adjusted to the darkness and the mess of blankets and pillows, some of which had slid off the bed to pool on the floor.

The bed was empty.

No Ivy.

She drew a sharp breath.

Had the girl taken off in the middle of the night?

"Shit." She ran her gaze around the room quickly as she said to the child on her hip, "Don't listen to that," before tearing through the upstairs, room after room, and calling Ivy's name as she opened doors to the bedrooms, bathrooms, and closets.

Where was she?

Down the stairs she raced. "Ivy?" she called as the dogs came to life, stretching as they rose from their beds. "Ivy?" She swept through the rooms on the first floor with the efficiency she'd learned at the academy regarding how to clear a house of suspects.

As she passed through each room, starting in the living and dining rooms, then down the hallway through the kitchen and family room, checking the laundry area and closets and finding no one, she began to panic. "Ivy," she yelled again, and under her breath, "Where the hell are you?" She ended up in the garage where her Jeep sat unattended, ladders hanging on the walls, dog food stacked in plastic bins, no sign of life.

Frantic, thinking the worst, remembering that the girl had been attacked *after* her parents had been killed, Pescoli returned to the kitchen, where, looking through the window near the back door, she spied Jeremy's truck.

Where he'd parked it the night before.

The cab was covered in a white blanket from the night's snowfall.

She paused, glanced at the calendar she kept near a built-in desk, and frowned, carrying Tucker nearer to read the notes. Wasn't he supposed to be in class this morning? Didn't he have Intro to Psychology at eight? A quick check of the clock on the mantel suggested he was running more than a little late. The class, at the junior college forty-five minutes away, had started half an hour ago.

"Oh, shi—" She caught herself this time as realization dawned.

Jeremy had evolved in the past couple of years to a good student. His grades had bottomed out in high school, but since that rocky time in his life, he'd turned around, caring about his future, talking law enforcement, which worried her but, in general, finally becoming responsible.

Only one thing could derail him.

Sex.

Quickly she bundled Tucker into his snowsuit and threw on her down jacket, then headed outside to the exterior staircase that led to the apartment over the garage.

On the landing she pounded on the door. "Jeremy?"

Nothing.

She rapped harder.

Bang. Bang. Bang!

Still nothing, not a sound from within, though the dogs in the house had started barking, their muted yips audible. "Come on," she said, and louder, "I know you're here."

She stomped her feet in the cold, then listened and heard something—feet hitting the floor, then the slow, steady tread of her son approaching.

The lock clicked and the door swung open a crack.

"About damned time."

Her son stood in the doorway, blocking her view to the interior as he firmly held the door in place, barely keeping it ajar.

"I know she's in there."

"What?"

"Ivy. I know she's in there."

"What'd'ya mean?"

"Oh, for the love of God, don't play dumb with me," she snapped, then, for a second worried that the girl was truly missing, that she wasn't in Jeremy's apartment but out in the wintry wilds of Montana. On the run. But staring at her son, those thoughts quickly vanished.

Bare-chested, Jeremy was wearing jeans that hung low over his hips. His dark hair was askew, his strong chin shadowed by several days' growth of beard, and he was definitely barring his mother not only entrance, but visibility, into his abode. "I know what's going on and, for the record, I don't like it." When he didn't budge, she added, "Are you out of your mind? She's seventeen. Barely legal."

His lips tightened.

"And your cousin. Your *first* cousin!"

A muscle started working in his jaw, but for the most part, he was unmoved and she was sick of the one-sided debate while standing with her baby in the freezing cold.

She pushed past him and, thank God, he didn't resist, allowing her into what was essentially still part of her house no matter that he thought it was completely separate. Fast-food wrappers, water bottles, and soda cans were overflowing from the garbage can, his game controller wired into an old TV and left on the floor, the cushions from his hand-me-down sofa also on the worn carpet, and the area smelled of stale pizza and dirty socks. But the odor and mess didn't make her cringe. Nope. It was something else that caused her guts to cringe.

In the darkened corner of the bachelor apartment, tangled in the messed covers of his bed and propped on his pillows, eyeing Pescoli sullenly, was her niece.

Pescoli's heart sank, her worst fears confirmed.

"What the hell is going on here?" Pescoli said, trying to keep her voice low, though of course she knew. It was obvious. But at least Ivy was still in the clothes she'd been wearing the night before. Had she scrambled into them when Pescoli had pounded on the door? Maybe, but she looked somewhat put together. No bra was left forgotten on the floor, no shirt turned inside out due to being hastily donned.

Jeremy lifted one shoulder. A casual gesture though the cords on his neck were visible. "We crashed here."

"You crashed? There?" She pointed to the bed.

"Yeah."

"And you two . . . ?" She waggled a hand between them.

"Nothing happened, Mom."

"Yeah?"

"We didn't do anything," he said, insolence visible.

"You expect me to believe that?"

"It's the truth. We, just, you know, watched a movie and . . . slept."

"Together."

"Yeah."

Was that a hickey on his neck? A bruise forming just above his shoulder? Had Ivy left her mark? Had she done it on purpose? Dear God, the girl could be involved in her own mother's murder. Pescoli's insides were churning. This was not good. Not good at all and here her son was, defending himself, defending her, when they didn't know a thing about each other. For a split second, Pescoli saw her sister's image, as if Brindel were in the room with them, which was absolutely nutso.

Closing her mind to what her sister might think

were she still alive, how horrified she'd be, Pescoli shifted Tuck from one side to the other. She wanted desperately to believe Jeremy, to trust that he wouldn't cross that forbidden line, but here in the litter of Coke bottles and beer cans, of clothes left forgotten on the floor, of textbooks shoved across the table to make room for an iPad, she remembered her own sex drive when she was his age.

"Nothing happened," he said again, more firmly. "Not a damned thing."

"Let's say for the sake of argument I believe you. But the deal is that as long as she's staying here, with me? She stays in the house, in her room. Got it?"

"I'm right here, you know," Ivy said resentfully. She'd wrestled her way out of the duvet and was standing, barefoot, her short brown hair sticking up. Blinking against bits of mascara lodging in her eyes, she added, "He's right. We didn't do anything." Her face was pulled into a little-girl pout and she swept a finger under her lower lashes.

"Why am I hearing a 'yet' at the end of that sentence?"

"God, Mom, you always think the worst!" Jeremy crossed his arms over his chest and she noticed the muscles in his shoulders. Somewhere along the line he'd become a man.

"I thought you had a girlfriend," Pescoli said. "Rebecca Something or Other."

"Becca Johnson and she's *not* my girlfriend." But he had the decency to blush.

"And you." Pescoli's gaze swiveled to her niece. "You've got a boyfriend."

"No, I don't." Ivy looked at her aunt as if Pescoli had just dropped in from Jupiter. "I told you Troy and I broke up."

"Around Thanksgiving, yeah I know, so you said. But he said that you'd taken up with someone else."

Rolling her eyes and shaking her head, she said, "He's such a lying sack of . . . such a liar! I *don't* have a boyfriend. I already told you that! I made one up so that Troy would leave me alone. Remember?"

Pescoli did. She'd been double-checking, baiting the girl.

As if she understood Pescoli's motivations, Ivy, petulant pout in place, stepped a little closer to Jeremy and despite the awkward situation, and the damning conversation, he, almost instinctively unfolded his arms and dropped one comfortingly over her shoulders.

"Haven't you heard a word I've said?" Pescoli asked tightly.

Stay cool, Regan. Don't make this worse.

Ivy snuggled closer.

"This is not happening," she told her son, and ignored the nagging voice in her head. "And you." She focused hard on her niece. "Go into the house, the main house, right now and get ready. You've got a police interview in a few hours and before that we have to pick up Sarina at the airport."

"I don't need to go to—"

"Yes, you do." Pescoli was taking no lip from this girl even though Tucker was starting to fuss. "Get a move on," she ordered. "Now."

"Fine." Ivy sent Pescoli a hateful glare.

"Wow, Mom." Jeremy scowled sullenly. "Way to be a dictator."

"Yep. That's what I am. A dictator. And in my house, we play by my rules. All of us."

The baby began to cry softly, but for once, he wasn't the son that needed her attention. Ivy found her boots and trundled down the exterior steps and to the back door, pausing to cast a glance that was both sultry and victimized to Jeremy before heading inside.

Pescoli had to appear calm when deep inside she was furious. And scared. Somehow she needed to get through to her son. She had to change tactics. "Look, Jer, I understand that you feel a need to protect Ivy. So do I. She's been through a lot." She had to tread carefully here. She couldn't come unglued. Couldn't start barking orders and edicts or try to shake some sense into his thick, sex-addled brain. The worst thing she could do was forbid them from seeing each other because it would be like forcing them straight into each other's arms. The whole star-crossed lovers thing. Which was so damned appealing, especially to young people.

"But she's fragile. Emotionally in knots," Pescoli said, not adding that she was also untrustworthy and probably lying to all of them. "What that girl witnessed, what she's dealt with . . . We have to be very, very careful."

Was she talking to Jeremy? Or herself?

"I was only trying to help," he said, and narrowed his eyes, as if searching his mother's face for a lie, a crack in her empathy.

Somehow she managed to hide it.

"Let's just be smart about this," she said, cajoling him even though she wanted to strangle him for being such a dimwit. "For her sake. Ivy's in some trouble as it is until this whole thing is cleared up, so you and she need to cool it, keep everything aboveboard and don't bring her up here. She's only seventeen. You can see her in the main house."

His face clouded over, features hard. He wanted to argue, but didn't.

Tucker was starting to wail and she rocked him on her hip as she asked, "Aren't you supposed to be in class?"

"I decided to cut today." *Because of Ivy.*

"Maybe you should rethink that. Get moving and make the next one. And you've got work later, right?"

"You don't need to remind me, Mom. God, I'm an adult."

"And you're still technically under my roof, rent-free while you're in school and working, so I'd be careful if I were you. No reason to blow a good deal."

His jaw tightened. "You don't like her, do you?"

"Ivy? I hardly know her. You hardly know her."

"I know you're trying to manipulate me. Pretending to be all worried about Ivy when you're really trying to manipulate her, too. Doing the whole cop thing. Don't you think I see that? Jesus, you're so transparent."

"No 'trans' about it. I'm a parent. Period. Your parent. And I don't dislike Ivy. She's my niece and she just lost her mother. I've lost a sister."

"But you don't trust her. Ivy, I mean. I see it in your eyes." He was shaking his head, running a hand through his hair. The way his father, Joe, had done when he'd been frustrated, and he'd been frustrated a lot. At his young wife.

Her marriage to Joe Strand had been as passionate as it had been rocky. Mercurial emotions. At this age, Jeremy was the spitting image of his father, but thankfully he had a cooler head than either of his parents when they'd struggled through their early twenties.

"Right?" he prodded.

"I just don't know what she's going through," Pescoli said as the baby started to really wail, wriggling in her arms.

Jeremy's lips twisted wryly. "I knew it. That's your problem, Mom. You don't trust anyone. Not even someone in your own family."

"Trust is earned," she said, walking outside again. "You know that." But his arrow had hit its mark, or pretty damned close. Pescoli had a problem trusting anyone. "You'd better get going. There's still time to catch your next class."

Taller than she, he stared down at her. "It's just so damned cool to have a mom who knows your whole schedule."

Her temper flared. "And it's just awesome to find my son in bed with his cousin." She gave him one last piece of advice. "Just keep it in your pants, Jeremy."

"I said nothing happened!"

"Keep it that way."

"Oh, like you did?"

She froze. The air went still for a second. He was right, of course. Twice she'd gotten pregnant before she'd married. Acts of passion she didn't regret. But he had a point. Their gazes clashed and she whispered, "Low blow, Jer."

"Yeah. Well. Now you know how I feel." He slammed the door so hard it banged shut.

The garage shook.

A heavy clump of snow fell off the roof and the baby started in her arms.

She heard the lock engage.

Great. She'd blown that argument. "Come on," she said to Tucker as she made her way down the steps. "Let's just hope your brother gets smart when it comes to girls."

And what were the chances of that? she wondered as she stepped inside and started peeling off her jacket.

Pretty damned close to zero.

Chapter 24

God, her aunts were morons. Well, maybe not the cop. She was pretty sharp, but Collette and Sarina were so predictable, so emotional, and, Ivy thought, so able to be tricked. She didn't like the word "manipulated," but she knew with the right display of emotion, she could wrap Sarina around her little finger.

Standing a step behind Aunt Regan in the Missoula airport, she watched Sarina, with the strap of an overnight bag slung over her shoulder, come scurrying from the terminal where they were waiting, idling in Regan's Jeep.

They both got out and Sarina let out a little cry, dropped her bag, and surrounded Ivy in a bear hug. "Thank God you're okay!" her aunt's voice cracked. "We were so worried. Oh, honey, I'm so, so sorry about your Mom and Paul." And then the waterworks started gushing as Sarina burst into tears of . . . relief? Grief? Joy? Worry? Who knew and who cared. Ivy put up with the hug, being rocked back and forth as Sarina held fast as if she'd never let go.

"I can't park here all day," Regan said, and Sarina finally released her niece.

"I know. It's just that I was *so* worried."

"I'm fine," Ivy lied.

"Oh, honey, how could you be?" Sarina gave her a hang-dog, I-know-your-pain look, which was ridiculous. No one knew how she felt. No one ever could.

Regan said, "We've got to meet Detectives Paterno and Tanaka in a couple of hours. Are you hungry?"

"Starved, but what else is new. I've been counting calories again . . . I hate it."

Ivy crawled into the backseat while Sarina took shotgun and Regan drove. During the trip, Ivy suffered through at least a thousand questions from Sarina.

"Why didn't you call?"

"Where have you been?"

"Is there anything we can do?"

"Why did you go to New Mexico? What's there?"

Sarina finished with, "I heard about that awful attack; it was on the news. I'm so glad you were able to get away! Did you know him? The man who assaulted you? Oh, dear, he has a record, you know that? So don't worry about him lying about you. The police will sort it all out, I'm sure." Then a questioning look at her sister. "Won't they, Regan?"

Ivy, who'd been answering in nearly monosyllabic words just to get the woman off her back, was thankful that Regan had to take over. "Yes, the police will figure out what's going on. We always do," said Regan.

Well, that sure sent a chill through Ivy's soul. They couldn't find out the truth, at least not all of it, or she would be in deep shit. Swallowing back her fear, Ivy thought about the phone call she'd have to make.

"Give her a break, Sarina," Regan advised as the road veered along the course of the river. "She's going to have to go through all this and more once we get to the station."

"Oh, I know, but they'll see she's telling the truth and release her. And then I'll take her home. Get her settled in. Back to school."

"No," Ivy said, cutting in. Is that what the plan was? To dump her back with Sarina to San Francisco? To live with her ridiculous cousins, Ryan and Zach? Were they serious? No way. She had her own plans.

Sarina twisted in the front seat, half turning to look at her. "You have to finish your senior year and I've got room now." Her smile faded at that thought, but she kept going. "And we'll worry about college later. I know you've taken your SATs and Brindel had said something about . . . about . . . Oh, God, I'm sorry." She'd started crying again.

"All this can be sorted out later," Regan said firmly.

"I'm not going back." Ivy thought they should know at least that much.

"But, honey," Sarina said, her voice cajoling.

Regan cut in, "How about one day, no, make that one hour, at a time?"

"Fine." Sarina's lips twisted down at the corners as she stared through the window where snow was beginning to fall. "God, it's cold here."

"Just in the winter," Regan said.

"Maybe I should move, but . . . not here." She sighed and started rambling on about making a new start, of leaving the condo with "all its memories," then made passing references to some other cities in California, LA or Sacramento, or Lake Tahoe. "Anywhere," she finally summed up, "away from You Know Who and that woman."

So your husband cheated on you. Big effin' deal. It happened all the time. Ivy had seen it with her own mother, and how she'd turned away from the truth that her husband couldn't stay faithful. Sarina was acting as if she were the only woman in the world who'd had to deal with a jerk-wad who found some other woman more attractive.

Ivy leaned back in her seat and mentally prepared herself for her interview with the detectives from San Francisco. Having Aunt Sarina with her wasn't much comfort. The woman was brainless. Her thoughts turned to Jeremy. Now, he could help steady her through the interview but, of course, that was a no-go with Aunt Regan.

She feigned sleep and let the two women natter on. At least the guy who'd attacked her was in the hospital. She'd prefer him to be dead, but then she would be a murderer and that probably came with a whole set of new problems. She had enough as it was. More than enough.

Pescoli ignored the feeling that she was coming home when she walked through the front doors of the Pinewood County Sheriff's Department. She didn't want to dwell on the question of whether she would return to her job full time, or instead stay home with her baby, do a little private investigation on the side, partnering up with Selena Alvarez's fiancé rather than with her. That option seemed less appealing than returning here where real cops worked and hung out, where criminals were arrested and everything from grievances about property lines and teenaged parties to brutal homicides were tackled. Officers in uniforms mingled with plainclothes detectives and office staff, laughing and talking, digging through mounds of paperwork or squinting at computer monitors, answering phone calls or writing reports. Keyboards clicked, footsteps echoed down the halls, and the struggling furnace was still rumbling. She smelled old coffee and heard a snippet of an even older joke, a raunchy one Deputy Pete Watershed told. He was always mouthing off with off-color remarks or offensive jokes.

God, she missed this place.

Maybe not Watershed so much, but she missed just about everyone else.

Still, she couldn't get caught up in her own dilemma about her career, not when her niece was about to be questioned by Tanaka. They were setting up. Tanaka leading Sarina and Ivy into the interview room with its camera and window that looked like a mirror on one side but actually allowed a view of the room by officers and staff in the darkened viewing room adjacent.

The deal was that she and Paterno would watch through the glass while Tanaka conducted the questioning. Pescoli had been through the same routine hundreds, if not thousands, of times, standing near the glass, staring at the subject of the interview and trying to determine if he or she were telling the truth or hiding something while a camera and audio equipment recorded it all.

But today was different.

Because the subject was her niece, because now her own sister was dead, killed by someone unknown, and the question was not just how much Ivy knew about her mother's and stepfather's homicides but how deeply Ivy might be involved.

Usually, Pescoli was hoping that the subject would crack under questioning, that a confession to some brutal crime was forthcoming, but not today. Not when Ivy was about to be grilled.

She passed by Alvarez's office and saw the door was ajar.

"I'll just be a second," she said to Paterno, and stopped while the San Francisco detective walked farther along the hallway and around the corner to the viewing room.

Alvarez was at her desk, head bent over the computer screen, her black hair pulled back into a neat bun and shining under the overhead.

"You want something?" Alvarez's voice was clipped. She spun in her desk chair, her face a knot of frustration.

"Good to see you, too," Pescoli said.

Alvarez's expression softened. "Not who I expected."

"Carson Ramsby?" Pescoli guessed.

"That would be the one. He's . . ."

"Driving you nuts. Just like Brett Gage before him."

"Yeah, that partnership didn't last long. Ask Gage. I think I drove him as nuts as he drove me. And now, Ramsby. Worse. Could you just come back already?" Alvarez smiled faintly. "You're a pain in the ass, too, but at least you give me a little space. Don't suppose you came back to tell Blackwater to get your office ready?"

With a shake of her head, Pescoli said, "Just saying hi. I'm here with my niece."

"Ivy Wilde, I heard. What's her story?"

"That's what we're trying to figure out." Pescoli usually would tell her ex-partner everything. She rarely held back except for the times where she'd crossed the line, like recently with Chilcoate. Now, with Ivy on the list of potential suspects in the double-homicide, full disclosure was not an option.

"Tricky business," Alvarez said, then added, "Sorry to hear about your sister."

Pescoli nodded. She didn't have to put in that she wasn't close to Brindel. Alvarez knew. Because the truth was that Pescoli was closer to her ex-partner than she ever had been with any of her sisters.

"So what're you working on?" Pescoli asked.

"Much of the same. Hattie Grayson's making noise again."

"Ah." Hattie was now married to Cade Grayson, though she'd first been married to Bart, both of whom were siblings of Dan, Pinewood County's former sheriff and Pescoli's and Alvarez's good friend. It was Hattie's contention that both the brothers, Dan and Bart, were murdered as part of a dark conspiracy, even though Bart took his own life and Dan's killer had been brought to justice. "She never gives up."

"Tell me about it," Alvarez said, then frowned. "Where's the baby?"

"Home. With Daddy."

Her gaze grew wistful. "You know, I get it why you

want to stay home with him. If I'd had the chance . . ." She let her voice trail off and Pescoli knew she didn't want to talk about the son she'd given up so many years ago, when she'd been a teenager.

Pescoli changed the subject. "I hear you've got another pretender to the crown, right? Garrett Mays, claiming that he's the long-lost son of Brady Long."

"So the story goes," Alvarez said.

"They keep cropping up, don't they?"

"Hopefully this is the last one."

"Amen to that." She heard footsteps behind her, then a male voice. "Detective?"

Turning, Pescoli found Sheriff Blackwater beckoning her from the door of his office. "A word?"

"Later," she said to Alvarez, then slapped a hand on the doorjamb before walking the hallway to Blackwater's office. She still thought of the room as belonging to Dan Grayson. For half a second she even expected to see Grayson's Stetson hanging on a hook near the door and find his black Labrador retriever curled up in a bed in the corner. All of which was pure fantasy, of course, the dog in question probably now tucked into a spot near the fireplace of Pescoli's house with Cisco and Nikita.

Blackwater was single and never married, at least as far as she knew. Around six feet tall, he was still trim, in such good shape she guessed he might do fingertip push-ups in his spare time. His black hair was cut military short, his clothes pressed, pants creased to a knife's edge that she bet he ironed in himself. He closed the door and motioned her into a side chair. "I'll keep this brief," he said, and didn't bother sitting himself, just leaned against the big, battle-scarred desk that he kept neat as a pin.

"Good, because I need—"

"I know—they're waiting for you. For the interview with Ivy Wilde. I talked to Detective Paterno." He stared at her a moment, his lips folding in on themselves before his gaze slid away. "First. My condolences. It's hard to lose a sibling." He acted as if he'd experienced some kind of similar pain, but he didn't elaborate and in truth she knew little about his personal life.

"Yes. Thanks."

His eyes found hers again and any trace of empathy she'd thought she'd glimpsed in those dark depths had now vanished. Again he was the hard-ass she'd come to know. "So, here's the deal: I can't keep your job open much longer. A week, maybe two, and then I need to start interviewing. I've already sorted through some applicants and there are a couple who would be a credit to the department. They come with a list of references as long as my arm. Good men and women. I've checked them out. Any one of them would be an asset to the department."

Her insides clenched at the thought of him handing over her position, of giving up a career she'd fought so long to establish. "Good," she heard herself saying as she sat down.

"So you're not coming back." A statement. Not a question.

In her mind's eye, she saw her son, Little Tucker, smiling up at her, and in that same second, when she felt an overwhelming sense of love for the boy, she also experienced a pang at the thought of missing out on being there for his first tooth, or steps, or when he scraped a knee. She'd already raised two children nearly to adulthood and they, if they'd suffered, had survived and been stronger for it, but could she do it again? Should she?

"I don't know," she admitted.

The skin over his face tightened and she noted his fingers blanch as they gripped hard against the edge of the desk. "Well, figure it out," he ordered. "February first, I'm starting to interview."

He moved to the door. His dark gaze held hers as she stepped into the hallway. "Make a decision, Detective," he advised. "Or I'll make it for you."

* * *

The girl was a liar.

And a good one.

Tanaka would give her that.

She just wasn't sure where Ivy Wilde's lies were threaded into her truth.

Tanaka was taking notes on her spiral pad even though the session was being recorded. She sat on one side of the table, Sarina Marsh and her niece on the other. Ivy, wide-eyed and ashen-faced, had seemed almost demure throughout and had answered all the questions posed to her. But Tanaka wasn't buying it. At least not all of it. Ivy had told the same story she'd spun to Pescoli: She'd come home from a friend's, found her parents slain in their separate bedrooms, thought she'd heard someone upstairs, freaked out, and picked up a kitchen knife, which she'd subsequently dropped onto the street. After running through a nearby park, she'd taken BART, then because she was afraid for her own safety, she'd decided to leave the area. She'd taken a bus to Albuquerque where she'd run into Wynn P. Ellis, gotten the better of him, and again hopped a Greyhound that had the bad luck of breaking down and causing another nerve-wracking delay. She'd eventually landed in Missoula and, after catching a ride into Grizzly Falls, she'd ended up on dear old Aunt Regan's doorstep.

Most of Ivy's tale was true, Tanaka supposed; it lined up with the facts, but some of the story just seemed a little too pat, though Tanaka couldn't say why.

But she would.

It was Tanaka's job to sort fact from fiction.

And she was good at her job.

"So you went to Albuquerque just to throw off anyone who might have been following you, so they wouldn't track you down here. Did I get that right?"

"Uh-huh."

"No other reason."

"No." Now Ivy shook her head, her uneven haircut even more ragged in the harsh light.

"Do you know anyone in New Mexico?"

"No! That was the whole point! Geez, didn't you hear me? I was trying to throw off anyone who was looking for me."

"So you could come to Grizzly Falls."

"My mom always said if I was in trouble and couldn't get to her to . . . to call my aunt, the cop." She stared at Tanaka as if the detective was being intentionally thick-headed.

Tanaka changed tactics. "Tell me about the man who attacked you. Did you know him?"

"I never saw him before that night. But he was on the bus from LA. Watching me."

"Why?"

A lift of the shoulder. "I don't know."

"Did he follow you onto the bus?"

"Maybe. I don't know. I didn't notice when he got on or if he was on before me, just partway on the trip I saw that he was watching me. He wore sunglasses the whole trip, even in the dark."

"Are you sure you hadn't met or seen him before?"

"I told you: no." Her chin angled upward a little indignantly.

"Okay, let's go back to the night you found your parents. You said you heard someone in the house."

"Yes."

"But you didn't see anyone?"

"I told you, I ran."

"But you think it was more than one person."

"It sounded like that. Multiple footsteps at the same time, you know?"

"From how many people?"

Ivy sighed through her nose. "I don't know. Maybe two people, maybe more." She bit her lip and looked away, thinking.

"Do you think the man who attacked you was involved in the murders?"

"I don't know."

Tanaka wanted to keep poking at her story, especially the night of the murders. It was almost believable, but there seemed to be a lack of grief or empathy over her dead parents.

"Whoever was in the house must've had a key," Tanaka tried. "The housekeeper . . . Dona Andalusia, said that Mrs. Latham, your mother, always locked the house."

"Yeah, but not Paul. He didn't care so much."

"So the front door could have been left unlocked."

"Yeah."

"But your mother and Paul were in their bedrooms. It looked like they'd turned in for the night. Wouldn't they have locked the doors?"

"I guess."

Tanaka asked who might have had access to a key and Ivy mentioned all the family members along with the housekeeper.

"Anyone else?"

"I don't know. Don't think so."

"Did you loan your key to anyone else?"

"No, but you should ask Macon and Seth."

"Paul's sons?"

"They had keys and were always losing them. Geez, I can't remember how many times I'd get a call because they were locked out."

"So your parents kept the house locked."

"They weren't my parents," she said quickly. "Paul wasn't."

Tanaka eyed Ivy's tight face. "You didn't get along with your stepfather, did you?"

She lifted a shoulder. "He was a douche. Cheated on Mom."

"What about with you? How did he act with you?" Tanaka pressed, and saw a bit of concern in Sarina Marsh's eyes.

"Like he didn't care."

"Did he ever . . . touch you?"

"You mean, did he ever come on to me? Is that what

you're suggesting?" An expression of disgust contorted her face.

"You said he cheated on your mom, that he was a . . . let me see." Tanaka flipped back a page in her notebook ". . . that he was 'a douche.' Always flirting with other women."

"Not with me. He left me alone." She actually shivered at the mental image, then looked to the mirror on the wall, as if she knew Pescoli was on the other side, which of course she did.

"Is this necessary?" Sarina asked, her spine stiffening. Until this point, she'd been quiet, allowing the interview as, Tanaka suspected, Pescoli had ordered.

"I'm just trying to figure out what happened."

"I already told you," Ivy declared. "Over and over again. How many times do I have to say it? I found them. I ran. I thought someone was following me and I got on BART. You know it all, about Albuquerque and finally coming here. What more do you want from me?" She glared hard at Tanaka before throwing a baleful look again at the window, meant for Pescoli.

The interview continued for another half hour, but they learned nothing more and finally Tanaka said, "Tell me about Troy Boxer."

"We've been over this, too. We broke up. End of story."

Tanaka leaned back in her chair. "Did you know that he and his friend Ronny Stillwell are missing?"

"What?" Ivy asked.

"I thought that's why you came to Montana at first. To meet up with them."

"Uh, no." Ivy sounded almost bored and it was unclear whether it was an act or the real deal.

Her attitude irked Tanaka, who told her flatly, "Troy Boxer and Ronny Stillwell went MIA a few days ago. Neither man reported in for work, nor have they been at the rooming house for a couple of days now. Their landlord, George Aimes, hasn't seen hide nor hair of either of them, though their vehicles were still parked in a back alley."

Ivy stayed silent, absorbing the news.

"Have you heard from either of them?" Tanaka asked.

"No." But she sent a wild-eyed glance toward the window again.

"We're checking with other friends and coworkers, their family members, but so far no one has heard from them, nor have they responded to calls or texts. The calls just go to full voice mail boxes, the texts go unanswered." Tanaka waited a moment, then asked, "Do you think they might have been the people in the house that night, the ones you heard and who chased you? That they might have been there to rob your parents?"

"You think Troy and Ronny . . ." She vigorously shook her head, but there was the tiniest bit of fear in her eyes, and Tanaka felt as if finally she was zeroing in on the truth, but what was it?

"You said you took money from Paul's safe, that you knew the combination, but that you left everything else."

"Yes."

"Your fingerprints weren't on the safe."

"I was wearing gloves. It's January."

"And you stole the money *after* you saw the bodies?"

"Ye—I—don't remember."

"Because before there would be no reason to."

"Yes." Ivy was nodding slowly, wary of the trap.

"So even though you saw your mother and her husband murdered and thought the killers might be in the house, might come after you, you took the time to go to the wall safe, put in the combination lock, and then pick out a stack of cash."

"Yes."

"All while the killers were coming down the stairs."

She licked her lips. "I didn't know where they were, I just worked fast."

Sarina Marsh had twisted her head to stare at her niece as if she finally understood the cracks in Ivy's heretofore pat story. She placed a hand over her niece's. "Honey," she said quietly, "I think we should stop this. You need an attorney."

"I didn't kill Mom or Paul." Her voice cracked and tears shone in her big eyes. "I didn't. You believe me, don't you?"

"Of course I do," Sarina said, then turned to Tanaka. "We're done here. She has the right to an attorney and she's requesting it." Before Tanaka could argue, Sarina said, "Now," and stood. "Ivy has told you all she's going to say until she confers with counsel."

And that was that. Ivy climbed to her feet, but her legs seemed wobbly, and Tanaka, unable to keep the girl for further questioning, opened the door and ushered them to the hallway where Regan Pescoli was waiting.

Chapter 25

"So where's the baby?" Joelle Fisher asked as Pescoli walked with her sister and Ivy past the reception desk. Joelle's blond hair was so pale as to be almost silver and she had already donned red-heart earrings that dangled and matched her nail polish and red heels. Joelle always dressed as if she were about to attend a holiday party and it didn't matter that Valentine's Day was still a month away. "I can't believe you would come to the station without him."

Pescoli said, "This is official business."

An arch of Joelle's eyebrow called Pescoli's situation with the department into question, the situation Sheriff Blackwater had so pointedly reminded her of.

"My niece, Ivy Wilde. She's my sister's daughter. Brindel Latham."

The name Latham brought the receptionist up to speed and her shiny lips rounded into a silent O. She understood "official business" even though Pescoli hadn't returned to duty.

"Well, bring him by when you can," she said, and clipped off, high-heels clicking as she headed toward the break room.

Ivy, Sarina, and Pescoli walked outside where Pescoli could brood. She'd watched the interview and once again decided that Ivy was hiding something, that she was somehow involved. And the link was Troy Boxer. There was still something going on between those two, no matter what Ivy said, no matter that this morning she'd been all about Jeremy.

Outside the snow was starting again, falling in big white flakes that had begun covering the cleared pathways and plowed parking lot. "Does it ever quit?" Sarina wondered.

"For about six weeks in summer," Pescoli said.

"Very funny. Ha. Ha."

Pescoli backed the Jeep up, switched on the wipers, then drove out of the parking lot, leaving the station where she'd spent so many years.

"So I wasn't kidding about an attorney," Sarina said. "Watch out!" she ordered, seeing the traffic light turn red and the van in front of their car hit his brakes. Sarina, too, pressed her foot to the floor as if she were driving from the passenger seat.

Pescoli had plenty of time to stop, sparing a fender bender by some distance.

"Sorry. Automatic response," Sarina said. "I spent the last year and a half teaching Ryan to drive. Not an easy trick in San Francisco, and now Zach's about to turn fifteen and clamoring to get his permit. Guess who'll have that task? Certainly not his fa . . . well, You-Know-Who, as he's busy 'finding himself' or off on his new adventure." She snorted derisively and muttered, "Selfish ass."

Pescoli eased off the brake as the light changed and followed the van through several intersections when Sarina got back to the point. "As I was saying before you nearly rear-ended that Econoline, I think Ivy needs a lawyer."

"What about you, Ivy?" Pescoli asked, and checked the rear-view mirror to catch her niece's eye.

"For what? I didn't do anything!" Ivy said again, angry. Then, "Well, I did take Paul's money, so I guess that counts as *some*thing, but that's all." She flopped back against the seat and said, "It wasn't as if he was going to need it anyway."

Sarina's head whipped around. "That's a bad attitude," she said. "Have some respect."

"I didn't like Paul. I'm not going to lie about it just because he's dead."

"But your mother?"

Ivy didn't answer, but her demeanor changed and sadness chased across her eyes. Sadness, grief, and just a hint of guilt. What the hell did the girl know? And why was she hiding it? Pescoli gripped the wheel a little tighter as they headed out of town, the road winding through the foothills and rising sharply. From the backseat she thought she heard a soft whisper. "I loved my mom."

Pescoli's heart twisted. She was so conflicted when it came to her niece. Yes, Ivy was manipulative and had secrets, but she was still a child. "She doesn't need an attorney. Not yet. She was just making a statement."

"In one of those interrogation rooms," Sarina said.

"Interview rooms."

"I'm just sayin'." Then, turning in her seat again, Sarina added, "And we need to discuss you coming home. I think you should live with us. Get back in school, you know, try to get back into your routine with your friends and—"

"I know!" Ivy glared at Pescoli in the rearview. "You're not going to make me, are you?" Her phone buzzed and she looked at the text. "God, it's Macon. Again. Can't he just leave me alone? Can't everyone?" Her fingers danced over the tiny keyboard and Pescoli inwardly cringed at what she imagined the text might be. She could find out, of course. Chilcoate was still on the clock, still monitoring all the phones and computers associated with Brindel's family, and now that Ivy was using her phone again, maybe Pescoli would finally find out what was in her niece's head. Whatever it was, she was pretty certain she wasn't going to like it. The more she knew Brindel's daughter, the more of a mystery and a worry the girl was.

Sarina frowned as Pescoli turned into the lane leading to the house. "You want her to stay here?" she asked.

"I think it's too early to make any permanent plans."

"But she lives in San Francisco. She's only seventeen."

"Almost eighteen!" Ivy spouted from the backseat. "And then I can do what I want."

"You need to finish high school and then there's college," Sarina was saying almost by rote.

"I can get a GED! I don't have to go back, and I don't want to. Do you know what that would be like?

Everyone would know about what happened. I'd be . . . stared at and whispered about. And not in a good way. I'm not going."

The house came into view, and Sarina, about to argue with Ivy again, decided to clam up. Instead she stared through the window. "Oh, Regan," she said in surprise. "This is . . . this is really nice. And the lake . . ."

Of course she'd never seen the place. She'd never once visited Montana, not even when Pescoli was going through the death of Jeremy's father, or the births of her children, or during her divorce from Lucky Pescoli. Regan had never felt the need to keep in close contact with her sisters, but maybe that had been a mistake.

Ivy flew out of the car as soon as it was parked and hurried inside. Pescoli and Sarina followed and, of course, were greeted by the excited barking and yips from the dogs, and Santana, in jeans and a long-sleeved T-shirt, who was kneeling near the fireplace and stacking a small pile of split fir. Within the firebox the embers of last night's fire were glowing against fresh tinder.

"Hey," he said, and tossed off his gloves.

"I brought company." Pescoli cocked her head toward Sarina, then petted a wildly yipping Cisco, who was doing terrier pirouettes at her feet. "Whoa, big fella. Take it down a notch, will ya?"

"Getting to be a habit with you." He smiled. "First Ivy and now . . . Sarina, right?"

"Yes." Sarina was nodding, taking him in.

"Finally." He stuck out a hand, took hers, and shook it. "'Bout time we met."

"Yes," she said.

"Sorry about Brindel," Santana said, letting go of her hand.

"Me too. She was . . ." Sarina's voice threatened to break, but she found a way to hold herself together as Pescoli walked to the couch where Tucker was starting to rouse and fuss.

"Hey, little man," Pescoli said, picking him up.

Santana glanced at his son. "He's been a pill."

"This guy? A pill? No way. Not in a million years." Pescoli nuzzled Tucker and he sneezed, then looked surprised, then broke into a big, toothless grin. "See?"

"A mother's touch," her husband grumbled. "I'll be back in a while. Got to go check the stock at the Long spread. Had a problem with a frozen pipe earlier."

"The kids?" she asked before checking the clock. Bianca wasn't due back from school for another hour and Jeremy should be at his job. "Never mind."

"Okay." With a wave he was off and Sarina was making come-to-mama motions with her fingers at Tucker.

"Let me hold him."

"He probably needs changing," Santana called back on his way out.

"Not a problem for me," Sarina said. Pescoli handed him into her outstretched arms, then pointed to a makeshift changing table positioned in the corner near the television.

"Diapers, wipes, cream . . . whatever he needs over there."

Sarina wrinkled her nose at Tucker. "I think we can handle this, right?" Then to Pescoli, "He reminds me of Ryan, when he was this small. It just goes so fast, doesn't it?"

"Yeah," Pescoli said.

Ivy, pretending not to be paying attention to the conversation, had been petting Sturgis near the back door and the dog was responding, his black tail whipping back and forth. But as Sarina cooed at the baby, Ivy's expression turned a little darker, the corners of her lips twisting almost imperceptibly. When Sarina giggled and started making baby talk, Ivy gave up her feigned interest in the dog and, thinking no one would notice, rolled her eyes as if she thought her aunt was an idiot for all the attention she was lavishing on Tucker. Without a word Ivy patted her back pocket, checking for the cell phone, then made her way toward the staircase, her footsteps echoing sharply as she hurried up the steps.

Pescoli watched it all, silently, wondering.

Sarina looked up from the changing table and caught the end of her quick exit. "Poor thing," she whispered. "She's been through so much. I'm not just talking about losing her mother. Lord knows that's hard enough. We've all felt the pain. But then what she suffered through in Albuquerque, too? When she was just trying to get away? And now, after she makes it here, to family and safety, she's treated like a criminal."

And maybe for a good reason, Pescoli thought. "Poor thing" or not, she was the key to finding out what happened to her mother and stepfather.

She considered calling Tanaka or Paterno, but felt they wouldn't tell her anything. Alvarez wasn't a part of the investigation and Ivy had clammed up.

But there were still two sources, if she could convince either of them to help her. The first was Chilcoate with his ability to hack just about any damned thing. And then there was Jeremy. Could she use her own son to get what she wanted?

You bet.

When it came to catching a killer.

"Here." Sarina handed the baby back to Pescoli. "I need to call Collette and bring her up to speed. She'll want to know what's going on."

Pescoli gave her a halfhearted smile. Just what she needed. Her other sister back in the mix.

Sarina added, "Then I want to talk to Ivy. Alone."

Be my guest, Pescoli thought as Sarina, tapping her fingers across the face of her cell phone before placing it against her ear, followed after her niece up the stairs.

Tanaka sat in the rental car at the airport in Missoula as Paterno turned it back into the agency. Her thoughts about the case had been interrupted by a phone call from Bonita, the neighbor girl who was in charge of Mr. Claus, while she was here, in the frozen tundra of Montana.

In performing her cat duties Bonita had discovered a decapitated, partially chewed mouse left on the little rug in front of the bathroom sink, a trophy displayed proudly.

"Disgusting!" Bonita, the thirteen-year-old neighbor, reported.

"You're right. Did you take care of it?"

"Uh—yeah."

"It's in the garbage? Or down the toilet?"

"I put a paper towel over it. I couldn't do anything else. I was almost puking just looking at it. I couldn't touch it."

"It's still in the bathroom."

"Unless he ate it. Yech. Why would he do it?"

"Kill the mouse? That's his job."

"But he could . . . I don't know, eat it or bury it or whatever it is they do."

"He did what they do. Look, don't worry about it. I'll be home in a few hours and I'll take care of it."

"Oh . . . okay. And you'll pay me then?"

"Yes," Tanaka said, staring out the windshield and watching a plane descend through the cloud cover. "I'll stop by your apartment."

"Good. Cuz me and my friends are going to get mani-pedis tomorrow."

Is that what thirteen-year-olds did these days? "Okay." She hung up feeling out of touch with the world. When she took on a case like the Lathams, she became uber-focused, and while the earth spun, and people had normal lives of husbands and children and run-of-the-mill jobs, she spent every waking hour trying to track down a killer.

That was good, wasn't it?

The world kept spinning because everyone did his or her job.

Hers just happened to be intense, trying to bring the most heinous of offenders to justice. As was the case in the Latham murders.

Through the window, she saw Paterno motioning to her and she climbed out of the car, double-checked to see that she had her laptop and briefcase, then pulled her coat tight around her torso and stepped onto the snowy parking area where an attendant in a puffy jacket halfheartedly walked around the vehicle searching for any damage.

A gust of wind swept over the lot, tugging at her hair, and she thought for a second that she and Paterno should stay here, that there had to be more of a reason for Ivy Wilde to come here than to seek shelter and safety with an aunt she barely knew. That just didn't make any sense.

But nothing about this case did.

No damage was found to the rental, so she and Paterno walked into the terminal, the chill of Montana winter chasing after her.

"You're not happy," he said once they'd passed by the stuffed bear standing on hind legs behind a glass case.

"What's with all the dead bears?" she asked. They'd eaten lunch at a place called Wild Will's situated near the Grizzly River, the dining area being decorated with stuffed heads of long-dead animals, and in the entrance, greeting potential customers stood a stuffed grizzly bear on its hind legs. If that hadn't been enough, it had been dressed in a toga, a hunter's bow spread awkwardly through the massive claws of a great paw, a pink quiver slung over one of its muscular shoulders. The arrows peeking out of the quiver sported glittery red hearts rather than feathers as fletching. Tilted jauntily over one ear was a crown with red jewels, and absurdly, a set of white wings had been spread across his back. Like the damned thing was supposed to be Cupid for the upcoming Valentine's Day.

"Bear country," Paterno said.

"So leave them in the country. And alive, thank you

very much." She threw the airport's taxidermied beast a dark glare. "Where is PETA when you need it?" She was in a bad mood as she headed toward security and her gate. As much as she disliked being here in bone-cold Montana this time of year, Tanaka couldn't shake the feeling that she shouldn't be leaving, that there was more to her case here in Montana than Ivy Wilde.

She just couldn't put her finger on it.

Yet.

But she would.

She tossed her coat into a bin on the conveyor belt with her briefcase and laptop, sensing she'd be back.

"Come on, come on!" Jeff Baylor, a few steps ahead, half turned to wave at Becca Johnson, encouraging her to keep walking. In snowshoes. Which she'd never worn before. In the freezing cold. And it was snowing again. Snowing pretty hard. This trek into the frozen wilderness was his idea, of course, and she'd gone along with it primarily because she was *beyond* pissed off at Jeremy Strand, the boy she was currently crushing on.

Maybe he wasn't crushing back, she thought with more than a smidgeon of disgust. Sure, he'd been interested. They'd gone out a couple of times, hung out a few more, and he'd seemed crazy about her. Or so she'd thought when they were making out in the back of his pickup. But it could be she'd been wrong about him. It had happened before. There was a good chance he was just one more man/boy who was only into the budding relationship for a hookup.

Becca had thought about going all the way. She'd

come close, but had stopped before things went too far. Such an intimate act hadn't seemed right at the time when they'd been rolling around in the back of his truck, discarding their clothes wildly, and kissing all over their bodies. She'd put the brakes on, saying as much. Not wanting to be denied, he'd asked her to come back to his apartment, to a real bed. She'd been tempted, only to learn that his "own place" was really just attic space over a garage attached to his mother the cop's house. Jeremy's mom, his father, and sister all lived in the same place, just a couple of slabs of sheet rock offering the privacy she needed.

Nope, didn't sound romantic at all. She'd put the kibosh on that idea.

"It's not like that," he'd assured her when, that night, she'd rehooked her bra and said she'd better get home. "It's really my own place. Separate door. Separate lock. C'mon, Becca, we could spend all night together."

"Nah." She'd shaken her head.

"We could wake up together. I'd like that." He'd seemed earnest. Kind. Loving. But she'd taken a swift reality check. Her mother would totally freak out if she wasn't home by midnight.

"I have to get back," she'd explained. "Mom works an early morning shift. I've got to watch after my brother." With a sigh, she'd run a hand down his cheek and felt just the hint of stubble. "I'd like to, really. But I just can't."

Jeremy hadn't pushed her after that, just driven her back home, the two-bedroom cottage Mom rented in town, just three blocks from the river and around the corner from a mini-mart. Becca had hoped the relationship would endure, that maybe, just maybe Jeremy Strand might be the one. In college and working, too, determined to become a cop or a criminal lawyer, Jeremy had aspirations, a future that she daydreamed about making hers as well.

She'd been wrong, of course, but all of a sudden, just this week he hadn't returned *any* of her texts or calls and then she'd caught a glimpse of him driving some girl she didn't recognize through town.

Heartbreak. She was heartbroken and mad.

So, forget him.

Now she plunged her poles angrily into the soft powder.

Of course, neither of them had said anything about exclusivity, so here she was with Jeff Baylor, whom she liked just fine but wasn't really interested in, and trying like crazy to get past the pain in her chest whenever she thought of lying Jeremy Strand.

"Becca! You coming or what?"

"Give me a sec," she muttered, forcing herself to keep up with him in the knee-deep snow. She was breathing hard, her breath fogging as snow fell and collected on the curls that escaped from her wool cap. "Where are we going anyway?"

It seemed like they'd snowshoed for miles, and the light was fading fast. The forest, shadowed though not dark due to the blanket of white covering the ground, loomed around them and she was getting a little worried. If they returned the way they'd hiked in, it would be nearly an hour to get back to Jeff's crossover SUV.

"It's just up here," he said. "There's a creek with kind of an abandoned cottage. It's cool. I saw a cougar up here once."

"What?" she nearly squealed, stopping in her tracks. "You're kidding, right?"

He turned and grinned, his eyes bright, his smile, in the scruff of a beard he was trying to grow, widening. "Sorry."

"Not, funny, Baylor."

"Okay. Come on . . . no big cats, I promise."

"And you know that how?"

"My uncle owns the property. We used to come up here before he died."

"So he doesn't own it anymore."

"Technically, no. But my cousin does. Trouble is, he lives in Miami. Never gets up here anymore. At least that's what Mom says."

"Fine." She trudged on, starting to sweat despite the cold air, breaking new tracks in the pristine wilderness. It was quiet up here, hushed in the snowfall, though she thought she could hear a creek gurgling in the distance. Her breath was a cloud as they turned and she realized they'd been following more than a trail—a path wide enough for a vehicle to pass through the stands of fir and pine. Also, the trek they were making seemed slightly lower than the surrounding drifts and she could feel the snow packing down, as if on a layer of tracks, ruts made by some vehicle before the last snowstorm.

"You said your cousin was in Miami?"

"Last I heard."

"Like in Florida, you mean."

Jeff tossed her a look, begging the question, *Are you for real?* "Of course. Florida. Is there any other?"

"Could be," she muttered under her breath. She

crossed the ruts and a shiver skittered down her spine, almost as if she'd walked across someone's grave.

Jeff was ahead of her, striding quickly into the gathering gloom.

"Hey! Wait a second," Becca called. "I don't like this." They were supposed to be on a trail that cross-country skiers used, one that cut through national parks or forests or something, but now they were on land owned by his cousin? Did he even know where he was going? "You said there was a cottage here somewhere?"

"More like a cabin. Rustic, y'know. With an outhouse."

"Great."

"My grandpa and uncle used it for hunting. Didn't need indoor plumbing."

"Everyone needs indoor plumbing."

He grinned again, his face ruddy from the cold and exertion. He was cute with his blond hair and wide smile, but he wasn't Jeremy Strand.

And you're a damned idiot still thinking about him.

Jeff said, "Come on, it's just around the next bend. Maybe we could warm up in the cabin. It's got a wood stove, I think."

That's probably filled with birds' nests or bats or squirrels or mice or raccoons . . .

"Hurry up." He was moving faster now and she had redoubled her efforts as she struggled to keep up with him. As they trekked deeper into the woods she felt a need to stay close to him. Not that he would ever leave her out here. He was a jokester, right, big on pranks, but he wouldn't. . . .

Her legs were beginning to ache as they rounded the

bend. He suddenly stopped dead in his tracks, and she almost ran into him.

"What the fuck?" he whispered.

"What?"

"What is that doing there? No one is supposed to be up here."

She followed his gaze and noticed a pickup, parked in a small clearing, the cab and bed covered in three or four inches of snow. "It's a truck. So what?" Didn't it just mean someone else was up here either snowshoeing or skiing or maybe even hunting even if it wasn't the season? Bad as it was, the fact was that poachers hunted in these hills year round.

"No one's ever been here before."

"Maybe your cousin is back," she said, but even as the words were out, the hairs on her nape raised, and though she didn't see or hear anything, she thought she sensed a presence nearby, something evil and dark. She shivered. "I think maybe we should leave."

But he was moving forward. "Something's wrong about this."

She felt a little tingle of dread. "Look, Jeff. If you're trying to scare me again, mission accomplished."

Was that rustle the wind sighing through brittle tree branches, or something else?

He kept moving cautiously forward.

"And if this is a joke, it's not funny."

"No joke." He'd reached the truck and was scraping away the snow, peering inside when the door that hadn't been quite latched creaked open.

A man slid out, landing hard in the snow.

Becca screamed.

Jeff leapt back. "Holy shit!"

And then she saw the blood, red splotches covering his jacket. His face, distorted and nearly blue, was twisted to look at her.

She screamed again, the sound tearing through the forest.

The bloody man didn't so much as twitch.

"He's dead. Shot." Jeff's eyes were bulging from his head as he peered into the cab. "Oh, shit, there's another one in there."

"What?"

"Another dead guy."

He backed up so fast that he nearly knocked her over. "Come on!"

Heart pounding, fear nearly paralyzing her, Becca fumbled for her phone, drawing it from her pocket as Jeff grabbed her hand and pulled her back the way they'd come. Still holding on to her pole, she nearly fell, juggling the iPhone and her pole. Both items dropped into a heavy drift. "Come on!" Jeff said, grabbing her hand and tugging. "Leave it!"

"No." She lunged for her phone.

"Fucking leave it!" He was practically shrieking, his eyes wide with fear. "That guy was shot! So was his buddy!"

Her pulse hammered in her ears. "But we need to help—"

"They're beyond help! Whoever did it could still be here. Oh, Jesus. Oh, Jesus." He was dragging her now, pounding through the snow, and she was scrambling through the drifts. "They were murdered, Becca! We have to get out of here. Oh, Jesus." She didn't argue, just kept up with him, moving as fast as she could, nearly running in the snowshoes as best as she could, pushing her one pole into the deep powder, the landscape now seeming treacherous.

Vicious.

Something evil lurking in the shadows.

Dreading what she might see, she glanced over her shoulder half expecting to witness the dead guys stumble out of the truck and zombie-walk after them. Or . . . as Jeff had said, whoever shot the men could still be around. He mentioned the cabin. . . .

Darkness was closing fast, Jeff's SUV a mile or so away. At any moment someone could jump out from behind a tree and . . . oh, God.

Adrenaline fired her blood, urged her forward. Her legs ached and her lungs burned but she didn't care. Nothing mattered but escape. If only they could break out of the woods, make it to the car before the murderer who had killed the two men caught up to her.

She thought she heard a keening wail and nearly fainted till she realized it was her own howling voice. She clamped her lips shut and scrambled away as fast as she could.

Chapter 26

"We don't have any sample of Brady Long's DNA," Carson Ramsby explained, as if Alvarez, seated at her desk and looking over an autopsy report, didn't understand basic genetics. "We'll have a helluva time refuting Garrett Mays's claim."

"Or substantiating it. Not that it's our problem." Alvarez looked up and saw that he was standing in the doorway to her office. Dressed in a puffy ski jacket and a watch cap, he was obviously on his way out of the office. *So go already.* She tried not to let Ramsby bug her, but he did. Plain and simple. The guy just got under her skin. Worse yet, earlier today, Alvarez had seen Pescoli, her old partner, standing in the very spot Ramsby now occupied. It was funny, she thought, and a tad ironic that Pescoli had, at the onset of their partnership, bothered Alvarez as well. Alvarez had always gone by the rules; Pescoli never had. But this guy—Ramsby—he wrote the book about going by the book.

He was forever second-guessing Alvarez and remarking that whatever she was doing wasn't precisely protocol.

You didn't know how good you had it, she thought now.

"See you tomorrow," he said.

She grunted a quick and thankful, "Bye," then noticed that he hadn't left at all. When she looked past the open door and a few steps down the hallway, she spied him brown-nosing his way into Sheriff Blackwater's office.

Did the kid have no shame?

What about a better place to be?

Wasn't there a girl to chase? A brew to drink? A sporting event to get lost in? Wasn't that what normal twenty-something males did?

But then there was nothing normal about Carson Ramsby, ex-jock, but with an IQ that was supposedly off the charts. She'd seen no evidence of that, at least none that she would admit to, but that was the rumor.

Her phone rang and she picked up automatically. "Alvarez."

"It's Rule," the deputy said on the other end of the line. "You better get out here. And by here, I mean on a little to nothin' logging road off Cougar Pass, near an old hunting cabin." He gave her the exact locale and explained, "I got a call about a couple of kids out snowshoeing and coming across what they thought were a couple of dead bodies and they were right. Apparent gunshot victims."

"Murder-suicide?" she thought aloud.

"Don't think so. Just by the first look at the wounds I don't even think they were killed in the truck where the kids found them, but that's for you and the forensics team to figure out."

"Where are the kids now?"

"Huddled in my SUV."

"Keep them there. I'm on my way."

"Got it."

Alvarez grabbed her service weapon, strapped it into a shoulder holster, then forced her arms into her jacket. Double-checking for the gloves and hat she kept stuffed into a pocket, she headed for the exit, just stopping long enough to check out one of the four-wheel-drive vehicles owned by the county.

Ramsby caught up with her at the desk. "Double?" he asked.

"That's right. How'd you know?"

"Rule called the sheriff after he got hold of you and the crime techs."

"Good. Then let's roll."

He fell into step with her. "What happened?"

"Don't know more than that. Guess it's up to us to find out." She was already pushing open the back door that led to the employee lot where personal cars and department-issued vehicles were parked, collecting snow. She eyed her Subaru, but made her way to the department-issued rig and unlocked the doors. "Get in."

She thought he might want to drive—they'd had that argument before—but she was wrong. For once Ramsby did as he was told and rode shotgun while she turned on siren and lights and stepped on the gas.

"I got the papers," Bianca said as she helped clear the table. Dinner was finished, later than usual as Pescoli had driven Sarina to the airport. Ivy was refusing to leave. For now, her aunts agreed, she could stay, though why she wanted to relocate to Montana was a mystery. Her insistence that she didn't feel safe anywhere near San Francisco and that Pescoli was her only relative who lived far away just didn't hold water as she barely knew her. The fact that she insisted her mother had advised her to seek shelter with Pescoli if something happened to her and Ivy was in trouble, rang a little truer. Now, of course, there was the Jeremy factor, too, whatever that meant.

Dear God.

Ivy had already headed upstairs. Jeremy, presumably, was still pumping gas at Corky's Gas and Go, the local gas station/mini-mart, but he was due home at any time. The baby, usually crabby this time of night, was seated in his bouncy chair on the island, watching the action from his elevated position. And Sarina was now at the airport awaiting her flight and probably on the phone with her kids or Collette, still upset that she hadn't been able to convince Ivy to return with her. Their private conversation hadn't apparently gone well. Whatever had been said upset Sarina, but she'd departed as planned, leaving Ivy in a sullen mood where the girl had barely spoken a word as she'd picked her way disinterestedly through a taco salad that Bianca had put together during Pescoli's airport run to Missoula.

"Did you hear me?" Bianca demanded.

"Yes. You said you got the papers. What papers?" Pescoli was wiping the counter, loading the dishwasher, but paused to look at Bianca.

"The ones to legally change my name."

"You're really going through with it?" Pescoli tossed her wet towel into the sink.

"I told you I was." Bianca glanced at Santana, who was bent over, pulling on his boots near the back door, dogs swarming around him as he got ready to feed the stock. "Just my last name. I'm getting rid of the Pescoli part." She hesitated, staring at her stepfather. "If it's okay with you. I'll change it from Pescoli to Santana."

He didn't straighten, just looked from his stepdaughter to his wife, then back as he tugged on the top of a boot. "This isn't my call, Bianca," he said. "Of course it's fine with me, you know that. I think of you as my daughter as it is. No matter what your name. But this is something between you, your dad, and your mother."

"Lucky doesn't get a vote," she said stubbornly.

Pescoli picked up the baby, who had begun to fuss a little, demanding attention. "Lucky will be pissed and you'll have to deal with the fallout."

"I'm never talking to him again."

Santana jammed on the second boot and stretched to his full height. "I know you don't get this yet, but life is long, people change, time has a way of smoothing out the rough edges of your life."

"Or making more," Bianca said, reaching for a towel and wringing it between her hands.

"Just don't do anything you'll regret," he warned. "But as I said, it's fine by me."

"Mom?" she asked.

"Your call. But don't do anything rash."

"So I can be more like you?" she said, and Santana, reaching for his hat, smothered a smile.

"Yeah, that's your mom, always levelheaded. On a smooth, even keel." He slid the flat of his hand across the air indicating how even-tempered Pescoli was.

"Not so subtle point taken," she said to her husband as he whistled to the dogs and walked outside, letting in a rush of bitter cold air.

"So it's okay with you?" Bianca asked.

"Of course. Your name. Your life. But you probably have to tell your dad."

Bianca rolled her eyes. "Let him find out on his own. I said I wasn't talking to him again and I meant it." She slammed the dishwasher shut. "And as I said earlier, you might want to change your name, too. Once I'm Santana, the only person who will have the same one as you will be Dad. And everyone else will be Santana. Well, except Jer, but he doesn't really count."

"Don't tell him that."

"I mean he's almost out of the house."

"I'll think about it." And for the first time since deciding to marry Santana, she considered it again. There was a good chance that in this case, Bianca was right. Why the hell was she hanging on to a name that only brought heartache, pain, and fury with it? If Bianca really went through with it, so should she.

She fed and changed the baby and was about to put him down for the night when her cell phone chimed. Withdrawing it from her back pocket, she saw Alvarez's number on the screen.

"I think you better get up here, to Cougar Point," Alvarez said grimly as soon as Pescoli answered. "There's something you need to see." Then, before Pescoli could ask why, she added, "We've found two bodies, nearly frozen solid, left in the cab of a truck. Double-homicide. Looks like the victims might just be Troy Boxer and Ronny Stillwell, the two men Paterno and Tanaka were looking for."

Pescoli didn't waste any time. She texted her husband, left the baby with Bianca with little explanation, then tore out in her Jeep, following the directions she'd received from Alvarez straight to the spur of the old logging road. Police vehicles, blue and red lights flashing, beams reflecting on the snow, were positioned near the entrance to a narrow lane, crime scene tape strung between the trees. A fire truck and ambulance were parked just on the other side of an open gate, and a little deeper into the woods she saw a panel truck for the crime scene unit. A deputy was posted at the gate and barred anyone from getting by.

Pescoli wasn't the first to arrive. A television crew had already set up with Talli Donahue, the blond reporter from KBTR, standing in front of the tape, her cameraman recording her report. She wasn't alone. Manny Douglas, the reporter for the *Mountain Reporter,* was already on the scene. Dressed in an oversized ski jacket and matching insulated pants, he was seated in his older SUV and seemed to be dictating into his phone. At the sight of Pescoli's arrival, he threw open the door and, as she got out of her Jeep, demanded her attention.

"Detective Pescoli," he called. "Are you back on duty?"

"Not now, Manny."

"But are you here because of the murders? Two people, yes? Males. Have they been identified? Is that why you're here?"

Talli heard the commotion and held up a hand to the cameraman, cutting off her planned report.

"Detective Pescoli!" she shouted, "could we talk?"

"Not right now," Pescoli threw over her shoulder, hoping both the TV reporter and journalist would take a hint.

"Afterward?" Talli pushed.

Manny, not to be outdone said, "Is there a serial killer on the loose again? The people of Grizzly Falls and the surrounding county deserve to know."

He was right of course, and considering the fact that this part of Montana seemed to draw nutcases, psychotics, and killers like a huge magnet, there was always concern.

Pescoli stopped for a moment, felt the soft touch of falling snowflakes melting on her face. She saw Talli's microphone thrust forward and Manny holding his phone out to record anything she would say. She, who was no longer on active duty, she who might not have a job with the department by the end of the month. She stared right into the camera's lens. "I'm sure the public information officer will give a statement as soon as possible. I can't."

As she turned to duck under the tape, the reporters didn't give up. Questions were thrown at her rapid-fire, one after the other.

Manny: "Can you confirm that there are two victims?"

Talli: "The first report was that they're both males. Is this a possible murder-suicide?"

Manny: "Could these murders be linked to any others? Is the killer still at large? What do you want to say to the public?"

And on and on.

Pescoli ignored them and walked up to the deputy in charge of holding the line, keeping the press and lookie-loos at bay. She knew the guy, who didn't hassle her and let her pass, probably due to Alvarez's orders.

She followed a trail of many footsteps to round a bend.

The snow-covered forest should have been quiet and serene, the silence only disturbed by the sound of a gurgling creek that hadn't quite frozen over. Instead a small clearing was a hub of activity with EMTs, cops, and firemen all working the scene, some off to the side, one woman deputy smoking a cigarette down to its butt, just out of the perimeter of the roped-off grid where techs were sifting through the snow. Another deputy was on his cell phone, pacing between two pines and casting glances at the pickup truck that was at the center of it all.

"Pescoli!" Alvarez broke away from a cluster of cops. She was bundled in department-issue winter wear and the same kind of booties over her shoes that Pescoli had donned.

"Hey."

"Let me show you what we've got." She led the way down a trail broken in the snow to the side of the pickup where two bodies, stiff and covered in frozen blood, lay.

"Troy Boxer and Ronny Stillwell," Pescoli said as she studied the faces. She'd met Boxer and seen pictures of Stillwell. "What the hell are they doing here?"

"Exactly what I was wondering." Alvarez used her thumb to point at the truck. "Stolen."

"Figures."

"But not in San Francisco. This one was taken here and we're doing some checking but we think a similar one was left in the parking lot from where this one was taken. It could be that Boxer and Stillwell traded out one for the other, through different states, switching plates, to cover their tracks. I've got Ramsby on that theory."

"You find anything on them?" She was thinking of the guns and jewelry and cash taken from the Latham house, some piece of evidence linking them directly to her sister's death.

"Nothing. Not even ID, but we recognized Boxer from information Tanaka left, so ID-ing Stillwell was a no-brainer. We assume they had weapons. Those are gone, but we've found some casings so we'll double-check, and they should have had some kind of baggage, but again, not found. No cell phones, not even burners, no laptops, not a damned thing. Looks like the truck was cleaned out by whoever took the time to put the bodies in it. And the murders didn't happen while our two dead boys were sitting in it."

"Why did they go to all the trouble?"

"Unknown, but maybe intended to come back and drive it somewhere to hide it. You know, put it in an old barn or shed, drive it off a cliff or into the Grizzly River, but then again, that's just conjecture."

"What about the killer? Any idea?"

"Not yet, but the murders happened on this property . . . over there. We found pools of blood, mashed grass under the snow." Alvarez pointed to a spot in the clearing where Mikail Slatkin, one of the investigators, was painstakingly going over the ground. "Not in the cab of the truck where we found the vics. No shattered glass suggesting they were shot through the window, no blood spatter inside, so even if a window was rolled down or a door opened, they weren't shot there. The nature of the wounds, where the bullets hit the body, suggests they were killed in the clearing. There were also drag marks where whoever killed them took the time to put them in the truck." She frowned, eyebrows knitting as she stared at Pescoli. "Boxer and Stillwell were placed in the truck for a reason, but I don't think it was so that they would be found. This is too remote."

Pescoli nodded, getting into the case. "So why were they up here? They drove. Did someone hide in the cab and force them up here, then shoot them?"

"No. Other tire prints." Alvarez pointed to a set of tracks that was being painstakingly cleaned of fresh snow. "We're hoping the weight of the vehicle compacted the snow to ice and that we can get pictures and even take a mold. We'll see." She rubbed her jaw beneath a nose that was turning red. "I think they came up here to meet someone, an accomplice, and there was a double-cross." Cracking her neck, she added, "The connection of course is Ivy Wilde. First she shows up here, after fending off an attacker, no less, and then these two"—Alvarez hooked a gloved thumb toward the pickup—"appear. Dead. Not just a coincidence."

"No."

"We'll need to talk to her."

"I'll bring her in tomorrow."

"Tonight." Alvarez's jaw was tight. "With or without that lawyer she was requesting earlier today."

"Okay. But if these guys were killed in the last forty-eight or seventy-two hours, she's not a suspect. She's been under my watch from the time she got here. Someone's always been with her."

"Even at night?" Alvarez asked.

For a split second Pescoli thought about how she'd found Ivy in Jeremy's bed. "Yeah. And she doesn't have wheels."

"You have horses."

"Oh, Jesus, now you're reaching, Alvarez."

"Am I?" she asked, and Pescoli couldn't argue the fact that Ivy could have "borrowed" one of the horses or vehicles, though she was pretty sure someone would have noticed.

The sheriff walked up and Pescoli thought he might throw her off the case, remind her that though she was still on the county's payroll, she wasn't assigned to active duty. She was wrong. Blackwater nodded to her and said to Alvarez, "The MEs made the evident decision that the victims died of gunshot wounds, but there will still be autopsies, of course." Then to Pescoli, "You need to bring your niece in for questioning, ASAP. Again. She's squarely in the middle of this mess, whatever it is."

"Yeah." Pescoli was nodding.

"Is she your ward?"

"Not officially. She has a father."

"He needs to be informed."

Pescoli thought about Victor Wilde and his new family. "He's kind of out of the picture."

"So get him back into it. He's legally responsible."

"Okay. Ivy's not going to like it."

"You think I give a flying fuck what Ivy likes? Four people are dead, detective, including your sister. From what I can tell, the link to all four is Ivy Wilde, so get her the hell to the station." He didn't smile as the skin stretched tight over his bladed cheekbones. "Got it?" His dark eyes narrowed as if he expected her to argue.

She didn't.

He was right.

If only in this case.

She couldn't wait any longer.

Things were getting too out of control.

Ivy took a deep breath and glanced around this, "her" room in her aunt's house, but of course it was never her room, never would be. Until she was eighteen she had little say in what was to become of her. The cops had been brutal this afternoon. If that Asian detective had her way, Ivy would be behind bars. Of course she was innocent; she hadn't had anything to do with her mother or Paul's deaths, well, not directly. But the cops might create a case that didn't exist, plant evidence or whatever. It happened all the time on cop shows on TV.

She worried her lower lip. But, even if they didn't go that far, they would likely send her to live with her father. Oh, God. She thought of Elana, the self-important bitch who ruled that house and her three daughters. They were all sniveling brats, but Larissa, the oldest, she was the worst, always creeping around and staring at Ivy as if she'd just shown up from Jupiter rather than the heart of San Francisco. God, they were irritating.

Or, maybe she would be sent to live with Sarina and her boys. No. She couldn't let that happen.

Swallowing back the dread that inched its way up her throat, she stopped breathing for a second. Over the pounding of her heart, she heard nothing to indicate anyone was nearby. As far as she knew, her aunt was out, her uncle still doing some late-night chores, and suspicious Bianca tucked in her room since she'd put the baby to bed.

So no one should bother her.

The house was quiet. Even the damned dogs weren't making any racket.

Good.

Heart pounding, Ivy punched out the numbers she'd been given and waited.

One ring.

She bit her lip.

Two rings.

Come on. Answer.

Three rings.

Panic began to rise. What if she had the wrong number? What if something had gone wrong? What if she'd been duped. She swallowed hard.

Four rings.

"No!" she whispered, holding her cell in a death grip.

Then a click and a recorded voice. "I'm sorry. The party you are trying to reach is no longer at this number. Good-bye."

Click.

The connection was broken.

Ivy wouldn't believe it. Punched out the numbers again. More carefully. "Answer," she breathed into the phone as she walked to the window and stared into the darkness. Snow was falling, harder than it had been, drifting against the sides of the stable and barn, nearly covering Jeremy's truck.

Jeremy's truck . . .

She smiled.

He was back.

When the recorded message started to play in her ear, she disconnected. *Plan B*, she thought. What did one do when Plan A fell through? You fell back onto Plan B, which, in her case, was Jeremy Strand.

Chapter 27

"Becca Johnson?" Pescoli repeated as they walked toward the car where the people who had discovered the remains of Boxer and Stillwell now sat. "She's one of the kids who found the bodies?"

"Right. She and Jeff Baylor, whose family owns this piece of property, or at least did until recently. Looks like there may have been a sale. I've got Ramsby working with Zoller on it." Sage Zoller was one of the younger detectives who was into all things high tech.

So, she was going to finally meet Jeremy's girlfriend, the one he'd been so crazy about for a few weeks according to Santana, before he'd come across Ivy Wilde. How odd that they'd meet this way, but then Grizzly Falls was a small town.

Alvarez stayed back to let Pescoli act as lead as they headed toward the idling SUV where the two teenagers were huddled in the backseat, a deputy with them. Pescoli felt a little buzz of excitement running through her veins, that feeling of expectation that always came with trying to unravel the strings surrounding a mystery, the part of the job she loved.

At the vehicle, they tapped on the foggy glass and the officer behind the wheel rolled down the windows. "I'm Detective Pescoli," Regan said, peering in at two frightened teenagers. The boy was blond and fair, his eyes pale, reddish whiskers starting to show. Becca Johnson appeared as freaked-out as the boy, but she was darker-skinned, black curls escaping from a pink stocking cap, her eyes round and wide, a deep chocolate brown. "I'd like to ask a few questions." Of course it wasn't exactly kosher as she wasn't active in the department, but no one argued with her.

"You're Jeremy's mother," the girl said once Pescoli had settled into the passenger seat, feeling the warmth from the heater, a nice change from the blistering cold.

Brown eyes regarded her warily. "Uh-huh. I take it you know him."

"We . . . dated."

"Past tense?" Pescoli asked.

She lifted a shoulder indicating that whatever relationship they might have had was now in limbo.

"And you?" Pescoli asked the boy.

"I, uh, I don't know him. We just came up here to snowshoe, y'know. My cousin owns this place. He, um, he lives in Miami and no one should be here and . . ."

He rambled on, launching into a story about how they were innocently snowshoeing and how they came across the bodies, then took off and, once they were at their SUV, called 9-1-1. They waited for the deputy, who brought them back to this area and, after calling their parents, asked them to stay until the detectives arrived.

". . . and that's all I know," Jeff said, wrapping up his story.

"The truck doesn't belong to your cousin?"

"No. He's in Florida. . . . Well, I don't know. He could be up here, but those guys, the dead guys? They aren't him. Thank God."

"You know them?"

"No!" Jeff nearly shouted, and Becca was vigorously shaking her head.

"Can we go now?" Becca asked, gnawing at her lower lip. "This place is bad. Gives me the creeps."

"Of course it does!" Jeff rounded on her. "Because you saw dead guys! Jesus, it's not the place, Becca, it's what happened!" He must've heard his voice rising because he looked down at his hands. "Sorry. We're just both weirded out."

Regan nodded. "I don't blame you for being weirded out. Anyone would be."

"We've answered questions with like three cops. There's nothing more to add," Jeff said, and Becca nodded her agreement.

She'd taken off her stocking cap during the impromptu interview, her dark curls springing around her face as she moved her head, her fingers twined in the pink wool of her hat as if they'd never let go.

After a few questions that led nowhere, Pescoli said, "Okay, thanks." To the deputy sipping coffee behind the steering wheel, "I'm done. If Alvarez says it's okay, they can go."

"About time," Jeff muttered, and Pescoli could feel

Becca's gaze following her as she made her way back to Alvarez, who was embroiled in a conversation with Carson Ramsby.

"Should she really have talked to the witnesses?" Ramsby hitched his chin toward Pescoli, his face a mask of disapproval.

"It's okay," Alvarez said.

He wasn't convinced. "But—"

"But if there are any problems, I'll take the heat," Alvarez said firmly.

"I'm taking off anyway," Pescoli said, watching as the half-frozen bodies of Troy Boxer and Ronny Still-well were zippered into body bags.

She'd started back to her car when Blackwater caught up with her, walking with her out of the crime scene.

"I know," she said. "You want me to get Ivy and bring her down to the station."

"The morning will work," he said.

"You're okay with that?" She glanced at him as they passed by the deputy posted near the entrance to the spur. "I thought you wanted her in tonight."

"I do. But I have to be practical, right?" He slashed her a smile without any mirth, white teeth showing in the dark. "She may need a lawyer and we have to get our minds around what went down here tonight. Get our facts together."

"You think she pulled off a double-homicide in San Francisco, took out her mother and stepfather, then came here and what . . . killed some guys who she followed here, or followed her here? She's seventeen."

"The Menendez brothers were eighteen and twenty-one."

"She's a girl."

"There are women killers," he argued, "but I don't think she's a serial killer." He stopped and placed a hand at the crook of her elbow so that she would face him. "I do think she's involved, though, directly or indirectly, and you do, too. Also, I know she's killed once."

"What do you mean?"

"Ah. You don't know yet."

She braced herself.

"Wynn Ellis died a few hours ago. Massive heart attack, probably brought on by the trauma he went through when she set him on fire."

"Oh." Pescoli felt as if she'd been kicked. "That was self-defense."

"The camera footage showed the struggle and he definitely was the aggressor, but that doesn't mean there won't be an investigation. You know how that goes."

She did. Not only as a cop but as the mother of a daughter who had taken another's life in a deadly struggle.

"So bring her in tomorrow, with a lawyer, and she's going to need someone as a guardian, so you'd better call her father. He needs to be with her." In the darkness she saw Blackwater's stern face. "Whether he likes it or not, he needs to be responsible for his kid. He needs to support her, no matter what she has or hasn't done."

With that he stalked toward his rig and held up a hand, warding off questions as both Manny Douglas and Talli trailed after him, and another television van rolled onto the spur. Pescoli didn't waste any more time. She slogged through the snow to her Jeep and slid into the now-cool interior.

Within seconds, she'd switched on the ignition, cranked up the heater, and set the wipers in motion. A quick U-turn and she was driving home, snowflakes dancing in the beams of her headlights, the old logging road covered in white, tracks of the vehicles disappearing in the soft, ever-falling snow.

The clock showed that it was after ten, an hour earlier in Northern California where the Wildes would probably be settled in for the night. Pescoli was going to interrupt Victor Wilde's life with his second family.

Too bad, because, damn it, once again Blackwater was right.

Victor Wilde needed to come to Montana to collect his kid.

And to support her. She was his flesh and blood. His daughter.

It was time for Ivy's daddy to step the hell up.

After stepping out of the shower, Bianca wound a towel around her wet hair and wondered if she should change the color again. Throughout high school she'd dyed her hair, everything from blond to black to a cool shade of magenta. But she was over it now and discarded the idea nearly as soon as the notion popped into her head. In less than nine months, she'd be in college. Hopefully somewhere far away. Somewhere warm. Like Southern California or Arizona, anywhere but here.

She glanced out the bathroom window, saw in the exterior lights that it was still snowing, and sighed. Usually she liked the winters, but now . . . she needed to get away from her crazy family, especially her father. However, she had to admit that it was ironic that she was thinking of LA and sun and palm trees in an effort to put distance between herself and her father as his current wife was the one who had put the idea into her head. Michelle, the epitome of the blond beach beauty, had insisted Bianca would love it in Malibu or San Diego or Santa Monica, anywhere she could be near the ocean. Now Michelle and Lucky were splitting up.

For the briefest of seconds she felt sorry for her dad. Not only was he losing his wife but his daughter as well. But she tamped that thought down. Luke Pescoli would land on his feet. He always did. And he only really cared about "Numero Uno" as he would sometimes call himself.

She let the towel fall, sprayed detangler into her massive curls, and carefully combed out her still wet hair.

Then she slipped down the hall and, after checking to see that the baby was sleeping in his crib, saw that Ivy's door was ajar. Just a crack.

Was she crying?

Bianca inched a little closer and heard the muffled sobs.

She grimaced, wondering what to do.

Drawing a breath, she tapped lightly on the girl's door. "Ivy?" she whispered, pushing against the panels to find her cousin wrapped in the covers and blinking back tears. "Are you okay?"

Ivy sniffed, blinking, swiping a finger under her eyes to catch the running mascara. "Fine," she said, when they both knew it was a lie.

"But . . ."

"Yeah, but." She cleared her throat. "But my mom is dead. My dad's a total jerk and everyone is trying to get me to go back to San Francisco to live with Dad and Elana . . . or Aunt Sarina. Worse yet! And . . . and I just found out that the douche bag who jumped me and tried to rape and rob me in New Mexico *died.* I saw it on the Internet. So . . . yeah . . . but maybe I'm not so fine."

"I'm sorry," Bianca said.

"Are you? Really?" She gave her cousin a hard look.

"I killed a guy, too. Someone I knew. When he . . . well, he was going to kill me."

Ivy said, "Really? But you were here in Montana, right? Mommy was a cop and could help you out?"

"Yeah, I know, but I—"

"Just leave me alone." Ivy's face turned from sadness to a dark anger and her lips flattened over her teeth. "Okay?"

Bianca hesitated.

"Okay?" Ivy repeated, in a deep-throated whisper.

"Sure. Fine. It's your life."

"Exactly!"

Bianca lifted her palms, irked by Ivy's mercurial moods. "I was just trying to be nice."

"Then go be nice somewhere else. Maybe with your cop mom. Or your ultracool cowboy of a stepdad. I know you don't get along with your real dad, but at least you've got a decent guy who seems to care about you."

Bianca didn't respond.

"Yeah. Thought so. Just leave me the fuck alone."

Bianca did. Closing the door behind her, she started back to her bedroom, but Ivy, as much of a pain in the butt as she was, had a point. Bianca had been feeling sorry for herself, she was so pissed at her loser of a dad. But she did have Mom and Santana. She flopped onto her bed and pulled out her Kindle. She should start working on an essay that was due in English next week, but she couldn't make herself. She thought she heard Ivy crying softly again, but this time she put earbuds in her ears and listened to music as she opened up chapter eight of the latest Stephen King novel and got lost in a world of her own.

On her way home, there was little traffic, but the snow continued, tiny flakes dancing and twirling, forever falling in the glow of her headlights.

Pescoli called Victor Wilde and explained what was happening with his daughter.

He was less than thrilled.

"Oh, no," was his response. "She murdered that man?"

"Self-defense. There are tapes of the attack proving her story."

"Thank God."

"Nonetheless, she needs you. Not just legally, but emotionally."

"What do you want me to do from here?"

"I want you to get on the next plane to Missoula, rent a car, and come and get her at my house," Pescoli said with forced patience.

"That's not possible. I can't just—"

"Yes, Victor. You can. You're her father, and until other arrangements are made, her legal guardian."

"No, no. I—I can't leave my family and my job."

"She's your family, too."

"You can't just expect me to drop everything because she's gotten herself into a little mess."

"Is that what you call it?" Pescoli's blood was starting to boil. She felt her back teeth gnash and she forced herself to relax as he went rambling on.

"I have obligations here, Regan. You know that. Three daughters."

"Who, last I checked, still have a living mother."

He had no answer for that, and as she waited for some response she heard what sounded like another muted conversation in the background, as if he were holding his hand over the phone and talking to someone. Elana, no doubt.

"Victor? Call Ivy!" Pescoli shouted. "Tell her you're coming."

"Well . . . um . . . what?" More muffled conversation with his wife. Then he was back. "So what about the will?" he asked, his voice clearer.

Pescoli's heart sank. It was about the money. Of course. Wasn't it always?

"All of this is going to cost a pretty penny and I assume Ivy will inherit from Brindel. It was my understanding that no matter what happened to her mother she'd . . . what?" More garbled, muted conversation as,

Regan guessed, the most recent Mrs. Wilde was making her instructions to her husband clear. He finished with, "All of this is sounding very expensive."

"Victor, you sound like a man who is doing everything possible to shirk his duties as a father and is now bartering his own kid's inheritance in the process. Just get to Grizzly Falls by tomorrow at noon. Hire a lawyer for Ivy. I'll e-mail you some good ones I know of, and then we'll go from there."

She hung up before she went any further. She told herself to calm down, but dealing with the likes of Victor Wilde pushed her blood pressure into the stratosphere.

"Supercilious, self-involved son of a bitch," she muttered, taking a corner a little too fast and feeling the Jeep slip a bit. Catching her reflection in the rearview mirror, she muttered, "Cool it, Pescoli," and eased up on the gas.

Nearer her house, she punched in Chilcoate's number and put him on speaker phone. When he answered she said, "This is Pescoli."

"I know." As ever.

Faintly in the background she heard a rock band classic playing. Pink Floyd, she thought. *Another Brick in the Wall*. Recorded long before Chilcoate ever thought of being a rebellious teenager. She pictured him in her mind's eye, at his computer, fingers flying, scruff of a beard covering his chin, cigarette smoldering in a nearby ashtray, curly mop of hair bouncing to the driving beat. All the while he was wearing headphones connected to his computer and phone and scanning several screens at once, digging deep into the dark web, into places she suspected were dangerous.

He asked, "What do you need?"

"Information on Troy Boxer and Ronny Stillwell."

"You got anything to start with on them?"

"Age and recent address, last employment. Maybe more information later."

"Let me guess, these were the John Does found dead in the woods near Cougar Pass."

"That's already out?"

He didn't answer and she let it pass, saying instead, "So, if you can get phone records, credit card information, anything. And find out if and how they're connected to Paul and Brindel Latham and Brindel's daughter, Ivy. I know Boxer and Ivy dated for a while, but if there's any other information you can find, let me know."

"That it?" he asked.

"For now."

"Call me back in about six hours."

"At four or five in the morning?"

"I crash after that. Till noon."

"Okay." She cut the connection just as she rounded the final bend to her home where, through the curtain of snow, she saw her children's vehicles. Good. Everyone was home. Everyone was safe.

It was comforting to see evidence of her family's safety after witnessing two dead bodies, victims of some unknown violence.

In the house, she peeled off her jacket, hat, and boots, then convinced the dogs that they needed to go back to sleep. She cracked open a Coke and drank three swallows as she made her way upstairs. Both Ivy's and Bianca's doors were closed, no light emanating from under either one, and when she peeked in at Little Tucker, he was sleeping soundly, on his back, arms flung wide.

She smiled, thought about picking him up and nuzzling him with a good night kiss, then reminded herself of age old wisdom: Let sleeping babies lie.

Shutting the door softly, she walked into her bedroom where the television was glowing and Santana, dark hair rumpled, head pressed into his pillow, lay on the bed.

"'Bout time," he mumbled.

"Yeah, a tough one. I'll tell you all about it."

She stepped into the bathroom, stripped, and washed her face and eyed her robe, then thought better of it. Instead she walked naked across the bedroom, only pausing for a second to stare out at the snowy night. She eyed the lake and felt a chill, so she rubbed her arms.

Why did this calm vista, the powdery drifts and icy water, large snowflakes falling, make her nervous and wary. A tingle ran up the back of her arms and she squinted through the glass and into the dark as she had before. Just as in the past, she saw nothing.

"Are you going to stand there all night, or what?" Santana had levered himself on an elbow and was watching her every move.

"Or what," she said as he clicked off the TV with the remote and she nestled into his arms. In her home. In her bed. With her husband. Where they were all safe. His lips found hers in the darkness, his tongue gently probing her lips, and she let go, shedding all the tension, grief, and worry of the recent days as she warmed beneath his touch. One of his hands slid down her spine, to cup a buttock and draw her tight against his hardness. In that moment, with her pulse pounding and desire throbbing through her brain, she gave herself into the heat and raw sexual desire that always accompanied the feel of his callused hands scraping against her skin.

As she arched against him, she wondered how she could have gotten so lucky with this man as they made love and the world drifted away.

Chapter 28

The bed was empty, the room cold, the house quiet.

Too quiet.

Without opening her eyes, Pescoli flung an arm out but, of course, Santana was already up, out with the horses. . . .

She stretched.

The silence was blissful and so rare.

Actually it never existed.

She opened one eye and glanced at the clock.

Seven thirty-seven.

And no one but Santana was up?

Odd.

Rolling over with the faintest memories of sex still swimming through her consciousness, she peered at the baby monitor, but the image was blurry. Again. She really would have to replace it.

She climbed to her feet and stretched, then realized she was naked. She smiled as she grabbed her robe from the bathroom and wondered why the house seemed so cold. Opening the door to the hallway, she checked the register and saw that the temperature had dropped another few degrees. She hated to think that the furnace had given up the ghost, but no, she heard it running.

Again, she noticed the quiet.

She pushed open the baby's room and saw the reason for the coldness as the window was open, blinds raised. "What the . . . ?" A jolt of panic stabbed at her heart as she turned.

The baby's bed was empty.

She fell against the wall in fright, then immediately stood back up, telling herself not to freak out as she walked to the crib and saw that Tucker wasn't in it.

He's with Santana. He has to be. Even though Santana never wakes him, this is the one time. . . .

She flew out of the room and down the stairs, her bare feet pounding along the hallway.

Maybe the baby is sick. Santana is taking care of him. Didn't want to wake me.

But even as she ran, she knew that the scenario was unlikely.

Calm down. Tucker is fine. He is. He has to be.

"Santana?" she said as she reached the first floor. Why weren't the dogs barking? *Don't lose it. Everything's fine.* "Santana?" Where the hell were the dogs? "Santana?" No response.

The family room was empty.

No dogs.

No baby.

Her heart was thundering in her ears, panic surging.

Keep cool. Just look for them. Santana's probably in the stable, the dogs with him. Maybe he's taken Tuck with him, to allow you to sleep in. But . . .

Up the stairs she flew, first sweeping the baby's room again, then back to the bedroom where she grabbed her phone and texted her husband:

Where R U? Have you got Tuck?

Next she walked to the hall and threw open the door to Bianca's bedroom. Her daughter was there, lying on the bed, curled inside the covers, hair visible over the pillow, no baby anywhere in sight. "Bianca!" Then she noticed the earbuds in her daughter's ears. She crossed quickly to the bed and shook Bianca's shoulder.

"Bianca!"

She stirred and groaned. "What?"

"Do you know where Tuck is?"

"What?" She yanked out one of the earpieces. "Tuck? No." She was squinting now, one eye pried open, her face twisted. "Isn't he like in his bed?"

"No."

"Where is he?"

"I don't know. That's why I'm asking you."

A yawn. "Maybe Santana's got him." But she was stirring now, stretching an arm over her head. "Oh, God, what time is it? I've got to get to school . . . wait." She shoved herself into a sitting position as slumber finally slipped away. "What're you talking about? Tucker's missing?"

"I don't know. I mean, yes, he's not in his crib but Santana might have gotten up with him." That possibility seemed more remote than ever, but she clung to it. "Get up. Get dressed. Forget school. We need to find him."

She stalked to the guest room and didn't bother knocking, just opened the door. The interior was dark. She flipped on the lights. "Ivy? Have you seen—?"

The bed was empty.

It looked slept in, or at least used, but it was definitely empty.

"Oh . . . oh, no," she whispered. She checked the closet before backing out of the room and yelling, "Ivy!" A dull roar started at the base of her skull and moved through her brain.

Had Ivy taken Tucker?

But why?

And to where?

Frantic, she called out again, "Ivy! Ivy!"

"Mom!" Bianca appeared in the door of her room, hair still mussed, her oversized sleeping T-shirt rumpled and falling to her knees.

"She's gone."

"What? Who? Ivy? But I saw her last night." As if she thought her mother might be lying or, more likely, was blind, she checked the guest room herself. "Uh-oh."

"Uh-oh, what?"

When Bianca turned to face her, she swallowed. "She was in here last night. I heard her crying and I tried to talk to her, but she just got mad because I had a mother and she didn't, then she told me to leave her alone."

"And you didn't tell me?"

"You weren't here."

"Did you mention it to Santana?"

"No."

"Why the hell not?" Pescoli demanded.

"Because I just thought she was in one of her moods. You know," Bianca said, getting her back up a little. "She's always upset about something. Not the most stable person I know."

"She just lost her mother and her stepfather. And now the guy who attacked her is dead. She has a right to be upset."

"And now you do, too?" Bianca threw back, her eyes showing that she'd been wounded. "You can't find Tucker, so you're taking it out on me?"

Pescoli stopped short. She was right. "I'm sorry. Now, we just have to find your brother. And Ivy."

Her cell phone buzzed and she glanced at the text. From Santana.

What RU talking about? I'm with the horses. He's asleep. In his room.

"No," she said aloud, as if her husband could hear her. "He's not." The phone rang in her hand. Santana had given up on texting.

"Tell me you're kidding," he said.

"I'm not. He's gone. So is Ivy."

A swift intake of breath on the other end of the connection. "Son of a bitch," he muttered. "I'll be right in."

She was already making her way to the stairs where she ran down the steps and raced through the kitchen, not bothering to take down a jacket as she threw open the back door and ran outside. Up the stairs to Jeremy's loft she hurried, through the snow, slipping slightly on the icy steps. She tried the door, found it locked, and pounded wildly while calling his name. "Jeremy! Open up!" When there was two seconds hesitation, she thumped more loudly, her bare fist aching from the cold and the pressure with each hit.

She hauled back to strike the door again when it was opened suddenly and Jeremy stood in the doorway. Dressed only in his boxers. She didn't wait for him to ask anything, just pushed her way past him and into the dark interior where, of course, Ivy was in the bed. Lying on her stomach, this time without her shirt or bra. Rousing, she grabbed the edge of the comforter and squinted at the open door.

"Mom!" Jeremy said. "Some privacy! What're you thinking?"

"Where's Tucker?"

"What?" Jeremy said, then, "You can't keep barging in here and—"

"Where the hell is your brother?" Snow melting on her cheeks, desperation burrowing in her heart, she glared up at her son willing him to have the answer. But the expression on his face was blank, even confused. He was staring at her as if she were stark, raving mad.

Oh, no. No. No!

She turned her attention to Ivy, cowering, holding the covers over her bare breasts. She stalked to the side of the bed and glowered over her niece. "Where is he?"

Ivy's eyes were round. "I don't know."

"You didn't see him last night?"

"No . . . Jesus, what are you saying?"

Jeremy was still standing near the open door, snow and cold air blowing into the room. "Mom, really—"

"He's gone!" she cried, her voice cracking as she straightened and the reality bore down on her. "Jeremy, Tucker's gone!" Tears clogged her throat. She sent a scathing look at her niece, saw a lacy red bra in the tumble of clothes on the floor, picked it up, and flung it onto the bed. "Get dressed!" she ordered. "Both of you, downstairs." Blinking hard, she fumbled her way to the door. "We have to find him. We have to find him!"

Pescoli was a wreck and Alvarez didn't blame her. When the panicked phone call came in, she was at her desk and heard the break in her ex-partner's voice as she explained about the missing baby.

". . . we checked the monitor, but it's been on the fritz and it looks like whoever it was came in through the window."

"Wasn't it latched?"

"I think so? God, it's freezing outside and who would do such a thing?"

Alvarez hadn't been able to answer it then, nor could she now, in the middle of Pescoli's family room while a forensics team went over every inch of her house. Regan's husband was beside her, an arm over her shoulders, but he seemed as shell-shocked as his wife. Pescoli's kids were gathered in the room, Bianca in a recliner and her brother on the footstool, Ivy Wilde looking small and frightened in an oversized chair and wrapped in a comforter.

"We found marks against the side of the house. It looks like a ladder was used and then whoever it was pried the window open. There's a partially visible print on the carpet where a wet boot left debris," Alvarez said.

"I keep all the ladders in the shed. It's unlocked," Santana admitted, guilt evident on his face.

"Why would someone take a baby?" Bianca asked, and a dozen answers flitted through Alvarez's brain. None of them good: Revenge. Envy. The black market. A couple who is barren and desperate. Or much, much worse.

"We don't know," she said, but caught the fear in Pescoli's eyes. She knew. All cops did.

And they all watched the clock.

Though Alvarez had no idea who would be so brazen as to steal a child in the middle of the night with so many people and dogs around, she couldn't help but wonder if the abduction had something to do with Ivy Wilde. Was her appearance on Pescoli's doorstep just a coincidence . . . or . . . ?

From the corner of her eye she saw the girl in the big chair, looking shell-shocked. Caused by guilt? Or the tragedy she'd witnessed?

As the crime scene techs pored over the house, she questioned every member of the family, learning nothing more. Santana had been in the house all night, until morning, when he was watering and feeding the stock. Bianca had been asleep in her bed, wearing earphones, but admitting that something, some kind of bump had woken her for a second before she'd fallen back asleep sometime near four in the morning. Ivy, feeling blue, had sneaked over to Jeremy's room above the garage sometime after midnight, but she hadn't thought to check on the baby and she swore she knew nothing about his abduction. Just like everyone else.

And yet he was gone.

Snatched out of his bed on the second story.

The baby monitor was working only part of the

time. There was an image of someone near the crib on the recorder, but it was pixilated and grainy and was more a shot of darker gray shadows in a dim room.

What the hell had happened?

Who would take Pescoli's baby?

Someone who had it in for her?

Someone who despised Santana?

Or just someone who had wanted a child for whatever nefarious purpose?

"We have to find him," Pescoli whispered, her voice raw. "We have to." She lifted her head and met Alvarez's eyes. "Whatever we have to do," she said with dark determination in her eyes, "we have to find my son."

The baby was a pain in the ass.

He cried all the time. All the time.

No matter how many bottles of formula she fed him, or how many times she'd changed his diaper or clothes, he wailed.

Nonstop.

How did mothers stand it?

She paced across the "nursery" where he was lying in the bed she'd purchased, staring up at her with big teary eyes.

Somehow, this wasn't going as she'd planned.

Oh, she was certain that Pescoli was suffering at the loss of her child, but really, was it fair that *she* had to suffer, too? She shot the crying kid another look, then tried again with the little stuffed bunny she'd bought, touching his cheek with the fake rabbit's nose, letting one lopped ear trace across his cheek, but the kid was having none of it. He was flailing his little arms and crying and hiccuping and . . . it was too much.

"Sleep it off," she told him, and crossed to the other room, slamming the door behind her, trying to mute out his screams. What was wrong with him anyway?

Could he really tell that his mother wasn't around?

Well, too effin' bad. "Get used to it," she yelled through the closed door, then donned earbuds and plugged them into her iPhone, cranking up the music, a Beyoncé song she liked, until she could hear nothing but the music pounding through her brain.

That was better.

Now that she could think again, she felt more than a slight bit of satisfaction that Pescoli was probably as freaked out as she'd ever been.

And that, despite hanging on to the shrieking brat, was worth it.

Well, until he wasn't.

She thought of the lonely little gravestone on the hillside overlooking San Francisco Bay, where her own son lay deep in the ground, and her heart twisted. If only she'd had the chance to raise him.

This one is yours, now. It doesn't matter that he was born to the cop and her husband—he's an infant, you could raise him, have the life you dreamed of. Hurting him to hurt her would be wrong. She's going to be in pain anyway. Remember how you felt when you didn't know where your own infant boy was? The questions that plagued you, the blackness that took hold of your soul? The abject loneliness and despair you experienced every waking hour.

That's what she feels.

And it will come to her tenfold because she knows

he was taken from her on her watch. Aside from desperation, Pescoli will feel deep, soul-numbing guilt. And really, what could be better?

Tit for fuckin' tat.

Besides you really don't want to kill a baby. No, no, no. Shooting Boxer and Stillwell, that was a necessity. They would have turned on you. And being the orchestrator of Brindel and Paul Latham's death, that was all part of the plan. To start the ball rolling. A little shock wave to put Regan Pescoli on alert.

She knows now that the person who stole her child is capable of murder, so her pain has doubled and tripled and more. With each second, her excruciation increases, like a blade twisting deeper and deeper.

So enjoy it.

The baby will calm down.

He will be yours.

And Regan Pescoli will grow old with the pain and guilt of never knowing what happened to her child.

Perfect.

Chapter 29

Pescoli thought and hoped, even prayed, that a ransom call would come through. The police had set up the call center, the FBI was on their way, and Pescoli waited, staring at her home phone, keeping her cell charged at her side, checking the mail when it came, hoping for some sign that whoever had taken Tucker would return him. She and Santana weren't rich people, but they could scrape together some money, borrow if they had to, do whatever it took as long as they got their child back.

It didn't happen.

Until nearly three PM.

When she saw a car approach and a man get out. He was bundled in a long coat, scarf, and cap pulled down low over his eyes.

"Let me get this," Alvarez warned when the doorbell rang, but Pescoli was already hurrying to the foyer, her heart pounding in expectation, Santana just a step behind her.

"Pescoli! Stop!" Alvarez tried to intervene, but as the doorbell chimed, and the dogs got wind of a visitor, Pescoli reached the door and flung it open, all three dogs bursting onto the porch.

"Hey! Call them off!" Victor Wilde recoiled, hands over his head, as he eyed the pups as if they were a pack of rabid wolves.

"Down," Pescoli ordered sternly. "Hush! Sit." Nikita and Sturgis did as they were told, butts on the porch floorboards, tails unmoving, but Cisco, damn him, yipped and barked, his stiff little terrier legs propelling him around Wilde's feet. Rather than scold the dog, Pescoli reached down and picked him up. "Sorry," she said, crushingly disappointed.

"Ivy's here?"

"Yes."

"Is she ready to go?"

Pescoli was petting her little dog's head, trying to keep her mind in the moment when all she could think about was Tucker and what had happened to him. "Go where?"

"Home. You said to come and pick her up and I'm here."

"It's not going to be that easy," Pescoli said, and stepped back into the house as Santana, in stocking feet, whistled to the two larger dogs. They always barked their fool heads off at the sound of the bell, but last night, when everyone was sleeping, they hadn't recognized that someone was sneaking into the house.

Her heart ached as they walked into the family room, Santana shutting the door and herding the big dogs, Alvarez, after introducing herself, leading Victor inside.

"What's going on?" he asked, as he noticed the cops and forensic techs who were wrapping up examining the baby's room.

"The Santanas' baby is missing."

"Missing?" he repeated, almost as if the idea were distasteful. "Missing?"

They'd stopped just inside the family room where he was unwrapping his scarf when he spied his daughter, now seated on the ottoman with Jeremy, burrowed close to him, his big arm over her shoulders. "Ivy," he said, forcing a smile.

She whispered, "Hi," but didn't meet his eyes.

Nor did he step forward to close the gap between them. But when had he ever? He asked, "What happened to your hair? It's . . . different."

"New style," she said with more than a little contempt in her voice. "Very cool and in."

"If you say so." He didn't even catch her sarcasm.

Ivy shot a glance at Jeremy as if to say: *See? This is what I have to put up with.*

Victor pulled off his gloves and shoved them into his pocket. "I came because your aunt said you were in some kind of trouble."

"I didn't do anything!" she burst out.

He held up both hands, palms out. "I didn't accuse you of anything."

"But they have," she declared, her chin jutting forward as she tossed a hand at Santana and Regan. "They think I took their kid!"

"We didn't say that," Santana corrected tensely. "We were questioning everyone here at the house. And anyone else." To Victor, he said, "We just want to find our son. If Ivy heard or saw anything she needs to let us know."

"I've told you like a thousand times, I don't know anything!" She was on her feet, her head swiveling back and forth as she looked from Santana to her father. "Jesus, I was up in Jeremy's room with him. What more of an alibi do I need?"

Victor jerked as if slapped. "You *sleep* with him?" His gaze moved to Jeremy, who at least blushed as he climbed to his feet, towering over Ivy's father by three or four inches.

"I care for Ivy," said Jeremy.

"For the love of God, Regan, are you out of your mind? And, Ivy, what do you mean about an 'alibi'? Why on earth would you need an alibi?"

"She has her own room here," Regan said, though at the moment she didn't care a whit about Ivy and Jeremy and their sleeping arrangements. All that mattered right now was her baby and his safe return.

Victor said, "But you said—"

"I know!" Regan snapped, her nerves shot. "She has her own room but she prefers to be with Jeremy so she sneaks over there with my son's blessing."

"Geez, Mom!" Jeremy interrupted, stepping closer, Ivy, at his side, clinging to one arm. "Stop already. It doesn't matter."

"You allow this?" Victor was shocked as he swung his gaze back to Pescoli. "Them sleeping together, doing God only knows what. What's wrong with you?"

"What's wrong with *me*?" Her temper spiked and she was suddenly hot all over, angry, her fears and worries chased away by fury. She stepped closer to her ex-brother-in-law and held his gaze with her own. "I'll tell you what's wrong with me, Victor. I'm trying to take care of your daughter and my own two older kids while helping out in the murder investigation of one of my sisters to start with. The dead bodies are piling up and now . . . my son who isn't yet six months old is missing, stolen out of his bed in the middle of the night. That's what's wrong with me. You want to take this further?"

Victor went silent as Santana stepped between them and said, "Regan. Just stop, okay? This isn't helping."

"I don't care." She wasn't finished. "At least I'm here for my children. I—" Her voice cracked and her knees wobbled as she realized she hadn't been able to save her son. Being home, in the very house with her child, hadn't been good enough. She'd felt the evil watching her, known it existed, and yet was stunned when it had struck, snatching her innocent babe. She buried her face in her hands and might have collapsed except Santana's arm was around her shoulders and he helped her to the couch.

"We'll find him," he said. He tipped her chin up with a finger to stare deep into her eyes. "We will find him."

"Promise?" she asked, knowing it was foolish.

If he hesitated it was for less than a heartbeat. "Promise."

But deep in her heart, she knew they were only words. She was too much of a realist to trust a promise made out of desperation. She sank against Santana on the couch and let Alvarez handle the situation for once. She noted it was still snowing outside and that the dogs had settled into their beds by the fire. Someone had made coffee but she didn't know who or when, just smelled it for the first time. The forensic team was closing up shop, having gotten all the evidence they could, and she and Santana were still without their son.

Her throat ached and her heart felt as if it were in a vise. She tried to focus on the scene playing out in her family room, but all the while her distressed mind returned to the questions:

Who did this?

Why?

Where was her baby?

Was he all right?

And, oh, dear Lord, would she ever see him again?

Santana's arm around her tightened, his fingers firm over her shoulder, and she was brought back from her soul-crushing thoughts to realize that Victor, still standing near the ottoman, hadn't bothered to take off his coat. "Look, you've got a lot going on here," he said to the room at large. "Ivy should get her things together and then she and I'll leave, get out of your hair."

"No!" Ivy held Jeremy's arm in a death grip. She shook her head, the uneven layers of her hair shifting in the light from the table lamps that someone had turned on. "I'm not going back."

Victor's face reddened. "Of course you are."

"No!" Ivy was on her feet, small fists balled. "You can't tell me what to do."

"I'm your father!"

"Is that what you call it?"

"Hey," Alvarez said sharply. "Everyone chill out. Okay?" Alvarez turned to Victor. "Ivy can't leave. Not yet. She needs to answer some more questions at the station. I thought you understood that."

Victor's shoulders slumped a little. "Regan said something, but I thought with everything else that's going on it might be postponed."

"We still have a double-homicide to investigate. Detectives Paterno and Tanaka are on their way back here. Should arrive by midafternoon and then we'll wrap this up as quickly as possible."

"I already talked to them," Ivy complained.

"Before Troy Boxer's and Ronny Stillwell's bodies were found." Alvarez watched the girl for a reaction.

Got none. But Victor was perplexed. "Who are they?"

Alvarez explained, "Your daughter dated Boxer."

"Yeah, well, it was a *long time ago*," Ivy said, finally letting loose of Jeremy and folding her arms belligerently over her chest.

Alvarez said, "If two months constitutes a long time."

"It wasn't a big deal," Ivy said, but Jeremy's expression changed from rebellion to wariness. Pescoli, despite her worries, noted that her son seemed to finally catch a glimmer of what he'd gotten himself into.

"Are you kidding?" Her father looked aghast.

Ivy expelled a puff of air in disgust. "You people . . . I knew him and he ends up dead and somehow I'm the bad guy?" A dark pout clouded Ivy's features. "We hardly dated."

"So, you're going to help us out by telling us everything you know." Alvarez's smile was even, but held little warmth. To Victor she said, "If you want an attorney present during the interviews, now would be the time to call one."

* * *

"I can not believe we're here again!" Tanaka said as she and Paterno left the Missoula airport in their rented SUV.

Paterno was driving through the ever-falling snow and she tried to relax, which proved impossible. She'd barely had time to get her notes together on the Latham murders, interview a witness, go home and take a shower and feed Mr. Claus before she'd gotten the word that Boxer and Stillwell had been found, human popsicles this time, rather than the shish kebab that Wynn P. Ellis had become. "The department is going to flip with all of these trips."

"Be positive, would ya?" Paterno said as he increased the speed of the windshield wipers, the snow falling thick and fast. "Think of all the air-miles you're amassing."

"You're retiring. Hey, here's an idea. Maybe you could forget Mexico or wherever and retire here in Montana. Maybe ice fish."

"I don't think they ice fish here. That's like Minnesota."

"Is there a difference?"

He laughed. "Pretty big one, I think. Just don't confuse the states with the locals."

"Wouldn't dream of it," she said. "These people run around with shotguns and rifles and whole arsenals in their trucks."

They drove south out of town and, as they had on the plane, discussed the case, going over the particulars and theorizing about Ivy Wilde's part in the murders. Tanaka didn't see her as the shooter. It just didn't make any sense. Most of her story had held water, proven by cameras, witnesses, and evidence. She'd left San Francisco because something had gone terribly wrong at her house. She hadn't pulled the trigger, and possibly didn't know that murder was in the cards, but Tanaka would bet five to one that she was a part of what might have been a planned robbery. One of the neighbors, Margaret Rinaldo, had seen one of the A-Bay-C Delivery vans cruising through the neighborhood twice when she was walking her miniature schnauzer.

"They're hard to miss, you know," Margaret had said when she'd phoned in. "Practically neon yellow, if you know what I mean. I think I saw the van, once the week before the murders—oh, my, I can't tell you how upsetting this is. We live in a *nice* neighborhood, you know. Safe. And this . . . oh, dear."

"You saw the van a second time?" Tanaka had asked, trying to steer the older woman back on track.

"Oh, yes! It was about two, maybe three days before all the trouble, you know."

"The murders."

"So sad. I can still hardly believe it. I remember because I was waiting for a package to be delivered. I do a lot of online shopping. So easy these days, not like when I used to wait for Sears, Roebuck as a little girl, but I suppose you're too young for that. Anyway, I'd ordered a couple of books on line and they were supposed to be delivered and I heard a van on the street—I was at the piano about to sit down for a practice. I play, you see, have since I was a girl in New York, and I heard the rumble of a truck's engine and peered through the curtains and the van passed going very slowly."

"The A-Bay-C Delivery van."

"Yes! I thought he couldn't find the address and imagined there was some kind of change of transfer companies as I usually get my packages through UPS, so I stepped out on the porch and Keizer, that's my dog, he starts barking his fool head off, but the van just drives past my house and the Lathams' and goes up the street. Oh, wait! And that's the thing. It turned around and came back by."

"Did you get a look at the driver's face?" Tanaka had asked, barely able to breathe.

"Yes. I think so. He had a cap on, of course, and a big yellow coat, the kind they wear."

"Do you think you could pick him out of a set of pictures?"

"I'm not sure about that."

But she had. Tanaka had brought two six-packs of head shots of various men, including Boxer to the Rinaldo home and while Keizer had sniffed cautiously at Tanaka's boots, probably smelling Mr. Claus, who had done circle eights at her feet before she'd left the apartment, Margaret Rinaldo had picked Troy Boxer out of the head shots Tanaka had displayed on the older woman's antique dining room table. "That's him all right," she'd said, tapping a manicured finger on the picture of Boxer. "I think I've seen him before, with Brindel's daughter." Her lips pursed and she'd twisted a graying curl between her fingers. In a low voice she'd added, "She's a bit of trouble, that one." Then sighing. "But they all are. Those older boys of Paul's?" She clucked her tongue. "And Ivy? Well, her last name is Wilde and I'd say that's more than fitting."

Margaret hadn't been able to pick Ronny Stillwell's

picture out of the photographs, but fingering Troy was enough.

The way Tanaka figured it, the robbery had gone bad, the Lathams were murdered by Stillwell and Boxer, each one shooting a victim, then something had happened and Ivy had interrupted their plans. Maybe a confrontation when she found out that they'd killed her parents? Maybe that hadn't been part of the plans? Or had they then decided to kill her to shut her up? For some reason they'd come to Montana as had she. Had she managed to kill the two men, gun them down, then take the time to stuff their bodies into a truck and leave them there in the wilderness? Tanaka hadn't figured the ending out yet, but it was coming to her. She felt that little tingle inside that suggested she was close, the case was coming together.

Ivy Wilde was the key.

And like it or not, she was going to unlock the rest of the mystery that was this case.

Pescoli felt like a zombie.

Once she and her family were alone in the house, she walked through the rooms, distraught, ending up in Tucker's nursery, staring at his empty crib. She held his blanket in her hands, twisting it, lifting it to her face so she could drink in the lingering baby scent of him, and fought like hell to keep from crying.

Sarina had called and wanted to take the first flight back to Missoula, but Regan had asked her to stay in San Francisco, and when that hadn't worked, Regan had put Santana on the line. He'd been calm and firm.

". . . we're doing okay, Sarina. No, it's not great,

far from it, but we'll let you know when we locate Tucker. . . . What? . . . Yes, that's right. The bodies were identified. Boxer and Stillwell . . . yeah, I know. But Ivy will be fine. . . . Victor's here for another interview with the sheriff's department. What . . . yeah, but that's the way it is. He *is* her father. . . . No, Elana didn't come. Well, at least she didn't come to the house and he didn't say so . . . probably stayed with her daughters. . . . Of course, and thank you, we'll let you know, but we'll be fine." With that lie he'd hung up. They wouldn't be fine.

Not until Tucker was home.

Collette, too, had made a requisite sisterly call of concern, but the conversation was short. "I'm here for you, if you need me. I can hop a plane in a heartbeat. Just let me know what's happening."

Now, Pescoli went into the bathroom, still clutching the blanket, counting how many hours it had been since he'd been stolen. "Why?" she whispered, and stared at her reflection in the mirror. She looked gaunt. Drained. And though someone—Alvarez?—had suggested she talk to a doctor about a prescription for antidepressants or something, she'd refused.

She needed to feel the pain.

She needed to sense this raw scraping of her soul.

She needed to experience the anguish of guilt that ripped through her.

She was supposed to be resting. She'd told Santana that she needed time alone, to pull herself together, maybe get some sleep, but of course that had proved impossible. Her thoughts were swirling, her worries immense, sleep elusive.

Her phone jangled and she jumped, heart leaping to

her throat. She almost called for Santana, who was downstairs, when she saw the number: Chilcoate.

"Hello?" she said, her heart beating a thousand times a minute, her hands shaking. Did he have something for her, something that would lead her to her missing child?

"You didn't call me."

"Oh, Jesus. I forgot." She wanted to pour her heart out to him, but bit her tongue, anxious for whatever information he'd discovered, knowing instinctively that he, the loner and hermit that he was, wouldn't understand. "What did you find out?"

"There's a phone number that was called weeks ago, then suddenly stopped. To Boxer. Lots of calls up until the end of November, then nothing."

About the same time that Troy Boxer and Ivy Wilde broke up.

"Yes?" she said.

"It belongs to a woman named Lorna Percival."

The name didn't ring any bells. Pescoli's heart nosedived. "Lorna Percival?" she repeated.

"I can't find much on her. It's kind of like she just suddenly appeared on the radar about six or seven months ago. She lives in San Francisco supposedly, but the address I checked shows a strip mall. Probably one of those mailboxes with a suite number attached, no physical address, and her credit card statements go there."

"But she has statements."

"Uh-huh. Probably got the cards with fake ID and recently, get this, she's been in Montana. Not many charges but a couple at a mini-mart. Corky's Gas and Go."

Pescoli's knees went weak. The station where Jeremy worked? The woman who abducted Tucker was brazen enough to frequent the small store and gas station where Jeremy spent over twenty hours a week?

Her blood began to pulse in her head.

The woman, this Lorna Percival, was taunting her. Playing with fire on purpose. She thought of all the times she'd felt eyes upon her and knew that horrible woman had been watching the house, plotting her malevolence. And the boldness of using a ladder and forcing open a window when Pescoli and her husband were in a room down the hall, a daredevil flaunting her skills, rubbing it into Pescoli's nose.

She dropped the blanket.

Stared at the woman in the mirror, the broken down mother with the phone pressed desperately to her ear.

"You still there?" he asked.

"Oh, yeah." She felt a bit of her old self returning. "Do you have a picture of her? Of Lorna Percival? She had to have some kind of government ID to get a credit card, I would think. So is there a driver's license?"

"I'll send it to your e-mail address. It will be encrypted but you'll be able to open it, just . . . you know."

"It will be hard to trace the source. Yeah, I know. What about the dates on those receipts? They should be dated and time stamped." And there would be security camera footage at the mini-mart.

"I'll send them as well."

"Anything else?" she asked.

"Not yet. You want me to keep looking?"

"Yes!"

"Okay." He was about to cut the connection when he added, "Oh. Hey. I heard about your son. The baby?" Of course he had. "Just want you to know, I'm sorry. And . . . and we'll get the son of a bitch who did this."

"You bet we will," she said, talking as much to the woman in the mirror as to the man on the other end of the connection. "You damned well bet we will."

Chapter 30

Padgett Long!

Jesus. God. Padgett Long?

Pescoli stared at the photo that came in through her phone. The woman's image on the driver's license looked different, of course, had aged, but Pescoli would recognize those intense blue eyes anywhere. The hair was different, curly black hair now short and streaked, blond on blond, but still she was recognizable.

Lorna Percival was effin' Padgett Long.

Rocking back on her heels in her bathroom, Pescoli felt the fury rise within her. Why would this woman steal her child?

Hadn't she been locked up in some mental hospital? Mountain View? With its tall fences, electronically locked gates, and panoramic, serene vistas of the nearby hills?

What was she doing here, stealing *her* baby?

The last Regan had heard, Brady Long's sister had

been mute, speaking only in prayers, but then what did she know?

The evidence was clear.

"You bitch," she whispered, glaring at the photo on her phone.

So do something!

Get your kid back!

Almost on automatic, she went to her closet, unlocked the gun safe, pulled out the case for her service weapon, and unlocked it as well. When the case sprang open, she picked up her handgun, tested its weight, then slapped in a clip, grabbed her jacket, and put the weapon in her pocket.

She flew down the stairs and found her children, both shell-shocked, watching television, some reality show, which was just fine. "Where's Santana?" she asked.

Jeremy looked up. "He said he had to check on something at the Long Ranch. That he would be back in an hour or so."

Her heart froze. This was not good. "When did he leave?"

"I dunno, maybe fifteen minutes ago? He went in to check on you, but you were resting, so he told us to 'sit tight' and 'take care' of you."

"I'm fine."

One of Bianca's eyebrows raised. "No, you're not."

"As fine as I can be." She started for the door.

"You're going somewhere?"

"Yeah."

"Where?"

"Over to the Long Ranch. I need to talk to him."

Jeremy's brow furrowed, his eyebrows slamming together. "Santana said that you should—"

"I don't care," Pescoli cut him off sharply. "I want you to lock the doors. Don't let anyone in. No one. Except Santana and me. Got it?"

"Why?" Bianca asked with growing alarm.

"I think Padgett Long has your brother and I'm going to get him back."

"Who's Padgett Long?" Bianca asked, but Jeremy remembered.

Jeremy said, "That crazy chick? Brady Long's psycho sister?"

"That would be the one," she said tautly, another layer of ice surrounding her heart. Padgett was certifiably crazy and there was no telling what she would do. And it seemed as if Padgett was blaming Pescoli for all her troubles when she alone was at fault. It was true that Pescoli had killed the man who was Padgett's protector, a twisted murderer who had earned the name of The Star Crossed Killer. And now, it seemed, Padgett was seeking her revenge.

"Shouldn't you call the police?"

I am the police. With great forbearance, she managed to not snap that out and said instead, "I will. On my way to the Long Ranch."

"There are reporters at the main gate," Jeremy said. "Santana told us. He closed the gate to keep them out, so if you have to stop and unhook it, they'll want interviews."

"I'll take the back road, then. The one Santana uses that links the property." The rutted lane was wide enough for farm equipment, though usually reserved for horseback riding.

"He won't like it."

"He'll get over it." She reached for the door, then eyed the dogs, heads raised, ears cocked, waiting for a signal from her. "Keep the dogs with you, okay?" Before either kid could respond she was through the door and into the garage. She backed her Jeep onto the lane and, instead of driving around the lake to the county road, she turned the other way, nosing her rig into the opposite direction, slamming it into gear. "I'm coming," she said through gritted teeth. "And I'm taking my kid back, you bitch."

This time Alvarez was the officer who interviewed Ivy and she didn't pull out any of the stops. The girl was seated with her father in the same room as before, but Alvarez questioned the girl while Tanaka and Paterno watched through the two-way mirror into the room. Her father was with her, as was a slim, balding attorney dressed in various shades of brown: chocolate-colored jacket, tan shirt, dark brown slacks, and a beige tie—all of which seemed the exact same hue as the thin strands of hair covering his pate. His name was Gregory Knapp, a local guy who'd moved to Grizzly Falls five years earlier and with whom Alvarez had crossed paths a couple of times before.

Ivy was as sullen as she'd been before, still unwilling to say much, playing the victim, but her father was having none of it.

"Just tell the truth, all of it," Victor told her, "and whatever trouble you land in, we'll sort it out."

She stared straight ahead and crossed her arms over her chest.

"Really, Ivy," he said. He tried to touch her shoulder but she shrank away.

Alvarez asked her again what had happened the night of the Latham murders, and Ivy had gone over her story again. Nothing much changed in the telling, so Alvarez went on to new questions about Troy Boxer and Ronny Stillwell. Ivy kept to her story, insisting she barely knew Troy, had only briefly dated him, had just met him at a party. He was older, could buy beer, and she thought he was funny, until the relationship went sour.

"What happened?" Alvarez asked.

"I got bored with him, okay?"

"And he with you."

A lift of her shoulder. "I guess."

Alvarez heard her phone buzz, but ignored the incoming text. Instead she took the file on the desk and opened it. Inside were gruesome pictures of Troy Boxer and Ronny Stillwell. Shots of them in their blood-soaked clothes and shots of their naked, dead bodies, bullet holes and all.

She laid them on the table.

"Oh, God!" Ivy said, closing her eyes and turning away after one quick look. Horror stretched her eyes wide.

"What do you think you're doing?" Victor asked Alvarez, staring at the photos, his face ashen.

Knapp's lips flattened into a barely moving line. "Is this necessary, Detective?"

Alvarez ignored him. Focused on the girl.

Ivy was shaking her head. "No . . . no."

"This is what happened, Ivy, to the people I believe were working for the same person you were."

"No . . ." But from her expression, she was already putting two and two together, already starting to realize the danger she was in.

"Look at these pictures, Ivy," Alvarez insisted. "We already took out the bullets from the bodies and compared them. Two guns were used, one to shoot Stillwell, the other to kill Boxer. Since the bullets retrieved from Stillwell's body match those that were located inside your stepfather, Paul Latham, the crimes are linked. We know that. The bullets we extracted from Stillwell weren't a match to any we had on file. Our working theory is that Boxer killed Stillwell with the same gun he used to take your stepfather's life. Then, whoever they met in the woods here in Montana killed Boxer with his gun, after Stillwell was dead or nearly dead."

Ivy was shaking her head, trying to deny what was obvious. "No," she whispered, and her nose began to run. She wiped it with the back of her hand almost not realizing what she was doing.

Alvarez pressed a little harder. "Then, once they were dead, or at least incapacitated, the killer hauled them both into the truck and left them there, either to bleed out and freeze to death or just be put in cold storage."

Ivy started quivering uncontrollably.

"Maybe he was going to return and drive them into the river or hide them somewhere nearby, but couldn't take care of it at the moment. Maybe he was interrupted, but in the meantime the bodies were discovered."

"I can't believe this," Ivy said, but the way her face was twisted, it was obvious she did. She knew that whoever was behind the scheme was capable of murder. Alvarez was finally getting through to her.

"Do you know who they were meeting?"

"No." But her answer was shaky, unconvincing.

"That's probably a good thing, because I believe that this person, the mastermind, is cleaning up his business, taking care of loose ends, killing anyone who might identify him."

Tears starred the girl's lashes.

"No one who knows him is safe," Alvarez said with dead calm. "Even you. I believe you're next on his hit list."

The dam broke. Tears began rolling down Ivy's cheeks. "Not from *him*," she finally said, glancing from her father to her attorney, her voice raw and trembling. "From *her.* She's . . . she's a woman, and I swear I thought, I mean I thought she only wanted Paul's guns and some of his money. . . . He was her doctor when she was sick and a real ass. . . . She said he, you know, intimidated her. Sexually. And she figured he owed her. I believed it. Paul was such a douche. I hooked her up with Troy and he found Ronny. I thought I could leave. Take some money and run . . . Troy and I even broke up so there would be no connection."

"And you supplied him with a key?"

"Yes, but no one was supposed to get hurt. I swear!" The words were tumbling out now, and though her lawyer tried to break in, she barreled on, "And then . . . everything went upside down and I got home and found Mom and Paul like they were." She was sobbing now. Broken. "No one was supposed to get hurt! Or killed! She told me that. Swore to it. *Swore to it!*" Ivy buried her face in her hands and began to wail.

"Who is she?" Alvarez demanded.

The lawyer said, "Wait a second. I want to confer with my client. If she has information I want—"

"Lorna," Ivy said through her hands, her face still hidden, her shoulders shaking. "Her name is Lorna Percival. I met her at a clinic, when I was going through, well, you know." She parted her fingers to glance up at her father. "Before I went to Dr. Yates."

When her father looked at her blankly, she let out an anguished laugh. "My *shrink*, Dad. Dr. Yates is my doctor."

"This is enough," Knapp charged. "I need to confer with my client. She's said much too much already."

Alvarez didn't argue. She'd gotten what she needed. A name. Now they were getting somewhere. "Turn off the camera, and the audio," she said, staring at the window with the two-way mirror where, she knew, as did everyone in the interview room, that other officers including the detectives from San Francisco were watching. "Pull the curtain."

She walked out of the room intent on joining the others in the darkened area when she pulled her phone from her pocket and read the messages that had come in while she'd been interviewing Ivy. They were from Pescoli and they made her blood run cold.

Padgett Long has my son.
Her alias is Lorna Percival.
Heading to the Long Ranch.
Requesting backup.

Pescoli parked at the edge of the compound, next to Santana's truck.

The house seemed quiet as she approached and she kept a hand in her pocket on her pistol, ready to use it if she had to. Her blood was pumping, adrenaline rushing through her veins at the thought of finding Padgett with her child.

If she would just hand Tucker over . . .

The door to the house opened and she froze, bringing her firearm up.

"Whoa, Pescoli, don't shoot me," Santana said. "Trying to make yourself a widow?"

She didn't find his attempt at humor the least bit funny. "Why are you here?" she asked, suddenly wondering.

"The other day when Bianca and I were riding, I thought there was someone inside, but there wasn't. And then the baby missing . . . I just thought I'd double-check."

"And?"

He shook his head.

"But Padgett's involved."

"Who? *Padgett?*"

"Don't ask me how, but I know that Padgett Long has been in town. I suspect she is connected to Ivy somehow and she has an alias. Lorna Percival. And I think she took our son!"

His dark pallor turned a few shades whiter.

"I'll fill you in later. Now let's go back through this house. I have to see for myself. I've had this feeling lately that our house was being watched . . . by some malevolent presence, that something evil was out there and it was coming from this direction. Humor me, please," she pleaded, even though Santana was just intently listening. "Then our baby was taken and I learned Padgett Long was back."

"Okay." Santana was short. "And there is a trail of dead bodies from here to San Francisco."

She nodded jerkily and Santana let them inside where it was warmer and still as death. The place, despite being furnished, felt empty. Abandoned. Brady Long's couches and chairs, desks, tables, and lamps were clean and polished, the carpets vacuumed, the counters clean, no dust collecting, but the house still felt unused.

They walked softly from one room to the next, listening and searching. Pescoli's gaze swept every nook and cranny and she kept her hand on her pistol. Was she wrong? The living area and den, kitchen and laundry room, all empty. The bedrooms, too, looked as if they hadn't been slept in, though the beds had been made and towels hung in the adjoining bathrooms.

Even when they snapped on the lights, Pescoli felt nervous about being in the home, as if she were stepping on someone's grave.

Not that she cared.

All that mattered was finding her son, and as she walked through each empty, unused room, she felt her hopes die a little. If Tucker were here, wouldn't she hear him, sense that he was near?

Please, please, please, she thought, straining to hear any sound out of the ordinary, hoping to catch a glimpse of something, *anything* that would indicate he was nearby. But all she smelled was the slight scent of pine cleaner and she saw nothing that would suggest a baby had been in the house. No diapers or missing socks or forgotten pacifier lying in a corner.

Finally they were back in the kitchen, standing near the island, and she looked outside to watch the snow falling in fat flakes.

"He has to be here."

"I've looked in the outbuildings, too," he said, raking a hand through his hair, and she saw that he'd aged in the past few days. The lines around his eyes and mouth seemed deeper, the few strands of gray in his hair seeming to have doubled overnight.

He snapped out the lights and, as Pescoli took a step toward the door, she heard a squeak.

"What was that?" she asked in a whisper.

"What?"

"I heard something." She glanced at the ceiling. Had the sound come from above? "Is there an attic over this part of the house?"

His eyes narrowed. "Maybe. There's room, although—"

Creeeaaak.

This time the sound was louder.

Pescoli froze and craned her neck to stare at the ceiling.

Santana's eyes narrowed.

He grabbed her arm and held a finger to his lips, then led her through the laundry room to quietly open the door to the garage. She followed, hand on her gun, silent as a wraith beside him as they passed through another door to a mudroom where he pointed to the ceiling. There, tucked against the wall, was a pull-down ladder, cord hanging.

She glanced at the floor, black and white tiles, shining where they'd been recently polished. Visible on the squares were two marks, about eighteen inches apart, where the stairs had scraped.

She met Santana's eyes and gave a quick nod.

Santana pulled hard on the cord.

The collapsible stairs came tumbling down with a loud bang.

Both Santana and Pescoli flattened against the wall, bracing themselves for what might be a hail of gunfire.

But there was nothing.

Everything remained still.

"Come out!" Pescoli ordered. "Police!"

Still nothing.

"Bring me my son and come down these stairs, Padgett!" she ordered, but Santana wasn't waiting. He started up the stairs.

"Wait!" she called, then handed him her pistol.

"This is the police!" she yelled. "We know you're up there. Come out now with your hands over your head!"

Santana crouched low, then peeked over the edge of the attic, the pistol beside his head.

"Don't shoot!" a panicked male voice yelled. Footsteps scrambled overhead. "For the love of Christ! Don't shoot!"

Chapter 31

"Who the hell are you?" Santana demanded, lowering his gun as he saw the panic on the kid's face, his hands raised over his head under the three single bulbs lighting the attic space. The second the words passed his lips, he knew the twenty-year-old standing in a corner of the dark attic was none other than Garrett Mays, who claimed to be Brady Long's son.

"I'm Garrett," he said, and damn if he didn't look like Brady. Tall and lanky, straight dark hair, big worried eyes. "Garrett Mays. Who're you? The manager guy—right?"

"Nate Santana. What're you doing here?"

"Camping out on the family property."

Camping was right. Spread against the far wall was a crumpled sleeping bag, a small duffle, and all surrounded by wrappers for candy bars and fast food along with empty cans and bottles.

"More like trespassing and breaking and entering to

start with," Santana said, and waved Pescoli up the stairs.

She was already climbing up and hoisting herself onto the unfinished floor.

"I didn't mean to do anything wrong or anything illegal. I just wanted to see what it was like, y'know." Mays took a step closer, then stopped as he focused on the gun still in Santana's hand. "I never got to be a real son to my dad, you know. I never even met him. Mom and him, it was like a one-night stand or something. She, um, she never would talk about it much."

"You asked her who your father was?" Santana looked threatening in the harsh light.

"All my life, but she wouldn't say. It was weird, y'know. She wanted me to call this other guy Dad, Harold Mays. She took up with him when I was twelve. But it never felt right, not even when he adopted me. After college I just started looking around—they've got all those tests you can take. DNA. Where you spit into a test tube and send it to a lab and they link it up. Turns out I matched with some relative of Brady Long's and, through the process of elimination and some digging, I got hold of people here, and I figured it out."

"Just like that," Santana said, still skeptical. But if Garrett Mays was acting, he was putting on a performance worthy of an award. Then again, it was all so far-fetched.

"There's a legal process," said Pescoli.

"I knew Brady. He never said he had a kid," added Santana.

"He didn't know. That's just it."

Pescoli put in, "Why wouldn't your mother have come forward? Tried to collect child support?"

"I don't know." Garrett shook his head.

"Ask her," Pescoli told him. "Now that you have all this new 'evidence,' put it to her."

"I did. But, it was kinda too late. She's got early-onset dementia. Can't remember shi—anything. She's only fifty-three and . . . and it's awful. She still knows me, and Harold, but it's iffy. Sometimes she's clear as a bell, the next time she looks right through you."

Convenient, Santana thought. But the family resemblance was strong.

"This is the story you expect us to believe?" Pescoli asked.

"Why would I make it up?"

"The fact that Long had money played no part in that decision?" Santana asked.

He flushed. "Well, sure it did. But, man, I also really wanted to see what it's like out here. I'm from Chicago and this is waaay different, all the cowboy, Wild West shit, er, I mean stuff."

"Including that belt buckle," Santana pointed out as he'd spied Brady Long's favorite silver buckle, cut into the shape of Montana, a gold star not exactly where Helena, the state capital, was, but fixed more to the left side of the buckle, the western edge where a lot of the Long family copper mines and logging camps were located.

The kid had the decency to look sheepish. "I saw it downstairs and thought, 'well, he's not using it anymore,' right?"

"Enough!" Pescoli said, and he actually jumped

back a step. "What do you know about our son? Our baby?"

"What?"

"He's missing. Someone stole him out of his nursery last night."

He blinked rapidly. "You think I had something to do with it?" he said, his mouth dropping open. "What would I do with a little kid?"

Pescoli started to advance, but Santana put a hand out, caught her by the elbow.

"Is there anyone else here?" Santana asked.

"Just the maid. And you, sometimes." He was looking a little frantic now. "I mean it, I'm sorry about your kid and all, but I had nothing to do with it." Then he stopped. "Well, but . . ."

"What?" Pescoli demanded.

He licked his lips. "This morning I thought maybe I heard someone downstairs. It was still dark so I just stayed up here. I hoped they'd go away and they did."

Santana's pulse jumped, and beneath his fingertips he felt the muscles of his wife's upper arm tense.

"I didn't hear a car or anything, but . . . well, it was kinda crazy, but I thought I heard a woman's voice whisper, 'In a few hours, it'll all be over,' or something like that, but the wind was blowing and it rattles the shingles up here and I was kind of dreaming about my mom, and I thought it was like her voice . . . and then I woke up, so maybe I imagined it."

Pescoli started to sag, but Santana held her up and he felt her straighten, find some inner strength.

"Oh!" Mays said, as if he'd suddenly remembered. "There was a little bit of plastic that I saw on the kitchen floor and I picked it up, didn't want the maid to get suspicious. It's right here. . . ." With an eye on Santana still holding the gun, he went cautiously over to his snarl of bedding and clothes, knocked over a beer bottle that rolled across the floor, then found, under what looked to be a wrapper for a Reese's Peanut Butter Cup, a small bit of yellow plastic: a one inch in diameter ring. Once again Santana felt his wife sag against him.

"It's Tucker's," she said, her voice strained. "The ring that holds his set of plastic keys."

Santana's throat closed. He remembered his son hanging onto the ring, swinging the colorful keys in one tiny fist. Pointing to the ring, he rasped, "That was here?"

"Yeah, by the refrigerator, kind of poking out from underneath it."

"But you didn't see the baby?" Pescoli pressed.

He lifted his palms. "That's all I know."

"You need to tell the police," Pescoli said. "I mean officially. I'm with the Pinewood Sheriff's Department, Detective Pescoli, but you need to go down to the station and tell the officers there what you know."

"Pescoli?" Mays repeated. He brightened a little. "Then you must know Lucky, huh? Like you're his sister or something, right? Sister-in-law?"

Every muscle in Pescoli's body froze. "Lucky? You know Luke Pescoli?"

"Sure," he said.

Santana thought of Lucky cruising down the street on the ridge where the Long Museum took up so many blocks of prime real estate.

"How?" his wife asked, her voice low, her eyes zeroing in on the man still holding the small yellow ring. "How do you know Luke Pescoli?"

"Remember I told you I got with some locals to help sort out how I'm related to the Longs?" Garrett Mays said. "The guy who helped me? Who actually looked him up? That was Lucky."

Would that kid never shut up?

Padgett picked him up and jostled him, changed his diaper and fed him again. God, what did he want? She was second-guessing herself and hated it because things hadn't gone completely as planned. She was confined by the kid so she really couldn't enjoy all of Pescoli's agony. Why the hell hadn't she been on TV, standing next to her cop-friends and melting down, weeping and begging for "whoever took my baby" to please return him unharmed. Padgett needed to hear the desperation in Regan Pescoli's clogged throat, see the fear and absolute dread in her eyes.

But things had gone screwy from the moment she'd decided that Boxer and Stillwell needed to be taken out. They'd been useful players in what had been the start of it all. But again, she'd misplayed her hand, thinking that Pescoli would be miserable when she found out her sister had been murdered.

That, too, hadn't worked out exactly as planned. Yes, the killings had brought Pescoli into play, which Padgett had wanted, but she'd thought the cop would be more affected by her sister's death. Originally Padgett had thought about killing the sisters one by one, closing in on Regan Pescoli, but that plan had been too complicated and took too much time. She'd been too impatient, wanted to get right to the heart of the matter so that Pescoli would suffer the longest by not knowing where her baby son was, or if the kid were alive or dead. Was he suffering? In the country? Spirited away?

Even now Padgett smiled at the thought of the torment she'd brought to the woman. Served her right. But now things had changed and she felt a little undone. Unsafe. She needed to leave Grizzly Falls with the kid. Maybe stop in various places and send pictures of the baby crying in distress from all over the country. Freak Pescoli the fuck out. Twist the knife.

But she'd have to make a getaway.

And there was one more loose end before she left town:

Ivy Wilde.

The girl could ID her and that would be bad.

Ivy would have to join her boyfriend and Ronny Stillwell in the deep beyond.

But also she saw now that she was going to have to give up her fantasy of making Regan Pescoli twist in the wind for the rest of her life. It was too dangerous. If Padgett got caught they'd send her back to that mental hospital, or worse yet the women's prison in Billings. That would be no good. And there was capital punishment in this state. God, they wouldn't actually put her on death row, would they? A woman?

Of course they would.

Women's rights, gender equality.

And the needle.

Lethal injection.

No way.

No fuckin' way!

Not as long as she had a breath of life in her.

And a clip of fifteen rounds.

Moving briskly in the dark, she hurried back into the "nursery" and found the kid on his back staring up at her, but at least he was no longer screaming. "That's a good boy," she said in this cold room with its forgotten machinery and covered windows. With one hand on her pistol, she touched the top of his head with her other, fingers smoothing his crown of dark hair. So like his father's. "You keep quiet now."

He followed her with his eyes, again so like his father's, and Padgett felt a little chill of apprehension climb up her scalp, like the tiny legs of a dozen spiders crawling through her hair. She slipped out of the room, the heebie-jeebies lifting the hair on her arms.

Of course the kid started bawling again.

At the top of his damned lungs.

She double-checked, making certain the gun was loaded.

"Hush!" she screamed at the baby, and that only sent him into a louder wail. "You have to shut up!"

For the first time since losing her own son she thought that maybe she wasn't cut out for motherhood after all.

"I know where Tucker is," Santana said.

"What? Where?" Pescoli turned to face her husband. How could he have suddenly come up with the answer to their son's location? They were still standing in the attic, Garrett Mays packing up his things, the police on their way. Not only had Pescoli texted Alvarez, but she'd called her ex-partner once she'd discovered Mays and the key ring, and connected Lucky to the kidnapping. Alvarez was sending the cavalry.

Her insides were cold as an arctic storm when she thought of her ex. How could Lucky be so heartless to be a part of a kidnapping? She wanted to wring his neck over and over again. Her fingers itched to surround his long neck.

"The Long Museum."

"What? How?"

"What better place to hide out than in plain sight."

"But people go in there all the time."

"It's closed now, though. For the winter."

"Let's go," she said, her heart a stone. If Padgett hurt her son . . . If she so much as touched a hair on his little head—

"I'll drive," Santana said as a county vehicle, siren blaring, approached.

"Let me handle this."

They walked outside just as the SUV stopped, and with the engine idling, Pete Watershed stepped onto the snow-covered parking area. Night was falling fast, the sky dark, the snow, no longer falling. Watershed was wearing his perpetual scowl, his eyebrows drawn together under the bill of his cap. "Sorry, I'm late. Hold-up on the highway."

"It's fine. We've got to go," Pescoli said. "But Garrett Mays, here, was trespassing, camping out in the attic over the garage. The Long estate may or may not want to press charges, but you need to secure the property and take him down to the station for a full statement, let him cool his jets."

"Okay. But you're leaving?"

"We'll meet you there."

"Alvarez is heading this way," Watershed said. "She got hung up with the detectives from San Francisco."

"I'll catch her when I get to the station."

"You're going there now?" Watershed asked.

"Soon. First we need to stop in town at the Long Museum."

She didn't wait for any further arguments and, as Mays was exiting the garage, Watershed had his hands full.

They climbed into Santana's truck. His face set and grim, Santana drove into town, motoring as fast as he could down the county road and into the upper tier of Grizzly Falls where traffic was heavier. With each passing mile, Pescoli felt her anxiety ramp up a notch, her heart thud painfully.

Was Santana right?

Would they find Tucker there?

Would he be safe?

"I'm going to kill Lucky," she said as they turned down the street to the Long Museum.

"Not if I get to him first."

"I'm not kidding."

"Neither am I. Between what he did to Bianca and now this? However he's involved I'd like to—"

"String him up by his balls," she finished for him. "And that would just be for starters. Trust me, all that torture on *Game of Thrones* wouldn't hold a candle to what I'll do to him if anything happens to Tucker. Anything."

"No arguments from me."

As Santana found a spot to park on the street, she watched other cars pass, moving slowly, drivers on their way to their own lives, their own problems, not a clue that her world had stopped.

The gates to the old estate were locked, the museum closed, but Santana, as caretaker for the Long estate, had secured a set of keys and was allowed on the property for some maintenance. He was always supposed to let the board of directors know before he visited, but not today. He parked across the street, and even before he cut the engine Pescoli was out of the passenger side and cutting across the slow-moving traffic to the fenced property. Santana followed quickly, working a key into the lock of the ornate wrought-iron gate, and they slipped through.

The snow was undisturbed, the manor rising above the frozen grounds, the blanket of white pristine, no sign of footsteps. "I hope this isn't a wild goose chase," she said under her breath.

"Got any better ideas?"

That was the problem. If this didn't work, if they didn't find Tucker here, today, when would they?

Don't think that way.

Be a cop. Not a mother.

But it was impossible, and as they walked to the side of the property and let themselves in to what had once been a servants' entrance, she was fueled by fear for Tucker. The blood pulsed in her ears. She drew her weapon. Through the kitchen they moved, past a marble counter, its top covered with utensils from a bygone era, past a stove that looked to be a hundred years old, and into a butler's pantry. Behind the glass doors of the cupboard were stacks of white dinnerware, still on display though no one would ever use one of those plates again.

She thought of Garrett Mays and wondered about him. Was he really Brady Long's son, Padgett Long's nephew? Would he someday lay claim to all of these artifacts, challenge his family's gift to the city?

She felt a breath of cold air and shivered, wondering if, as local lore claimed, the ghosts of the long dead walked through these rooms.

Ridiculous.

Or was it?

They fanned out in the dining room with its long antique table, then came back together through a music room, where a spinet was gathering dust. Beyond the mullioned windows, past a few low-lying shrubs, was a view of the river with the lower tier of Grizzly Falls sprawled upon its shores. Lights winked in the darkness, brilliant specks lining the shore of the dark wedge that was the river.

Inside, there was no sign of Padgett, nor of Little Tucker.

Please, please, please that she could find him. Alive. Well.

Santana nudged her and they kept moving.

In the foyer they walked beneath a huge chandelier dripping with crystals and passed by umbrella stands and pictures of Brady Long's ancestors. Across the marble floor and through a drawing room where small sofas clustered near intricate tables and lamps, they came across another door that opened to the kitchen.

Nothing.

No sign of her baby.

Her heart ached.

And the house was so quiet.

Even the furnace could barely be heard, though the rooms were kept warm enough that Pescoli's jacket began to be uncomfortable.

She ignored the pang that cut through her soul.

Kept moving.

Kept searching.

Kept silently praying.

On soft footsteps they climbed a massive split staircase opening to the second floor. There the rooms were kept as if to accept guests, the beds made, the lamps lit. Only the ever present dust spoke of disuse. Her heart nearly tore when she spied the nursery with its antique rocking horse, Victorian dollhouse, and oversized tricycle. Again, Santana gave her a little prod and they walked through a master suite and several bathrooms.

Not a hint that anyone had been inside since the doors closed after the tourist season.

It'll be okay. You'll find him.

She had to believe it. Had to think she would see her child again.

Ignoring the rope disallowing visitors to the third floor, they made their way up to the servants' quarters under the eaves but found only unused furniture and pictures, the place dusty and forlorn, as if no one had set foot up here in decades.

There was nothing on any of the floors aboveground, and as they explored the basement staircase, Pescoli's heart sank. Dark and dry, dust and dirt.

Nothing but mouse traps, some with furry little victims, and more forgotten furniture from times gone by, lives once lived.

"Son of a bitch," Santana said as they climbed back to the first floor.

"He's gone," Pescoli said, miserable at the thought.

Don't go there! You have to find him. Don't give up.

"We're not done yet," Santana said, and she thought he was just being stubborn.

"There's the laundry house and toolsheds," but there was little hope in his voice and the night seemed close, as if behind these closed gates they were in another world. The snow had begun to fall again. Slow, lazy flakes drifting from the sky. In another situation, she would have found joy and beauty in the landscape. Tonight she felt bleak.

"Let's go." Pescoli started for the laundry house and Santana fell into step with her, cutting a path through the snow.

What had her grandmother once told her when her grandfather lay dying, pale and thin beneath sheets as he breathed in horrible rasps? "Where there's life, there's hope."

She had to cling to it. Clenching her teeth, she waited as Santana found the right key to open the door. She heard the lock snap open and she told herself not to get her hopes up. There was no sign of life within.

This, of course, was another wild goose chase.

Chapter 32

They were here?

For the love of Christ. How the fuck did they know to come here?

Padgett had hazarded a peek through the curtains and nearly fallen through the floor of the ancient laundry facilities when she saw Pescoli and Santana leaving the main house, the museum for God's sake, and break a path through the snow to the very spot where she was hiding out.

Shit!

In a flash, everything she'd worked for was about to be lost. She'd dreamed of tormenting Pescoli for years and now it was going to end here? No way!

She worked fast, thankful that the kid had finally worn himself out and for once wasn't screaming his fool head off.

She figured she still had the upper hand for a little while longer if she played her cards right. She unlocked the back door, would make her escape down the path that cut along the steep hillside to a parking garage where her vehicle was parked near the river. Her eyes were used to the dark and so she eased over to the fuse box, as old as it was, and pulled the main lever, cutting electricity to the box, insuring that no lights would turn on if they hit the switch. She slipped her small mag light into her pocket, and with her gun in one hand, she slid her high-intensity flashlight out of her pocket and held it between her teeth. She lifted the baby from his crib just as he was starting to wake and fuss and eased around an old wringer washer with a huge tub. When she looked over the rim, she had a full view of the door.

She heard the key turn in the lock.

Then she pinched the kid.

The door opened just as Pescoli heard Tucker scream.

Without thinking she flew inside the room and heard Santana call out, "Regan! Stop!" as he pounded against the wall, fumbling for the switch. "Shit, there's no lights!"

"Tucker? Baby?" she cried, banging her shin into something, a washtub? Pain ricocheted up her leg. It was dark as pitch in here and her child was crying, screaming. Her heart wrenched.

"Regan, it's a trap! I can't get the lights—"

"I'm here. Honey, I'm—"

A spark of light simultaneous with an ear-splitting blast.

Blam!

The laundry house boomed with the sound. Regan flew backward, the gun flung from her hand, her body slamming into wooden cupboards. Pain screamed up her back and she slithered to the floor.

She'd been hit. Hit.

The gun . . . where the hell . . . ? She turned in the direction that she'd heard it skitter across the concrete.

"Regan!" Santana yelled.

Blam! Another shot, this one to the wall where chips of concrete sprayed the area.

Oh. God.

Blood oozed from her torso.

"Oh, Jesus, Regan!" Santana yelled.

The baby shrieked.

"Don't move, Santana, or I swear to God, I'll kill your kid right here and now." Padgett's voice was low. Evil and thick, as if she were drunk, but the meaning was clear.

"Let him go," Pescoli yelled, but her voice was faint, and though she was scrambling to get up, to strip her son from Padgett's arms, to break free . . . she couldn't get her feet beneath her.

Her feet slid in something slick.

Was it her own blood? She touched her abdomen and felt the wetness, warm and oozing.

She sensed Santana moving closer in the dark. Could he jump Padgett? Risk it?

If only she could get to her gun, if only—

Click!

The room was suddenly awash with light.

Emanating from the intense lens of a flashlight.

Pescoli blinked.

A bright circle of light, enough intensity to light up the room, nearly blinded her. She held her arm over her eyes, tried to focus to the darkness beyond the flashlight. Squinting, she pleaded, "Don't hurt him! Please, Padgett. Do not hurt him."

Tucker, momentarily shocked to silence, started screaming again. As Pescoli adjusted to the light she saw her child, red faced and terrified, clutched in Padgett Long's arms. She had his squirming little chest pinned to hers, the flashlight in her mouth and her gun aimed straight at Pescoli. "How does it feel," she mumbled around the flashlight, "to lose your son like I did?"

Her arm still held against the light, Pescoli's mind raced. She had to keep Padgett's attention on her, not the screaming baby. If she just could move. Her gun was only inches away. Lying useless under an ancient sink.

With all her effort, she tried to ease toward it, stretch out her arm.

"Don't even think about it," Padgett warned.

"Drop the gun," Santana said. "Drop the gun and give me Tucker."

"As if," she said around the flashlight. But her gaze had moved to Santana.

He kept talking. Low and sure, barely moving forward.

Pescoli stretched. Her fingertips less than an inch from the butt of her weapon.

"Just listen, Padgett," Santana said, his own gun drawn, but unable to shoot as the baby was Padgett's shield. How could he be so cool, so quietly determined, when she was going crazy, wanting to scream, to yell, to pummel her son's abductor with her fists. She forced her body to move, but it wasn't enough. Damn it. And the world was spinning, the gun so near but so far. . . .

"You said you lost a son, you know what it's like. Don't do this."

Pescoli inched her body closer to her pistol. Her fingertip swiped the butt of the gun.

"I said, 'don't even think about it,'" Padgett shouted, turning, her weapon leveled at Pescoli again.

Pescoli froze.

"That's better."

Was Santana still moving ever so slowly forward? He was still six or seven feet away from Padgett and the baby, an old wringer washer, Padgett's cover, between them.

"Drop the weapon," Santana said again.

"Nuh-uh. No way." Padgett's attention was split for a second, then she focused on Regan again. "Do you feel it? Like I did? You ruined my life," she muttered furiously, her teeth still clenched around the flashlight. "You killed him. The only man I ever loved."

"He was a cold blooded killer."

"And he protected me. He cared for me. And the baby . . . I had to give up the baby. His baby." She was getting more amped up by the second.

"I had nothing to do with that," Pescoli said..

"I gave him up at that horrible place in San Francisco. Cahill House. You know the one. They said they'd give him to a good family and I couldn't care for him, that I wasn't fit and he *died!* Did you know that? My son died." Tears filled her eyes. "And then you killed him. The man I loved. My son's father."

"His body was never located," Pescoli said.

"But we all know he died in that icy lake. And it's your fault."

"He kidnapped me," Pescoli said, but it was no use trying to talk sense into this crazy woman.

"Because you were getting in his way! No, no, this is all your fault. Don't try to turn it around. And the upshot is because of you, Detective, I'm all alone. No son. No protector." Her gaze moved to Santana. "While you have both." Her lips twisted in an evil smile as once again her eyes focused hard on Pescoli. "So now," she said. "So now you know what it's like. To lose a child. To feel the pain."

Oh, God. Would she really murder an innocent child? Little Tucker? Pescoli's heart drummed with dread.

The gun. So close.

Pain radiated from Pescoli's midsection and she blinked to stay conscious. She was fading, but she remembered Padgett had never been right, not after a boating accident when she'd nearly drowned. But now Padgett blamed her for all the trouble in her life. Disturbed as she was, she was trying to get even.

And Tucker would pay.

No, no, no!

Gritting her teeth, she said, "Padgett, okay. You blame me. I understand. Then kill me, if you have to. Do it. But let Santana have the baby."

"Are you crazy?" Padgett asked around the flashlight, then laughed coldly. "Oh, no, that's me. The girl who nearly drowned and spent half her life being mute in a mental hospital only to come back to reality and find her son, her only damned son was dead! I waited fifteen years. And then . . . then I discover it was all for nothing."

Did Santana take another step forward?

So, Padgett said, "So, no. I'm not giving Santana his son." She eyed Pescoli's husband. "We go way back, don't we Nate? You were Brady's friend. You remember how he was. My brother. Well, half-brother. Nonetheless, he tried to kill me, you know. In that boating 'accident,' where I lost consciousness and ended up in the loony bin. I had to play at being mute and stupid and out of it. Locked up with people who really were psychos. Weird as hell, all of them. And then I heard that Brady had died and I was free, it was like a new lease on life. Except that was wrong. I got out, tracked down my son and found out that he was dead!" Did you hear me, 'Dead!' and I never knew. No one told me. Each year his birthday would roll around and in my head I would sing 'Happy Birthday' to him, wondering what he looked like, how he'd grown. I knew when he should have gone to school and worried about him and it was all a big, horrible waste of time. A fantasy, because I didn't know that he'd died! Oh, God, I still don't know why . . . or how . . ." Her voice cracked and then she shook her head, forced herself to calm down.

When she collected herself and she spoke again, her voice was brittle as ice. "Handing your boy back to his father would be too easy. It's touching that you're willing to die for your kid, but it's too late for that. And I want you to feel my pain, experience what it's like to lose a child." She shook her head. "But you won't feel the pain long, will you? From the looks of you, I'd say you're going to die anyway. And soon."

"No." Santana was staring at Padgett and his son, or was he looking beyond the halo of light that surrounded her? "She's not going to die. She can make it. I just need to call for an ambulance."

"Try it," Padgett said as he reached for his cell phone. She waggled the baby.

Tucker howled, his little feet dangling.

Pescoli forced herself to inch more upright. She had to plead with this woman, do whatever she could to save her child.

"Padgett, please," Santana said, but he didn't seem to be looking right at her.

But how would she know? The world was spinning. Pescoli tried to maintain, to hang on. "Just give the baby up," she murmured weakly, seeing a shadow, some movement in the dark behind Padgett. Was it a trick of light? Or her own fading consciousness playing mind games with her?

Santana warned, "Padgett, you don't have to do this. Leave the baby and we'll call an ambulance for my wife. You can leave."

"Oh, sure." Padgett laughed then.

The lights were dimming, the world spinning. Pescoli slid off her elbow.

"Uh-oh, looks like wifey isn't going to make it after all." Padgett stepped from behind the big washer to get a better look at Pescoli as she bled out.

The room swayed. Pescoli gathered all of her strength and flung herself forward.

"No!" Santana warned.

Pescoli's fingers grabbed the butt of her weapon.

"Shit!" Padgett cried over the baby's wails . . . and was there something else? The faraway sound of sirens? Padgett must've heard it too. For a split second she wasn't focused on Santana or Regan.

Santana yelled, "Now!" and lunged.

Regan saw him fly through the air to tackle Padgett, knocking the gun from her hand and the flashlight free, grabbing his son to hold Tucker to his chest in a quick tuck and roll.

Padgett screamed. "Nooooo!"

Santana crashed against metal bins, the sound echoing, her poor baby shrieking.

The flashlight rolled crazily across the floor, the light spinning as if she were in a fun house. With an effort, her hands quaking, Pescoli trained her weapon at Padgett, who, too, was on the concrete floor, dazed from being taken down. "Die, bitch."

"No, don't!" Another voice? Alvarez's? "Pescoli, don't!"

But she ignored the warning. Leveling her gun at Padgett Long, intent on killing the woman who had dared steal her son, she watched as the creature, with the tables turned, started to cry and push herself back, scuttling away.

Pescoli flipped off the safety with difficulty but she aimed at the broken, terrified woman staring at her.

"Don't! Regan!" Santana yelled. "I've got him. Regan, please. I've got Tuck!"

I want her dead.

But she glanced over at her husband and son. They were safe. Tuck was safe.

All the breath rushed from her body and her arm went limp. The gun fell from her hand.

The world spun off its axis.

From a far distance she heard, "Regan . . . *Regan!*" Santana. It was Santana.

She tried to say something.

No words came and she felt as if she were drifting above herself, leaving her body. But it was okay. Santana had Tucker . . . nothing else mattered.

She was floating, looking down, and saw Alvarez appear, her service weapon drawn, aimed straight at the cowering woman. "Padgett Long," Alvarez said with authority. "You're under arrest."

Epilogue

Two weeks later, Pescoli said, "I feel like an old woman," as she sat in Santana's recliner after being released from the hospital.

"You are. Forty's right around the corner," her husband reminded. He was on the floor in front of the fire, playing airplane with a giggling Tucker and in clear danger of being drooled on. Fortunately Cisco was nearby, ready to clean up any of the baby's messes.

"Don't remind me."

He didn't. Nor did he bring up how lucky she was to be alive. She'd been gut shot by Padgett Long that horrible night two weeks earlier and she'd nearly lost her life. As it was she'd been life-flighted to a Missoula hospital and survived, though she'd lost her spleen and her ability to ever conceive another child.

She could live with that.

No bones had been damaged, no vital organs destroyed, and she had her boy back. That's all that mattered.

Padgett Long had been arrested and would never be released into society again, and Ivy Wilde was back in San Francisco dealing with the court system, her father and stepmother—a just punishment on its own to Ivy's way of thinking, or so Jeremy had related to her. His short-lived infatuation was over and he'd wanted to take up with Becca Johnson again, but so far Becca had refused.

Pescoli didn't blame her.

Detective Tanaka, that hard-ass, seemed intent on getting the DA to prosecute Ivy as an adult. Sarina was having a fit about it. Sarina was also lobbying to come to visit Pescoli again as Pescoli had missed the dual memorial service for Brindel and Paul, but so far it hadn't happened and Pescoli was grateful for that. If she heard one more story about "You Know Who," she might just puke.

Meanwhile Bianca was waiting until she turned eighteen and then she was going to stick it to her father and change her name legally. And as for Lucky, it turned out he hadn't done anything illegal, this time around, had just responded to a Facebook inquiry made by Garrett Mays and together they had discovered Garrett's connection to the Long family. Of course he was in it for a cut, but what else could you expect from her ex-husband, the con man's con man?

And yes, it was true, she thought as the fire crackled and the dogs slept. Garrett Mays was indeed the son Brady Long hadn't known existed. What that meant to the Long estate and Padgett's share was anyone's guess as Mays was already hooked up with an attorney and making his claim.

Pescoli didn't care much how it turned out.

She glanced at the window, saw the reflection of the cozy room, and felt an inner peace. The feeling of malevolence, that something evil was hovering across the lake, was gone. Finally.

She had experienced an epiphany the night she'd come so close to viewing heaven from the other side of the pearly gates—that is if heaven was actually where she would have ended up; she wasn't so certain of that—and that was why she couldn't give up her job.

Some people had expected that her near-death experience and near loss of her infant son would have made her retreat into the safety of her own home, and increase her need to spend more time protecting her family. But she'd gone the other way. She'd chosen to be proactive. No mother should ever have to suffer the terror she'd gone through, and thank God the police were there to save them all. If it hadn't been for Pete Watershed telling Alvarez where Pescoli had gone, things might have turned out differently. But between what Watershed conveyed and what she'd learned from Ivy Wilde, Alvarez had driven to the museum, taken stock of the situation, and sneaked into the laundry facilities through an unlocked back door. Santana had seen her and known help was there, but Regan had kept fighting to take Padgett down.

They'd all been lucky.

Pescoli owed her life as well as her son's to Alvarez and the sheriff's department.

So she was returning to the force as soon as she was well enough. Probably just around Valentine's Day when Joelle Fisher would be making sure everyone on the force got a small heart-shaped box of candy or something like that. Maybe Joelle had the right idea after all. Celebrate life at every opportunity.

Even Santana had agreed to her return to the job. He'd just been grateful both she and Tucker had survived.

"Hey, how about giving me a break?" Santana suggested after one last hoisting of his son over his head. He rolled lithely to his feet, still holding his son. "Can you handle it?"

"Of course I can. Let me have this little man."

He handed Tucker over before walking to the refrigerator and pulling out a beer. "You want something?"

"Nah, not now." She was staring at her son. "Later."

The baby wriggled and smiled at her, showing off his first little tooth. "You know, Tuck," she said, "you're the best. Don't let anyone tell you differently."

The back door opened and Bianca walked in. Cisco gave a quick little bark and the big dogs thumped their tails. "I heard that," Bianca said as she dropped her backpack onto the floor and hung her jacket on a peg near the garage.

"It's true. He is the best. And when you were his age, honey, you were the best."

"Yeah, right."

"And what about me?" Santana asked from behind the kitchen island. His eyes twinkled and a bit of a dimple showed as his lips twitched.

"You." She grinned at her husband and shook her head. "It's a sad story. You're the worst, Santana. You always have been and you always will be."

"Guess we'll be bad together," he said suggestively, comically waggling his eyebrows at her.

Bianca threw her gaze to the ceiling. "Gross."

Pescoli ignored her, smiling at the man she loved. "Wouldn't have it any other way."

Dear Reader,

I hope you liked *Willing to Die*, the latest edition in the Montana "To Die" series featuring Detectives Alvarez and Pescoli, two of my favorite characters. I love returning to Grizzly Falls just to catch up on them and their ever-changing families! I see a few more books in their futures and I'm hoping you'll want to catch up with the detectives next time around.

Currently I've got another book on sale. *Paranoid* is available now in hardcover and e-book. It's a story set in Edgewater, Oregon, with a whole new set of characters. Rachel Ryder is a divorced mother of two rebellious teens whose past comes back to haunt her when her stepbrother reaches out from the grave or so it seems. She is convinced that she killed him and the strange text messages saying "I forgive you," freaks her out. Add to that the chilling fact that classmates who graduated with her are dying, one by one in hideous deaths. She's always been unsure of herself and the current brutalities push her closer and closer to the edge of insanity. Her ex-husband Cade is a detective frantically trying to solve the crimes of the present, along with the mysteries of the past before Rachel, the target of a deranged killer is murdered or loses her mind. *Paranoid* is a fun book; I think you'll like it.

Also look for my sister Nancy Bush's next book, which is available now. *Bad Things* is the story of Kerry Monaghan who grew up in the small, outwardly serene town of Edwards Bay, Washington. She's returned to her hometown just after her stepbrother's violent death. He's not the only one who's been brutally murdered. Others in their circle of friends are being picked off, one by one, and it seems as if they are linked by a dark obsession that has turned deadly. Kerry along with sexy Cole Sheffield the local chief of police are determined to find the killer, but as the sand runs through the hourglass, to Kerry's horror, she might just be the murderer's next target. *Bad Things* is a high-octane, fast-moving thriller that I think you'll really get into!

I'm also working on several projects for the future, including a new novel featuring Detectives Rick Bentz and Reuben Montoya set in New Orleans. Many of you have written asking me when their next book will be available and it's looking like 2020! I'll keep you posted. It's been a long wait, I know, but hopefully worth it.

For updates on these books and more, please check lisajackson.com or find me at readlisajackson on Facebook or Twitter. I'll post excerpts, host contests, and keep you apprised of the publication schedule. I hope to see you there!

In the meantime . . .

Keep reading!
Lisa

Some mistakes you have to live with . . .
One victim succumbs to an overdose. Another is brutally bludgeoned to death. Each, in turn, will pay. Because you never forget the friends you make in high school—or the enemies . . .

And others . . .
In the wake of her stepbrother Nick's death, Kerry Monaghan is visiting Edwards Bay. Kerry has just returned to the small town overlooking an arm of Puget Sound that she left before high school, though not before falling hard and fast for Cole Sheffield, now with the local PD. But Nick's death may be more than an accident. And soon there are others—all former teenage friends, linked by a dark obsession.

You will die for . . .
With Cole's help, Kerry sets out to learn the truth about what happened to Nick. But within Edwards Bay is a shocking legacy built on envy and lust—and a secret that has unleashed a killer's unstoppable fury . . .

Please turn the page for an exciting sneak peek of Nancy Bush's

BAD THINGS,

now on sale wherever books and eBooks are sold!

Prologue

Patient: *Bad things happen, Doc. Bad choices. Bad decision making.*

Doctor: *You think the decisions you made are bad?*

Patient: *If things had turned out differently, I might have made different choices. But fate took the wheel. You know that.*

Doctor: *It's hard to blame what happened on fate.*

Patient: *Oh, don't worry. I know what I did.*

Doctor: *Let's talk about your motivation.*

Patient: *Sure. Then you can write up some notes about my homicidal behavior, look smart and serious, and go on to your next case.*

Doctor: *I'm here to get to the truth.*

Patient: *Sorry, Doc, my story is my story. Not for public consumption.*

Doctor: *Anything you say here is private.*

Patient: *Doctor/patient privilege? Tell me another one.*

Doctor: *I'm your doctor. You're—*

Patient: *You're the brain digger. Digging, digging, digging away. You don't think I know what you're doing?*

Doctor: *Okay. Let's pivot for a minute and talk about those bad decisions you made.*

Patient: *You tell* me *one bad decision you've made, Brain Digger. Maybe then I'll tell you what you want to know.*

Doctor: *All right. That's fair. Well . . . I've already cheated on my diet this morning.*

Patient (short laugh): *You haven't killed anybody? Hurt them? Called them out?*

Doctor: *No.*

Patient: *Then you're not on the same playing field, Doc. You're not even in the same ballpark.*

Doctor: *Tell me about the bad things that have recently happened.*

Patient: *The ones I caused? That's what you're really thinking. Well, this is going to take awhile.*

Doctor: *I'm here as long as it takes.*

Patient: *As long as you get paid, right? Well, fine, Brain Digger. This is a story about Nick Radnor. Some of us believed he was something special. He's certainly always believed it. And the whole damn town bought into his act. But I found him out for the faithless bastard he really is. That's what my story's about, Doc. Bad choices for a bad guy everyone thought was good.*

Chapter 1

Diana Conger woke up with a sense of deep dread. Her mouth was a sewer and her head ached. Once again, she'd had too much to drink . . . among other things.

It was dark, the middle of the night, the wee hours of the morning. Throwing her legs over the side of the bed, she stumbled into the bathroom. Her stomach quivered as she leaned over the toilet, spitting. After several minutes and some hard breathing she sensed she wasn't going to throw up after all. Holding onto the counter to balance herself, she carefully searched the jumbled memories of the past few hours: the bar-hopping, the dancing, the flirting, the recreational drug use . . . That was her, wasn't it? In the restroom of Forrest and Sean's bar? With those old classmates, taking pills and yeah, snorting coke, or something? She grimaced. She'd really told herself she was going to get it together after the class reunion meeting that was such a mind-numbing, cluster-fuck. Those people . . . the ones she'd gone to high school with . . . She'd thought they'd all surpassed her in life, but it turned out they were just as messed up and clueless as she was. At least most of them were. There were a few stand-outs. The ones she'd always known would do well, although Josie Roker was sure one crazy bitch. The way she went on about Nick, like they were an item? What about that husband of hers? But she wasn't as nuts as Egan Fogherty. There was something seriously wrong with that guy. He'd been weird all through high school. Cute, but weird. But Josie . . . she acted all pure, but the way she was around Nick said she wanted to screw his brains out. That last bit was from Killian O'Keenan who'd used something a little more explicit than "screw" in his description. But then Killian always had something kind of mean to say when he wasn't standing by, silently intimidating. What did Miami see in him? Was it just that they'd been together since high school? Well, okay, he'd held up well and had still had a hard body, amazing guns. When he stood back and surveyed the room, Diana's eyes invariably traveled to his upper arms, which could really get her juices going. But maybe that was what it was with Miami—Mia Miller, who'd been nicknamed Miami, a combination of her first name and the beginning of her last—maybe it was all about sex. Well, Diana could admit that she'd made some serious mistakes when it came to sex herself. But at least she didn't act like a *virgin* like Josie.

Diana rinsed out her mouth with water from the tap, then made a face. She was pretty sure she'd made it back to her apartment tonight by the grace of God. She struggled to remember how she'd gotten home and gave it up, as it made her head hurt. She'd taken Uber to the first bar where she'd met her friends, so she hadn't driven herself back home.

Her hand touched the door jamb for a moment as she oriented herself, then she left the bathroom, stepping across the carpet to her bed, smelling the scents of lavender and grapefruit from the incense sticks in the vial on her night stand. Slipping beneath the covers she snuggled down with a grateful sigh.

She buried her face into the pillow as her head began to ache again. She stretched her arms out . . . and encountered another body in the bed.

Diana froze. Heart racing, she lifted her head, her eyes searching through the dimness. There was a sliver of bluish illumination glimmering through the gap in the curtain over the sliding glass door that led to her bedroom deck; the closest exterior streetlight shining in. Leaning forward, she saw the back of a man's head. *A man.* She slid back carefully, one hand reaching for the light switch. She hesitated before she flicked it on, her galloping fear beginning to slow. This wasn't the first time she'd brought a guy home and then forgotten about him. That kid she'd brought home last summer, a couple years below her in high school, Jimmy.

She leaned over her bedmate. Noticed the way his dark hair waved around his ear. Oh, Christ! Holy Mother of God. It was *Nick Radnor.* Josie's Nick. Well, not really hers. She *was* married. But the object of her desire, and well, Diana's, too! He was the one classmate of theirs who'd made it *big*. Something in the tech field. Lots and lots of money. Diana nearly forgot her jumping stomach and aching head. A smile spread across her face. Well, well, well . . . Things were looking up. She recalled dimly that she'd run into him somewhere earlier in the night . . . Had he been with Miami? Or . . . Forest or Sean, at their bar? Josie had been there . . . but they weren't together . . . Nick stayed away from her because she was married . . . although everyone kind of thought they were having a secret affair. . . but he was here now. In her bed. How had that happened?

Diana had run with the high school gang. None of them had ever really separated, those that had stayed in Edwards Bay. They hung out at the same bars with the same friends. God. It didn't bear thinking about. She'd met up with Nick at the third bar . . . wasn't it? They'd all gone to The Whistle Stop first and the Thai place. Kerry had been there, too. Nick's sister . . . stepsister . . . really. She didn't know Kerry all that well because she wasn't a classmate, hadn't gone to high school with them, but she'd been around tonight, hadn't she? Jesus. It was tough to remember. Felt like a dream.

But *Nick!*

Oh, Lord she'd scored big tonight. He was THE GUY from high school. And he was divorced from Marcia now, too, though honestly, even if he was still married, Diana wouldn't have much minded. Josie could play her virgin games all she wanted. Diana could admit her morals were fluid when it came to sex. But Nick and Marcia *were* divorced. Miami had told Diana that Nick and Marcia barely spoke to each other anymore. Marcia had moved back to Edwards Bay, and when Nick visited from Palo Alto, he didn't come anywhere near her. Of course, Miami wasn't exactly trustworthy when it came to rumors, but who cared anyway. Good times were few and far between these days, and Diana was ready to make the most of this opportunity. She was eager to climb atop him and make love like rabbits. Oh, man. What a notch on her belt. She couldn't wait to tell Miami and Josie all about tonight!

She leaned over him and whispered in Nick's ear, "Fancy meeting you in a place like this."

Slipping a leg over him, she turned him on his back, astride his naked body.

His eyes were open.

And his tongue lolled out of his mouth.

And his skin was . . . cool . . . cold.

For half a beat she didn't breathe.

"Nick . . .?" she whispered, terror running through her veins.

Oh, no . . . no . . . no . . . NO!

Diana scrambled away from him, her mouth open on a silent scream. Her insides shriveled. He was *dead*. A corpse. A cold, naked body *in her bed*.

She staggered backward, slamming into the wall. A thin, keening wail rose from her soul, an almost inhuman sound. She stumbled back into the bathroom, slamming her shoulder against the jamb in her haste. The jolt of pain stopped the wailing.

Leaning over the toilet she puked her guts out.

Then she lay on the cool floor tiles and shook all over. There was a pounding on her door. *Bang, bang, bang.* Alan, her neighbor, shaking the doorknob.

"Diana! You in there? You okay?"

He'd heard her shrieking through the paper-thin walls.

She continued to shiver. Didn't answer. Stared with horror through the bathroom door to the side of the bed and the dead man she knew lay on top of it.

"Diana!"

She wanted to call to Alan, tell him she was fine. She didn't want him here. She was freaked out and sick and needed to think . . . to remember . . . to consider.

What happened?

Did you cause this somehow?

The shock of pure terror morphed to a new kind of fear. The coke . . . and other things . . . behind the Blarney Stone . . . they'd all been there . . . She remembered the toe of her boot getting caught in the gap of the deck floorboard. A small, screened back porch for employees only, but Forrest and Sean owned the place and they allowed them to be back there.

"Diana?"

His voice was softer now, unsure. She kept quiet, though her heart was beating so loudly in her ears it sounded like thunder.

She heard his footsteps head back to his apartment.

You're going to have to move.

But what to do now?

Gathering up all her courage she crawled from the bathroom to the chair at the far side of the room. Don't look, she told herself. Don't look. DON'T LOOK.

But her head swiveled and she peeked over the top of the bed to see Nick Radnor's dead body. With a squeak of horror, she slipped her purse from the chair, spilling the contents onto the rug. The strip of light through the balcony curtains landed directly on the tiny pill canister attached to her keys.

She grabbed up her cell phone, hugging it tightly. Who could she call? What should she do?

What time was it?

Three a.m.

Shit.

She felt like she was going to throw up again and drew several deep breaths, exhaling slowly. Okay . . . okay . . . who?

With shaking fingers, she scrolled through her call list. One of the guys? Maybe Randy? He was a good friend to Nick, wasn't he?

But thinking of Randy Starr of Starrwood Homes brought her back to Kerry Monaghan, Nick Radnor's stepsister, who worked for Randy. Or, was it a half sister? No . . . definitely step . . . she was pretty sure.

You should call one of your friends to help you, not Kerry.

What friends? she asked herself hollowly.

She crouched on all fours for ten seconds, listening to her own breathing.

Books by Bestselling Author

Fern Michaels

__The Jury	0-8217-7878-1	$6.99US/$9.99CAN
__Sweet Revenge	0-8217-7879-X	$6.99US/$9.99CAN
__Lethal Justice	0-8217-7880-3	$6.99US/$9.99CAN
__Free Fall	0-8217-7881-1	$6.99US/$9.99CAN
__Fool Me Once	0-8217-8071-9	$7.99US/$10.99CAN
__Vegas Rich	0-8217-8112-X	$7.99US/$10.99CAN
__Hide and Seek	1-4201-0184-6	$6.99US/$9.99CAN
__Hokus Pokus	1-4201-0185-4	$6.99US/$9.99CAN
__Fast Track	1-4201-0186-2	$6.99US/$9.99CAN
__Collateral Damage	1-4201-0187-0	$6.99US/$9.99CAN
__Final Justice	1-4201-0188-9	$6.99US/$9.99CAN
__Up Close and Personal	0-8217-7956-7	$7.99US/$9.99CAN
__Under the Radar	1-4201-0683-X	$6.99US/$9.99CAN
__Razor Sharp	1-4201-0684-8	$7.99US/$10.99CAN
__Yesterday	1-4201-1494-8	$5.99US/$6.99CAN
__Vanishing Act	1-4201-0685-6	$7.99US/$10.99CAN
__Sara's Song	1-4201-1493-X	$5.99US/$6.99CAN
__Deadly Deals	1-4201-0686-4	$7.99US/$10.99CAN
__Game Over	1-4201-0687-2	$7.99US/$10.99CAN
__Sins of Omission	1-4201-1153-1	$7.99US/$10.99CAN
__Sins of the Flesh	1-4201-1154-X	$7.99US/$10.99CAN
__Cross Roads	1-4201-1192-2	$7.99US/$10.99CAN

Available Wherever Books Are Sold!

Check out our website at **www.kensingtonbooks.com**